BOOKS BY WILL MURRAY

Tarzan: Return to Pal-ul-don
King Kong vs. Tarzan
Doc Savage: Skull Island
The Spider: The Doom Legion
Wordslingers: An Epitaph for the Western

FORTHCOMING:
The Wild Adventures of Sherlock Holmes

The Wild Adventures of Edgar Rice Burroughs™ Series ❾

TARZAN®
CONQUEROR OF MARS

By
WILL MURRAY

Illustrated by
Romas Kukalis

Altus Press • 2020

Tarzan, Conqueror of Mars © 2020 Edgar Rice Burroughs, Inc. All rights reserved.

Cover illustration by Romas Kukalis copyright © 2020 Edgar Rice Burroughs, Inc. All rights reserved. Map of Barsoom by Jason C. Eckhardt copyright © 2020 Edgar Rice Burroughs, Inc. All rights reserved.

Trademarks Edgar Rice Burroughs®, The Wild Adventures of Edgar Rice Burroughs™, Tarzan®, Lord of the Jungle®, Tarzan of the Apes™, Lord Greystoke™, Tarzan and Jane®, Jane Clayton™, Jane Porter™, John Carter®, John Carter of Mars®, A Princess of Mars®, Gods of Mars™, Warlord of Mars®, Dejah Thoris®, Tars Tarkas®, Carthoris™, Woola™, Barsoom®, and Jason Gridley™ owned by Edgar Rice Burroughs, Inc., and used by permission. The Doodad symbol is a trademark of Edgar Rice Burroughs, Inc., and used by permission.

THANKS TO

John Bruening, Gary Buckingham, Christopher Paul Carey, Jeff Deischer, Joe DeVito, Laurence G. Dunn, Dave McDonnell, Henoch Neethling, Don O'Malley, Ray Riethmeier, Jim Sullos, Jess Terrell, Cathy Mann Wilbanks, and Edgar Rice Burroughs, Inc.

COVER ILLUSTRATION COMMISSIONED BY
Henry G. Franke III

No part of this book may be reproduced or utilized in any form or by any means, electronic or mechanical, without permission in writing from the publisher.

First Edition — January 2020

DESIGNED BY
Matthew Moring

Like us on Facebook: "The Wild Adventures of Tarzan"

www.edgarriceburroughs.com
www.adventuresinbronze.com

For Edgar Rice Burroughs—

Who might have written this
adventure long ago....

TARZAN, CONQUEROR OF MARS

Chapter 1

Sobito Escapes

IN THE brilliant canvas of diamonds comprising the African night sky, the planet Mars stood apart, burning steadily, a beckoning red beacon of mystery.

There was no moon to rival its light. The East African jungle was exceedingly dark and eerily quiet. Absent were the customary sounds of the jungle at night. Predators were not prowling, as was their wont. The rolling yip of the hyena was not heard. Birds roosted in silence. Even the insects kept a respectful hush.

Usha the wind held his all-pervasive breath. It was as if all of nature dared not breathe.

Nothing seemed to move. Not a leaf trembled. But high in the upper terraces of the trees, something did stir.

More silent and stealthy than Histah the snake, a sinewy figure crept along, a creature that barely disturbed the leaves as it moved among the crowns of close-packed trees. Something that was in the shape of a man, but which moved like no other man who ever walked on two legs.

This demigod of the forest slipped artfully from branch to branch in absolute silence. Starlight showed naked limbs, but only glancingly. Beneath sun-bronzed skin, supple muscles like molten steel rolled with each stealthy motion, then subsided, becoming uncannily still.

Gray eyes peered about. Human eyes, yet savage withal. These were the eyes of a hunter. They belonged to one man, and one man alone.

Tarzan of the Apes was on the hunt.

Sensitive nostrils quivered as they tasted the evening air. But there was no wind to carry jungle scents to the majestic countenance of the ape-man. Odors lingered aplenty. But not the odor of the jungle lord's quarry.

Tarzan held still. At his side, the hunting knife that had belonged to his father sat firmly in its sheath, its horn handle faintly burnished by starlight.

Across his back was slung an antelope-hide quiver, so packed with fletched arrows that none rattled together. A hardwood bow lay across his scarred back, its confining string pressing against his magnificent chest.

None of these weapons were necessary to take in hand. Not just yet.

A heavy scent came to his nostrils then. That of a lion, the so-called king of the beasts. But no lion, no matter how kingly, ruled the jungle as did Tarzan of the Apes, who was rightly called the Lord of the Jungle.

No concern touched Tarzan's bronzed countenance as he tasted the musky odor of Numa the lion. For he feared no lion. Nor any other animal born in Africa. Many lions had he slain in his time. His hide bore the silvery stitch-marks of their fierce claws and fangs. Yet he still lived, and they were no more, except that their dead meat had fortified his living muscles.

Tarzan listened intently. His black-haired head swiveled about until his sharp ears detected the faint pad-pad-pad of a ranging lion. Numa was all that was abroad in the night. Tracking its stealthy footfalls with his ears, Tarzan noted that the soft-footed feline was stalking toward the west. It was perhaps one hundred yards ahead of him.

When he had fixed the relative position of Numa to his own, Tarzan slid forward, slipping toward the east. Not out of caution, but for other reasons....

THE OLD man smelled the lion as well.

He squatted on the ground in an attitude that bespoke of a craven heart. There was not much to him. He consisted of old bones and stringy muscles connected with tendons that stood out tensely here and there along his sun-blackened skin. His features were wrinkled in the extreme, and the face paint that he had applied earlier in the day was now smeared and streaked with sweat.

He wore only a G-string of turtle hide. Affixed to this was a leather pouch that hung heavily. He had no other weapon, no knife, no spear—no apparent means with which to defend himself.

This wizened old man was either exceedingly brave or unsurpassably foolhardy. For no one who walks on two legs goes out to the jungle unarmed. At least, not if he has any choice in the matter.

Old Sobito had no choice in the matter. He had lately escaped from the village of Tumbai, where he had been a prisoner for nearly a year—all but a slave after being deposited there by the forest devil that was Tarzan of the Apes.

Sobito's feud with the ape-man went back to the reign of the Leopard Men who had terrorized this district and threatened the peaceful Utenga tribe. The fearsome Leopard Men were no more, banished from this world by the Lord of the Jungle. Tarzan had surrendered defeated Sobito to the village where he had once been a crafty witch doctor for just punishment. Sobito had fully expected to be slain. But the village chief, Lobongo, had decreed otherwise.*

Sobito and other medicine men of his ilk often terrorized unlettered natives with their mumbo-jumbo. Wise Lobongo wished to teach his people the folly of heeding the pronouncements of witch doctors.

So instead of putting the craven Sobito to death, Lobongo had caged him. Made him an object of ridicule—reducing the cowed wretch to the status of less than a dog. And so Sobito

---

* *See* Tarzan and the Leopard Men *by Edgar Rice Burroughs.*

had passed his miserable days for nearly a year, subsisting on scraps thrown to him and rainwater he captured on his tongue by thrusting it out through the bamboo slats of his rude jail.

During that long year, Goro the moon waxed and waned without surcease. The monsoon rains arrived, pouring out their afternoon libations. Invariably, the oppressive heat returned. Came the day when the lashings of the cage had become frayed from exposure to the jungle extremes. So Sobito carefully plucked at certain splintery threads until he was confident that he could worm out of his prison after dusk.

The emaciated captive had waited for a night which lacked a visible moon. He would have preferred cloud cover to obscure the plentiful starlight of the dazzling African night sky. But he needed to take care to wait another dozen suns until the lunar orb hid her cold face again behind a stupendous cloud bank.

And so simply by plucking at the leather lashings with broken fingernails and yellow teeth did Sobito the witch doctor create an opening large enough to squeeze his squirming dusky-skinned body through. He did not bother to seal the ragged orifice behind him. His absence would be noted soon enough. Once the sun rose in the morning, there would be no concealing his escape....

In his calculations, the wily old sorcerer had made an error. Possibly a fatal one.

Sobito had assumed a full night's start on his presumed pursuers. Yet Fate had other designs—as she so often does....

A young man had woken in the middle of the night. Unable to regain a satisfactory state of slumber, he had gone for a midnight promenade about the village.

Thus did Orando, son of the chief, notice the witch doctor's empty prison less than an hour after Sobito had made his careful escape.

An alarm was sounded. Tom-toms started pounding. The chief was swiftly aroused from sleep by the insistent drumming.

Lobongo gathered together the sleepy villagers, took stock of the situation, and made a fateful decision.

"The old rascal is without food or weapons," proclaimed Chief Lobongo. "He will not get far. We will not chase him. Let the lions and hyenas do that work. There is no doubt but that they will. Another day, or perhaps two, we will find his carcass rotting in the sun. We showed him mercy, and Sobito repaid us with disrespect. He was a cannibal in his heart, anyway. Let his withered limbs serve as a paltry feast for whoever finds him first...."

And so the headman consigned Sobito to his presumed destruction, never once suspecting that it would be other than what his imagination had conjured up.

For Tarzan of the Apes was passing through this district. To his ever-alert ears came the shouts of discovery. The ape-man had heard everything, and so learned that the witch doctor—whom he had more than once before captured—had again escaped the justice of the jungle.

But no one escapes the justice of Tarzan. Not even a witch doctor.

Now the jungle lord well understood that Sobito was more of a fraud than he was a medicine man. Sobito knew jungle herbs and their uses. He claimed to talk with ghosts. But many witch doctors claim that. Inasmuch as only they could hear these disembodied voices, this claim was difficult to refute.

AS HE had moved through the night, the wily old fraud paused to capture certain mushrooms, uncommon leaves he recognized, and other tools of his disreputable trade. He gave a low yip of pleasure when found a kingo root, said to confer upon one who knew how to wield it mastery over all others.

His captors had not taken from him his medicine bag. They had, however, emptied it, returning it to Sobito as a contemptuous gesture of his new state of impotence.

Sobito now squatted in the dirt, pausing to catch his breath and pick over his discoveries. Here were sundries that he could work with—once he had time to prepare them properly....

Suddenly smelling a prowling lion, Sobito seized in his bony fingers a clutch of mint leaves. Hastily he crushed these, and smeared the bole of a nearby pepper tree with the meager juice.

The freshening smell wafted upward but failed to disperse. There was no breath of wind to disperse it. The air was still and exceedingly oppressive.

Still, Sobito thought craftily, the juice might do its natural work.

Leaving the crushed mint leaves among the roots at the base of the tree, the old man slipped away into the encroaching darkness....

A magnificent lion stepped into the small clearing not long after that, paused and sniffed at the tree with interest. Its yellow-green eyes gleamed with feline appreciation. Purring throatily, the big cat rubbed its whiskers against the knobby tree trunk, first on one side and then on the other.

Then, having picked up the scent of the pungent juice lingering on withered old fingers, the lion padded on, slinking in the direction of the witch doctor's flight....

FEAR CLUTCHED at his pounding heart when old Sobito realized that despite his imagined cleverness, he was being stalked by the unseen lion.

For he had smeared the old pepper tree with the leaves of a small bush that is known throughout the world under different names, one of which was catmint, and the other catnip. Its fragrance was irresistible to felines of all species. Leaving the juice on a tree should have stayed the lion's hunt. Instead, it appeared to have barely delayed it.

The steady padding came to Sobito's age-shriveled ears as he slipped between the trees. He recalled a stand of trees where the trunks grew close together. He shifted in the direction where memory guided him. His thought was the lion might be hindered in his stalk by the close-pressing boles.

Farther to the east he ranged, not running—for he knew that if he overexerted himself, he would fall prostrate to the ground and have no chance against the remorseless lion who tracked his scent spoor with unerring ability combined with seemingly tireless patience.

Finally, canny Sobito found the closely grouped stand of forest trees. There, he insinuated his scrawny form, crouching down and becoming still. Yet he trembled. The sweat of fear oozed from every pore. He commenced crawling on his wrinkled belly like a creeping serpent.

From time to time, Sobito looked up, seeking a low-hanging branch by which to hoist himself up into the foliage. But no convenient branch presented itself. Besides that, the old witch doctor had been starved to the point where his physical frame was but a ghost of its former self. Strength was sorely lacking. He could no more climb a tree than he could flap his arms and seek refuge in the night sky….

Frequently, the old man turned his head. But he saw nothing but shifting shadows. He wished for a moon in the sky, but at the same time, he feared what the lunar light might show him.

At length, Sobito summoned up all shreds and vestiges of his courage and forced himself to his feet. Creeping carefully, ancient back bent, he advanced, soon picking up his pace when no predator pounced.

On and on he rushed, not quite running, his cracked and naked feet pressing down on hard roots and dried vegetation. Fatigue began to make his scrawny muscles ache.

Once, when he turned his head, Sobito thought he spied luminous green eyes. Because he did not care to see any such impending vision, he tore his gaze away and blundered on before confirming his most dread fears.

Trailing him, the patient lion padded in calm pursuit. The creature appeared to be in no hurry. Nor did it veer from its unwavering path.

There was no doubting the lion's intentions. With remorseless casualness, the beast was stalking him.

Just when it seemed as if Sobito's destiny was to be captured by the unseen lion, he blundered into a clearing.

THERE WAS no forest canopy here. Only open sky. Starlight filtered down, steady and stark. The sky seemed to be full of brilliants, glinting and ever-changing in their twinkling light.

Only red Mars burned steadily, near the constellation called the Serpent.

Fearful of being caught in the open, with no chance to spring with his last ounce of breath into the trees, Sobito hesitated at the clearing's grassy verge.

His dark eyes wide with mounting terror, he surveyed the clearing.

Something stirred in the trees on the opposite side. Something that shifted amid the still leaves. Something that could not clearly be discerned.

Next came a rustling high in the leafy crowns. Certain branches shook as if a wind had sprung up. But nothing like that was transpiring.

Cold gray eyes peered down from those shaking branches.

Without further warning, a bronzed form dropped down to land lightly in the dirt, superb physique enveloped in shadow.

The figure was human enough, yet a giant, especially as compared to the old medicine man. He was naked except for a loincloth of antelope hide. And his weapons were not in his hands.

Face a determined mask, Tarzan of the Apes padded forward confidently.

"It was an ill-omened star that rose upon your fortunes this night, Sobito," intoned the ape-man. "Otherwise, you would have chosen a more propitious night in which to make your escape. Instead, you have run into my arms, and are once again at my mercy."

"*Tarzan!*"

Grim words followed that quavering exclamation like a pronouncement of jungle doom.

"You are a slippery one, Sobito. Tarzan is tired of capturing you, only to have you slip free again. Perhaps it is better to leave you to the tender mercies of Tarzan's jungle friends."

Sobito's mouth dried at those words. Deep within him, he felt a sharp quailing. A cloudy coldness settled into the pit of his empty belly.

Jungle rumor had it that this sun-bronzed white man ruled a tribe of great apes of unsurpassed ferocity. Tarzan had been raised by them, it was further whispered. Legend claimed that he was more ape than human. If he cast Sobito into their hairy hands, the scrawny old witch doctor knew that he would be torn limb from limb. He had seen apes, baboons and chimpanzees do exactly that to hapless humans who fell into their clutches. They were literally ripped asunder while still living.

Considering that unhappy prospect, the old medicine man did the only sensible thing that came to his mind. He turned tail and ran screaming back the way he had come—back toward the stalking lion.

Sobito had seen lions pounce on antelopes and even human beings. In contrast to the great apes, they were merciful. Their terrible fangs went for the living throat and tore it out, leaving the victim to die swiftly, and in considerably less pain than being torn limb from limb.

A grim smile touched the bronzed countenance of the ape-man when Sobito bolted. Surprisingly, Tarzan did not give pursuit. He merely padded barefoot after the frightened old witch doctor, striding as purposefully as the hunting lion who pursued the same prey.

Sobito plunged into the jungle cover, blundered about for a bit, his shrill shrieks of mortal terror echoing only briefly.

There came a commotion, followed by a struggle. It was brief.

Ere Tarzan had passed through the clearing, a great tawny lion with a luxurious mane as black as a thunder cloud emerged from the outlying trees, emerald eyes gleaming.

Ferocious jaws clamped like a living vise, dragging Sobito by one of his emaciated legs. The old witch doctor beat the ground with his empty hands, crying out in inarticulate frustration.

A cool smile touched Tarzan's ruggedly handsome features.

"I see you have met Jad-bal-ja, who is the faithful companion of Tarzan," said the ape-man with a trace of humor in his voice.

Jad-bal-ja dragged Sobito forward and released him at Tarzan's feet.

Thereupon, the old witch doctor gathered his arms and legs into a ball and began begging for mercy in a wailing voice.

"Please do not consign me to the apes of your tribe!" he cried piteously. "I beg you, mighty Tarzan. I will go back to my cage and trouble you no more."

"You will go back to your cage if I permit it," returned the bronzed giant. "Tarzan has not yet decided your punishment. You are a nuisance, a pestilence in this jungle. Were it not for my mercy, Sobito, you would be but a pile of bones being eaten by ants long before now."

"Do not cast me to the hungry ants, O merciful Tarzan," Sobito wailed piteously. "I do not wish to be eaten by any creature you command."

"Tarzan should simply break your neck and be done with it," mused the ape-man.

The terrified witch doctor was at the end of his emotional tether. He proved this with his next words. "If you break my neck, I will consider you to be merciful."

As Sobito awaited the stern justice of the jungle lord, the trembling witch doctor threw his fleshless arms before his face.

Tarzan said coldly, "Stand upon your two feet, craven one. Tarzan will march you back to your cage. Unless you prefer to be dragged through the jungle by Tarzan's hungry friend."

Reluctantly, the old witch doctor gathered his wits together and clambered to his feet. He looked up into Tarzan's unmoving face and it was like looking into the countenance of some forest god of antiquity. The features of Tarzan combined a noble cast with an indescribable quality that was not so much bestial as it was feral.

Tarzan lifted a muscular bronzed arm and pointed into the darkness of the woods.

"Turn about and march," he commanded. "Do this!"

Shakily finding his footing, Sobito looked up into the night sky and hot tears of shame mixed with rage leaked down and smeared the pigments he had applied to his wrinkled face.

And he said quaveringly, "I was once a man of spiritual prowess. I wielded influence. Men feared me. Now I fear you."

Tarzan returned calmly, "All of the jungle fears Tarzan of the Apes."

As he trudged along, the wizened one slipped fingers into his medicine bag, and slipped from it the twisted length of kingo root, believed to confer power upon wise men who prepared it properly. But the witch doctor had not had time to do any such thing, so he fingered the root wishfully, not malevolently.

LIFTING HIS eyes to the night sky, Sobito noticed the planet Mars, which he knew as Meriki.

In his primitive religion, Meriki was a god of wrath. A thunder deity, and the hurler of lightning bolts.

How much of Sobito's wicked craft consisted of guile is difficult to say. But other tricks of his trade were not so much tricks as they were a species of wisdom, even if it was a perverted wisdom.

As he stared at Meriki burning high above, Sobito's withered lips rose in mumbled prayer, simultaneously squeezing the kingo root.

"O mighty Meriki," he whispered. "Strike down my enemy with your irresistible magic."

Tarzan heard these words, and understood them.

"Tell your god good-bye," he said firmly, "and commence your march back to captivity."

Sobito breathed a muttered curse and then tore his eyes back to Earth. Woodenly, he turned, and took three halting paces, his back to the remorseless jungle lord.

Stepping around the golden lion with its threatening black mane, Sobito walked with heavy tread and with every footstep he laid the curse of Meriki upon his tormentor in low, vehement words.

Tarzan and Jad-bal-ja fell in behind the quaking witch doctor. There was no concern in the ape-man's clear gray eyes as they followed Sobito. The old wizard was thoroughly cowed. No resistance remained in him. Only resignation and an inner rage about which he could do nothing.

At a word from his master, the Golden Lion lifted his head, got in front of Sobito, and led the way back into the forest.

Having no choice, Sobito walked meekly behind the switching, tufted tail, head bowed in abject defeat.

They progressed for a time, masters of the woodland trails, and unchallenged by its inhabitants.

THERE WAS no warning rumble, no cloud in the sky. Just a searing flash of light.

Perhaps it was a bolt of lightning. If so, it was strangely, glaringly scarlet.

The bolt struck Tarzan just as the ape-man felt the hairs on the back of his neck and forearms lift in warning. Accustomed to nature, Tarzan recognized the atmospheric warning that told that a gathering lightning bolt was about to strike the vicinity.

His muscles coiled tensely, preparing to spring from the path of danger.

But no one, not even Tarzan of the Apes, could move as swiftly as Ara the lightning.

A searing hot bolt enveloped the bronzed giant, striking him down. He crumpled wordlessly to the dirt.

JAD-BAL-JA, TOO, had sensed the impending danger.

The powerful lion jerked its great head about—just in time to behold the clearing explode in red light. A light so hot it blinded him.

Roaring, Jad-bal-ja thrashed about, momentarily unable to see, terrified by the force of nature's unleashed fury.

And while the Lord of the Jungle lay felled by a power greater than he, and the lion who served him flashed about in the ensuing confusion, wily old Sobito slipped between the trees, his yellow teeth gleaming at his wholly unexpected good fortune.

As he raced through the night, clutching his kingo root, the vile witch doctor gave thanks to his fearsome god.

"Take the soul of Tarzan into your embrace, O Meriki. Make him your prisoner for eternity. For you are mightier than he."

Chapter 2

"I Am Still Alive."

TARZAN OF the Apes never heard the crack of thunder that came in the aftermath of the abrupt lightning bolt that so forcefully struck him down.

Momentarily, his senses swam. All was blackness. For all intents and purposes, his brain was paralyzed—devoid of all emotions, all sense impressions. No thoughts troubled his mind. Therein existed only a still black void of nothingness.

Presently, he became conscious of a sharp snapping sound, as if a taut wire had parted. This was followed by a rushing sensation, then a penetrating coldness that was unlike anything the ape-man had ever before experienced.

These unnatural sensations came and went quickly.

Awareness was swift in returning.

Without knowing how this had come to be, the jungle lord felt unfamiliar ground beneath his naked back. It was not grassy, nor was it stone. Rather, it was soft and slightly spongy.

Opening his eyes, Tarzan observed that it was yet night. The stars wheeling above his head were exceedingly clear and plentiful, yet the light they shed was faint. At first, he paid them little attention, being for the moment more concerned with his physical and mental state.

Tarzan sat up, and found that he could do so with no difficulty. He felt strange. He could not account for the odd sensation, nor trace its origin. But he lived. That was sufficient to begin with.

Looking about, Tarzan scrutinized an unfamiliar expanse. Nowhere to be seen were the familiar jungles of the African continent. He saw, not a forest clearing, but a flat plain that appeared to stretch monotonously for miles all around. The absence of strong light made this difficult to discern, but the ape-man sensed a great emptiness all around him. Not a fringe of trees did he descry.

His questing hands clenched at the ground. He tore at it, bringing clumps of some vegetable substance to his face. His intelligent eyes studied the matter and he concluded that he lay in a bed luxuriant with moss. This natural carpet was a yellowish color. It was unlike anything he had ever encountered over the length and breadth of Africa.

Releasing the stuff after first smelling it, Tarzan stood up with care.

The ape-man discovered several things at once that baffled his ordinarily agile brain.

First, he was entirely naked. His loincloth was gone, as was the scabbard that held his hunting knife. Gone, too, were his longbow and full quiver of arrows. Lastly, his mother's locket no longer depended from his sinewy neck by its gold chain.

Starlight painted the area immediately around him and the ape-man quickly discerned that his missing possessions were not in evidence.

The realization that he could not account for his present whereabouts caused the jungle lord to take a sudden breath. When the air flowed into his lungs, it carried with it a faintly chemical tang resembling ammonia. This air was thin, dry, and uncomfortably chill.

As he became accustomed to his surroundings, Tarzan's skin began to react to the unfamiliar environment. He shivered. This was something that rarely happened, even in the rainy season, which in Africa was seldom very cool, and never cold. This air felt chill on his bare skin.

Searching the sky, the ape-man studied the heavens. He perceived no moon, but neither did he expect to find Goro, who had been smothered by clouds. Yet the blanket of clouds had vanished, exposing a star field of vast extent. His sharpening gaze took in the myriad constellations, and something akin to wonder passed over his sun-bronzed countenance.

Like many who dwelt in nature, Tarzan knew how to read the night sky. He did not recognize the arrangements of stars overhead. Some possessed a vague familiarity, but taken as a whole, this was not the night sky of Africa, England, North America, nor any other land he had ever visited.

A fresh shiver coursed through his magnificent frame, but this time it was not actuated only by the cold.

Had he stood in Tarzan's place, a civilized man might have rejected the evidence of his senses. Doubt, denial, refusal to accept facts would have waged war in his brain. For civilized men are conditioned to a more fixed environment than one who dwells openly out among the elements.

The strange smell of the air combined with the cold and the alien stars above convinced Tarzan of the Apes that he no longer stood on the planet Earth. He wasted no time in mental struggle. He saw what he saw and he smelled the odors passing through his nostrils. It was but a small leap from the recognition that he was no longer in Africa to the firm conviction that he had awakened upon another world.

As if to underscore that fact, something swept across the night sky at great speed. It appeared to be a moon. Smaller than Earth's solitary satellite, it hurtled the breadth of the sky with impressive celerity, bringing a silvery shine like that of Goro, and illuminating the distressing emptiness of his barren surroundings and making shadows crawl in the great carpet of moss-like vegetation spreading in all directions. No features dotted the circular horizon.

The ape-man cast his mind back to the moments before the thunderbolt struck him down. He remembered also Sobito the witch doctor compliantly marching back to his rendezvous with captivity while beseeching his thunder god, Meriki.

A grim smile touched Tarzan's well-formed lips.

"Sobito's sorcery is indeed mighty," he breathed. "Tarzan took him for a fraud. If he is a fraud, he is the luckiest fraud to ever walk the Earth."

So saying, the bronzed giant gave vent to an ironic laugh heard by no one. Relieved of that emotion, he soberly confronted the astounding prospect of being alive on another world.

As far as the eye could see stretched a flat, dreary expanse of moss and lichen. It appeared to be endless, but, in fact, the weak starlight illuminated barely a quarter mile around the ape-man.

Setting out to investigate his new abode, Tarzan took two careful steps, mindful that the moss might harbor anything from sharp stones to small creatures.

The ground was soft and cool beneath his naked soles. Gaining confidence in the firmness of the terrain, the ape-man attempted to pick up his pace, knowing that vigorous movement would be necessary to keep his body warm in the chilly atmosphere.

With his next springy step, Tarzan left the ground.

A momentary astonishment seized him. He had not intended to leap into the air, but the simple act of pushing against the ground with his feet propelled him into the atmosphere at an oblique angle.

Twenty feet. Thirty. Nearly forty feet he soared, until gravity took hold once more. It was a weaker gravity than that to which Tarzan was accustomed. He felt lighter than his customary weight.

Landing awkwardly, he rolled and sprawled to a stop upon soft ground.

Taking care, the bronzed giant found his feet and attempted to progress. Since he could not see very far in any direction, any point of the compass seemed as provident as any other.

This time Tarzan moved more carefully, but the result was virtually the same. Four steps convinced him that he had control of his locomotion, but with the fifth he was again flying, describing a shallow arc that brought him ignominiously crashing back to the ground.

This time, Tarzan took matters into his own hands.

Tensing his steely muscles, he kicked backward with both legs—with the startling consequence that he then soared over sixty feet into the night. This gave him a greater view of his surroundings—which were both depressing and dismal.

The vast carpet of ochre moss seemed to stretch to infinity. He saw no signs of hills or other such natural features. More distressingly, the ape-man perceived no trees. Not even a solitary bush.

As gravity flung him back onto the mossy ground, Tarzan momentarily despaired for his survival. The night air was still and brought to his keen nostrils no smell of game, no scent of plants. Worse yet, there appeared to be no bodies of water in this section. The abundant starlight would have made visible any standing pool of water, had one existed.

This time the long fall back to the springy surface afforded Tarzan the opportunity to twist about and land on his feet. The success of this maneuver gave him confidence and he bolted back into the sky.

Each time the ape-man landed, he managed to do so under increasing control of his body.

Gaining confidence through practice, Tarzan leapt from position to position, covering great distances in astonishingly short order.

Alas, none of this swift progress gained him anything other than a soft cushion of moss in which to alight.

Pausing to rest, he squatted down and seized a clump of the matter. He sniffed it carefully. The odor was faintly disagreeable. But since the air smelled of chemicals, this might have been a trick of the atmosphere.

Cautiously, Tarzan rolled the yellow moss on his tongue. It tasted worse than it had smelled. Slowly, he chewed a bit, washing it about the inside of his mouth, tasting it for several moments before deciding to swallow.

The stuff produced no immediate ill effects, but neither was it satisfying to stomach or palette. Since it was plentiful, the ape-man decided to partake of it no further. When he became unbearably hungry, Tarzan would brave the taste of the stuff again. By that time, he reasoned, he might have little to lose, even if the moss was inimical to survival.

Standing up once again, the bronzed giant decided to test his limits. He broke into a swift run, then kicked downward at the ground with his right foot.

It was impossible to measure the height of this latest leap in the dark of night, but his senses told him that he achieved something quite close to seventy feet before the now-familiar sinking feeling took hold anew, warning Tarzan that he was returning to the ground.

Timing his landing was difficult. The ape-man struck the ground forcefully, unable to keep his feet, and consequently rolled several yards before shrugging off the dying momentum of his fall.

This experiment taught Tarzan one important thing about his new dwelling place. If predators were present, he possessed the ability to outpace them. Survival, then, was a matter of foraging for food more than it would be a battle to avoid being eaten.

A civilized man might have taken that for cold comfort, but Tarzan of the Apes was more akin to the great apes who raised him than the human mother who had birthed him.

If there was food in this strange place, he would find it. If plants grew, he would risk consuming them. If beasts roamed, he would find a way to slay them and discover if their meat was palatable.

But that was for the future. Tarzan's immediate concern was water and warmth.

Confidently, he set out to locate both.

Chapter 3

STRANDED

WERE THE situation not so dire, Tarzan of the Apes would have found humor in his predicament.

Marooned on an unknown planet, he bounded from place to place like a two-legged grasshopper. Had there been any such insects common to this world, the ape-man would have given them a run for their money. In fact, he would have hunted them and eaten his fill. As a young boy of the tribe of Kerchak, Tarzan enjoyed having a belly full of grubs. As a man, he preferred antelope meat or boar steaks. But he would subsist upon insects, if only he could find any.

From time to time, Tarzan paused in place to take stock of his surroundings. As the strangely grouped stars wheeled remorselessly overhead, a second moon appeared. This one moved more slowly through the night sky, its shape irregular. This lesser moon gave a weaker light than her sister satellite, but the result was distressingly the same.

Moss as far as the eye could see, appearing to undulate with an eerie animation of contrasting shadows created by the swiftly speeding moons.

The possibility that this world consisted of nothing but flat plains coated in moss began to gnaw at Tarzan's innate confidence.

As the second moon passed overhead, a new realization came to him. Despite having been raised in the jungle, and choosing to dwell there in early adulthood, Tarzan of the Apes was not an ignorant savage. He knew well of cities. He had read books, many of them learned texts. Scientific thought was not something unknown to him.

Of all the planets in the solar system shared by his natal world, only one was known by Earth astronomers to be illuminated by two moons, a greater and a lesser one.

Tarzan spoke their names aloud in a quiet breath.

"Phobos and Deimos."

Casting his mind back for what he knew of them, Tarzan recalled that their names meant "Fear" and "Terror."

This, and a half-familiar array of stars overhead, told the ape-man that he had somehow been conveyed to the fourth planet from the sun, orbiting next to the Earth. This red world was known to be smaller than Earth, and exerting a diminished gravity, as well as a less robust atmosphere. All of these clues assembled themselves in Tarzan's brain.

"This is Mars."

Once again, Tarzan's mind harkened back to the old witch-doctor who worshipped Meriki, who was identified with the Red Planet. The ape-man did not pointlessly wrestle with the seeming incomprehensibility of how he had been transported to this distant sphere. The facts had presented themselves to him, and he at once had accepted them without quarrel. In the jungle, a traveler may encounter a hungry lion or a lurking python at any time. When confronted by a ravenous lion or some similar beast, one had but two choices: to flee or fight for one's life. Typically one had only a split second to make a decision and to put it into effect.

There was no luxury in denying reality when it was intent on devouring one alive.

Tarzan of the Apes now stood upon the barren surface of Mars. That fact was undeniable. And so, the jungle lord accepted it. For what other choice had he?

Little was known for certain about the Red Planet, Tarzan reflected. Astronomers had long thought it to be a dead world, uninhabited by anything like the race of man. Much of it was believed to be desert. Looking through their telescopes, men of science had thought they discerned canals, which mistakenly led them to suspect water flowed on the Martian surface.

Surveying the prospect about him, the ape-man saw no canals or any signs of water, flowing or otherwise. Nothing moved but shifting shadows. A silence greater than he could recall enveloped the spectral expanse. The absence of sounds smacked of lifelessness.

Again, a dismal uncertainty seized his heart. In Africa, Tarzan was the Lord of the Jungle. The forest was his home, the animals of the untamed realm his subjects. He knew every branch and leaf, and each stream. All of his life, he had learned the ways of the jungle. Tarzan was supreme in his own environment.

Now he stood naked and alone in a land where there was no jungle, no streams, no game. For the first time since he was a hairless balu, Tarzan felt as if he were lord of nothing. It was an ugly, empty, unfamiliar feeling. And the ape-man instinctively detested it.

Gathering his mighty muscles, he essayed a running leap and so cleared an expanse of vegetation that stretched nearly fifty feet. Again and again, he vaulted skyward, changing direction from time to time, seeking something other than yellowish barrenness.

If there were animals upon the ochre surface of Mars, he was eager to find them. If they were greater than he, he would fight them, and eat them if he could. And if the strength of Tarzan of the Apes was not sufficient to best these unknown creatures, well, the law of the jungle invariably prevails, whether one dwells in a jungle or not.

In the struggle for life, Tarzan preferred to fall in battle, not from thirst or starvation, which he considered to be an ignominious and unworthy fate for a jungle lord.

The idea that Mars harbored human life was a possibility so remote that the ape-man gave it little consideration. He was not the first intelligent human being to take at face value the opinions of scientists. Tarzan knew that no man born on Earth had ever visited Mars, and therefore such lofty pronouncements should be taken with a grain of salt. But the prospect of encountering men appeared increasingly remote.

Hours of necessarily frenetic exploration availed Tarzan of the Apes absolutely nothing. Try as he might, he spied no signs of life, smelled no spoor, and heard no sound other than that of his own breathing.

The Red Planet, it seemed, was devoid of animal life.

Succumbing to this realization, Tarzan gave up. Dropping back to the soft ground, he gathered together sufficient moss to make a comfortable bed and lay down to sleep the remainder of the night away.

By this time, both moons had left the overhead sky. Only wan starlight illuminated the boundless plain, which was flat as far as the eye could perceive. The darkness would have been absolute to any other. But the powerful lenses of the ape-man's eyes could make out the scant features comprising the near distance.

Believing himself safe from predators, Tarzan fell quickly asleep, concluding that further exploration might better await the illumination of Kudu, the life-giving solar body that the Earth shared with Mars.

And so Tarzan slept, warmed by the moss that he had piled both atop him and beneath his bronzed form, for he had no other protection against the bitter cold of the Martian night.

Twice more the irregular moons appeared, the greater one seeming to flee her pursuing companion, washing the mossy carpet for a few hours before dropping below the flat horizon and plunging this strange world into near darkness.

Through these intervals of alternating lunar brightness and Cimmerian darkness the jungle lord slept soundly, his slumber troubled by neither dreams nor nightmares. Such was the mind of Tarzan of the Apes that even cast away on a remote world, bereft of everything that gave life meaning, his sleep was undisturbed by the cares of the day. For he knew that with each sunrise came new opportunity and new adventures.

WHILE UNBEKNOWNST to him, many miles to the west as Earth men perceived distance, something living plodded across the flat landscape, moving on decapod feet, drawing closer, ever closer....

But Tarzan heard it not, for the rarified Martian atmosphere did not carry sounds as easily as did Earth's oxygen-rich air....

Chapter 4

Beasts of Barsoom

CONSONANT WITH the suddenness of the sunrise in Equatorial Africa, morning broke on Mars with such breathtaking celerity that Tarzan of the Apes sprang to his feet the instant the climbing solar orb blazed in his face.

The sudden act precipitated him at a forty-five degree angle from the makeshift moss bedding which had insulated him through the Martian night. The ape-man was forced to throw out all four limbs in order to catch himself when he fell back to ground.

The risk of landing on his head and possibly breaking his neck was proving to be an ever-present danger. If he desired to navigate the Martian terrain successfully, Tarzan understood that he would have to become master of his powerful body as it operated in the reduced gravity of the Red Planet.

Regaining his feet, Tarzan looked about him. The atmosphere was already suffused with the warmth of the newly risen sun. Bathing in its crimson brilliance, Tarzan experienced strange sensations.

This was indeed Kudu, the familiar sun. But she was smaller than the sun of his earthly existence. Shrunken, but no less bright. Her warming rays touched his bare skin and he began to shake off the chill that had crept into his bones.

Seen in clear light, the moss carpeting the endless plain took on more color, but the hue was still a pale yellowish. Where there was open ground, it was the color of mud. But mud suffused with a rusty reddish hue.

If Tarzan needed further evidence that he stood upon the fourth inner planet of the solar system, the rust-red soil provided that proof.

As the diminutive sun climbed into the sky, the ape-man peered about, perceived nothing to suggest life awakening. In the jungle, the sun heralded the morning cries of birds, the drowsy drone of insects. But here, nothing of that sort reached his ears.

Not yet discouraged, he once again took to the skies, springing upward like a magnificently muscled bronze grasshopper, alighting wherever gravity deposited him.

Eventually, Tarzan spied a feature in the western distance that loomed above the dismal plain. Landing, he oriented himself to face this elevation and propelled himself in successive hops toward it.

The act of continually leaping and landing, cushioning himself with each maneuver, seemed not to tire him very much. Tarzan of the Apes was exceedingly strong for a man, but here on Mars his muscular prowess and endurance seemed at least trebled.

Finally alighting close to the mount, he observed it at a careful distance, knowing that it might conceal a burrow or cavity into which some Martian creature might have sought refuge.

It consisted of a rocky outcrop that did not quite seem to be stone. It displayed a slightly organic aspect, and its delicate hues blended from blue to a pale purple. It was certainly not metallic, nor was it quite mineral, although its coloration suggested otherwise.

Approaching carefully, Tarzan found that he could walk with greater confidence. It required more restraint in the use of his leg muscles than was his custom. But he was no longer propelled into the sky at the slightest misstep or excess pressure.

Coming to the edge of the natural feature, the ape-man circumnavigated it, and saw that it consisted of irregular surfaces that seemed to be fused together, as if different substances sharing a common identity had somehow come to be one substance.

There were dark orifices visible here and there, but the surface of the mound was dry and dusty, suggesting that it was a natural feature abraded by the Martian winds, which keened so faintly as to create a constant susurration that barely impinged upon his hearing.

Tarzan inhaled the dry air and again the perpetually present chemical tang masked whatever odors he might have otherwise detected. But there seemed to be something in the air he had not previously smelled. The scent spoor reminded him of nothing in his previous experience.

Kneeling down, he seized a crusty extrusion, gave it a sideways twist. A piece of the substance colored blue broke off. Lifting this to his face, he examined it intently.

A flicker of surprise touched his gray eyes. Observed up close, he recognized the twists and whorls which comprised the substance's outer surface.

"Coral," he said aloud.

There was no question of it. This ancient mound had once been submerged in a body of water and unknown sea life had formed coral. This sample displayed characteristics unlike any coral that Tarzan had encountered back on his home world. But it was unmistakably allied to brain coral. The matter was dense, having the consistency and feel of calcium.

Stepping around the mount, Tarzan looked for a piece of stouter stuff to serve as a weapon, but also thin enough to be harvested. He found such a piece, a horny extension that snapped off with a sharp kick of his naked heel.

The horn broke easily, but Tarzan had forgotten himself. The recoil of his action threw him backward, and he went skating along the surrounding moss.

Managing to brake his headlong flight using clutching hands and arresting heels, the ape-man sat up, and again looked about him.

He now realized that he had been traversing the bottom of what once had been a vast sea during an epoch when Mars was younger. *Had the planet retained any of its water?* he wondered. It was vital that it did. Vital to his own survival. But thus far Tarzan had seen no evidence of it.

Returning to reclaim the horn of coral, the jungle lord continued on his way. Inasmuch as he felt the need to relearn the art of walking, he walked.

A growing sense of enormity came over him as Tarzan made his way through the barren mossy expanse. The sun continued to rise, increasing the warmth of his surroundings with welcome speed. The chill night was now gone. Having no obstructions, the solar rays touched everything, but only Tarzan of the Apes showed any signs of life.

From time to time, he paused to kneel and scratch around in the moss, seeking ground moisture or grubs. He found neither.

Squeezing a clump of mossy roots produced a bitter fluid that Tarzan spurned at first taste. Yet the ape-man reasoned that for moss to grow, there must be some moisture feeding it. The skies were cloudless, as far as he could perceive. But that did not mean it did not sometimes rain on this strange world.

Carefully standing up anew, Tarzan reflected that rain was probably the most welcome thing he could experience at this juncture in his trek across the disagreeable face of Mars.

Tiring of his slow walking progress, the bronzed giant again took to the skies, this time endeavoring to shoot straight upward, in order to see beyond the far horizon.

During one of these upward perambulations, the jungle lord spied something moving over the mossy former sea floor.

His view of it was necessarily fleeting, but it appeared to be an animal. There was no mistaking this fact, even though its bodily configurations appeared distorted to his eyes.

Upon landing, he shot straight up again, this time as high as possible, and cleared nearly seventy feet. For his skill in leaping was growing in proportion to his ability to manage ordinary walking.

The thing he perceived was low and flat in appearance. From a distance, he judged it to be the size of a juvenile hippopotamus. It had something of the shape of one as well, but there the resemblance evaporated into fantasy.

For one thing, the beast owned ten limbs, five set at each flank. The head might have been that of a frog, had frogs grown to excessive proportions. The hairless thing was walking along on its busy feet, showing a speedy locomotion that belied its bulk. Its coloration was reddish-yellow, shading to a pale gray at the belly.

Tarzan of the Apes did not know what it was, but this fantastic beast represented meat. And red meat saturated with hot running juices was what he craved most in life.

Clutching the jagged horn of blue coral, he shot back into the air and hopped toward the thing in a series of prodigious bounds.

As he drew near, the ape-man perceived that the creature's mouth was open and the frog-shaped maw gleamed with three rows of needle teeth that reminded him of those of the tiger shark.

Tarzan had fought sharks before, and always successfully. He did not fear this beast's fangs.

Four successive leaps put Tarzan within striking distance of the perambulating creature. A fifth would precipitate him upon its colorful back, putting him in a position of advantage.

TARZAN DID not execute that fifth leap, however.

His attention went to a mound of coral not far distant from the strange creature. By this time, the Martian sun was bathing everything in its glorious radiance. From a distance, Tarzan spied something stirring amid the confusion of purplish-blue coral.

It seemed to him to be antennae or feelers groping out of the orifices. Instantly, he went on guard. From out of these orifices jutted something that was rubbery in substance and a translucent violet in hue.

The ten-legged creature walked along, oblivious to what was transpiring. But Tarzan halted, sensing danger.

Rising slowly, the inhabitants of the long-dead coral reef ascended silently into the light. Whereupon, they inflated like bladders.

To describe them intelligently would be to commit folly. To human eyes, they suggested violet jellyfish or perhaps cuttlefish. Rubbery tendrils hung below the swelling bodies, which must harbor a natural lighter-than-air gas such as hydrogen, for once they had fully emerged, they flowed up into the thin air and by a means of propulsion that was not evident, they floated toward the oblivious creature in the manner of a swarm of deformed bees.

Tarzan moved no muscles as he watched. The silent things descended upon the creature and their tentacles commenced to lash out, striking again and again on the dorsal surface of the steadily plodding thing.

Abruptly, it broke into a run. Its speed was something to behold. A cheetah would have envied it. An antelope would have been proud to move so swiftly on its four fleet legs as this cumbersome creature propelled itself upon ten feet.

But its speed availed it not. The floating phantasms had inserted their tentacles—or perhaps they were flexible stingers—into the flesh of the terrified beast and being thus anchored, were pulled along with it like balloons tied to a locomotive.

The frog-faced monster could not escape. It ran and ran and then commenced to careen in frantic circles, falling and rolling on its heaving sides and attempting to crush the stubborn violet bladders attached to it.

Fatigue soon overtook it, and Tarzan suspected that mere fatigue was not the entire cause. The way the bladders convulsed, expanding and contracting in pulsing waves, made him think of fat spiders injecting a struggling fly with their venom.

Panting its last, the stricken creature rolled over and lay still. Its hairless flanks ceased to heave and its noisy snorting abated.

Then the jellyfish detached themselves and floated to one side. There they hovered, waiting patiently. Tarzan could now discern delicate frills decorating the creatures. Set longitudinally as well as latitudinally along the oblate bodies, these wavered and appeared to be the external organs that enabled them to navigate the thin air.

With surprising swiftness, the fallen beast began to expand, bloating up enormously. The ponderous creature slowly rose, lifting skyward, buoyed by gases that were fast expanding within its body cavities.

Crying out, flailing its weakened feet, the thing rose helplessly into the thin air, higher and higher and higher until it could climb no more. There it twisted and turned in an agony of futility, a prisoner of its unnatural buoyancy.

Rising to join it, the jellyfish creatures attacked it once more, this time piercing it at all points, releasing the pent-up gases until they had vented outward with a prolonged and ghoulish hissing.

No longer buoyant, the hapless hulk crashed back to the surface, screaming and bellowing by turns.

It landed with a loud thud in a clump of moss. There it lay still, eyes wide and glazing over.

As Tarzan watched fascinated, the violet things descended to feed upon the corpse. Propelled by their fin-like frills, they swarmed about the carcass, and the sounds that came from their feeding were grisly and unfamiliar to the ape-man's ears. As he watched, they steadily grew fatter in girth, becoming bloated themselves.

During this feeding, one of the swelling creatures took notice of him. Detaching itself from the fresh meal, it floated lazily in Tarzan's direction.

From it came a low and eerie whistling. At that sound, other jellyfish quietly detached themselves and followed in the leader's wake.

Recognizing his peril, Tarzan lifted the horn of coral and flung it at the lead creature, knocking it from the sky. The bladder of a thing landed with a mushy plop, but did not rise again.

Whipping their tentacles frantically, the others redoubled their efforts and Tarzan swiftly recognized the hopelessness of his position.

Turning, he bounded to the north, landed successfully and jumped back into the sky without hesitation. He did this six times. And when he looked back over his shoulder in mid-leap, the weird violet bladders were distant flecks pulsing in unison against the undulating ochre plain. Tarzan knew they could never overtake him, so the ape-man kept moving, satisfied at last that he had discovered that Mars supported forms of life that promised future meals, if only he could hunt them down.

Chapter 5

THE DRIVERLESS CHARIOT

LONG BEFORE the noon hour, the Martian day had heated up to a degree that reminded Tarzan of his home plantation, but without the extreme humidity of Africa's equatorial zone. Perspiration became a second skin, making his bronze epidermis shine.

This unrelenting sunlight made the ape-man thirst. Still no sign nor sound of water presented itself. No scent of it either. But who was there to say what the water of this weird place would smell like?

Clouds were absent, foreclosing on any promise of rain. Usha the wind sounded differently here. The familiar feeling of being upwind or downwind was not the same. Compared to his beloved jungle, Nature spoke a different tongue, one Tarzan had difficulty understanding.

A slow frustration began to gnaw at the ape-man's thoughts. He stood so completely out of his natural element that he was beginning to question his ability to fend for himself.

True, this doubt existed only in Tarzan's mind—a mere mustard seed. Yet he knew if he did not make progress, it would sprout.

Despair was not something Tarzan customarily felt. He had been trapped in dank dungeons for long months, exiled in faraway lands, yet always managed to persevere. But that had been on Earth, a place of forests, streams, and plentiful game.

The deserts of northern Africa had given the ape-man travails such as he now faced—thirst, hunger, and similar privations. But when he roamed those sands, Tarzan contended with the familiar flora and fauna of his own world.

Here on Mars, almost nothing was familiar. Natural sounds were almost wholly absent. Usha inhaled and exhaled so softly that the ape-man hardly noticed the absence of the wind's soft susurration after it had abated. Only Kudu the sun, shrunken to a fraction of her usual splendor, reassured him. Warm as ever, but otherwise unhelpful.

Pausing to rest, Tarzan took up a clump of moss and squeezed its rootways in one fist until moisture ran out into his open palm. These yellowish juices were meager. But sufficient droplets fell that he licked his palm and was grateful for the scant moisture provided, despite its brackish taste.

This operation went on for nearly an hour, when Tarzan's ever-alert ears were smote by a sound that was both strange and familiar.

Muffled by the soft undulating carpet of ochre moss, it came to his attention softly at first. This was the monotonous turning of wheels. They creaked as they rolled along, and that incessant sound now carried to Tarzan's keen hearing.

Lifting up to his full height, the bronzed giant directed his attention toward the commotion.

To his astonishment, he saw what looked at first to be a stupendous elephant lumbering along. The thing was a dun-colored juggernaut of rolling muscle and ponderous bone. In its wake rumbled a chariot of impressive size, three wheels turning as the monster stepped along, one set forward and two rolling on either side. The wheels did not appear to be constructed of wood or metal but of some other composition that showed indications of age and disrepair.

The size of the chariot suggested that the owner was a giant. But no one could be seen driving the contraption, whose rounded front was covered in strange designs having no meaning to him. The vehicle appeared to be fashioned of a metal that resembled iron, and might well have been iron.

Springing in the direction of the apparition, Tarzan covered a great distance in a short time, hopping upward and landing on soft ground where he could. Once, upon alighting, he skated in the vegetation and scraped his skin in an open patch of reddish soil.

At length, he came to a spot well ahead of the monstrous beast of burden and its abbreviated train.

Observing closely, the creature resembled a mastodon of Earth's ancient past. But this behemoth was no earthly pachyderm, nor anything ever birthed upon Tarzan's natal planet.

For one thing, it appeared entirely eyeless. The head was a great knob of brown hide, featureless for the most part. Nor did there seem to be a mouth. Instead, three trunks extended from the otherwise blank center of its face. They bore some resemblance to elephant trunks, but they had just as much in common with octopus tentacles, or perhaps the scaly bodies of constrictor snakes.

The central trunk—if it was, in fact, such—most resembled that of an earthly pachyderm. It was long and flexible and ended in an orifice that consisted of a pad perforated by three natural holes. Two of these apertures pulsed with its breathing. Evidently, these were nostrils. But the larger hole at the base of the pad showed a double ring of small triangular teeth. Obviously, this was the beast's mouth.

The appendages on either side were slimmer but no less flexible. These ended in round orbs that opened and closed as the thing plunged along. The eyes had a generally orange look to them. Each appendage waved about sluggishly. The tentacles looked up, around, and even up and over its back to peer behind it. They moved independently of one another and seemed capable of perceiving more than one mental picture at a time.

This told Tarzan of the Apes that evolution had produced in this monster pachyderm an ability to see in all directions at will.

Such a configuration could only mean that the great beast was perpetually on the lookout for predators.

What manner of predator could fell such a mighty thing was for the moment beyond the ape-man's powers of imagination. But he had no doubt that such a creature existed on the Red Planet.

TARZAN STEPPED into the path of the oncoming beast and lifted a hand in the warning.

"I am Tarzan of the Apes," he proclaimed loudly. "Halt!"

The jungle lord spoke in the language of the elephant, whom he called Tantor.

Tarzan had little expectation that this elephantine monster would understand him. But he thought it was worth the expenditure of effort to try.

So he was not greatly surprised when the formidable behemoth continued lumbering ahead, its optical tentacles swinging forward and fixing on him. They opened and closed slowly, but showed no sign of recognition or any other discernible emotion. Nor did it utter any vocalization.

The ground shook with its thunderous tread. The thing did not possess hoofs, but rather pads. In that wise, it was not that much different from Tantor. But it went about on six gigantic legs, having an intermediate set mid-way on its flanks.

Seeing that the thing would not halt, Tarzan bent his knees and launched himself toward it. He cleared the thing's bald skull and landed in the driverless chariot it was patiently transporting across the Martian surface.

But it proved not to be entirely empty. The flat metal bed of the chariot was a litter of dry bones, suggesting that its driver had perished long ago. He spied no reins, no apparent means of guiding the beast of burden to steer the chariot along. Tarzan could not fathom how the chariot was controlled. He put that mystery out of his mind as he rooted around among the bones.

The bronzed giant soon unearthed a great skull, one grotesquely out of proportion to what would belong to a human being. Despite its general human configurations, it spouted a pair of great curving tusks, resembling polished white porcelain.

Lifting the osseous relic to the sun, Tarzan examined it from all perspectives and tried to envision what the bony head looked like when clothed in flesh. That it was human-like in some respects was undeniable. But the upcurving tusks reminded him of Horta the boar. Perhaps there dwelt giant men on this world whom evolution had favored with the blood of the wild boar.

Tarzan thought that the tusks would make serviceable weapons, even if they would be difficult to wield, so he wrenched them loose, shattering the desiccated jaw, and dropped the skull amid the litter of bones.

Taking inventory of them, he found an extra set of arms, but thought little of that. The possibility that giants existed on this featureless world who naturally grew an extra pair of arms did not cross his mind.

There were no weapons to be found in the chariot, nor any provisions, only a few ornaments of beaten metal that might have been armbands or fetters. It appeared that the chariot had been attacked and looted long ago, its driver slain, and possibly butchered, leaving only his picked-clean bones to bleach in the sun and the dumb beast of burden to pull the chariot across the Martian wastes like a funeral procession of one.

Perhaps, wondered Tarzan, the Martian mastodon was conveying his late master home. Instincts higher than those guiding most men often inhabited and motivated the lower animals.

The ape-man decided to see where the creature took him. In this decision, he was aided by the absolutely bleak landscape that promised nothing of value.

And so becoming accustomed to the monotonous groaning of the three great wheels, Tarzan cleared a space on the floor, and waited patiently while the uninviting landscape rolled by.

All during the ape-man's investigations, the behemoth had lumbered on, seemingly uncaring that it had acquired a passenger. From time to time, the massive mastodon employed its central trunk to snatch up bunches of moss, chewing noisily and conveying the mulch to its belly via pulsing constrictions along its sinuous length.

It did not pause to dine, but remorselessly plodded on, never stopping, never resting, a rolling engine of meat and muscle propelled along by brute instincts that were unfathomable to the ape-man, who was familiar with the ways of the elephant tribe, but who found this Martian brute to be more mechanical in its base instincts than animal.

To pass the time, Tarzan tossed out of the back of the chariot the bones that had been its only cargo. After giving it a final examination, he discarded the skull last. It shattered upon impact.

The bony relic did not present in its brain case or heavy jaw evidence of a high-minded race of men. Again, the ape-man attempted to envision what manner of biped this might have been in life. But all his imagination could conjure up was a boar in the form of a giant man, which he mentally named Horta-mangani, which in the language of the apes who reared him meant Great-boar-men.

When he was done, Tarzan stood holding the two curved tusks of polished ivory. They felt strange in his fists. As weapons they were no doubt formidable when attached to the jaws of their owner, but held in hand, their curving configuration severely limited their utility as stabbing weapons. Until the jungle lord could fashion something more blade-like, they would have to serve.

Tarzan wondered if he was destined to encounter such a fearsome man-monster during his trek across the face of Mars. If so, he did not fear such a meeting. For Tarzan of the Apes feared nothing....

Chapter 6

The Martian Lion

HUNGER WAS a steady, ceaseless gnawing in the belly of Tarzan when the mastodonian draught animal pulled into view of a cluster of small hills.

These hills were not composed of coral deposits but appeared to be natural upheavals of the rusty soil of Mars. Tarzan studied them intently.

Nothing seemed to move in their vicinity, although sunlight brought forth gleams of something resembling diamonds. No birds of any type flew about the area. Nor was the drone of insects heard. The sounds of Mars appeared limited to the soft sigh of the wind, which rarely encountered any obstacle that produced audible wind effects.

The mastodon was moving perpendicular to the hills and appeared to be uninterested in them. By contrast, the ape-man was eager to explore the low range. He wished there was a means by which to urge the elephantine animal north so that he could explore the intriguing feature at his leisure.

Feeling a growing frustration, Tarzan pointed in the direction of the hills and shouted, "Turn! Tarzan demands that you turn, beast."

Whether the creature heard was not immediately clear. A single eye-stalk whipped up and floated over the beast's rolling back. The uncanny orb regarded Tarzan without expression.

Leveling a bronzed arm, the ape-man indicated the distant rolling hills.

In response, the tentacle waved once, then swept around and gaped at the hills. The round eye appeared to find nothing of interest, for it lingered but briefly, whereupon the sinuous appendage returned to its forward-facing position.

Now Tarzan knew that he could hop off the rolling chariot and leap to the hills in short order. No doubt he would subsequently catch up to the wagon in time. But hunger created in him an impatience with the limitations of life on Mars. Nor could he properly gauge how long his strength would hold out unless he found substantial sustenance.

In his frustration, Tarzan's imagination pictured the lumbering beast turning toward the hills.

To his utter astonishment, the creature mechanically adjusted its plodding feet and shifted in that direction!

Perhaps it was a coincidence. Perhaps it was a delayed reaction to the ape-man's arm gestures.

As the plodding creature changed direction, Tarzan's impatience caused him to wish that the beast of burden would pick up its pace.

Almost immediately, it did! The ponderous revolving chariot wheels rumbled more rapidly, its forward rolling motion increasing noticeably.

Desiring to test this phenomenon, Tarzan called out, "Halt!"

The creature did not halt. It kept rolling. Tarzan then folded his arms, intending to see if a delayed reaction manifested. The brute might own a sluggish, slow-comprehending brain roughly such as dinosaurs were reputed to possess.

After several minutes passed, Tarzan unfolded his arms and visualized the living juggernaut pulling up to a halt.

The response was virtually instantaneous. The creature stopped short. The trailing chariot lurched once, whereupon all motion ceased.

Tarzan scrutinized the broad back of the thing and wondered.

Could the creature have read his mind? Was it possible that it was sensitive to thought waves? Science had never proved such mental waves existed, but their existence was strongly suspected.

Wishing to test his control further, Tarzan imagined the creature's right eye-stalk looping around to regard him once more.

In short order, it obeyed! Satisfied, the ape-man silently commanded the creature to show him both of his eyes. The other tentacle looped around and two gaping orange orbs stared at him, opening and closing independently in an attitude of obedient expectancy.

There was no question in Tarzan's mind but that the creature was awaiting further instructions. Mentally, he gave them.

"Go to the low hills yonder."

Lurching back into motion, the creature reoriented itself with some difficulty and trundled in that direction.

Tarzan stood on a raised driver's platform that permitted him to see over the curving rail of the chariot. Otherwise, he could not peer over its high, ornate sides.

With the strangely scented air of the Red Planet coursing in and out of his lungs, the bronzed giant stared ahead and scrutinized the hills.

They were not impressive in shape—except insofar as they were virtually the only bit of vertical topography that these former sea bottoms boasted. Tarzan did not expect much of those uninviting mounds. But any feature that differed from the monotonous ochre moss promised novelty, if not sustenance. Of the two, the ape-man much preferred sustenance. But he would also welcome any opportunity to explore fresh terrain.

As the creature undulated along, it slowed to a creeping crawl, as if hesitant.

"Faster!" thought Tarzan. And the obedient beast picked up its lumbering pace.

But before long it again slowed to a crawl.

Now Tarzan of the Apes understood beasts of all types. And even this alien creature exhibited behavior that he recognized from long association with African wildlife.

The behemoth hesitated to advance not because it was lazy but because it feared something. A predator, no doubt.

Respectful of the creature's innate instincts, the ape-man permitted it to proceed at its own pace despite his eagerness to explore and forage for food.

Amid the litter in the chariot was a flat band of whitish metal, broad and ornate. Along its hammered surface were empty indentations and hollows suggesting that stones or jewels had formerly been held in place by metallic tines that were now deformed or missing.

Its purpose was unclear, but by prying it open and then bending it to conform to his waist, Tarzan fashioned a crude belt. The heavy metal bent readily under his animal strength.

Retrieving the curved tusks from the chariot bed, the jungle lord inserted them on either side, so that if danger showed its face, he was prepared to leap to the attack and make use of his newfound weapons.

On and on rolled the chariot, drawn by the reluctant elephantine dreadnought, ever eastward.

As the hills drew closer, Tarzan noticed that the eye-stalks became more animated. Independently of one another, they swept around, looking by turns toward every compass point. The orange orbs were clearly seeking early warning of something that the creature feared above all other things.

Yet nothing untoward transpired. The hills loomed closer and closer, and soon Tarzan by mental means commanded the brute to come to a complete halt. It did so.

Stepping off the chariot, the ape-man landed squarely on the ground, and walked confidently toward the hills. On either hip, the recurved tusks moved with his easy, rhythmic stride.

Pleased that he was able to hold his feet on the ground, Tarzan marched confidently up to the mounds. Stepping into them, he saw that they consisted of tight-packed red soil, in which extrusions of what appeared to be clear quartz glinted in the beating sun.

Kneeling, the jungle lord examined these outcroppings with his practiced eye, but they appeared to be no different than earthly quartz. The hard substance, he knew, could be chipped and fashioned into arrowheads, or even crude but wicked blades. But he would require rudimentary tools to fashion them.

Questing about, Tarzan found nuggets of quartz that might be suitable for his purposes. Arrowheads, of course, would be useless unless he could find wood and feathers, as well as suitable cord with which to fashion a bow. Because Tarzan had not yet discovered any Martian forest did not mean that such did not exist.

The ape-man's more urgent need was for a straight cutting blade. So he took care to select two long lengths of quartz, excavating them with his bare hands.

Laden with these, he jumped back to the chariot, landing perfectly in the back. There, the ape-man deposited his prizes and prepared to return and scavenge more.

A long, thin, piping snort came from the blunt head of the mastodon-beast. It abruptly backed away, knocking Tarzan off his feet. And the dry air was suddenly filled with a musky scent.

Tarzan could not place it. Nor did he expect to. It was wholly unfamiliar to his experience.

Climbing back to the raised platform, the bronzed giant seized the railing in both hands and swept the surroundings with his keen gray gaze. He took notice of the fact that the monstrous mastodon did not direct his vision skyward at any point. The questing orbs scanned the surroundings laterally but tended toward the ground.

This behavior communicated to the ape-man one unassailable fact: that any threat would come from the ground, not from above.

Taking hold of his tusk weapons by their comparatively thin roots, Tarzan made certain they were properly positioned and ready to be drawn if necessary.

The musky scent creeping through the thin atmosphere grew more ripe. Whatever was out and about was fast approaching.

Tarzan issued a mental command for the creature to come to a complete halt. This, it did.

Climbing atop the rail and balancing thereon, Tarzan shaded his flinty eyes with a sun-burnished hand, the better to see clearly.

Because the vista was so flat, the bronzed giant reasoned that any threat would come from the hills. It was a foregone conclusion that anything of sufficient size to attack the chariot hauler must be formidable. Otherwise, the creature could not be brought down.

Almost as soon as the thought manifested in his brain, it seemed to birth a result.

SOMETHING APPEARED on one of the near hills. It was long and sinuous of body, and seemingly without fur except that around its face bristled a wild halo of hair, generally reminiscent of the mane of an African lion. In that particular, it reminded Tarzan of faithful Jad-bal-ja, whose magnificent mane was also ebony.

If this was a lion, the evolutionary forces that dominated the Red Planet had produced a creature far more ferocious than any terrestrial feline. For it was larger than a bull elephant, although not as tall, being constructed for stalking. Its orbs were green and protuberant, and they fixed upon the mastodon with an emerald glare. Avarice gleamed in those eyes.

Abruptly, the creature leapt from its perch, and came charging down on ten synchronized legs.

Lifting its central trunk, the Martian mastodon gave forth a long weird wailing cry, almost of despair.

Mentally, Tarzan commanded it to run.

The beast wasted no time. It threw itself forward, describing a half circle as it fled from the low hills, with the pounding predator tearing in its direction.

By that time, Tarzan of the Apes had vaulted skyward, simultaneously extracting the ivory tusks from his makeshift belt.

Less than a day marooned on Mars, the ape-man had fully mastered his ability to leap and land where he wished. The fact that the charging lion-monster was moving with unnerving alacrity did not hinder Tarzan's expert bound.

Miraculously, he landed atop the creature's long twisting body. Dropping to his lean, muscular haunches, the bronzed giant lifted a recurved tusk in each fist and brought his arms sweeping downward and inward, where the natural points slid unobstructed through the creature's rib cage, after first piercing the thick tawny hide.

The ten-limbed monster stumbled, then reared up, its snarling face twisting about. The ape-man had landed at mid-back, where the beast's yawning teeth could not reach. Wildly, the jaws clamped and snapped as the creature roared in baffled futility.

Releasing the embedded tusks, Tarzan wrapped mighty legs about the creature's barrel chest and clutched at its thick hide, so he could not be thrown off.

For all its ugly length and multiple feet, this Martian lion was agile. It twisted about like a crocodile, and like a crocodile its rows of vicious teeth snapped and clutched at empty air, missing Tarzan by mere inches.

When it saw that it could not reach its anterior tormentor, or break loose, the lionine creature attempted to throw the jungle lord by bucking and rolling. Reaching down, Tarzan pulled free one of the tusks, which was now slathered with gore.

Clasping it by the root in both hands, Tarzan brought the ensanguined point down on the portion of the spine directly before him. He did not expect to accomplish much damage with his first thrust, but to his amazement, the tusk drove in deeply, parting the twisting spinal column as if it were held together by gum and not tough tendon and muscle.

Rearing back on its hindmost set of legs, the lion-monster screamed long and loud, and the sound echoed off the hills, reverberating throughout the quiet Martian atmosphere.

That mortal cry—for it was plain that the creature was mortally wounded—was its last living utterance.

Giving a final rolling flounce, the thing flipped over on its side, legs jittering, its gristly tail beating madly.

Tarzan stepped off, and walked around the creature.

The face was hideous to behold, and the green eyes glared at him for several moments. Then the angry light in them faded, and the protuberant orbs half closed. The legs settled down. Finally, the whipping tail gave a final flop and then moved no more.

Stepping up to the beast, Tarzan placed one naked foot firmly upon its sinuous flank, and threw back his black-haired head. Lifting his voice, he gave forth the weird scream that was his call of triumph.

Now, for the first time, the kill-cry of the victorious bull ape resounded in the thin air of the dying planet, Mars.

Chapter 7

"Tarzan Is No Ghost"

TARZAN OF THE APES stepped off his kill and examined it from every angle.

On Earth, the lion was known to him as Numa. The crocodile was called Gimla. In his naturalistic conception, the ape-man took this vanquished beast whose carcass he intended to exploit to be more lion than crocodile but also reminiscent of the latter in the sinuous length of its body and elongated ferociousness of its snout.

On Earth, Tarzan had tasted of both lion and crocodile meat. Of the two, he much preferred the former. But he was presently in no position to be choosy.

Stooping, he retrieved one of the curved tusks and studied it. The blood that coated its ivory surface was the same scarlet hue as the blood of Earth animals. That much was a comfort.

With his tongue, he tasted the strange creature's blood and found it more salty than lion blood, but still good to the taste. He licked the tusk clean, found its mate piercing the creature's tawny flank, and rolled the creature off its other side so that he could perform the same task.

The ease with which the carcass rolled surprised him. He judged the beast to weigh in excess of eight hundred pounds.

After he had licked the second tusk clean, Tarzan knelt and drank from one open wound. Inserting one of the tusks after replacing its mate in his belt holster, the ape-man jerked the ivory tool around in the creature's vitals, managing to break several ribs, which he yanked free.

Warm meat clung to these ribs. He began chewing. The taste was strange; it wasn't like Numa at all. Nor was it reminiscent of Gimla's gristled meat.

Nevertheless, Tarzan devoured what he could, and then returning to the open wound used both tusks to peel back a length of hide. The tools were not appropriate to the task, having no edges. So Tarzan again holstered them, gripped the nap of the pelt tightly in both bronzed hands and began wrenching back.

The hairless hide was tougher than lion skin, but Tarzan's gorilla-like strength was more than sufficient to peel off a portion, exposing the muscles of one rear leg.

Having nothing to cut with, he fell upon the leg and began biting out great gobs of meat, chewing carefully, and becoming accustomed to the taste. The flesh was not as stringy as lion meat, and this met with Tarzan's approval.

As his belly filled and renewed life again flowed through his veins, the jungle lord spoke aloud.

"Tarzan is no ghost."

He had begun to wonder if he had been wandering through some strange abode of the dead, if the eerily quiet planet was where men's souls convened when they died. But now he started to suspect otherwise.

The ape-man's lower face was stained with gore when he finished his meal. He stood up and looked about.

He saw the chariot poised at a standstill. The mastodon-like behemoth was half turned toward him, its eye-stalks intent upon Tarzan's bloody business. One blinked. The other followed suit.

The bronzed giant sent his thoughts to the animal. At first, it did not respond. Lifting an arm, he waved for the thing to return, and again formed pictures in his mind of the beast returning.

Slowly, reluctantly, the creature transferred its orientation back toward Tarzan and his conquest. It plodded along gingerly, its eye-stalks sweeping about, obviously on the alert should a second predator appear.

Tarzan returned to the monster's hide and tore lose another patch with his bare hands. By this means, he began to collect the raw material with which to make garments. A loincloth would have been preferable, but he lacked a sharp edge with which to cut the pelt into appropriate lengths. Thinking of the bitter Martian nights, the ape-man decided he would have to be satisfied with blankets of this Numa-Gimla hybrid creature.

At last, the chariot pulled up. Tarzan mentally signaled for the lumbering dreadnought to halt, which it did with a nervousness that could not be denied.

It had been Tarzan's hope that he could somehow drag the carcass into the back of the chariot and thus carry with him sufficient food for the near future, since there was no predicting when next he might encounter an edible animal.

Taking the creature by the forepaws, he began to drag it away. It came so easily that he increased his efforts, hoping that its weight would keep him from flying off the surface of Mars.

Attempting to wrestle the thing around, he discovered that he could lift it with relative ease. Stifling his astonishment, Tarzan concluded that the low gravity of Mars lent him enormous strength in comparison to his earthly state.

With only a little muscular effort, he was able to lift the inert beast into the back of the chariot.

Immediately, a pair of gaping eye-stalks swept up and over the back of the mastodon of burden, and studied the dead lion-creature with animated intensity.

Tarzan communicated to it that the lion was deceased and would trouble them no further.

No sooner had that thought left his brain than the flexible eye-stalks transferred their attention to his bronzed frame. They wavered, dipped, and looped, as if seeing him for the first time.

Inasmuch as these orange orbs were always perfectly round, except when the lids were shut, the emotion conveyed was not terribly one of surprise. But now the black pupil widened to an extreme, all but swallowing the surrounding orange iris and conveying a kind of faceless incredulity.

Tarzan communicated a simple thought to the dumb brute.

"I am Tarzan."

That the monstrous mastodon perfectly understood was never to be known, but apparently it was satisfied by what it had perceived. Its tentacular eyes looked back, then faced forward. There it waited on its six ponderous legs for further instructions.

"Take me to where dwell people such as myself," commanded Tarzan.

The beast did not move. This caused Tarzan to believe that there were no people on Mars such as himself. Of course, this could be a simple misunderstanding.

"Take me to the abode of those who drive such vehicles as this chariot," he amended.

Here, the mastodon started forward anew. It moved about as if aimless and then fell upon a specific heading, like a ship finding a true compass direction.

As the creature lumbered on its purposeful way, Tarzan thought of the living ships of the desert, the camels. They invariably filed toward water wherever it existed. The ape-man wondered if this creature knew where water pooled.

"Take me to a place of water," he added.

The many-legged brute did not deviate from its course. Tarzan hoped that meant that water resided at its destination, or at least along the journey path. Concern that no significant water existed on Mars continued to plague his thoughts. While the blood of the lion creature was refreshing in its way, water would be necessary for life. And the blood contained in the carcass was even now leaking out slowly. In time the hot Martian sun would bake it into an unpalatable ooze not fit for human consumption.

As the chariot rolled monotonously along, Tarzan took up his scavenged pieces of quartz and used them to scrape the fat from the inside of the lion-creature's hide. This took some time and when he was done the ape-man draped the two sails of skin along the side rails where the burning Martian sun would begin the task of curing them.

It was exceedingly hot now. Once again Tarzan was thirsty for clean water with which to wash the salty taste of fresh blood from his mouth, which was becoming sticky due to the dry air. But no water presented itself along the way.

The knowledge of Tarzan was not limited to jungle craft. But the ways of the jungle were best known to him. As he watched the shrunken sun begin to dip in the sky, he wondered when night would fall. He had no way of knowing. His knowledge of Mars was exceedingly limited. He scraped his memory for details, but no useful ones came to the surface of his mind.

Tarzan could not remember the estimated duration of the Martian day. He only knew when it came, it would doubtless arrive with little warning.

AND SO it did. Long hours passed before the Martian sun set. Kudu had no sooner touched the horizon than it was gone and a velvet blackness settled over all.

Brilliant stars that dazzled the eyes like fields of scattered diamonds appeared as if some great celestial hand had tripped an electrical switch. Before long, the greater moon of Mars tore across the sky, sending its all-pervading light across the dried sea floor, putting the stars to shame, each and every one.

In the twinkling brilliance of this alien firmament, a planet arose. Tarzan knew the planets as seen from Earth. This sphere was not Mars, of course. Nor was it Jupiter or Saturn. Its hue was blue.

With a nostalgic pang of recognition, the bronzed giant realized that he was looking at his home planet.

"Earth," he whispered to himself.

There lay the jungles he knew best. Somewhere on that distant blue gem no larger than a freckle, lived his beloved wife, Jane. As well as his son, Jack, feared as Korak the Killer.

The jungle lord wondered what they must be thinking now. Did they believe him dead? Was Tarzan, in truth, deceased? Had he been fatally struck down by Sobito's vile sorcery, only to be transmigrated to the planet Mars? Was death, then, simply a change of planetary habitation? Tarzan had never dwelt long upon the subject and so had formed no fixed opinion. He had been exposed to the tenets of Christianity, but his beliefs were primitive, if not primal. He acknowledged a supreme being, whom he called Mulungu, but gave Him little thought, believing Mulungu to be remote from His Creation.

The ape-man felt of his naked hide. It was solid to the touch. The steely strong muscles rolling beneath the sun-baked skin were palpable and unaltered.

"Tarzan lives," he decided. "He is still flesh and blood, yet somehow reborn on another world." Intrigued by the fact that he had materialized on Mars without his loincloth and trusted knife made the ape-man wonder if he had also left his mortal body behind.

If so, had it been discovered? Did Tarzan's beloved family and friends know him to be dead? If his mortal clay lay inert and unbreathing upon the Earth, did that mean that he was forever barred from returning?

Tarzan of the Apes did not know. But he was determined to discover the truth of his present state. For dead or alive, if it were possible to be restored to his natal planet, the Lord of the Jungle would find a way. He would not cease searching until the time of his death on Mars, if such a time ever came....

Thinking these morbid thoughts, the ape-man commanded his steed to stop dead in its multiple tracks. Disembarking, he set about harvesting yellow moss with which to make a nest in the back of the chariot. Upon this he threw the raw blankets of lion hide. Satisfied that he was as safe as it was possible to be, he mentally commanded the obedient mastodon to resume his trek, which the dumb creature was only too happy to oblige.

With the grumbling of revolving wheels before and on either side of him, Tarzan fell asleep while the moons of Mars hurtled overhead, throwing their brilliant ever-shifting illumination that troubled not his slumber. One soon disappeared over the horizon, leaving only its lonely pursuer to illuminate the undulating moss with stark light.

Chapter 8

The Guarded Grave

FOR THE remainder of the moonless African night, and far into the next day, Jad-bal-ja the Golden Lion ranged about the forest, emerald eyes open but unseeing.

The searing red lightning flash that had struck down Tarzan of the Apes had blinded the magnificent beast. Fortunately, a lion depends as much on its canny sense of smell as it does its vision. Too, few creatures who prowled the forest would dare to molest a full-grown lion, no matter how impaired.

Unable to see, or hunt, or find his way about the jungle trails, Jad-bal-ja lay down on a bed of ferns and slept deeply into the heat of the day. Insects buzzed about him, and his tail switched lazily so that he flicked them away without realizing it.

Jad-bal-ja awoke to the buzzing of these infernal pests, shook himself, and clambered to his feet. His optic nerves had recovered from lightning-shock. He could see again. He looked about, recognized a stand of trees, and trusting his broad nose to help navigate, padded back to the clearing from which he had been forced to flee nature's fury, eventually returning to the side of his master, Tarzan of the Apes.

SOBITO THE wily old witch doctor was making his way back to the clearing.

He had passed the night safely and undiscovered by the warriors of Orando, son of Chief Lobongo of the Utenga tribe.

But now these warriors were beating the brush, and it was not safe to be about.

These noisy operations forced him back in the direction of the clearing. Into his wicked brain crept a thought.

Tarzan of the Apes was dead. His body lay back in that clearing, inanimate and without respiration. But Tarzan carried with him a great long blade of Sheffield steel. All of Africa knew the strength of the bronze hand that once wielded that knife. There was plenty of juju in that blade. It had been a symbol of authority throughout Africa. And an instrument of swift and cutting justice, if not retribution.

And so Sobito hatched a plan to regain his lost influence. If he could steal that knife off the cold corpse of the ape-man, and attach the proper medicine to it in the form of feathers and herbs, his old power would be restored to him.

It was an audacious scheme, but had not his prayers brought down the wrath of Meriki, the fiery red star, upon the head of Tarzan himself, laying him low for all eternity?

It seemed to Sobito as if his deity had blessed his scheme.

So he crept back to the jungle clearing, ever watchful, careful as he had never been careful before, until at length he emerged and saw the prostrate form of Tarzan of the Apes lying upon his stomach, his profile pressed into the dirt.

A moment's careful study showed that the bronzed giant did not breathe. Yet he was whole. No flies buzzed about his corpse. No hyenas had gnawed at his well-developed limbs.

That in itself was passing strange. The jungle did not spurn a convenient meal. Yet there Tarzan lay, intact and untouched, his knife at his side in its rude leather scabbard.

Satisfied as to the state of his recently vanquished enemy, Sobito crept up and snatched away the knife, along with its scabbard. A chain of golden links showed at the nape of the ape-man's neck, gleaming seductively. This, too, he snatched, vanishing into the woods with his prizes. The witch doctor did not look back. He would never look back from this day forward.

Tarzan of the Apes belonged to the past. The future belonged to Sobito. Of that, he was quite confident.

WHEN JAD-BAL-JA the Golden Lion at last reached the clearing, Sobito was nowhere to be seen. His unclean scent was present in the air. This brought a disagreeable growl from the feline's parted jaws.

Spying Tarzan lying inert, the loyal lion advanced, and pressed his nose against Tarzan's body. Gently, he nuzzled it, attempting to move the limbs, but achieving no positive results.

Life and death are so closely entwined in the jungle that when one is encountered, there was no mistaking its reality. Jad-bal-ja the Golden Lion saw soon enough that his master was cool to the touch and not breathing.

A roar that mixed defiance with disappointment emerged from his lifted mouth. The tufted tail switched angrily as if to strike out at the one who had done this terrible thing.

Jad-bal-ja paced in anxious circles around Tarzan's corpse, as if uncertain what to do.

A hyena happened to pass that way and peered out from the low ground cover to see if the lion had made a kill that could be looted once it had eaten its fill. The scavenger's narrowed eyes fell upon the bronzed white man's body and saw that it had not been eaten. So he sat down to await the inevitable.

Instead, the luckless creature was sent yipping into the forest when the lion bounded after him, chasing him away. But he thought no more of that once he had distanced the sprinting feline, for lions were of that disposition, proud and selfish.

There would be time enough for the hyena to return to sample the lion's unfinished meal once night had fallen. For that was the way of the jungle. What one did not finish, another would consume to the last morsel. Nothing was wasted in the jungle.

Returning to his master's side, Jad-bal-ja nuzzled it one more time. Satisfied that nothing would bring the ape-man back to vibrant life, he began tearing at the soft soil, pawing patiently until he had excavated a trench large enough to accept the body of the muscular giant.

It was not unusual for a lion to dig a hole into which to deposit an unfinished carcass in order to return for it later. But this body had been tasted by no scavenger, not even a passing fly.

So when Jad-bal-ja stepped to the other side of the pit and began pushing Tarzan into it with his broad muzzle, it was a strange and unnatural thing to behold—had any creature of the jungle beheld it.

No sooner had the body rolled in, than the Golden Lion started filling the hole, going from one side of the trench to the other carefully, almost tenderly, replacing the soil until the body of Tarzan of the Apes was entirely covered, protected from passing scavengers of all species and sizes.

Once this was done, Jad-bal-ja sat down upon the shallow grave like a guardian animal spirit. His eyes peered about watchfully, his tail switching and his purpose abundantly clear.

Nothing would disturb the grave of Tarzan of the Apes. Nothing would be allowed to consume the flesh of the Lord of the Jungle. Jad-bal-ja's job was to see to that.

Patiently the magnificent lion sat waiting. But even he did not know for what he waited… he knew only loyalty to the man who had raised him up from a helpless cub….

Chapter 9

The Ruin

TARZAN OF THE APES awoke suddenly.

His eyes snapped open, every jungle-honed sense alert. He lay in the interior of the great three-wheeled cart, warmed by dried moss and thick hides.

No scent came to his nostrils suggesting danger. He sat up, looking about him.

Instantly, Tarzan realized what had awoken him. The chariot's massive wheels were no longer turning. And this absence of reassuring sound had roused him from slumber as surely as if the growl of a predator had impinged upon his hearing.

Coming to his feet, he climbed atop the forward platform that permitted him to see over the high rails of his vehicle. The greater and lesser moons passing through the Martian night sky illuminated all.

The ape-man discerned at once that they had passed from the vast sunken floor of the ancient evaporated sea and were halted at a rise that might well correspond with a long-vanished shoreline. Stone projections ran from this higher elevation. Their walls were high, sheer and steep, yet perfectly illuminated by the greater moon. They seemed to have no clear purpose.

Peering over the brutish head of the tireless mastodon, Tarzan saw the unexpected, and his heart leapt with excitement.

For less than a mile ahead rose a fabulous sprawling city, whose towers and blocky battlements shone like alabaster in the Martian moonlight. He discerned no lights, but given the hour, thought little of their absence.

One solitary eye-stalk switched back and regarded him roundly.

Pointing the way ahead, Tarzan gave the telepathic instruction to proceed. But the beast declined to advance. A second orange-orbed appendage swept around and joined its mate.

At the same time, the central trunk that was employed both for breathing and eating climbed high. The sounds that came from it suggested that the creature was sniffing the thin air cautiously.

Tarzan did the same.

The odors he detected were heavy and musky, suggesting inhabitants of some type. Dwelling as he did in the African wild, the ape-man had learned to distinguish by sense of smell alone the white man from the black man, based primarily on their diet, which saturated the perspiration that leaks from their bodies.

The scent spoor hanging in the air suggested neither race.

Collecting the long curved tusks that were his only weapon, Tarzan restored them to his metallic belt and prepared to meet the mysterious manlike race whose tusks resembled those of wild boars.

Again, Tarzan gave the telepathic instruction to advance to the gates of the city.

Once more, the great mastodonian beast of burden declined the silent entreaty.

Leaping onto its back, Tarzan directed his right arm ahead, pointing peremptorily.

"*Go!*" he commanded aloud, forgetting himself for a minute.

The mastodon refused. It then evidenced a behavior the ape-man had yet to experience. Lowering its belly to the dirt, it folded its short legs and took the attitude of a Missouri mule demonstrating a fit of stubbornness.

Tarzan recognized that nothing he could do would impel the beast to advance. So he dropped off its back, gave a reassuring pat on the forepart of its featureless skull, and proceeded ahead on foot.

The strong odors emanating from the city grew heavier, and less pleasant to inhale. As he progressed, Tarzan realized what the stone projections must be. Ancient jetties, or possibly artificial breakers! As he examined them in passing, he wondered if they might have served both purposes in the long ago epoch when the ocean tides crashed against wharves that now no longer existed.

Putting these artifacts behind him, the ape-man continued his padding, barefoot progress.

The entry to the city consisted of an open gate on either side of which stood two poles of some unknown greenish substance resembling jade. Atop each one of the uprights was set a fearsome skull. The skulls were virtually identical to that which he had found in the Martian chariot when he first claimed it. The curved tusks were similar to the ones inserted into his metal belt. If anything, they were larger and the bony craniums, broader and more robust.

Tarzan judged that when living the owners conceivably stood a dozen feet or more in height, their massive skulls more than double the size of that of an average man of the Earth.

The presence of the twin skulls suggested that the inhabitants of the city, if any, might not have been men, but other beings who regarded them as enemies. For who would set the skulls of their own kind as a warning to intruders at the gates to their own city?

Tarzan's thoughts flashed back to Africa and tribes who had done the same. Yet as he regarded the skulls, he could not shake the inner conviction that they did not belong to any ken who built this city.

Stealthily, Tarzan advanced, keeping low, his bare feet making no sound and his eyes ever watchful and alert.

As Tarzan crept forward, he listened. He heard no sounds, not even the scattering of vermin, and was struck by the fact that there were no guards in place. Yet the entry gate was not closed. In fact, upon closer inspection, it appeared that the original barriers had long ago been swept away, perhaps by age and natural deterioration.

Passing through the empty gate, the ape-man was unmolested.

Upon entering, an overwhelming sense of foreboding mingled with antiquity swept over his senses. He could not account for it. But it was as if he had entered a tomb.

Pausing briefly, the bronzed giant looked about and saw that the buildings stood in disrepair. Ancient dust had accumulated in crevices. The pavement beneath his feet was cracked and broken, with missing paving stones resembling absent teeth.

This, then, appeared to be a ghost city, long since abandoned by its inhabitants. Its silence was that of an ancient crypt.

Considering his surroundings, Tarzan decided on a fresh course of action. Bending his knees, he sprang for the tallest of the towers, one that was decorated by windows which were entirely devoid of glass. No cracked panes or surviving shards reflected the ever-shifting moonlight.

Into the night air he sailed, landing perfectly upon the tower's rounded summit.

THE NOISE of his arrival was not soft. And as Tarzan knelt and surveyed the ruins all around him, he saw that he was not far from the central plaza. The ape-man looked for places where water might pool, but perceived no reflections of either moon anywhere.

This was further proof that the city was uninhabited.

And yet, a heavy scent reminiscent of musk wafted to his sensitive nostrils, which were never mistaken. Creatures of some sort inhabited this ruined metropolis. Whether human or otherwise, Tarzan could not be certain. But nothing in the scent spoor smacked of human beings.

Taking hold of the roof's rounded rim, Tarzan set himself to swing out and in again, determined to enter the tower interior.

With an agile twist of his body, he thrust his sinewy legs into the aperture, swiftly transferring his steely grip to the molding of the window frame.

After this was accomplished, he let go.

Based upon his observations, the ape-man had deduced that the city had been built by humans more or less of his stature. This was evident from the dimensions of the windows and doors he perceived.

Consequently, Tarzan expected his feet to encounter flooring just under the windowsill. Instead, he found himself plummeting downward, whereupon he landed ignominiously in a dark chamber of unknown size, scrambling to his feet in an instant.

His arrival caused a great commotion among the inhabitants of the Stygian space. There followed a frantic skittering and scampering, and Tarzan was suddenly beset by myriad teeth.

Striking out in the darkness, he brought down one bronzed fist, encountering a creature which squealed in pain as his knuckles drove it back against the wall.

Another sprang upon his back and he could feel its hot breath. His right hand leapt for his tusk weapon, and drove it up and around and over his shoulder, delivering a death blow. Obscene claws detached themselves from his naked back.

Whirling on a fresh assailant, Tarzan extracted his second weapon, and drove in toward the sound of its hissing.

The curvature of the tusks forced him to sweep the weapons around where he was normally accustomed to stepping forward to deliver a straightforward stabbing strike, or thrusting downward. This fluke proved to be fortuitous since the ape-man had no clear sense of the size or shape of his attackers.

The point of one tusk pierced something low to the ground, and it screamed in fear and anger combined. Stepping back, Tarzan kicked it away. And the kick brought forth an audible crunch of bone. It was a very satisfying sound but one which upon the Earth the ape-man would not have been able to manage.

Other shapes swarmed about him. Tarzan kicked at them, brought down his tusk points one at a time, seldom missing. The metallic smell of blood came to his nostrils, while the sounds that arose beside him swiftly settled down and then died away.

In short order, Tarzan of the Apes stood alone among the unseen creatures he had vanquished.

Carefully, the bronzed giant stepped toward a flow of chill air coursing over his naked skin.

His bare feet encountered things that reminded him of dogs in size, but absent any light, he saw no point in attempting to examine them by feel.

Tarzan walked along, feeling cold stone under his feet. Lifting both arms, he employed his ivory-tusk daggers as feelers. Stretching out his arms laterally, he heard the scrape of the ivory points along stone walls. He used these to guide him forward.

At length, he came to a turn in the passage which debouched to left and right. Pausing, he sniffed the air but detected nothing he had not previously scented.

Tarzan decided to go to the right for no reason other than it was convenient to do so. As he moved along this passage, a dim light showed up ahead. When he came to another turn, he found himself in a passageway whose walls were perforated by narrow notches some twenty feet above his head. These let in sufficient moonlight to show the way.

The smooth floor was littered here and there with grit and loose debris. Bones lay scattered about, but they were not large. They seemed to belong to some animal he could not identify.

As he moved ahead, Tarzan became consumed by the thought that he was prowling in the lower reaches of the tower building. But this seemed to be a cellar and not a proper floor. The ape-man had been consigned to underground dungeons in the past and this labyrinth reminded him in both sight and smell of those unpleasant occasions.

He came at last to the end of the passage. Instead of a wall, he saw a ramp curving upward. Carefully, he ascended this, his pantherish shadow preceding him.

When he came to the floor above, the jungle lord saw something curled up in a corner. It was a creature, somewhat larger than a dog.

Tarzan endeavored to move past without awakening it, when the thing suddenly snapped its head around and the ugliest animal face he had ever seen glared at him.

The thing twisted about, got on its multiple legs, and charged in the manner of a pamba—a great rat.

Tarzan met it head on, drove one tusk down into the top of its skull, while the other swept up and under to impale its throat. Holding the thing in his cruel makeshift vise, he swung his torso about and sent the creature forcefully into a wall.

There it went into convulsions; its death throes were not prolonged.

Wiping the gore off his makeshift dagger, Tarzan took stock of the creature and thought that it might be some species of Martian rat, although that was really only a guess. The rank smell of the thing brought to mind a hyena or jackal.

Whatever the thing was, it was dead and its horrid sounds had convinced the ape-man that the things he had killed in the dark were of the same order.

Passing through the room, Tarzan continued his stealthy explorations.

He soon came to a chamber that was large and had been furnished in ancient times. The furniture had long ago fallen into ruin. He examined the remains and was pleased to discover that portions were built of some desiccated wood he could not identify.

A thrill of exultation coursed through the jungle lord. This meant that Mars supported trees. But as he held pieces of a chair in his hand, they crumbled with age. Did this mean, Tarzan wondered, that perhaps living trees belonged to the Martian past and not its present? The idea was disheartening, but the ape-man dismissed it as unimportant for now.

Dropping the rotted wood, he continued on, once again withdrawing his ivory weapons.

Tarzan found hangings on one wall. After he swept them aside, the rotting fabric came apart in his hands. Beyond was another chamber, this one quite large.

Hesitating upon its threshold, Tarzan was confronted by a musky odor in greater concentration and knew that he was not smelling one of the dog-sized Martian rats, but something larger and more formidable.

So it was with great care that he stepped into the room, which was still lit by high windows, narrow as those in a medieval keep.

Another chamber lay beyond this one, but the windows had been enlarged in some violent manner. For several of the slits stood gaping.

As Tarzan watched, a bulky shadow passed beyond one of them.

Something was moving. Something stupendous. A hulking thing that stood exceedingly tall!

As Tarzan watched, he perceived the profile of a head. Its outlines were familiar, yet disturbing. Disturbing because they were larger than they should have been.

Recognition vied in Tarzan's mind against incredulity. The creature could not possibly be what it seemed to be, or if real, the beast could not have achieved such a towering height.

While the bronzed giant wrestled with this conundrum, the shadow moved suddenly and a broad white face thrust itself into the broken row of windows like an angry moon.

The bestial countenance that looked down upon him dispelled all doubt from the ape-man's incredulous mind.

The face was as starkly white as the moonlight, but its bloodshot eyes were dark, deep-set and apish.

That albino countenance brought a sharp cry of recognition from Tarzan's lips.

"*Bolgani!*"

Chapter 10

The Tarmanbolgani

BATHED IN the weird, ever-shifting lunar light, the Gargantuan anthropoid visage was spectral in the extreme.

Tarzan stared unblinking, as if not accepting the evidence of his senses. His gray eyes widened with slow amaze.

The gorilla-like countenance yawned, exposing terrible yellow eyeteeth. The thing gave forth a tremendous roar, and two pale hands thrust through the crumbling wall at a point far below the stupendous beast's jaw.

The stony substance of the wall shivered to pieces. The monster stepped through the cascade of matter.

For perhaps the first time in his life, Tarzan took an involuntary step backward. It was not the sheer size of the thing, which rivaled that of the cyclops of Greek mythology, alone. For, despite Tarzan's ejaculation of surprise, this was not some species of albino Martian gorilla.

In the fleeting glance the ape-man stole before turning to make his escape, he saw that the monster stood upright and was hairless except for a shock of dirty ivory bristles sprouting from the top of its tapering skull. The wrinkled face of the behemoth was modeled on the configuration of an African gorilla's visage. There the resemblance ended.

For while the thickset body also displayed a general simian shape, it boasted not two, but four burly arms—the second pair set midway down its densely muscled torso.

The blunt-fingered hands were empty. The lower fists opened to clutch at the ape-man while the upper extremities batted away falling plaster and debris, producing a cloud of dust and grit.

Roaring again, it came on, intent upon capturing the ape-man.

Not out of fear, but through the natural instinct for self-preservation in the face of the unknown and the overwhelming, Tarzan retreated back into the adjacent chamber, and made for a passageway which he knew to be too narrow for the apish monster to enter and pursue.

Racing through the dusty detritus of a long-dead people seemingly of his own scale, Tarzan reached the passage, ran half its length and turned to see what the grotesque four-armed gorilla would do.

The trampling and crashing of ancient furniture reached his ears as Tarzan saw in the half light the pale face pressed into the open doorway. It glared at him. Growls issued forth from the giant mouth. Then it roared its gigantic rage, pounding its massive hairless chest.

Tarzan attempted to communicate with this Tarmanbolgani, or White-great-gorilla. The language of the Mangani and the tongue of their cousins, the Bolgani, was the same rough tongue.

Bringing a fist to his bronzed chest, he proclaimed, "I am called Tarzan. Tarzan of the Apes. Friend to all who belong to the tribes of apes. What are you called, Tarmanbolgani?"

Frowning and wrinkling its snout, the albino giant only roared back, making noises, not speech. The hideous face then withdrew.

A broad hand, remindful in size of a palm leaf, appeared next, and clutched repeatedly from the end of an elongated arm.

The Tarmanbolgani could not reach him, but neither could it see him.

Tarzan considered himself to be safe until he heard a sudden crack and realized that the thing was throwing its sloping shoulder hard against the separating wall. Fissures began appearing in the ceiling above him. The ape-man realized that if he did not discourage the white-skinned gorilla, it was certain to bring down the building on top of him.

Striding forward, Tarzan took hold of one of the creature's monstrous fingers, and giving a two-handed twist, snapped it loose from its knuckle socket. Inhuman strength lent him by the gravitational conditions of Mars made this fantastic feat possible.

Sudden pain brought a noteworthy howl, and the hand hastily withdrew. Sucking sounds came next. Tarzan understood that the creature, like many inhabitants on Earth, was sucking at the injured member.

Before long, another hand stretched out, groped blindly about. Encountering nothing, it formed a fist. The titanic fist began pounding the floor, shaking the unsteady building with an alarming and dangerous thudding.

Lifting his only weapons, Tarzan stepped in again, punctured the stupendous fist, drawing blood, and producing a similar reaction. The bloody fist withdrew, and the thing roared in baffled fury.

Other, more distant yells rose in answer.

This informed Tarzan unmistakably that this creature was not the solitary inhabitant of an abandoned city. This hideous specimen belonged to a tribe, no doubt a band formed of members exactly like itself.

Retreating further, the jungle lord made his way back to the base of the tower by which he had first entered the sprawling building. Looking up, he saw moonlight streaming through the open window into which he had breached the structure.

One of the fast-moving moons was now in a different position in the sky, and its spectral rays bathed the remains that choked the floor and made it sticky with blood.

As he had imagined to be the case, these were the remains of the giant ratlike denizens of this lower floor. Seeing that they had all given up their lives, Tarzan entered the compartment, after first holstering his makeshift weapons.

With a well-calculated upward leap, he gained the windowsill, grasping it with both hands. Hanging there briefly, he hooked his sturdy legs, first one, then the other, and straddled the open frame.

Swiveling his head about, the ape-man saw that the plaza was filled with more of the six-limbed brutes. They ranged about, screaming and searching, to clutch ledges that appeared to be made from rough stone, and thrusting wrinkled faces into open casements.

They were searching for their injured fellow, whose cries of distress continued to fill the night air. Some wielded crude stone clubs larger than a man.

Scanning the rooftops with his far-seeing gray eyes, the ape-man picked a sure path from the city which he judged to require only three successive leaps, two of which would land him on flat roofs while the final one was certain to deposit him outside the city gates.

Before he could put his plan into effect, Tarzan took time to study the lumbering brutes as they blundered about. He saw that while they could walk upright, it was common for these Tarmanbolgani to fall on four limbs, using the intermediate set of hands as an auxiliary set of feet. This naturally slowed them down, but also permitted them to peer into lower windows and doors in an effort to comprehend the commotion that had presumably aroused them from their nightly slumber.

The jabbering noises they made were incomprehensible to the Lord of the Jungle. No grunt, no bark, no fragment of expelled breath was understandable to him. If these albino Bolgani spoke a coherent language, it was not understandable to Tarzan of the Apes.

Having satisfied himself on that important point, the bronzed giant prepared to make the first of three overarching leaps that would enable him to clear the city proper.

But he never took the first leap. To his ears came another sound, a creaking of turning wheels.

And in through the skull-mounted entrance pillars came his faithful and obedient mastodon, which was being pulled along by its harness against its will. Two towering white gorillas dragged it without seeming to exert much effort in doing so. Others followed, beating their barrel chests and emitting rude noises and gestures.

At the sight of his only means of transportation—not to mention his sole store of meat—in unfriendly hands, Tarzan immediately resolved to free the beast if for no other reason than it had showed loyalty to him, becoming his only friend upon the Red Planet.

Filling his lungs, he released the weird shrieking war cry of the great apes of Africa, a sound that normally froze the blood. Nor did it fail to do so here, for the ranging albino gorillas of Mars all stopped in their quadruped tracks and peered about fearfully, hesitant to move before ascertaining the source of the alien outcry.

IN THAT tense tick of time, Tarzan leaped once, shooting into the night like an unleashed bolt. Gaining a roof, he crossed it in a series of agile bounds, and again took to the night sky.

The nimble ape-man landed in the back of the chariot, then sprang atop of the muscled-padded spine of his mastodonian companion.

Two gorillas dragging the reluctant beast failed to notice him, for his arrival was swifter than their sluggish reactions.

Throwing back his head, Tarzan again gave voice to the weird scream of the bull ape.

Against the terrible roars of the giant white gorillas, it was yet a mighty cry. Turning about and rearing up on their hind legs, the nearest creatures spied Tarzan and reached back with their multiple hands.

Out flashed the ivory tusk-daggers, piercing and scoring their hairless skin. Blood flowed; apish paws were pulled back in sudden surprise. Still clutching one weapon, Tarzan jumped from his moving perch and struck a mighty blow at the surprise-slackened jaw of the nearest ape. Stunned, it reeled backward under a forcible blow all out of proportion to the puny-looking creature who delivered it.

Grunting in astonishment, the Tarmanbolgani stumbled backward. He landed on his hairless muscular back; thereupon Tarzan sprang upon his heaving chest and inserted an elongated white fang into his throat, parting the jugular, which sprayed crimson in all directions.

Witnessing this prodigious feat, the gorilla's companion lunged, bending from the waist, and attempted to grab Tarzan by his comparatively small forearms.

Squatting briefly, the bronzed giant swept them aside, shot upward. The top of his head came into contact with his four-armed foe with such force that the snapping of neck bones came, followed by the loose toppling of the stunned white ape.

Its massive form crashed to the ground, nerveless arms flapping upward and then downward in a hapless gesture of defeat.

Jumping back atop his gigantic steed, Tarzan regained the chariot platform and, concentrating his thoughts, commanded the mastodonian brute to wheel about and seek egress from the city via its grisly, moon-drenched gate.

The creature moved at its best speed, but it was not sufficient for the required maneuver. Nor had Tarzan expected it to be.

A clutch of the white gorillas came stumbling in their direction, some of them brandishing stony clubs and cudgels. A blow from the least of these would crush Tarzan's skull like an eggshell. Of that, there was no doubt.

Despite that disagreeable fact, Tarzan raced toward his oncoming enemies, and allowing himself a moment of pause to tense his steely muscles, he sprang over their heads, clearing them easily, despite all attempts to bat at him with grasping paws and swinging bludgeons.

The bronzed giant landed several yards behind them. Turning, he lifted his hand to his mouth and yelled imprecations at them in the tongue of the great apes of his tribe. That he was not clearly understood was immaterial. The tone of his utterances carried the unmistakable force of his contempt and derision.

Outwitted and insulted, the six-limbed brutes turned and charged him, going on all fours where possible. Those with clubs hurled them at Tarzan, who nimbly leapt aside, dodging each one.

Darting toward one of the skating weapons, the ape-man picked it up in both hands. It was hewn from heavy stone, but neither its size nor heft proved unwieldy to one possessing Tarzan's simian muscular prowess. Like a baseball batter warming up, he swung it about and then let fly.

The cudgel struck an apish face in the center of its broad forehead, directly beneath the bristling white scalp, causing the heavy skull to rock backward with a snapping sound that told of a broken neck.

Waving both sets of arms spasmodically, the monster toppled backward, striking the base of its skull against paving stone; thereafter he did not rise.

Leaping for the other cudgel, Tarzan swept it up, displaying an effortless strength out of proportion to his comparatively puny tendons and muscles.

The glowering eyes of the white gorillas went wide with alarm when they realized the puny man-thing's muscular strength. Evidently, they had thought his previous maneuvers were incidentally successful. Now they understood what they faced.

Turning in place, Tarzan spun the ugly cudgel around, and this time the expressions on his enemy's wrinkled visages showed signs of fear and respect.

Flinching, not knowing when to expect the missile to come flying in their direction, they hesitated, and one of them fled in quailing panic, covering his brutish head with all four hands.

Tarzan let fly, this time aiming for the center of the group.

This compelled a pell-mell scattering among his simian foes, some bumping into one another, others throwing themselves prone.

The bludgeon sailed over their heads, which had sunk protectively between broad sloping shoulders.

While they were awaiting an impact that never arrived, Tarzan launched himself for the handiest roof, paused momentarily, then jumped for another, consciously propelling himself into the heart of the city, in the hopes that his chariot would be conveyed to safety.

But it was not to be.

From various points in the city, more of the nightmarish white giants emerged, yelling and screaming and carrying on. Soon their howling voices were lifted in a cacophony of inarticulate savagery.

One figure emerged, imposingly taller than all the others.

This apparition was different in other ways. His gorilla-like countenance carried with it in impression of higher intelligence. Circling his forehead, partially lost in his relentlessly stiff shock of hair, a band of shiny white metal encircled his cranium.

Spying this in the moonlight, Tarzan saw that it was made of the same metal that he wore around his waist. Moreover, precious jewels and gemstones studded it.

Perhaps the beast merely fancied grandiose ornamentation, but something about the way it moved, first on four lower limbs and then on two when he stepped out into the broad plaza, suggested that here was the king of this four-armed tribe of monstrous white gorillas.

The bull Tarmanbolgani lifted his voice—and all other voices fell still. When he spoke, his utterances carried the weight and force of command.

This satisfied Tarzan of the Apes that here was the leader of this stupendous tribe of alien gorillas.

Stepping to the edge of a parapet, the better to study the brute, Tarzan made an indelible portrait of unconquered humanity while painted by the shadow-shifting light of Mars's mismatched moons.

Even standing perfectly still, his weapons tucked into his metallic belt, and otherwise nude, the Lord of the Jungle presented himself with kingly carriage.

The searching eyes of the gorilla king caught the glint of Tarzan's belt and raised his brutish face. Their eyes met, locked, and neither antagonist showed a trace of fear in their depths.

The anthropoid eyes came into intelligent focus, all animal passions fleeing from its ghostly countenance.

To his utter astonishment, Tarzan heard clear words in his brain, words forming questions.

"Who are you, man-thing? How came you here to the city conquered by Murdank?"

Chapter 11

THE APE-LORD

NO FLICKER of astonishment touched Tarzan's gray eyes. His mien remained stoic in cast.

That the apparition staring up at him appeared to defy imagination was beyond refutation. But the ape-man had already accustomed himself to the sight of these bizarre, four-armed anthropoid colossi.

That one of them could communicate by mental means was striking by itself. But Tarzan had already experienced telepathy as it existed upon the Red Planet during his arduous crossing to this ruined city of a parched and dying Mars.

A question had been asked of him, although it was entirely voiceless. Concentrating his mind, the bronzed giant endeavored to reply in kind.

"*I am Tarzan of the Apes, mighty hunter, terrible fighter. Who are you?*"

The enormous albino gorilla did not deign to reply. Instead, he sent out another question: "*How came you to the city conquered by Murdank, Ape-lord of Vakanor?*"

"*Tarzan was conveyed here by chariot.*"

At that point, a subservient white gorilla dragged the resistant mastodon into the plaza and knocked it to its knees with a double blow of his right-hand fists.

The tentacle-faced behemoth collapsed, dazed by the unexpected blow. The pavement shook, and the dust of countless ages billowed up.

The subservient gorilla turned and started barking and grunting at the one who wore the metallic circlet about his shaggy brow. The latter did not reply by voice, but he stared at the other until the secondary gorilla nodded agreeably.

Turning his attention back to Tarzan, the gorilla leader sent out his thoughts.

"This is the war chariot of Churvash Ul, jeddak of the tribe of Vakanor, whom I expelled from his seat in this place. How came you by it?"

"Tarzan happened upon this chariot as it was making its way across a vast plain. It was empty, except for a pile of bones. So Tarzan took possession of it."

The ape-king showed his gleaming fangs, licking them lavishly with a tongue that was the color of calf's liver.

"These bones, were they picked clean?"

"Very clean," replied Tarzan.

Something like a laugh reverberated in Tarzan's brain and the ape-king told him, *"Little doubt of that, for Murdank ate the greasy flesh off those very bones, after first defeating the horde of Churvash Ul."*

Evidently, this creature was known as Murdank. Tarzan addressed him thusly.

"Murdank, it is Tarzan's intention to ride his chariot beyond these gates and resume his journey."

Resolutely, the ape-man folded his arms across his bare chest. At that moment, the night wind freshened, blowing cool air across his bronzed skin. Involuntarily, Tarzan commenced shivering.

The colossal white gorilla communicated, *"You think brave thoughts. But your hide betrays you. You tremble."*

"Tarzan of the Apes never trembles." So saying, the bronzed giant sprang from his perch and landed squarely before the towering Murdank.

So swiftly had he leapt that the lesser gorillas recoiled in surprise and perhaps some dull presentiment of fear, especially those few who had seen Tarzan's brutal handiwork minutes before.

Shifting his broad snout, Murdank gazed downward, and his upper arms lifted in surprise. The lower limbs formed fists resembling alabaster blocks.

"You call yourself Tarzan-ko-do-raku, man-thing. Yet Murdank has never before heard of you. What is the name of your tribe?"

Tarzan folded his arms anew. There was defiance in his steely eyes as he looked upward.

"Tarzan was raised by the tribe of Kerchak. Although he was born of a human woman, he was reared as an ape. Tarzan remains so."

"Your name is unknown to Murdank. Are you a panthan?"

"I do not know what that word means," replied Tarzan without speaking.

"You wear no harness. The panthan is a fighter without a harness, and without a cause."

"I am no soldier," returned Tarzan firmly. *"In the land where I dwell, Tarzan is war chieftain of the Waziri tribe."*

Murdank grunted skeptically. *"Are you a jeddak, or a lesser jed, O mighty one?"*

"Those words mean nothing to me."

"How many men do you command?"

"Tarzan does not command any army as you know it. He protects his subjects, man and wild beasts alike. But in his role as war chieftain of the Waziri tribe, he punishes those who are wicked."

MURDANK FROWNED with all of his weather-withered face. *"A mere jedwar, then. Do you hail from Zamadrung, or Uxfar?"*

"I do not know these places. Tarzan lives in the jungle. Tarzan rules the jungle."

Murdank wrinkled his pale, pugnacious snout. His nostrils flared. *"I do not know this word, jungle."*

"A jungle is a place of trees and plentiful game."

"Oh! You come from faraway Desh?"

"Tarzan comes from the continent of Africa, on the planet Earth."

Murdank's response indicated he comprehended what a planet was. Or had at least heard of the conception.

Under his stiff pate of hair, the beast's low pale forehead wrinkled. *"Murdank does not know of this Earth. Murdank knows only the planet on which he dwells, which is called Barsoom. Where is your planet in the sky?"*

Craning his neck around, Tarzan searched the strange night sky until his eyes fell upon a blue fleck of light, steadier than the diamond stars surrounding it.

"There. That is the Earth—the blue spark of light."

Murdank followed Tarzan's pointing finger and made a low growl in his throat.

"You are pointing toward Jasoom. No one lives there!" The ape-king said it in such a dismissive way that Tarzan saw no point in arguing. Evidently, it was a point that had been settled long ago on the planet Barsoom, at least among this weird Tarmanbolgani tribe.

Returning his scornful gaze upon Tarzan, Murdank grunted, *"Tell me about yourself, man-thing. You are obviously not a red man. Are you one of the Lotharians?"*

"Tarzan does not know what you mean by that. Tarzan is a Tarmangani, a white ape of the Mangani tribe. In the language of his people, Tarzan means 'White Skin.'"

Now Murdank shook with silent laughter. Clearly, he took Tarzan's assertion to be humorous.

"White Skin! Your hide is bronze." Observing the gooseflesh ripples passing along the ape-man's naked arms and legs, Murdank added, *"I should call you Thin Skin!"*

Once again, the stupendous four-limbed monstrosity shook with apparent humor.

Upon Tarzan's brow, the long scar earned in battle long ago against Terkoz the great ape sprang lividly into life. It burned like a jagged streak of lightning crossing his high forehead and temple.

Observing this phenomenon, Murdank ceased shaking in his mirth. The next words directed toward the ape-man were more measured.

"You have been in battle, I see."

"Tarzan is a mighty warrior. Tarzan has emerged victorious from more battles than Murdank owns fingers and toes."

Murdank's dark eyes shifted to Tarzan's midriff. *"About your waist you wear the metal of Churvash Ul, as if you have conquered him. Yet that is a lie. Only Murdank conquered Churvash Ul and his horde."* Tapping the bedizened circlet banding the crown of his brutish skull, Murdank added, *"This, too, belonged to Churvash Ul, but Murdank took it off his mortally wounded carcass. Then he feasted upon his muscle meat and organs in one moon, leaving only the bones, which I licked clean. After that, those bones were consigned to the dead sea bottoms in Churvash Ul's own chariot, in order to spread the word to all the green hordes that the city of Vakanor belongs to Murdank."*

Reaching into the metal belt, Tarzan plucked out the matched ivory tusks, now discolored with gore.

"Tarzan does not know Churvash Ul, but these are the fangs Tarzan took off the bones you claim to have cleaned with your tongue."

Stooping, Murdank started at the twin tusks. A gleam of recognition came into his dark, sunken eyes.

"Those were the tusks of Churvash Ul, who was delicious while he lived, for I did not let him finish dying before I commenced consuming one of his legs. Churvash Ul was less delicious with each limb, for it took me many suns to consume him to the bone." Murdank transferred his attention to Tarzan's bronzed limbs. *"Perhaps Murdank will eat you, too. There is not so much meat on your bones, so there will be no opportunity for them to spoil."*

Once more, the jagged scar upon Tarzan's brow flamed up.

Lifting his weapons higher, the jungle lord proclaimed, *"If it is Murdank's intention to eat Tarzan of the Apes, then be at it. I will wear your hairy scalp in a bundle about my loins when I am through with you."*

These bold words seemed to impress the hulking gorilla king. For he did not laugh this time.

Dropping his bestial features even lower, he looked into Tarzan's eyes and his thoughts flowed into the ape-man's receptive brain. These thoughts were very clear.

"You may or may not do such a bold thing, Tarzan-ko-do-raku, but you will never be an ape, much less an Ape-lord such as Murdank. You may call yourself an ape, but you are nothing but a man-thing, and a lowborn one at that. For you wear no harness, such as I do."

Murdank pounded his left breast with one fist of that side of his elongated trunk. Across the chest was a swath of hide similar to that of the leonine creature Tarzan had previously slain. At his throat was the bristling mane, now dry and matted. Across the front appeared to be burned symbols that Tarzan did not recognize. Evidently, this was a decorative garment, for he could see no practical use in it, inasmuch as it only covered his upper chest. Perhaps, like the kingly circlet, the decorative skin was a symbol of his status among his tribe.

For several long moments, the two steadily regarded one another, one looking up fearlessly while the other peered down with challenge deep in his sunken anthropoid orbs.

WITHOUT WARNING, Tarzan let out the war cry of the bull ape and sprang upward, jumping into the face of the totally unprepared Murdank. The great white gorilla recoiled in surprise, and all four arms swept in and up in an effort to capture the bronze-skinned attacker in midair.

They failed. Two pale palms clapped together like thunder. The others swatted about futilely, for Tarzan had hooked his ivory weapons into the metallic circlet, and lifted it free. It went tumbling away in the moonlight.

Tarzan's leap carried him over the bristling white hair, to land on Murdank's opposite side.

The self-proclaimed Ape-lord commenced tearing at his hair with all four hands, but found nothing to grasp.

All around, the subservient gorillas pointed, gesticulating at the fleeting bronzed figure that landed lightly, then spun about, curious weapons raised.

Ponderously, Murdank turned, his simian orbs shifting between the challenging figure of Tarzan and his kingly crown which lay desecrated amid the ancient dust coating the paving stones of the plaza.

Sweeping up all four of his burly upper arms, he charged.

Bending low, the bronzed giant charged in turn, but instead of leaping, this time he ran between the beast's pounding legs. As he passed between, he left behind one of the ivory tusks, hanging from the brute's groin, turning red with gore.

Howling, Murdank half turned, attempting to capture his wily antagonist. Then a pain shot through the injured leg, and he looked downward. Blood was coursing in rivulets down his right leg. He saw the tusk-root sticking out, and realized that he had been wounded.

Instead of screaming in pain or rage, he sent out his thoughts.

"Well fought, man-thing. You are a worthy opponent. More worthy than Churvash Ul and his green horde."

Reaching down, he extracted the protruding tusk, wiped his own blood off it, and threw it toward Tarzan. A bronzed hand swept up to recapture it in midair. The ape-man stood with both ivory weapons raised, ready for come what may.

All around him, the subservient gorillas had formed a threatening circle, but they showed no appetite to interfere. It was evident to Tarzan of the Apes that they had no intention of doing so. Out of respect for their Ape-lord, they intended to let Murdank settle his own quarrel.

Instead of attacking, Murdank covered his wound with the palm of one hairless hand and said to Tarzan, *"You call yourself a mighty warrior. It is evident to my eyes that you are as you claim to be. I will not eat you, Tarzan-ko-do-raku, although I am curious as to the exact taste of your bronze flesh. I will make you one of my bulls. You have shown your mettle. What say you?"*

Tarzan considered in silence. He had no wish to be a bull of a tribe of hairless six-limbed gorillas. These Tarmanbolgani were not his people. But Murdank did not appear to distinguish between Bolgani and Mangani. And Tarzan had no immediate place to go. He required food and drink, and later, directions to the distant forest of Desh of which Murdank had spoken.

Lowering his bloodstained ivories, Tarzan sent his answer through the ether.

"Tarzan of the Apes will be your bull. At least, until such a time as Tarzan chooses to move on. For Tarzan fully intends to return to Earth, which you call Jasoom."

"Good, good," grunted Murdank voicelessly. *"You may intend to return to Jasoom, as you say. But for now, you are a Barsoomian. And a respected jedwar in the tribe of Narag, subservient only to Murdank, Ape-lord of Vakanor."*

Tarzan nodded. Somehow, he comprehended the concept of the unfamiliar word, jedwar. It appeared to be the Martian equivalent to war chief, or perhaps general.

Murdank stepped back and retrieved his royal circlet. Placing it back upon his shaggy crown, he looked about, and sent his thoughts to his pensive brethren.

Curiously, Tarzan could not perceive his thoughts. Apparently, he owned the ability to direct his mental transmissions to only those whom he wished to receive them.

Now, however, Murdank broadcast his thoughts to all who had assembled in the broad plaza of the ancient deserted city.

"Welcome to the tribe of Murdank, this warrior who is to be respected. He calls himself Tarzan-ko-do-raku. In honor of his induction into our tribe, I hereby rename him Ramdar—Red Scar!"

The circle of titanic white gorillas broke out into something like applause. They clapped their hands together wildly. And not always were the clapping hands parallel to one another. They pounded their chests. They beat upon the backs of those on either side of them. If there was any dissent among this boisterous, jabbering band, it was not evident in their raucous revelry.

And so it was that Tarzan of the Apes, no longer bound to the Earth, became Ramdar of Barsoom.

Chapter 12

BLADES

WITH THE secession of all hostilities, Murdank and his ghost-white gorillas unceremoniously repaired to their sleeping quarters, which appeared to be scattered throughout the crumbling city of Vakanor.

The prodigious four-armed beasts left Tarzan standing alone in the plaza, evidently expecting him to fend for himself.

The ape-man strode over to his chariot and examined his steed. The mastodon of Mars slumbered noisily but did not appear to be seriously injured. Tarzan's fingers probed the broad apex of its skull where one of the Ape-lord's subjects had brought his fists crashing down with stunning finality.

The thick skull-bones of the creature's crown were whole and unbroken, its central trunk emitting a vague whistling noise consonant with respiration.

Satisfied on that score, Tarzan went exploring. He avoided the sleeping apartments of the Tarmanbolgani and spent over an hour scavenging.

His initial impression that human beings approximating his own size and stature had built this city was reinforced at every turn. But he saw naught of their images. No portraits, no carvings, nothing. Murdank had called the Martians red men. But there also existed another great race of men, who evidently corresponded to the boar-tusked skulls mounted at the entrance gate. These beings were obviously giants and the equivalent in stature to the stupendous gorillas of Mars. Tarzan wondered if they were apes as well. Instinctively, he doubted it.

During his search, he heard a gurgling suggestive of water. Locating its source, he discovered a stone grate set in the pavement of one narrow street. This arrangement suggested a sewer, such as would be found in an Earth city. But bringing his sensitive nostrils to the grate, he did not smell foul odors, but a freshness that might have been clean running water.

Using his curved ivory tools, he pried up the grating and managed to break off the tip of one tusk in the process. Throwing the useless thing aside, he completed his task with the other, wondering anew about the tusked colossus named Churvash Ul, who had once carried it in his enormous jaws.

Setting the grating aside, Tarzan eased himself down and landed calf-deep in water. Squatting carefully, he dipped his hands and gathered up a portion of the rushing stream. This, he lifted to his face. Sniffing the liquid carefully, he found its smell not unpleasant. Taking it up to his mouth, he drank carefully. The water was cold, and its taste slightly bitter. But it was not sea water, and so he drank it down, refilling his cupped palms time and again until he was satisfied.

Walking along the sluggish underground stream, the ape-man found that there were other grates, and some of these were open. Clearly this had been a water source in ancient times, and no doubt the great white gorillas of the Narag tribe continued to use it for that all-important purpose.

The labyrinth of waterways seemed to pass more or less directly under the ruin of a city from an unknown source. Conceivably, Tarzan reflected, it was all that remained of the once-vast ocean that had surrounded Vakanor in ancient times.

An upward leap brought him back to the surface and he continued his perambulations. Further investigation convinced the ape-man that the ruined outpost had been looted many times in the past and all that remained were broken furniture and other such detritus, all useless.

Since he was not at all sleepy, Tarzan continued exploring.

Luck was with him. The bronzed giant was investigating a tower when he saw something hanging from the ceiling, twenty feet above him—a complicated contrivance of some type. The chamber into which he had stepped was too narrow to admit one of the Tarmanbolgani—even one of the lesser specimens who stood under ten feet tall.

Appraising the construction of the tower, it appeared as if it had been subdivided vertically by floors long ago, but these floors had fallen away generations before. Worm-eaten planks littered the basement floor of stone in testament to that assumption. But with his ability to leap higher than they formerly stood, Tarzan was able to jump straight up and take hold of the intriguing thing hanging so high above his head.

Tarzan discovered that he clung to an elaborate fixture that might have been used to illuminate the uppermost floor, but by what means was obscure.

More intriguing was the fact that the fixture was composed of metal, leather, crystal, and glass. Studying it, he divined its construction and realized that it consisted of, not two crosspieces as he first suspected, but four equal blades vaguely similar to the propellers of an earthly aircraft.

Examining these blades, he discovered an amazing thing.

They were removable!

For each of the four extensions consisted of an aged leather scabbard covered in thin, hammered white metal. Jutting from the outer tips of each blade were heavy steel extensions recognizable as the hilts of swords. So cunningly were these wrought that the ape-man at first assumed that these were works of art created to mimic sheathed swords.

Hanging onto the hub by his left hand, Tarzan used his right to tug at the hilt of another extension. It slipped free with only moderate resistance.

He dangled precariously thus, holding a perfectly good sword, although it was not very long in length.

Pointing this downward, the jungle lord let it drop. Falling, it held its orientation, showing that it was well balanced, and impaled itself on the rotted wood of the collapsed flooring below.

Tarzan repeated the process with two more swords, and then twisting himself upward, kicked the last one loose. It fell to the ground with a clatter, still in its scabbard.

After knocking the scabbards loose, Tarzan let himself drop. The lesser gravity of Mars duly brought him back to earth, so to speak. He regained his feet and carefully examined his newfound arsenal.

One sword had survived the drop without damage. The scabbards were banged up. One was bent too badly to be used as a sheath.

MAKING A bundle, Tarzan took the best of these items in hand and carried them back to the chariot where the mastodonian brute continued to slumber the night away.

There, Tarzan applied the blade to one of the hides he had peeled off the lionine monster, until he had cut a breechclout, which he affixed to his metallic belt. He would have preferred his customary loincloth, but a short-sword was not the proper tool with which to fashion one.

The leather-and-metal scabbard was set with loose rings, and by prying them half open, it was possible to hook and anchor them to his belt, squeezing them closed once more by finger strength. Once the scabbard hung balanced to his satisfaction, Tarzan sheathed his blade.

Compared to his father's hunting knife, which he had carried since his youth long ago, the ape-man found the short-sword banging at his side a clumsy and awkward thing. But he gave thanks to Mulungu, the only deity he acknowledged, that he had found a serviceable metal blade on this barren and desolate world.

Studying the faint stars, tracking the speeding moons with his eyes, Tarzan attempted to gauge the hour until dawn. But he could not. The misshapen moons came and went repeatedly during their nightly rounds, making calculations difficult. That failure of conception brought his brows knitting together. For his inability to calculate such a simple thing vexed the ape-man as few things in his existence ever had.

Life on Mars, he realized, promised to be a process of learning unlike anything he had ever experienced.

As the light of the companion moons caused shadows to shift in nearly opposite directions, Tarzan considered his predicament.

A weird force had deposited him upon the surface of Mars, which its inhabitants called Barsoom. That much staggered his natural imagination. But now, upon this second evening on the Red Planet, hours before dawn broke over another full day of his new Martian existence, fortune had conspired to place him in the heart of a tribe of weird gorillas.

On Earth, the gorilla was the hereditary enemy of the Mangani—the great apes with whom Tarzan the Tarmangani was allied. Now he lived among them and, he assumed, would fight alongside them in the days to come.

He wondered what his ape mother, Kala, would think of him now if she could behold her little balu, White Skin, a member of a tribe of freakish gorillas as white and hairless as himself, but of fantastic configuration of body, beside which a full-grown Tarzan stood no more tall in stature than Tongani the baboon.

Ultimately, Tarzan was glad that Kala did not live to see this day. No doubt she would have cuffed him about contemptuously, and either abandoned him to his new tribe, or dragged him by his long black hair back to the shaggy security of the tribe of Kerchak.

When he exhausted himself entertaining these forlorn thoughts, the ape-man gathered about him the yellow moss of the old sea bed and threw over his shivering body the hide of the leonine creature he had slain, and on whose meat he intended to feed in the days to come.

Chapter 13

MURDANK'S TALE

TARZAN WAS rudely awakened by Murdank's bestial hands pawing at his bedding.

Springing to his feet, he seized the hilt of his sword and prepared to defend himself.

Almost immediately, he saw that there was no need. For Murdank loomed above, and two of his vassal apes were unceremoniously hauling the carcass of the Martian lion that Tarzan had slain on the previous day.

"Arise, lazy one," came the booming brain-thoughts of the Ape-lord. *"The sun is new and our bellies are empty. This tribute that you brought to Murdank will be our morning meal."*

Tarzan lowered his short-sword and concealed from the great white gorilla his thought that he had intended no such thing. Inasmuch as the ape-man was now a general in the army of Murdank, it would be rude not to share his meat. So he made no protest.

Buckling on the short-sword, Tarzan helped haul the creature into the plaza.

He was amazed at the absence of flies—or the Martian equivalent. Tarzan had begun to suspect that he had alighted in the vicinity of the equator of the half-dead Red Planet, for the days and nights were of nearly equal duration. Yet no insects troubled day or night. Perhaps they were plentiful at other latitudes, but here they lacked plant life and carrion on which to feed.

As the entourage lumbered toward the plaza, Tarzan directed his thoughts to the Ape-lord.

"What is this creature called?"

"It is a banth, a scavenger of the dead sea bottoms."

"Who built this city?"

"Men like you, but not like you. We do not know the color of their hide. Perhaps they were copper, perhaps black, perhaps yellow. The city was deserted long ago, before the time of Murdank's ancestors."

"How did you come to be Ape-lord?"

Murdank blew a derisive snort through his distended nostrils. *"You ask many questions, Ramdar."*

"I am new upon this world. I have much to learn."

They had arrived in the broad plaza of paved stones where the carcass of the banth was laid out.

Raising both sets of arms over his head, Murdank turned in place, clapping his twin sets of paws in a kind of syncopation that appeared not to be random.

"Ramdar does have much to learn. Murdank will teach him. But first, we eat."

From out of various warrens came in answer to the Ape-lord's drumming summons a number of females, distinguishable by their pendulous breasts and smaller statures. There were juveniles as well. But not many of those. As they assembled, Tarzan counted the tribe. They numbered less than thirty, of which most were bulls.

Addressing Murdank, Tarzan said, *"Permit Ramdar to cut the meat with his sword."*

The Ape-lord sat down and placed two hairless hands on his knees, while the upper pair pointed toward him.

"Such weapons are beneath the dignity of the great white apes of Barsoom. But since you do not have worthy fangs, Murdank gives you leave to wield the pitiful thing. And since you offer, you may cut up the meat, taking care to render to Murdank the best cuts."

Nodding, Tarzan began to butcher the banth. He did not know which were the best cuts of meat, so he simply made piles until he had all but eviscerated the ugly yellow beast.

Leaning forward, Murdank selected four handfuls and fell to gorging himself. The others then dug in, first the men, and then the women. Tarzan stepped in and took a cut of haunch, and then sat down to eat while jabbering juveniles picked over the scraps.

As they ate in silence, the ape-man observed them closely.

Despite their gorilla-like faces, their bodies were those of men, albeit burly men replete with an extra set of intermediate arms. Of apparel, they wore not a scrap. Only Murdank was clothed in any way.

As the meal progressed, Tarzan directed his attention to the Tarmanbolgani seated next to him and mentally asked, *"What is the name of the small animals that inhabit the lower regions of the city?"*

The beast did not reply, so Tarzan directed his question to the great white gorilla at his other elbow. No reply came from that quarter, either.

This confirmed what he had suspected, namely that the lesser apes were incapable of telepathic fluency. Only Murdank seemed to possess that uncanny power.

So Tarzan put a series of questions to the colossal Ape-lord.

"Mighty Murdank, how is it that your tribe cannot hear my thoughts?"

"They hear only Murdank's thoughts because only Murdank is practiced in the art of telepathy. Murdank is Ape-lord by virtue of his high birth, and that which came before the hour of his day."

"Ramdar does not understand," said Tarzan, using his new name.

"Before I was reborn, I lived as a Holy Thern. A man-priest of the Valley Dor. Had all gone well, I would have lived a thousand ords, but my life was cut short long before that. As a consequence, I was reborn as a white ape. But I retained some of my knowledge-learning

from my previous lifetime. The power of telepathy carried over with me. I used it to impress the tribe into which I was born, eventually rising to lordship for them all. You see, Ramdar, the great white apes are a fallen race, forced to inhabit the dead cities of Barsoom, for we have no culture of our own. Only a language, which we will teach you in time, so that you may converse with my subjects, in the course of your generalship."

Chewing silently, Tarzan nodded. He did not know what to make of the story told him, did not know what a Holy Thern was; nor was the ape-man particularly conversant with the doctrine of reincarnation, the supposed transmigration of souls.

And yet, he had apparently been struck down in death on Earth, and found himself whole and physically intact upon the planet Mars. He did not understand it. But he did not doubt it, either. Perhaps there was something to Murdank's tale.

"Tell me of the red men," invited Tarzan.

The Ape-lord grunted. *"Murdank knows little of them. They keep to their cities. Sometimes they fly over our heads in their sky vessels. But they do not visit Vakanor."*

"They have machines?"

Murdank nodded his ponderous skull. *"Chariots that fly. Since they do not trouble us, we pay them no heed. The green men trouble us greatly, however. They are very ferocious with their tusks and their sharp swords. Moreover, these metal blades are weapons which we do not comprehend. For us, the stone club is sufficient to dash the brains from the shattered skulls of all enemies."*

THE MEAL was coming to a conclusion and the juvenile apes were now gnawing on the bones of the dead animal. They cracked these bones open and fell to sucking at the sweet marrow. Tarzan helped himself to a few of these bones and did the same. He did not know when he would next enjoy a meal, so he decided that a full belly would be advisable.

"What do you eat apart from banths?" he asked.

"The zitidars," replied Murdank.

"Ramdar does not know what those are."

This struck the hairless Ape-lord as humorous, for his mental laughter rolled out around the plaza, causing the bodies of his subjects to shake in sympathetic humor. Murdank did the same.

"You have brought us a fine zitidar as tribute, along with this dead banth."

"The beast that drew my chariot hither is called a zitidar?"

Murdank nodded shortly. "The beast that drew the war-chariot of the green Jed, Churvash Ul. Since you will not be needing the chariot any longer, we will eat your zitidar next. After that, we will consume the last of our captives."

"Captives?"

Murdank sucked on a broken bone shard and then flung it carelessly over his sloped shoulder, where it went clattering onto the roof of a decrepit building.

"When we seized this city from the green men, we took prisoners, making them slaves. We ate the women first. For their flesh is more tender. We are down to our last male. So your coming was fortuitous. We can save him for a feast."

"I have never beheld a green man," commented Tarzan casually. "Only their skulls."

"They are not like us, nor like yourself. They are ugly. And their shes lay eggs that hatch smaller version of themselves, which are very tasty."

"Which do you mean—the females or the eggs?"

Murdank showed his yellow fangs in a grisly grin.

"Both," he grunted. "But I myself prefer to eat them before they hatch and grow. But at least the green men boast six limbs. Unlike the other pitiable man-things that resemble you."

"Ramdar would like to see one of these green men you consider to be so ugly."

At that, the Ape-lord closed one sunken eye and cocked his head in Tarzan's direction.

"Are you still hungry?"

Tarzan shook his head.

"Ramdar is merely curious."

Murdank grunted unconcernedly. *"Ramdar's curiosity will have to wait. Ramdar must first learn the ways of the tribe of Murdank. You should learn our tongue. For if you are to give orders on my behalf to my subjects, you must learn to be understood in our tongue."*

Again, Tarzan nodded. *"If I am to be a jedwar, on whom do you intend to wage war?"*

"Vakanor is the first city that Murdank has conquered. Once we eat the green man and the last of the ulsios, there will be no more food. We must find another city to conquer so that we can continue to eat."

"Are the ulsios the small creatures that dwell in the dungeons?"

Murdank nodded. *"They are. Ulsios are carrion beasts. Scavengers. Not very good to eat, but acceptable. When they are no more, we must march."*

"Is it far to other cities?" asked Tarzan. *"Ramdar came a long way and encountered no habitations."*

Murdank stood up, stretching his upper limbs. He seemed satisfied with his meal and so his humor was good. He showed his yellowing fangs.

"It is a very long march to anywhere on Barsoom. But there are rumors of a city to the south, which is inhabited. When our food is gone and our bellies commence growling, we will march toward that city. It is called Uxfar by the green men."

"Should Murdank not set out for that city carrying his food and not wait for his belly to growl?"

If his response was any indication, this thought had not occurred to the Ape-lord prior to this.

"Murdank has not given that point much consideration. Until recently, food has been plentiful. Perhaps Ramdar is correct in his thinking. But how would the tribe transport food over a long march?"

Tarzan was quick to reply. He pointed toward where the now-awake zitidar stood patiently lashed to the chariot of Churvash Ul.

"If we capture enough ulsios to fill the chariot, we may bear them along the march, and eat along the way."

Murdank wrinkled his brow in such a way that his royal circlet became slightly dislodged and the shock of hair on his head bristled whitely.

"But who will pull the chariot once we have slaughtered the zitidar?" His query masked his perplexed demeanor.

"The answer to that question is simple," replied Tarzan patiently. *"We will not eat the zitidar, not until we arrive at our destination. Perhaps not even then, if the city of Uxfar is full of food."*

Readjusting his kingly circlet under the stiff-haired apex of his skull, Murdank considered this idea at length.

"This is sound thinking. Murdank approves of your plan, Ramdar. You will make an excellent jedwar. Now go learn the tongue of my tribe, for my belly is full and I will sleep."

Thus did Tarzan of the Apes preserve the life of his zitidar, as well as the means by which he could, when necessary, escape the tribe of Narag. For by no means did he intend to while away his days as a jedwar of a tribe of slovenly Tarmanbolgani. He still saw himself as the Lord of the Jungle—even if the ape-man had yet to spy a solitary Martian tree.

Chapter 14

The Rise of Ramdar

OVER THE course of the following days, Tarzan of the Apes was tutored in the uncouth tongue spoken by the tribe of Murdank, Ape-lord of Vakanor.

It was not a difficult language to learn. Like that of his African great ape tribe, it consisted largely of grunts, barks, clacks, and similar vocalizations, yet there were words and combinations of words that suggested a rudimentary grammar. It was not by any means sophisticated, but it was serviceable for the needs of the six-limbed anthropoid colossi.

Their days consisted of exploring those portions of the city their girth permitted them to enter, and using their tremendous limbs to smash walls in order to get at the inner apartments. They drank the water from the underground waterway and ate any ratlike ulsios they captured and killed.

Those specimens that Tarzan had slain on his initial night of exploration were the first to be consumed. When these were exhausted, and their picked bones thrown into a heap, fresh victims were sought.

Tarzan led one such expedition, which involved cornering three of the specimens in a lower passageway. Thereupon, two gorillas fell upon the screaming vermin with their crude stone bludgeons, smashing them to a bloody pulp.

Having learned enough of the rough tongue to be understood, Tarzan next led an expedition in which he employed his sword to decapitate a single ulsio.

"We do not use such weapons," scolded one hairless bull, whose name was Foad.

"Yet behold," countered Tarzan. "The meat is undamaged and can be shared without waste."

"What if the bones are unbroken?" demanded another surly Tarmanbolgani.

"After the meat is consumed," suggested Tarzan, "the apes of Murdank can break the bones with their clubs and partake of the marrow."

This suggestion was met with reserved approval, but once Tarzan had shown the way, he was deputized to lead the hunt for meat henceforth.

Thus did Ramdar win the respect of the lesser followers of the Ape-lord, Murdank.

One of these lower subjects was a dull anthropoid known as Thagg. Thagg had been one of the bulls with whom Tarzan had contended during his first encounter with the tribe. Thagg had lost a finger to Tarzan's might.

For several days, he had gone around sucking at the broken member, but when it refused to stop aching, he had bitten it off with his own teeth and tossed it over his shoulder contemptuously. Thagg continued to suck at the bloody joint, but the pain lessened over time as the stump healed over.

If the great white gorilla bore any grudge, he did not show it in any outward behavior. Tarzan kept an eye on him anyway. These creatures reminded him more of the bolgani than his own tribe. In the ape-man's mind, they were a lesser order of anthropoid. Nature had given them an extra set of limbs, but this advantage did not extend to increased brain power.

Also, they appeared to be exceedingly slothful. Whenever their bellies were satisfied, they napped the Martian day away.

Over the approximately one Martian year of their occupation of the fallen city of Vakanor, they had systematically destroyed a good portion of it in their fumbling searches for food and water.

It was evident that if the supply of ulsios did not run out, the city would be reduced to a rubble in a matter of months, if not weeks.

Tarzan worried that the ulsios would be eaten to extinction before he could convince Murdank to load the chariot and set out on the trek toward the city of Uxfar. But the brutish Apelord showed no indications of harboring such ambition, except in his speech, which was windy.

IN HIS waking hours, Murdank held court in the great plaza and spoke boldly and broadly of his intentions.

"We will gather up as many ulsios as we can," he proclaimed at one juncture, *"and I will lead the tribe toward the next city. There we will conquer it."*

"What if it is inhabited by red men and not green men?" asked one gorilla in a worried series of grunts which Tarzan now understood.

Out of respect, the bull spoke aloud, so that the others of the tribe of Narag could understand.

Murdank replied mentally, *"Then we will eat the red man-things who inhabit that city. And if they are yellow, we will eat them as well. It does not matter what color they are. We will devour them all."*

"But," protested another, "if they are man-things, they will not fill our bellies well. Only green men fill apish bellies to their fullest extent."

"Then pray to whatever god you pray to that the city of Uxfar is inhabited by green men. Then we will eat our fill."

Another pale gorilla objected, "But green men are more ferocious than the puny red men. And what if their numbers exceed ours?"

Murdank deftly parried the question by communicating, *"If their numbers exceed ours, we may eat well for moons."*

Even the least intelligent of the subject apes understood that that was not the point of the original question. But Murdank had waved away any such concerns over being outnumbered. The titanic blowhard seemed absurdly confident in his plans.

Observing all this, Tarzan perceived that Murdank was a bit of a braggart. For when another gorilla asked if they were to begin the march today, he was told sullenly, *"No, not today."*

"Tomorrow?" asked another, scratching his chest with a blunt thumb.

"Perhaps," mused Murdank. *"When the time is right, Murdank will know. When Murdank knows, he will proclaim that day as the day of marching. Until then, we have sufficient meat to eat. We have no enemies here in Vakanor. That is all that matters today. It may be all that will matter tomorrow. After tomorrow, Murdank will decide. Now be silent, all. Murdank has decided."*

At the end of the parlay, Tarzan was convinced that Murdank was mostly talk, and exceedingly lazy. The ape-man waxed impatient. He did not mind sojourning with these creatures, for he was learning much of this planet called Barsoom. But he was also growing anxious to explore further. From what little he could glean, there were men of a higher order living in cities who had developed the means to traverse the skies. If they controlled such aircraft, it was possible that they had scientists who could help him return to Earth. If not, there might be people with whom he could dwell until he could devise a means by which to restore himself to his former earthly station.

Tarzan had no interest in eating the green man who dwelt in captivity and whom he had yet to meet, nor any other kind of man who lived on this forlorn world. Tarzan subsisted on meat almost exclusively, but he was not a cannibal. He would not partake of his fellow Mangani, nor his kindred human beings, regardless of their outer coloration.

Nor would he devour the zitidar who had befriended him and whom the bronzed giant saw as a means of crossing the trackless mossy plain when at last the time came to leave the exhausted city of Vakanor.

On this point, Tarzan's mind was made up. He would do none of these things, even if it put him at odds with the tribe who had adopted him and made him one of their own. For they were shambling, hairless gorillas, and nothing like his own clan of African apes.

Chapter 15

THE MAN-BOAR

FIVE MORE Martian days passed. To strike out, or not? That was the question on every ape's mind. And still Murdank, the blowhard of Vakanor, dawdled and boasted.

With each day, it became harder and harder to hunt and capture the scavenger ulsios.

"If we do not set out toward Uxfar soon," Tarzan told the Tarmanbolgani of his acquaintance in private, "we will be stuck here forever with nothing to eat except one another."

Tarzan was careful to make these comments out of earshot of Murdank, who often slept the day away.

The callow ape named Foad barked back, "There are still the green man and your zitidar. They will sustain us for padans, if we ration them."

"And after six suns have set," countered Tarzan. "What then?"

The hairless young ape scratched his bristled shock of hair and had no certain answer.

Tarzan told him, "Ramdar points out the obvious. To delay the march to Uxfar is the same as condemning us to eventual starvation. Unless we eat one another."

"Apes do not eat apes."

"Then what will hungry apes do? Lie down and expire?"

"The tribe of Murdank has always had food."

"What did you eat before you conquered the city?"

"Banth meat. Sometimes calot."

"What is a calot?" asked Tarzan.

Foad attempted to describe the creature, managing to get his point across, even if he lacked sophisticated descriptive words.

When he was finished, the ape-man was confident that the small, frog-faced creature he had encountered early in his Martian sojourn had been a specimen of calot.

"In my travels," Tarzan pointed out, "I encountered only one example of each of those animals. Given that banth hide matches the coloration of the plentiful moss, Ramdar may have missed a skulker. But not more than one to two. If we march soon, we can hunt banths after we have eaten the last ulsio. This will ensure our survival until we reach the other city."

It was midday and the hour was exceedingly hot. Even though Tarzan had come to believe that Vakanor was located beneath the equator, the nights were as uniformly cold as the days were torrid. He was by now anxious to move on from the crumbling ruin, for the zitidar was once again in peril, and every day's delay made the trek more risky, if not foredoomed to failure.

Days of dwindling provisions and lazy inaction had caused the subjects of Murdank the Ape-lord to become restive and disgruntled. Tarzan knew some had begun to grumble among themselves and issue muttered objections, but nothing had come to a head yet. Tarzan also understood that if the matter was not raised openly soon, Murdank might begin to suspect that Tarzan was agitating against him.

IN ORDER to head off that sort of trouble, the jungle lord approached Murdank after he had awoken from a prolonged afternoon siesta.

"Your subjects are restless," he informed the sleepy Ape-lord. *"Ramdar regrets to inform you of this fact, but feels in his heart that you must hear his words."*

Furrowing his brow, Murdank demanded, *"What is wrong?"*

"Everyone understands that the food supply has become lean. The marching order has been put off long enough. If we are to reach that city, the time to embark has arrived."

The Ape-lord narrowed his deep-set eyes. "You are my chosen jedwar, Ramdar. You are a mighty hunter, as you boast. Take a detachment of apes into the dungeons and find more ulsios. They breed exceedingly slowly, but they do breed in their burrows. Surely, there is more meat to be found, if you scrounge thoroughly."

"The tribe has grown tired of ulsio meat," replied Tarzan firmly. "Its taste makes their tongues thick and their appetites dull."

Murdank considered this.

"Perhaps it is time to consume the green man in captivity. Have him brought out. At once!"

Tarzan had not expected that argument. And it interrupted his plan. But having no choice, he turned and walked about and gave the order.

"Murdank has decreed that the green man-thing be brought out for inspection," Tarzan told a lounging trio he happened upon.

The lethargic trio looked interested. "Are we eating him today?"

"Murdank wishes to inspect the prisoner; a decision about his final disposition has not yet been made."

Tarzan returned to Murdank quietly excited, and patiently awaited the arrival of the prisoner.

It was brought out from the lower levels, driven by clubs, and in heavy chains that resembled rusty iron.

The ape-man's first view of a green Martian all but staggered him. During his adventurous career, Tarzan had been to strange lands where dinosaurs still roamed. He had battled surviving triceratops in the lost land of Pal-ul-don.* In Pellucidar, an underground realm beneath the North Pole, there were

---

* See Tarzan the Terrible *by Edgar Rice Burroughs.*

even more ferocious prehistoric creatures.* The ape-man had faced them all and quailed before none of them. In truth, he conquered many.

But this Horta-faced monster was of another order entirely.

Like the great white gorillas, he was tall and titanic in his proportions. They might have been different specimens of the same species, for the green man shared the double set of arms of the Martian Tarmanbolgani. Except that one arm was missing, the lower right limb. Over the stump, a bloody poultice of rags was swathed.

If anything, this Hortamangani—for Tarzan mentally considered him to be a giant man-boar—was even more hideous than the Tarmanbolgani, having a glossy skin that was the color of dark-green olives. Instead of a gorilla mask, the heavy features were grotesque in the extreme. The two red eyes were set high on its bald skull and moved independent of one another. Instead of a nose, two vertical slits formed thin nostril openings. The small ears sat on the headlike antennae, twitching the way Buto the rhinoceros moved its aural appendages.

From the lower jaw reared up a set of massive tusks that gleamed like polished white china, curving upward and inward, the points nearly touching the green forehead. The bite of the monster would have been fatal to any creature, but the configuration of those natural weapons suggested that they were used as a boar would its shorter tusks, for stabbing and goring.

The creature was naked except for the remnants of some sort of harness made of coppery metal and leather, and a filthy loincloth. It was not so tall as Murdank, but in fact was more on the order of some of the ape juveniles. He stood perhaps nine feet tall, for it was unmistakably a bull. No doubt his strength was tremendous.

The creature glowered in all directions, but he was overmastered and outnumbered by the ape bulls, who towered over him.

---

* See Tarzan at the Earth's Core *by Edgar Rice Burroughs.*

Under the brutal prod of primitive stone clubs, he was forced into the center of the plaza.

Tarzan turned to Murdank and commented, *"He is not so large as I expected. His skull is not as sizable as the specimens I have encountered thus far."*

Murdank shrugged elaborately. *"He is not yet full grown."*

That gave Tarzan an idea.

"If that is so, why would you eat him before he is fully grown? Would that not be a waste of future meat?"

The Ape-lord wrinkled his snout. *"Murdank is also tired of ulsio. Murdank's tribe is tired of ulsio meat. Unless you wish to sacrifice your zitidar, we must finish eating this green abomination. For I myself devoured his missing arm, which was tasty. As much as Murdank tried, I could not resist the temptation."*

The jungle lord saw the look of loathing that came from the green giant's hot red eyes as it glared at the Ape-lord. But the amputation of a limb appeared to have taken the fight from him, for the captive made no move to avenge its humiliating loss.

DIRECTING HIS thoughts outward, but also following them with sharp barks and grunts of the gorilla tribe so all assembled understood him, Tarzan pointed out, *"If we eat the zitidar, your ambition to conquer Uxfar will fall into ruin, just like this city around us. But if we gather up the last of the ulsios, and take this green monster with us, he may grow larger and provide much more sustenance later."*

Murdank snorted, *"Young green men taste better than older specimens. Although green women always taste good, regardless of their age and maturity."*

"Very well," said Tarzan, repeating himself aloud for the benefit of the other gorillas. *"We will have a feast. Let us also eat the zitidar. It may be the last good meal we enjoy in this city, for we have no future beyond this feast, except for the scraps left over and the odd ulsio we may or may not find. It will be a celebration of the victory*

of Murdank over Churvash Ul, for there will be no conquest in the future for our tribe."

Hearing this, the Tarmanbolgani king crashed two fists against his chest, the upper left in the lower right and then crashed the others the same way. For the first time, he bellowed in a deep, bestial voice.

"How dare you speak thus to me, Jedwar Ramdar! The power of Murdank will extend to far away Uxfar at the proper time. My ambitions will not be thwarted by a lack of meat. So say I!"

"It is not for lack of meat that the lofty ambitions of Murdank will be thwarted," countered Tarzan. "But there is still enough meat for the march to Uxfar. Murdank's ambitions can only be thwarted by a lack of will. Where is that will? Where is the fire that burns for conquest in the belly of Murdank, Ape-lord of Vakanor?"

Murdank bared his fangs angrily, and a low growl issued from his parted lips. It rose, but then died away—for even in his slow brain, Murdank realized the truth of the words of Ramdar, his bronze-skinned jedwar from distant Jasoom.

All around, the lesser apes took up the argument. Some raised war clubs. Others shook fists and waved cudgels, not at their Ape-lord, but at the hot, brazen sky.

"How many suns before we march, O Murdank?" Foad cried out.

"Yes, how many?"

Baffled, Murdank raised four burly forearms and cried out in a bellowing roar, "Let us feast and talk among ourselves while we eat."

"If we feast," Thagg pointed out, "we will only sleep afterward. But if we march, we will reach Uxfar one padan sooner."

"If we march now," insisted Murdank, "we must lose a night of sleep, for the day is growing late."

"Why put off what has been delayed too often?" another gorilla asked aloud.

Growing dissension took hold of the anthropoid tribe. Fists raised, clubs were shaken, but no threats were directed at the Ape-lord. But everyone saw which way the Martian wind was blowing. It was not blowing toward Murdank, but away from him.

Seeing that power and authority was slipping away from the grasp of the reluctant ape-ruler, Tarzan inserted a calm comment.

"If we march now, all arguments end. If we march today, we march with full bellies and will not need to sleep. Not the first night. We have a chariot to carry such ulsios as we can harvest. The zitidar walks upon six legs and the green man walks upon two. They will be our insurance against starvation should the march last longer than Murdank believes it will."

A renewed chorus of outcries rose up, scarred and broken-knuckled fists and stone clubs waving. The crowd was with Ramdar, although they knew it not. Nor did Murdank suspect that his own jedwar had stirred the cooking pot until it was boiling and on the verge of overflowing at his feet.

Seeing the way of things, knowing that he would lose face if he did not quell the unrest building up before him, Murdank, Conqueror of Vakanor, stood up, and spread his four great arms at oblique angles to his heaving chest and rendered his decision.

"Gather all the ulsios you can! Chain the green slave to the chariot. We will march when the chariot is piled with meat, living and dead. Let the word go forth that on this day Murdank the Conqueror has decreed that we seek our sustenance elsewhere."

Removing his short-sword from its leather and metal scabbard, Tarzan raised it to the sky and proclaimed, "For the greater glory of Murdank, Ape-lord of Vakanor and Uxfar!"

Clubs lifted in sympathy with the ape-man's gesture of feigned loyalty and subservience, and the great white gorillas of the Narag tribe howled and shrieked their excitement.

Turning to lead the hunt, Tarzan of the Apes repressed a knowing smile. Back upon the Earth, among the tribes of Africa, it was sometimes necessary for the young warriors of a village to compel the older chief to take the path of war. Sometimes leaders became complacent in the comfortable seat of their power, and reluctant to take risks.

So it was with Murdank, Ape-lord of Vakanor. But the jungle lord had showed him the way forward.

As he rushed for the lower regions of the ruined city, Tarzan caught the eye of the young green Martian and wondered if the creature understood the debt he owed to the bronzed giant now known as Ramdar.

Possibly; probably not. But it was Tarzan's intention to learn the creature's language and thereby apprise him of the truth, for he saw in the green man a potential future ally. Besides, Tarzan had no appetite to eat the flesh of the appalling manlike monster.

Chapter 16

Dag Dolor

AFTER THE white chariot had been laden with dead and dying ulsios, and the green captive chained to its rear rail, Tarzan of the Apes stepped on board the platform. Mentally, he directed his zitidar to commence the trek out through the greenish, skull-decorated gates of Vakanor.

The mastodon beast had become accustomed to the great white gorillas by this time. Under Tarzan's gentle reassurance, it no longer feared them.

So the ponderous draught creature commenced his peculiar undulating mode of locomotion by which his two sets of three feet began working together. There was something centipede-like about the way those legs synchronized in motion, seeming to flow rather than step individually once they achieved their customary pace.

Murdank was uncharacteristically silent as they left the ruined city. His pale face was stiff, but he carried himself almost fully erect at the start, soon transferring to his four lower limbs as he settled into his march.

His subjects did likewise after he set the pace, striding in two wings on either side of him, the bulls taking the lead, while the females and the juveniles trailed behind the chariot, which rolled along in the wake of the males.

They made a strange progression as they trudged into the Martian sunset. The burning red orb set steadily, suffusing the yellowish moss plain with a reddish tone that made it seem as if it were smoldering.

The mood of the bulls was boisterous; many beat on their chests with alternating fists, as if to project their fierce determination ahead of them and scatter any resistance before it was encountered.

Although Murdank kept his thoughts to himself, Tarzan read his uncharacteristic silence as worry. For all his bluff and bluster, the Ape-lord, in truth, had no intention of leaving the rough comforts of the ruined city until it was absolutely necessary. As a leader, therefore, he was but a braggart and a bully, despite his claim to be of a higher order than the bulls who followed him.

The rumbling of the three-wheeled chariot soon became a kind of unceasing accompaniment to their progress. Standing on the forward platform, Tarzan could not see so high as the larger Tarmanbolgani, but his perch enabled him to see far.

The ape-man continually scanned the horizon, looking for signs of the sun-bleached purple-blue coral that harbored the horrid bladder-like creatures that could float through the air. Neither coral nor the violet monstrosities showed against the ochre carpet of moss, nor did he smell the foul odor of their lairs. Knowing that the leonine banths roamed the parched sea bottoms, Tarzan continually sniffed the air for their musk while his far-seeing eyes swept the mossy streaks of yellow, where the massive creatures might crouch in waiting, their hairless bodies blending in with the unappetizing vegetation.

As they rolled along, Tarzan thought about the dying world on which he had become marooned. Once, these desolate plains had been the bottom of a surging sea or ocean, which seemed to have once covered unlimited expanses when Mars was young. Now there was nothing remaining except the yellow moss and patches of lichen, and what meager juice they yielded.

They had brought no water, for no suitable containers could be scavenged from the ruin of Vakanor. Some broken crockery had been found, but even if any of it had been whole, none would have lasted longer than part of the day, even brimming with water.

But water was not a problem for the striding white gorillas. Periodically, they snatched up clumps of moss, squeezed them in their fists, and licked the pale yellow moisture off their paws. It seemed to be sufficient for their needs.

From time to time, Tarzan turned about and regarded the green Martian who was forced to trudge along at the same pace as the chariot. The Hortamangani regarded him back, and the look in its red eyes was that of defeat. The olive-green face with its vise of upcurving and downcurving ivory tusks was ferocious, even in repose.

Tarzan attempted to send his thoughts to the green man, but if they were received, no answer was returned. It appeared that telepathy was selective on Mars. Some species were receptive, while others were not.

"Do you speak?" Tarzan asked the creature at one point.

The horrible thing regarded him coldly.

Tarzan pointed at his bare chest and said, "Ramdar!"

The creature did not respond. Tarzan repeated his name and gesture. Then he pointed at the massive olive chest and asked, "What is your name?"

The protuberant eyes grew sullen.

Tarzan indicated himself and repeated his name, "Ramdar." Then he pointed at the green Martian. "Name?"

A rumbling voice returned, "Dag Dolor."

"Dag Dolor," repeated Tarzan. The thing had a language, as well as a name by which it identified itself. That, along with its manlike but Herculean shape, suggested that it was at least semi-civilized.

The creature pointed at his mouth and made chewing sounds, indicating hunger.

As the chariot rolled along behind the wide-ranging albino bulls, Tarzan took out his short-sword and cut off a length of meat from one of the dead ulsios. He tossed it toward the creature who clapped the dead matter between three green palms, greedily eating the raw steak.

This action had gone unnoticed, so Tarzan repeated it. And then repeated a second time. After that, he turned around and ignored the green Martian, not wishing to be observed fraternizing with the prisoner, whose lowly status amounted to emergency provisions.

The lower limb of the sun touched the horizon, turning a hot orange color and sinking rapidly. Dusk was but a brief interlude. Abruptly, Kudu's vermilion crown vanished from view. Night clamped down not long after. It did so with a finality such that it was as if an ebon curtain had fallen across the heavens. That interval of darkness was relatively short but profound.

It was followed immediately by a sprinkling of stars appearing in the vault of the sky, whose dim illumination seemed insufficient for sunken simian eyes, but Tarzan's far-seeing vision was able to discern shapes and movement, if imperfectly.

First one, then the other, of the Martian moons put in their appearance, one careening across the sky like a misshapen meteor, the other seeming to pursue it. The cold illumination they brought emboldened the bulls heading the procession, who, with the arrival of absolute darkness, had come to a dead halt and began muttering uncertainly among themselves.

Tarzan caught up with them as they crawled along on their nether sets of limbs.

The Tarmanbolgani started sniffing the air. The talk that passed among them was of banths. Evidently, the leonine monsters were to some degree nocturnal, and roamed the dried-up sea bottoms by moonlight.

The bitter cold that belonged to the Martian night soon returned, but Tarzan was prepared for it. He had fashioned from the banth's hide a kind of cloak, which he wore pulled tightly around his neck. This, along with his breechclout of glossy banth hide, was all the protection the ape-man needed—not that it was particularly comfortable. But it would do.

Half the Martian night they marched, Murdank leading the way. He knuckled along in a straight line, meandering only slightly, as Tarzan watched him.

Beaming his thoughts to the Ape-lord, the bronzed giant inquired, *"How do you know the way to the city of Uxfar?"*

"By the listening with my magnificent brain for the thoughts of the city's inhabitants. They guide me as a star would guide me, if I knew the names of any single star. Though I do not comprehend their individual thoughts, collectively they sing. Their song is a summons. For I am their doom." Murdank's mental tone was matter-of-fact.

The statement impressed Tarzan for two reasons. One, it told him Murdank could detect thoughts across a vast distance, even if he could not understand them. Secondly, the Ape-lord appeared to understand the concept of navigating by the stars. Perhaps that was not such a sophisticated thing on a slowly expiring world such as this, reflected the ape-man. But it made Tarzan wonder again about Murdank's claim to have once been a member of a higher race of Martians.

It seemed as if Murdank could not passively read minds, only send out his thoughts and receive those thoughts sent back to him. Otherwise, he would have turned his head around when Tarzan was feeding the green man. Perhaps the lumbering Ape-lord could sense treachery, or dishonesty, in a companion, but that was no different than the natural instincts belonging to any other being who was sensitive to the behavior of others.

For it was Tarzan's aim to make friends with the green man and learn what he could of life on Mars, knowing that only by such knowledge could he make his way on this harsh and forbidding planet where trees did not seem to grow and fresh game was scarce.

Only once did Murdank turn around and regard Tarzan standing at the forefront of the white chariot as it rolled along the uneven Martian surface.

"Take care to guard the food stores, Ramdar. Without them, we will be forced to turn around and forsake our journey."

Tarzan thought back: *"Ramdar has great confidence in Murdank. The conqueror of Vakanor and the tribe of Narag will undoubtedly lead his own tribe to fresh conquests."*

The Ape-lord bared his teeth in acknowledgment, but there was a flicker deep in his dark eyes that Tarzan took to be regret over taking the path they now trod. But the braggart values his pride above all other things—except, perhaps, his skin. So Murdank swiveled his white-haired skull about to distant Uxfar, and resumed leading his shambling subjects through the night.

The first night's crossing transpired without incident. They encountered no banths, and as for the hillocks of dead coral, Tarzan spied one and brought it to the attention of the Ape-lord.

They skirted the mass, but nothing emerged from its low, brain-like surface.

Tarzan wondered if the horrible creatures who dwelt within were active only during the hot Martian day. It would seem so, he reasoned, since prey must be scarce and the thud and rumble of the passing of the gorilla horde could hardly have gone unnoticed.

DAWN BROKE with its breathtaking speed and brilliance. The ape tribe kept up its monotonous march until nearly midday when fatigue began to set in, as well as hunger.

Coming to a dead halt, Murdank lifted all four arms in the familiar fan-like gesture and announced that he wished heed be paid to him. Ponderously, he turned his great bulk about, and addressed his tribe.

"Hear me! Hear Murdank. On this spot, we will rest. We will eat our fill. We will sleep. Then we will march anew."

The formation of gorillas broke apart and made for the halted chariot. Reaching into the back, they jostled one another for their share of ulsio meat.

The green Martian was knocked to his knees when he reached in for a share. The apes grunted derisively at him and the green brute laughed back in a thunderous manner that puzzled Tarzan of the Apes.

Not caring for stringy ulsio meat, Tarzan let the Tarmanbolgani eat to their belly's satisfaction. They dragged out several carcasses and fell upon them with their teeth. Soon, the yellow moss bed was scarlet with gore. The breaking of bones came, and the sucking of marrow followed.

For his part, Murdank directed Tarzan to bring him an ulsio. *"A fat one,"* he clarified.

The ape-man reached in, pulled out a suitable specimen and, after balancing it between both arms, he jumped atop the back of his startled zitidar, and then leapt again to land at Murdank's dirty feet. Laying this upon the ground, he stepped back.

Seemingly, the white anthropoid experienced a measure of gratitude. *"Murdank will share this also with Ramdar, as a gesture of his respect for Ramdar's prowess,"* he communicated graciously.

Stepping back, Tarzan bowed his head. "And Ramdar, as a gesture of his respect for Murdank, declines his share. He will go hungry for now. It is Murdank who must eat. For the Ape-lord must keep up his strength. Take it now. All of it is yours. Ramdar has spoken."

Then Tarzan closed his mind so that the Ape-lord could not read the actual intent behind his words.

Grinning, Murdank fell upon the carcass and devoured it greedily.

Returning to the chariot, Tarzan quieted the zitidar, and then removed two steaks from an untouched carcass and fed them to the green man, who devoured them without any gesture or utterance of thanks.

Tarzan watched the man-monster and wondered as to its temperament. It did not seem to respond to kindness, although the ferocity of its face made it difficult to read its expression. The eyes remained sullen and sad. But that was all the ape-man could discern.

When the eating was done, the bloated-bellied apes sprawled about in the moss and fell to sleep. Their snores became a cacophony that would have prevented Tarzan from sleeping, had he the desire to do so.

Instead, he crouched in the back of the chariot, gesturing for the green Martian to squat on the ochre ground. The creature did so, pulling on his chain, causing the chariot to jerk under Dag Dolor's enormous muscular might.

Its size and girth were such, Tarzan realized, that it could have upended the chariot at any point by yanking at the chain. It could not have freed itself, but it could have impeded all progress. Yet it did not.

Tarzan attempted to communicate with the Hortamangani by using simple words and gestures. As the gorillas slumbered noisily on, Tarzan made little progress.

It was difficult to get anywhere with the green brute, and the things Tarzan desired to learn from him were more sophisticated than the simple concepts of names and food. But that is where he started.

Tarzan pointed to the pile of dead ulsios and asked, "What name?"

The creature replied, "Ulsio."

Tarzan indicated his cloak of banth hide. "Name?"

"Banth."

Indicating the beast of burden, he repeated the question.

"Zitidar," muttered the green man.

This told Tarzan that the names of creatures on Mars were common terms, at least between the albino gorillas and the green Martians.

The pale gorillas slept most of the day, which meant that they were picking up their camp, such as it was, in the last hour of the daylight.

Tarzan decided that this was probably a good thing, at least for now. It meant that the menace from the coral mounds would be nonexistent during the greater part of the march. And he could keep watch during the day, provided that he took catnaps in the rolling chariot from time to time.

As the ape tribe fell into formation, and their quadruped feet began pounding the ancient ocean floor in time with the rumbling of the triple chariot wheels, Tarzan glanced back at the carcasses of the devoured ulsios and wondered if their rotting stench would draw banths.

If so, the ape-man hoped that, in common with the African lion, the banth would be satisfied with found meat and would not exert itself to hunt for live prey.

Before they had gone the equivalent of a terrestrial mile, Tarzan looked back and thought he saw yellowish forms shifting and slinking among the clumps of moss. To his sensitive nostrils came the now-familiar sour musk of the banth. It appeared as if he was correct in his thinking.

No doubt whatever banths lurked amid the endless sea bottom, they were leery of attacking such a large tribe of fearsome bulls. Scavenged meat was much more to their liking.

Before night came again, the near horizon bulged upward, and the ape-man discerned the vivid purplish-blue of brain coral.

Murdank led his tribe toward it fearlessly, and Tarzan wondered if the Ape-lord understood the significance of the outcropping.

Turning to the green Martian, Tarzan pointed ahead and asked, "Name?"

The Hortamangani had been trudging along with its head bowed in an attitude of abject shame, no doubt over his captivity and ignominious station in life.

The creature lifted his head, followed Tarzan's pointing finger and saw the purplish-blue mass. The sullen eyes shifted as one, focused, and became uneasy, then flew wide with alarm.

"Denjuru!" he cried aloud. "Denjuru!" Whereupon it began yanking and pulling at its chains in a violent effort to break free.

Turning about to face forward, Tarzan commanded the zitidar to come to a halt. Eye-stalks windmilling in wild gyrations, it sought the source of the alarm. This caused the trudging apes to pause and look behind them.

Hopping atop the zitidar, Tarzan raised his hand and said to Murdank, *"The formation ahead harbors danger. Danger in the form of denjurus."*

Murdank looked back at Tarzan, then looked ahead and confessed, *"Murdank does not know of denjurus."*

Tarzan sent out his thoughts and this time tried to make them in the form of pictures.

No sooner had he transmitted those pictures than they became unnecessary.

For from the great mass lying in their path, a balloon-like creature ascended slowly, followed by another. Then another. All were a translucent violet.

Swiftly, but silently, a swarm of the things lifted into view and began beating toward them on their frilly stub wings.

Tarzan commanded his zitidar to turn about and retreat. But the creature did not need any such command; its entire body trembled when it saw what was coming.

In the rude tongue of the Tarmanbolgani, Tarzan shouted, "Retreat, retreat, retreat!"

Startled, confused by the unfamiliar sight and perhaps unimpressed by the danger of the silently floating tentacled things, the pale hairless apes of Murdank milled about, pointing and gesticulating.

"Kreegah! Bundolo!"

Having given the savage warning cry of his own tribe, Tarzan drew his short-sword and sprang high, prepared to take on the weird new adversary on their own terms, in midair!

Chapter 17

Denjurus

IT WAS unlikely that the floating jellyfish-form creatures possessed ears or aural faculties. Consequently, Tarzan's war cry rolled over them without notice.

But it had an impressive effect upon the great white gorillas of Murdank. Lifting their fists and clubs, the bulls followed Tarzan's vaulting leap to charge in his wake.

After some hesitation, even Murdank came erect on his dirty white hind legs and charged, his four arms shaking threatening fists.

The vanguard of pale apes and the leading denjurus closed rapidly.

Before they could engage, Tarzan plunged into the midst of the violet creatures, slashing and hacking with his sword, bursting them like bladders. They disgorged a distressing amount of malodorous viscous fluid, and dropped to the ground, hissing disconsolately.

Certain denjurus floated away from Tarzan, but others sought to surround him. The ape-man landed on the ground, and those floating creatures that descended were met with cleaving steel. They were decisively cleft in two, and otherwise dispatched.

But the numbers of the denjurus were not diminishing. Rather, they increased exponentially. More specimens emerged, wriggling from their tiny caves, expanding upon contact with the thin Martian atmosphere and lifting upward, seeking with waving tentacles convenient prey.

One floated toward Murdank—or it might be said that Murdank charged up to meet it. When the Ape-lord clapped his mighty hands, a denjuru was squashed between the flat palms, its violet remnants dropping to his apish feet.

Stone war clubs and bludgeons slashed the air, knocking others of their alien kind away, sending them crashing to the soft moss, where they flopped and deflated, hissing hideously.

After clearing the air about him, Tarzan again sprang high and thrust himself into a cloud of the airborne monstrosities. His blade slashed time and again. He found the sword a clumsy and unfamiliar weapon, being more accustomed to his hunting knife, which he would employ to hook into a foe, disemboweling him.

As the ape-man battled, he discovered that the short-sword was the perfect weapon for this purpose. It sliced and smashed and made short work of any denjuru that came within range of his vaulting leaps.

Seeing the prowess of Tarzan, the Tarmanbolgani horde gave forth resounding cries and blundered forward, confident that they could do the same. But not all of them carried bludgeons, and four mighty arms had not the same effectiveness as two hands wielding a sharp sword.

One juvenile was accosted by three denjurus, who fell upon him. Howling for his mother, he erected his upper limbs and punched outward in all directions, but in vain. Slender tentacles inserted themselves into his thin white hide, and suddenly he was swelling up like a balloon and lifting off the ground, all six limbs kicking and flailing, eyes mirroring simian terror.

In the mêlée, hardly anyone noticed this, and as the squalling ape-child floated higher and higher, a greater number of the denjurus followed, then sank their stingers into his bloated form, puncturing it. Whereupon he crashed screaming to the ground, attracting an even greater swarm to feast upon his broken body.

Additional denjurus fell on the milling gorillas. But there were more denjurus than there were apes and even more came oozing out of the long-dead coral honeycombed with warrens harboring colonies of the jellyfish creatures.

Unbeknownst to anyone, the green Martian, Dag Dolor, had snapped his fetters, reached under the pile of ulsios, and located one of Tarzan's extra swords. This he seized and used to defend himself. The olive-skinned brute showed deftness with his blade.

Soon, his massive feet were mashing the corpses of burst denjurus where they fell. None touched him. Where the sword did not slash and pierce, his remaining free fists struck mercilessly.

For his part, Tarzan of the Apes landed close, searched the battlefield and sprang toward the next largest concentration of the violet creatures. They came on and on, floating almost lazily. By some strange means, they were able to propel themselves through the air. Tarzan thought that they must sport siphons such as squid do and expelled air to push themselves about, employing their frills for navigation.

It was not the most efficient means with which to traverse the thin atmosphere, but the creatures depended more on numbers than on individual strength. Lone denjurus were easily discouraged, but like a swarm of bees, it was their numerical superiority that told the tale whenever they concentrated on a single foe.

As it happened, one group selected Murdank, perhaps because he was the largest of the great white gorillas and presented the most obvious target. They could hardly be expected to possess the animal intelligence to recognize the bedizened circlet of authority riding his sloping white-haired skull askew from his strenuous exertions.

Several of them slipped up behind him while the ape-king concentrated on fending off the attackers floating before his face. Murdank clutched his stone bludgeon in his uppermost hands and was swinging it about wildly. There was a little science in his efforts, yet also a good deal of panic. The fact that these creatures were unknown to him no doubt lent great urgency to his frantic efforts.

While he was engaged with an overwhelming number of the denjurus, beating them back handily, the ones congregating behind him advanced, thrusting their barbed tentacles into his thick hide, introducing whatever pernicious substance that caused the grotesque swelling.

Feeling painful stings, Murdank turned, roaring, and began flailing and thrashing with every limb not anchored to the ground.

At first, the tentacles did not inflict any more damage than to cause blisters to form along the Ape-lord's twisting back. Then more fluttering denjurus swarmed about his legs, his neck, and other spots that were not normally vulnerable.

In the end, sheer numbers and not brute force won out.

MURDANK WAS soon overwhelmed. Roaring, he crushed floating denjurus to his chest, smashed them against his muscular thighs, and punched them away with impunity. The Ape-lord did not notice that his body was swelling until one foot lifted off the ground and he waved all four upper arms wildly, struggling to regain his balance. Thereupon, the other foot lost contact with the Martian soil.

Bellowing, Murdank started floating upward. It seemed all but impossible that a creature of such titanic proportions could be made to float like a balloon, but the sheer number of denjurus that had injected their gaseous reservoirs into his helpless bulk overcame all protections lent to him by superior weight and size.

Stricken and helpless, Murdank floated up and up. This was hardly noticed amid the surging battle—then Tarzan observed what was unfolding.

Murdank slowly floated aloft, trailed by swirling, ever-shifting swarm-clouds of greedy denjurus.

When Tarzan spied the unfolding drama, he realized at once that there was no saving the flailing Ape-lord. Still, he coiled his muscular legs and sprang skyward, his sword upraised.

His leap was a tremendous one, and so well timed that Tarzan landed on Murdank's horizontal chest, which was now uppermost in his mad flailing, for the hapless Ape-lord floated upon his naked back.

Directing his thoughts, Tarzan communicated to Murdank his inevitable doom. He transmitted pictures into his mind, then added words: *"They will sting you until you burst, whereupon you will fall to your doom. Nothing can save you, Murdank. Not even Ramdar. However, out of loyalty to you Ramdar is prepared to spare you the agony of falling to your destruction, there to be consumed by these foul creatures. Murdank has only to say the word, and Ramdar will grant you this gift of mercy."*

As if uncomprehending, the titanic Ape-lord appeared to be bereft of words. His wide eyes stared skyward, all but unseeing. Crouching on his heaving chest, Tarzan looked into the stark orbs and forced his thoughts to penetrate the other's terrified brain. Murdank's powerful limbs grew heavy and ceased their futile struggles. He closed his dark eyes.

Finally, the defeated Ape-lord sent out his last mortal thought.

"Murdank accepts the mercy of Ramdar...."

Whereupon Tarzan brought his short-sword down with both hands and with a single oblique stroke, removed the Ape-lord's head from his burly shoulders. It dropped from sight, and the flood of blood pulsing from the stump of the exposed neck grew prodigious. It cascaded over the congregating swarm, forcing them down, while others, untouched, continued sweeping upward.

Tarzan dropped down into this noisome cloud, hacking and cleaving, bursting and deflating many before finally landing on the ground, entirely unharmed. The ape-man was forced to dodge out of the way ahead of the falling carcass. It slammed to the surface, shaking the ground all around.

After that, the flesh-greedy denjurus descended, making noises that chilled the blood and plucked up pimply gooseflesh crawling upon naked simian limbs.

There was so much to Murdank that virtually every denjuru pounced to feast upon his still-warm corpse. The gorilla tribe found themselves fighting empty air, their numbers no longer harried.

Thinking it was the better part of valor, Tarzan rushed back to the survivors, gathered them together and proclaimed, "Murdank is no more! He gave his life for all, so that we might live to conquer in his name. Ramdar is the new Ape-lord. Ramdar will lead the tribe of Narag forward, into the future."

Surprisingly, there was no dissent. The survivors had had a difficult time of it. And the sight of their stupendous leader, all but covered by the voraciously feeding denjurus, was sobering in the extreme.

Tarzan pointed to the south, saying, "We will skirt this accursed zone. Leave the dead. Resume the march."

Staring and wide-eyed, the surviving gorillas obeyed.

Returning to the chariot, Tarzan found the green Martian lying on the ground, his chest heaving from his exertions, but miraculously unharmed.

Tarzan got back into the chariot and commanded the zitidar to resume the trek. Glancing back, he waited for the Hortamangani slave to follow the chariot in its own way, no longer in chains.

Whether the massive green hulk understood Tarzan's intentions or not was immaterial at the moment. There was no advantage to remaining behind and becoming a target of the swarming denjurus, who were so busily feasting that they paid the marching great white gorillas no heed whatsoever.

By nightfall, they had put the colony behind them.

Tarzan rode at the head of the tribe, no longer a military jedwar, but leader of the tribe of Narag. Behind him trailed the dirty ragtag Tarmanbolgani who looked to him as their new Ape-lord, although he scarcely stood taller than their youngest stripling.

A strange destiny had made Tarzan king of the apes once more.

Chapter 18

The Jungle Beckons

FOR SIX days, Kudu hunted across the brilliant Martian sky. Each night, the dreary landscape was illuminated by the two moons, Phobos and her smaller sister, Deimos, washing everything in their unstable lunar light before disappearing, one following the other in their rounds. Tarzan had by this time learned their Martian names, Thuria and Cluros.

The dwindling ulsio meat supply soon ran out, which led to talk among the horde of eating the Hortamangani slave, Dag Dolor. This discussion devolved into the question of who would consume which surviving part, with some apes preferring the legs and others fancying the muscular arms.

Tarzan instructed his tribe to leave the green man alone.

"Save him for a dire emergency. I will hunt fresh meat."

Taking his short-sword in hand, the ape-man leaped high up and came down athwart his chariot. Springing forward, he cleared the zitidar's broad brown back. Across the silent landscape he hopped, giving voice to his weird and terrible cry.

The banths were of a disposition to lie flat on their bellies, hugging the yellow moss, in an effort not to be seen. In that, they were like the lions of Earth—even if their feline qualities were debatable.

Tarzan's feral cries roused them from their stealthy positions. They seemed to have no lairs, there being no such thing as caves or burrows out on the moss-covered plains that comprised the greater portion of the Mars Tarzan had come to know in the first week of his existence upon the barren planet.

Many of the fierce-faced banths were solitary, but some hunted in packs. Tarzan fell on the solitary ones, taking off their wild-maned heads with quick, powerful sword strokes. This accomplished, he gave forth with his resounding ape-cry of triumph, summoning his shambling, spider-limbed tribe.

By this time, Dag Dolor had been given limited freedom. The Tarmanbolgani came charging and blundering toward Tarzan's trailing cry. Behind them, the towering green Martian drove the chariot that suited him better than it did the comparatively diminutive ape-man from another world.

When they pulled up, Tarzan was butchering the headless banths, and the spidery anthropoids descended upon them ravenously. While they were so engaged, the ape-man spied another banth, for he knew two would not be enough to feed his unruly charges.

Taking off in aerial pursuit, Tarzan made short work of the beast, lopping off its fanged head before it sensed danger descending from the sky.

THE FIRST kill had been nearly consumed when he again sent out his weird victory cry and those who were hungry came galloping his way on their lower limbs, hooting and calling.

Once again, they arrived to fresh cuts of raw steak, which Tarzan had laid upon the moss. This time he made four piles, one of which he kept for himself. This he bore to the chariot, where he and the green Martian ate in relative privacy, rather more like civilized men than colossal hairless gorillas.

In the intervening days, Tarzan learned much from the Hortamangani. Dag Dolor had already told him the names of the moons and described some of the creatures that roamed the dying planet. The existence of many of these outlandish monsters the ape-man privately doubted, but neither would he have been astonished to have encountered examples of some of them.

That the Hortamangani belonged to a more organized tribe than the rough and ready Tarmanbolgani became plainer with each passing day. This chariot was one of their means of travel. They also rode upon massive horse-like beasts that the Martian called thoats.

"Describe these creatures," demanded Tarzan.

"They stand as high as I do at the shoulder," Dag Dolor said as he ripped at the raw red meat of the banth, his massive tusked jaws working as blunt teeth chewed. "Their color is slate. Their bellies are more yellow than the moss. They are controlled as the zitidars are controlled, by mental means. Only a warrior may ride a thoat, and they are not eaten for food, being very valuable."

"Tell me of the red men."

"The red man is the hereditary enemy of the green men. They are shaped like you are. But their skins are a reddish copper. And they are deformed like you are, lacking a second set of arms."

Tarzan let that observation pass unchallenged. He did not consider it an insult. In Africa, Tantor considered Tarzan's human nose to be a regrettable mistake of nature.

"Where do the red men live?" he questioned.

"In cities that they built."

"Did they build the dead cities?"

Dag Dolor shook his head. Strong sunlight made his curving tusks gleam.

"No. The ancients constructed those cities. No one living has ever encountered their descendants, whose skins are said to have been as pale as alabaster with hair the color of fire. The cities were built in the days when there was plentiful water and great seas. These long-dead white men sailed in large ships upon the broad water. Now there is no water and the red men sail through the air. Green men prefer to keep their feet firmly upon the ground."

"Do trees still grow on this planet?"

The Hortamangani bull responded slowly and reluctantly. Gratitude did not seem to be built into his temperament. Even though he was fed daily, and relieved of his fetters, it was clear to Tarzan that Dag Dolor would flee had he the means.

Finally, he imparted, "There are forests."

"Where is the nearest forest from this spot?"

Dag Dolor gave a negligent shrug and was slow in responding.

"Since I do not know where I stand upon Barsoom," he said at last, "I do not know where the forests lie from this spot. When my horde was expelled from the city of Vakanor, they scattered to the winds. I do not know where they camp now."

Noticing the deftness with which the green Martian had changed the subject, Tarzan asked, "Tell me of your people."

"My horde was the horde of Vakanor, whose jed was Churvash Ul. But Churvash Ul is dead. I do not know who leads the horde now, only that he commands a remnant of a once-proud tribe."

Tarzan interrogated the young Martian carefully, learning that the green Martians occupied different areas of the planet, forming warring hordes, much in the manner of the Mongols of Asia. The red men, by contrast, were largely city dwellers. The manlike Martians seemed to be in a perpetual state of war, for the green hordes battled with one another and with the red men, who also battled with one another, although there were alliances. These shifted from time to time, Tarzan gathered.

"The ships that sail through the air," asked Tarzan. "Do they also leave the atmosphere?"

Dag Dolor fingered one gleaming tusk, cleaning off traces of banth blood and licking the gore from his olive fingers. Shrugging, he rumbled, "The doings of the red men of the newer cities are of little concern to green nomads."

Because it was important, Tarzan pressed him on that point.

"Are any of their ships capable of traversing the void of space and journeying to other planets?"

The response was slow in coming, and when it came, it was disappointingly vague.

"I do not know. But I do not think so."

"What makes you believe that these sky ships do not travel to other worlds?"

"If they traveled to other worlds," Dag Dolor mused thoughtfully, "they would have brought back slaves and there would be people upon Barsoom who do not belong here."

It seemed like a reasonable point, so Tarzan dropped that line of inquiry. This was a question better asked of a red Martian, if he ever encountered one.

When the meal was concluded, the gorillas assembled behind the chariot of Tarzan, whom the Tarmanbolgani called Ramdar, and he commanded the zitidar to resume the arduous march.

During this trek, Tarzan had familiarized himself with the stars overhead and, by their light and changing positions, strove to maintain the heading that Murdank had established. Lacking the Ape-lord's telepathic ability to sense the minds inhabiting the city of Uxfar, he endeavored to not deviate from what he believed the correct path to be.

Came a time when the ape-man began to detect unfamiliar smells. They were not wholly unfamiliar, for they smacked of things he knew back in Africa.

These scents were furtive. They came and went. The first was the heavy smell of vegetation. Intermingled with this was the musk of unknown beasts. Sniffing the still air, Tarzan recognized none of these odors. He could separate one from another. But that was all that lay within the jungle lord's power. It was a weird feeling.

A low, brooding range of black crags showed to the south. Tarzan studied it by sunlight and moonlight as he journeyed, eventually ascertaining to his satisfaction that the smells were passing over the blunt peaks to reach his sensitive nostrils.

At one sleeping stop, the bronzed giant stayed awake, and went bounding toward the lofty ridge in spectacular leaps that brought him as close to the hilltops as he dared to range. He did not want his tribe to be found by a pack of banths, or worse, in his absence.

Reaching the lowermost peak, Tarzan managed to ascend its craggy face by jumping vertically from cliff to cliff until he reached a flat ledge, which proved to be a stony saddle bridging two taller elevations.

His heart began pounding in his chest when he looked down upon a completely different landscape than anything he had so far encountered during his enforced exile on Mars. His savage soul swelled.

It consisted of a circular valley, a depression that extended for many miles beyond this basalt escarpment, which swept around on either end to form a palisade ringing this vast basin. Tarzan spied what he took to be grass, but it was a purple on the outskirts, shading to a shocking scarlet hue deeper inland, remindful of certain tropical birds of the Earth. Exotic trees grew. None were recognizable. Except that they were undeniably tree-like.

The thin air brought varying smells. Pungent and indescribable, they represented the unmistakable smell of untamed woodland. Inhaling these mingled fragrances deeply, the jungle lord felt, for the first time since his inexplicable advent on the Red Planet, a loss of the homesickness that he had heretofore kept firmly suppressed.

The air was moist, and farther into the distance, steam hung low, obscuring the extent of the verdant basin.

Searching the basalt boundary on either side, the ape-man spied a break in the stony palisade imprisoning the place. A narrow section had collapsed and had fallen in, creating a passageway into the woodland.

IN THAT moment, Tarzan resolved to lead his strange gorilla tribe into this natural paradise. The city for which they were bound was an unknown thing. He was not eager to penetrate it with a small band of the apes, not knowing who defended it. Nor did the Ape-lord relish the thought of consuming its inhabitants, whether they be green, red, or any other hue that Martian flesh took on.

Dropping down the rocky black cliff, Tarzan reached the flat, barren ground and began traversing the landscape in increasingly exhilarating stages. The bronzed giant had become accustomed to this mode of transportation, and it was the nearest thing to flying like an eagle that his imagination could conceive.

Returning at last to the sleeping camp, Tarzan surreptitiously repositioned the chariot, giving the zitidar silent commands to move slowly and carefully until its three-tentacled skull was pointed toward the rocky range.

It was a day's march to the rock palisade. How the gorillas of Murdank would take the idea of abandoning the quest for Uxfar, which they hoped to pillage, for a more pastoral life in the jungle was uncertain. From everything he had gleaned from Dag Dolor, Tarzan gathered that the four-armed giants had forsaken the trees long ago, preferring to dwell in the deserted cities.

Had it been due to the inexorable shrinking of the forests that once carpeted the failing planet, owing to the receding oceans of eons past, or because of the inherent dangers of these sparse woodland patches, was an interesting question. It did not seem plausible that semi-savage gorillas would leave their natural habitat for the emptiness of depopulated ruins, but Barsoom was so evidently a dying planet that perhaps only the hardiest of Tarmanbolgani held the jungles to be their own. Or so reasoned the jungle lord.

Tarzan put the question to Dag Dolor, but the Hortamangani professed complete ignorance on that score. To him, the gorillas of Barsoom were man-eating savages that Tarzan had mastered in some way that he could not fathom.

Perhaps, the ape-man reflected as he lay down to sleep, the four-armed gorillas had never been arboreal. On Earth, the Bolgani spurned the freedom of the treetops. Despite their extra limbs, which would have been perfect for traversing the upper terraces of the forest, these Tarmanbolgani might harbor the same limiting terrestrial inclinations. The size of Martian trees was no doubt another factor. He could think of few earthly trees that would support their weight, which he estimated to be a quarter of a ton.

Upon awakening, Tarzan exhorted his indolent ape tribe to resume the march.

"Ahead lies hills. I scouted while you all slept. There is a pass through one escarpment. Perhaps it leads to the city of Uxfar."

Tarzan knew that it would not, but having phrased it as a possibility, he left himself the opening to be in error without losing face.

Organizing themselves with the women and balus to the rear, the tribe of Narag set off in a sullen silence contrary to their usual boisterous character. This told the ape-man that they were nearing the limits of their patience and endurance.

As the caravan drew nearer to the rugged hills, the smell of the jungle slowly infiltrated the nostrils of every participant. Turning his head from time to time, Tarzan watched the reaction of the colossal gorillas of Barsoom.

It soon became evident from their nervousness, their futile scratching and other signs, that these were not familiar smells. They had never known the forest, these fugitives from a sundered ruin.

Turning his head back toward the broken horizon, Tarzan smiled to himself.

No doubt it was time that these naked brutes reacquainted themselves with their natural roots. That they did not know the ways of the jungle was not a consideration in Tarzan's mind. He would teach them. When he was done with them, they would be true apes, even if they were a strange species of albino gorilla.

When the jungle odors grew pungent, even Dag Dolor became fidgety.

"Have you ever dwelt in the woods?" Tarzan asked him.

"I have never enjoyed the privilege, O Ramdar," returned the green Martian in a heavy and reluctant tone.

"Take heart," encouraged Tarzan. "No doubt there will be game aplenty for us to eat once we reach the trees."

"I would rather die on the moss like an exhausted zitidar," returned Dag Dolor, his shifting red eyes glaring in opposite directions.

Gazing back at him, Tarzan inquired, "Why do you say that?"

"My imagination tells me this."

"What does it tell you?"

"My imagination warns me that if there are things in the forest that we can eat, there are also creatures dwelling there that would consume us. For is that not the way of nature?"

Tarzan nodded, unconcerned.

"That is the character of jungles on Jasoom, so Ramdar does not doubt that it is the nature of a Barsoomian woodland as well. Ramdar is not worried. Ramdar looks forward to meeting the challenge that the jungle offers."

His voice low and rumbling, Dag Dolor added, "Let us hope that we do not all live to regret your enthusiasm."

Chapter 19

Rebellion!

A HALF a Martian day's march before they reached the circular palisade, Tarzan smelled a wholly new scent. A beast he had not yet encountered—perhaps more than one.

Turning to Dag Dolor, he inquired, "What is that smell?"

"I smell nothing," said the green Martian stubbornly. He still lacked the gratitude that should have inhabited someone who was no longer chained and now fed regularly.

Tarzan knew that his sense of smell was more acute than an ordinary man of Earth, having been raised by the great apes of Africa in a savage environment. So it did not surprise him that his nostrils were keener than that of a hulking green giant whose biology was not completely understood by him.

The albino apes resembling naked gorillas began to scent the thing sometime later.

Once again, Tarzan asked Dag Dolor, "Do you smell the creature now?"

The green Martian shook his head in the negative. But his furtive, independently questing eyes told otherwise. It stood to reason if the Tarmanbolgani at last detected the scent, it should have reached the queer slit-nostrils of the young Hortamangani. For it filled the air thickly.

Switching to the language of the great white gorillas, Tarzan inquired, "What beast does Ramdar smell?"

"Thoats!" came the shouted response. "Excellent eating. If they can be captured."

"Ramdar will capture them."

"Thoats run like the wind."

"Ramdar will leap like a greater wind," assured Tarzan. Eyeing the downcast Hortamangani, he added, "My subjects say they are thoats."

"I smell nothing," insisted Dag Dolor, and Tarzan's suspicions grew. The captive was denying the obvious, therefore he had some reason to do so.

Leaving the zitidar to plug along methodically, Tarzan leaped upward, as high as he could ascend. Numerous pairs of simian eyes followed him, as did those of Dag Dolor, which strained to track him.

Twisting in midair, Tarzan spied the creatures. There were three of them, grazing on yellow lichen. Two were the slate gray that the green Martian had described, their hairless hides shading to pale bellies and yellow at the feet. But one was as white as Dag Dolor's tusks, whiter than the thick hides of the albino gorillas, who accumulated dust and grime and were not fastidious about keeping themselves clean.

Landing safely, Tarzan paused briefly, then leapt skyward again. The long-bodied creatures did not notice him. They were facing away, their heads down, intent upon their eating. They were sleek-skinned and six-legged, with tails that were both broad and flat, tapering down toward the root, in a way that made the ape-man think of a beaver's tail, although the shape was not quite like that.

Two more prodigious bounds and the ape-man settled into a walking gait. He strode boldly up to the grazing beasts, endeavoring to remain downwind of them, for the terrain was too flat to permit stealth and offered no cover.

Tarzan studied the thoats at a distance, saw that their heads were generally horse or zebra shaped, but gashed by mouths that were prodigiously large. In size, they compared with African elephants in their mass and were slightly taller in stature, standing approximately ten feet at the shoulder. But beyond that, they bore little resemblance to the terrestrial pachyderm, having sleek and sinuous bodies. The ape-man then made up his mind.

Setting his pantherish leg muscles for a shallow leap, he sprang into the arid air, landing almost perfectly astride the white thoat's withers, as he would upon the broad back of an African elephant. The creature reared up half its long length, and Tarzan took hold of its thick neck, the way he would an unbroken horse.

The other thoats bolted in opposite directions. The ivory beast whirled and flung its torso about, but no matter what muscular convulsion it essayed, Tarzan could not be thrown from his high perch. His powerful legs clamped tight, holding firmly in place. The steely grip of the ape-man's fingers on its struggling neck muscles soon convinced the beast that it was overmastered.

Finally, the thoat quieted. Tarzan impressed upon the creature's brain telepathic commands that were firm but unthreatening. This beast was not as easily tamed as the zitidar, but eventually it settled down. Tarzan mentally directed it to traverse the distance back toward the waiting ape band. It galloped in the manner of a zebra, then settled into a steady trot.

When the apes of Ramdar spotted their diminutive bronzed Ape-lord riding a splendid white beast, they jumped up to their hind feet, shouting and waving their balled fists and war hammers in the air.

Excited, the bulls were cheering him on. For no ape had ever ridden a thoat. The concept was unknown to them. The specimen in question was of a size and scale equal to that of the colossal anthropoids. Tarzan's magnificently splendid musculature was dwarfed by the alabaster beast, but he controlled it effortlessly.

The slate-hued thoats followed at a paltry distance. Evidently, the white one was their herd leader.

When Tarzan drew up to the advancing gorillas, Dag Dolor stared at him very intently, his three surviving hands on the chariot rail squeezing spasmodically as if his emotions were boiling internally.

Tarzan noticed this but said nothing.

Swerving the thoat around to pace the chariot as it creaked along, the jungle lord told the green man, "I will ride this beast. The chariot is now your responsibility. The zitidar knows what Ramdar expects of it."

His square jaw clamped shut, Dag Dolor turned his attention to the plodding zitidar as it continued on its patient and enduring way. The less colorful thoats turned about and trotted on either side. After the terrifying four-armed apes did not attack, they ceased to look behind in wary shifts.

The spectacle that now forged toward the mountain pass was remarkable to behold. An Earth man astride a titanic bone-white thoat, flanked by other thoats and trailed by a chariot, followed by a rear guard of hammer-wielding great white gorillas constituted a formidable force on the move.

The sound of the thoats was surprisingly subdued, and Tarzan, looking downward, noticed they did not possess hoofs, any more than did the zitidar. The thickly padded feet lacked nails, claws or any equivalent. Hoofs were apparently not a Martian evolutionary development.

As they moved closer and closer to the escarpment, the pale apes of Ramdar grew increasingly restive.

"What is wrong?" asked Tarzan.

Thagg, the bull with the missing finger, barked back, "We do not like these smells. We fear them. We fear no red man or green man or other men. We fear only the unknown. Where are you leading us, O Ramdar?"

"To the far side of that range of cliffs," replied Tarzan calmly.

"What lies beyond the cliffs?"

"Food. Shelter. And possibly beyond that the city of Uxfar."

The great white gorillas growled and grunted among themselves. This last pronouncement met with their favor, but the pungent odors ate at their flaccid resolve. Accustomed as the apes were to the dusty ruins of the dried-up sea floor, the riot of vegetable and animal odors assaulting their twitching nostrils grew overpowering.

What they considered disquieting, Tarzan judged to be the familiar, even if the scents were as alien to his nostrils as they were to his six-limbed cohort.

"We will press on!" exhorted Tarzan. "Ramdar promises you full bellies once we breach those black cliffs."

Rumbling and muttering, the ghostly gorilla horde continued trekking. They were up on their hind legs again, although by this point so fatigued that they preferred to go on all fours. But they were entering the unfamiliar, preparing to penetrate the unknown, and so instinctually saw the advantage of their great height, the better to scan all around them, and to intimidate any threats they might encounter.

Tarzan's steady gaze was on the cleft passage, which had fallen into shadow, Cluros, the lesser moon of Mars, having dropped below the western horizon. For now it was night.

The ape-man might have been forgiven for not noticing out of the tail of his eye what Dag Dolor was doing. The Horta-mangani had fallen completely silent, and the grumbling of the chariot wheels continued to mask certain sounds.

Reaching back into the litter on the floor of the chariot, he seized a sword with his lower left arm and transferred it to his upper right fist, away from Tarzan's view.

Turning his attention to the nearest thoat, he sent out his thoughts.

The steadily galloping creature drifted over to the chariot's side and paced beside it for a time, patiently waiting, yet always remaining alert. It might have recognized the green man. And he, it. No nervousness hung about the creature as it ambled along on its sextuple padded feet.

WITHOUT WARNING, Dag Dolor bolted the light rail of the jouncing chariot and landed perfectly astride the thoat.

Wheeling, the creature raced ahead of the chariot, whereupon he charged Tarzan's pale steed.

Hearing this commotion, Tarzan turned in his perch, beheld the slate thoat coming and then saw the flash of cold moonlight on chill steel as the Hortamangani swept in, preparing to remove his head with a sideways stroke.

The ape-man extracted his own blade with quicksilver speed, brought it up and about, and parried the first blow. His strength was prodigious for a man of his size, and it was more than sufficient to stand up to the gigantic green Martian.

With two quick flashing strokes, Tarzan smashed the other's weapon into the soil, and then brought the flat of his blade against the Hortamangani's huge olive-skinned skull with decisive results.

No one was more surprised than Dag Dolor when he was unhorsed. He crashed into the dirt, where no spongy moss cushioned his fall.

Dropping from his steed, Tarzan marched over to the fallen and former friend and placed the point of his short-sword to the creature's pulsing jugular vein.

"What has come over you?" Tarzan demanded.

The disconnected eyes shut tightly. "I could not bear to see you ride the sacred thoat any longer," he breathed.

"Ramdar captured it. It is Ramdar's to ride."

"Before that, it was the thoat of Churvash Ul, Jed of Vakanor."

"What of it? Is Churvash Ul not dead?"

A smoldering anger drove the sullenness from Dag Dolor's tone.

"Dead to all, except to me, who is his only surviving son."

Tarzan's handsome features registered mild surprise. "You are the son of Churvash Ul?"

"Did I not just tell you this?" spat Dag Dolor contemptuously. "Since you have humiliated me in battle, you may dispatch me, for I do not care to look upon your tuskless bronze features any longer, you unhatched abomination of an ape."

Tarzan's blade did not waver. "If I slay you, my apes will eat you."

"If they consume me after I am dead, Dag Dolor will have no say in the matter. I no longer wish to suffer in captivity, a maimed slave to savages."

Tarzan placed one bare sole upon the creature's heaving breast. The weight of his down-pressing foot was greater than it seemed possible, given the bronzed giant's disadvantageous size as compared to his hulking opponent. The strength of Tarzan of the Apes in the weaker gravity of Mars was a considerable thing.

Dag Dolor had felt the power of the sun-bronzed Jasoomian before. Those steely thews had impressed him previously with their indomitable and irresistible might. But now, as he lay helpless under the heel of this puny creature who was one-third his bulk, the green Martian felt a helplessness wash over his struggling limbs that completely unmanned him.

As the ape-tribe of Ramdar gathered about, lifting their clubs and war hammers, Dag Dolor glanced around and saw that their fangs were bared to taste his flesh.

"Grant me one boon, O Ramdar. Cut my throat with a swift stroke. I do not wish to have my skull crushed by the clubs of these brutes. What happens after that does not concern me."

The white gorillas did not understand this speech, of course. But they could read the situation perfectly.

One barked, "Slay him swiftly! We will feast on his remaining limbs."

Tarzan hesitated. He had no desire to see the green man rendered to a mere pile of broken bones empty of all marrow. But now he could not trust Dag Dolor.

"Ramdar has a better idea."

The great white gorillas regarded him curiously. They were on the verge of attacking what they considered to be their next meal.

"Some of you fear to ride into the valley. We will send the green man ahead, and if he survives the passage, we will know that it is safe to follow."

"And after that?" grunted one.

"We will see what there is to eat on the other side of the cliffs. This green man is yet young and growing. The longer he lives, the larger he will become and the greater a feast he will offer to us when the proper time comes."

This satisfied the pale apes, for fear of the dark passage in wait beyond was greater than their hunger. And Ramdar had fed them well.

Removing his blade tip from the pulsing jugular, Tarzan stepped back and said to Dag Dolor, "Regain your mount. Ride ahead of us. What you do henceforth falls into the lap of the gods, if any such inhabit this barren planet you consider your home."

Not having understood the exchange between Tarzan and his barbaric gorillas, the green Martian hesitated, but then realized that to hesitate would be to be torn apart by the rending fangs of the savage white band. Climbing to his feet, Dag Dolor found his thoat, mounted it with practiced ease, and directed the creature to gallop toward the shadowy cliff pass.

Tarzan and his Tarmanbolgani watched him enter. Martian and beast were soon swallowed by darkness. Expectantly, they waited. For the sounds that followed would dictate their next course of action.

Chapter 20

"I Fear You Now"

AS LUNAR shadows fell upon the flat paddle of a tail on the white thoat, Tarzan dismounted and addressed his simian subjects.

"Since you fear to venture into the valley in the night, we will await the dawn, the better to scout as we file through the crevasse to the other side of the palisade."

"What if the green one does not return?"

"Ramdar does not expect him to return. But if he runs afoul of danger, we will hear his death shrieks, and we will know then that danger lies ahead of us to be met."

One great white gorilla grumbled disconsolately, "Danger always lies ahead to be met."

"And behind us, too," added another.

"Danger is always around us," echoed Foad. "This is why we abide in ruins."

"As long as Ramdar leads you, you need not fear," stated Tarzan.

These words were accepted in silence. But there was muttering among the ranks. Tarzan had rescued them from the floating denjurus, but not all of them. Nor had he preserved Murdank, who was of their species. These great white gorillas had not expressed any noticeable grief over the loss of their chief, and their confidence in their new Ape-lord was all but unbounded. But now he was leading them into uncertainty. Their simian brains struggled with that concept. They did not much care for it.

Deciding to take the opportunity to rest, they sat upon their haunches and laid down their weapons. They scratched themselves, muttered to one another, and rested while the youngest offspring nursed at the breasts of their mothers.

Watching them closely, Tarzan ruminated upon how much like terrestrial gorillas they were except for certain variations in their specific physical configuration. Their freakish hairlessness was unpleasant to behold, yet the tapered skulls with their sunken eyes beneath beetling brow ridges conformed to the Bolgani pattern, as nature made them. The ghost-pale skin and scalps of stiff white hair struck Tarzan as incongruous. When standing up, the Tarmanbolgani might have been mistaken for giant humans except for certain outlandish features. But when they hunkered down on their lower fours, they were most gorilla-like, other than their elongated torsos set with a bizarre extra pair of limbs.

Keeping his ears cocked for any sounds reverberating back from the darkened passage, Tarzan went among the thoats and examined them closely. More than any creature he had encountered of the lower orders, there was a suggestion of the equine about them, except for their multi-legged locomotion. In truth, they served as credible steeds.

Eventually, the second moon dropped out of the sky. After Cluros departed, darkness took over. But the interval was relatively brief. It was a nervous interlude regardless. The great gorillas fell silent, listening intently. Tarzan directed his attention toward the beasts of burden, sending them calming telepathic reassurances.

He thought again how strange it was that after only a week on the Red Planet he had managed to communicate with the lower animals, just as he had in his African homeland. This easy familiarity, however, did not detract one jot from his burning desire to return home, if that were in fact possible.

His only hope rested with the copper men of Barsoom. But since he did not know where their cities lay, finding suitable habitation where he could make for himself a bow and arrow set and spear, as well as eat more appetizing meat, was his highest goal.

The jungle had taught Tarzan of the Apes patience. It might take a month to learn if Earth was an achievable goal. It could take years. He did not have control over that, or over other factors that governed his strange new destiny.

But the ape-man would keep his goal firmly in mind, and follow it with single-minded determination until he achieved what he most desired in life, or surrendered fatalistically to this most disagreeable of fortunes.

Alone, Tarzan could make a life anywhere, even upon Barsoom. But he had a home back in distant Africa. A wife and son. Native allies. And loyal animals such as the faithful Golden Lion and little Nkima, the monkey.

No doubt all of these missed him by now. Unquestionably, they wondered as to his fate. But he had no means to communicate any of that to his beloved circle of friends and family.

Kudu appeared on the horizon, familiar yet strangely shrunken. As her rays of light suffused the Martian atmosphere and sent night shadows fleeing, Tarzan swung atop his massive white steed with a quick leap and wheeled the gigantic thoat about as if he had been doing so all his days.

"Dawn has come!" he cried out. "It is time to follow Ramdar."

Slowly, reluctantly, the apes scratched their dusty hides. Surly growls indicated their reluctance to face the day. Some had fallen asleep and sleepiness might have informed their sluggishness, but before long they were standing erect on their hind legs, making fists of bone and gathering up their stone mallets.

The march commenced anew. The thoats took the lead while the lurching zitidar resumed hauling the empty chariot, and the monotonous sounds that accompanied their lumbering progress were again heard.

Presently, they drew near the upflung morass of soil and stone that formed a natural escarpment. It reared some twenty to thirty feet above their heads, a frowning and forbidding mass as black as basalt.

Sunlight illuminated the cleft in its dark face, showing the way into the shallow valley, but nothing of what lay beyond, owing to an abrupt turn in the passageway.

Tarzan rode into this gash of a pass well ahead of the others. Again, he had the impression of an upheaval which had created the entranceway, thrusting stone and soil aside, which had long since settled. He examined the stony walls as they passed by. He saw again white quartz and was reminded of the store of quartz the chariot carried.

Those fragments would be chipped into spear points and arrowheads if he could but locate hard stones with which to fashion them. Wood to turn into shafts would complete his needs. Tarzan could not imagine any jungle that would not contain both of those items. On the other hand, he did not realistically know what to expect of a Martian forest.

So he rode ahead carefully, alert in every fibre of his being, his right hand not straying far from the jeweled hilt of the shortsword hanging from his metallic belt.

The pass was deep, and the way sloped downward into a shallow depression. The rocky barrier had concealed much of the greenery cupped within, since it lay below what passed on Barsoom for sea level.

When Tarzan emerged on the other side, he saw the tall purple grass growing tall and rank. Yellow fronds tipped it. The air was strikingly different from that of the desiccated sea bottom he had traversed. It was moist, humid, and pleasantly hot.

Beyond it lay a weird jungle dense with towering trees—none of which Tarzan recognized!

The morning had hardly blossomed, yet the jungle lord drank in the heady smells of this unfamiliar woodland. Sounds of insects and animals were entirely absent, however.

The first stand of Martian trees he entered was nothing like anything the Earth had ever supported. Their leafy colors were strange, almost beyond conception. Of course, the familiar hues of the rainbow were present, but in such combinations and shades that his earthly eyes wanted to make of them something completely alien to his experience. But that seemed to be a trick of clashing hues.

This was no forest such as the ape-man had conjured in his imagination, but a true jungle! How such an oasis of moisture could have flourished on arid Mars was difficult to account for.

Searching the vast sky, Tarzan sought signs of rain clouds. There were none. Whence came the water that fed these stout trees? Ferns were abundant. Vines choked the upper terraces of the trees. No answer presented itself. So he moved on.

THE TALL, purple grass had been trampled in a curving line where Dag Dolor had ridden his thoat. There was no mistaking the manner in which the wild grass was crushed by multiple padded feet.

Quietly dismounting, Tarzan extracted his sword and sent the beast ahead to follow the trail that Dag Dolor had blazed. Slipping off to one side, he crept through the untrampled purple shoots, keeping low, wary of ambush.

He no longer trusted the towering green Martian who had showed his true colors.

The thoat encountered no difficulties, and Tarzan emerged out the other side. To his mild surprise, he found Dag Dolor standing beside a strange tree, eating of its fruit.

Cautiously but confidently, Tarzan approached, and the green warrior turned and lifted the fruit in one hand, saying, "This is a somp. It is delicious."

Reaching up, he plucked a fruit and handed it to Tarzan, who accepted it. The ape-man sniffed the pulpy thing and saw that it was somewhat like a grapefruit with a thin, red rind. Peeling it, he sampled the juicy interior and found it to be sweeter than his personal preference, but acceptable.

Casually, Dag Dolor remarked, "This is a sompus tree. The somp is a delicacy. Very rare."

Pointing toward a spreading tree of much greater growth and size, he added, "That is a skeel tree. Its nuts are also delicious. You might like them better."

Tarzan walked over to the skeel tree and spied clusters of nuts nested amid the higher boughs. They were too high to reach, so he sprang into the tree with the agility of a monkey. As he ascended, the jungle lord realized this was the first tree he had scaled in more than a week. It felt good to feel branches in his palms and sturdy bark against his bare soles.

Finding a bough able to support him, Tarzan squatted there and plucked nuts off the lesser limbs. The shells were hard, and would not have normally given in to his finger pressure, but he was abnormally powerful in his digital strength and they soon surrendered.

The nut's meat was less sweet than the somp and therefore more to his liking. Tarzan chewed slowly, enjoying the unfamiliar taste upon his tongue.

By now, the sun was rising strongly and the drone and buzz of insects made themselves heard. Tarzan watched one flitter by, but it moved so fast he could not make out much of it except that it reminded him of a dragonfly. Its vivid color brought to mind a fresh lime.

Exploring the tree further, he jumped over to the adjoining crown, and immediately felt an unexpected coolness. In some strange way the leaves of these trees held the chill of the night even as the warmth of the morning was saturating the thin atmosphere.

A curious-looking creeper wound up around one twisting branch. Tarzan reached out to it. Amid its pinkish blooms, black eyes popped open. Strange thin hands unfolded. They grasped at a passing insect, and crushed it. The inhuman hands withdrew. Tarzan decided to seek another tree.

A reconnoiter of the immediate vicinity was called for, and the bronzed giant realized how ignorant he was of the ways of this lush woodland. The trees were entirely alien. That they had branches and leaves and trunks was the only thing they held in common with terrestrial trees.

Tarzan beheld his first bird, and it presented only a single oval eye in the center of its feathered head. That was unnerving enough that he declined to approach it. That solitary orb regarded him unwinkingly, and for all the ape-man knew, it saw in him a meal.

Dropping back to the grassy ground, he crept back toward Dag Dolor, who was quietly devouring his third somp fruit.

"These trees are unlike any that grow upon Jasoom," Tarzan commented in a matter-of-fact tone of voice.

The Hortamangani grunted contentedly.

"Where trees grow," remarked Tarzan, "there must be water."

Dag Dolor looked thoughtful for a moment and offered, "I have heard of a bush that gives milk. But I do not know what that plant looks like." He looked about carefully, studying the various trees, and Tarzan began to suspect he knew more about this jungle than he had previously let on.

Lifting his upper arms, he pointed with two huge index fingers, saying, "I think that is the tree over yonder. I do not know its name."

"Did you not say it was a bush, not a tree?"

"I do not recall," grumbled Dag Dolor. "My knowledge is not complete. I know only what I have heard from others."

Curious, but not entirely trusting, Tarzan walked over to the tree in question and examined it more closely.

The thing was not terribly tall, but its crown was thickly congested with triangular leaves that were a variegated yellow and green. Mixed in with this foliage were the dried husks of various insects. It made him think of the discarded meals of jungle spiders.

Sword in hand, the bronzed giant made a rapid circumnavigation of the tree and saw nothing that would produce milk. His newfound suspicion of the green Martian's motivations made him decline to investigate further.

Turning to go, he heard a brief rustle, and then felt a weight falling on his back. Pivoting swiftly, he sliced with his sword, blindly but purposely, but failed to encounter anything. The weight remained on his back and something was digging into it.

Using the flat of his blade, the ape-man swept the sword backward in an attempt to dislodge the hideous thing, but it would not budge.

Round and around he went, but the thing still clung to him. So Tarzan did the only thing he could think to do. He leaped straight up, managing to achieve over thirty feet in altitude, and then deliberately plunged back down, landing on his bare back.

Something broke open with a horrible sound, and a disagreeable odor emerged. The awful sense of pinchers digging into his back released.

Scrambling to his feet, the ape-man looked down upon the thing that he had tricked into releasing him.

It appeared to be a species of spider, but nothing on the order of the arachnids of his home planet. This thing boasted a dozen legs, and they reared up and then down from its ventral spine. Three of the legs were broken and the others were flailing madly, attempting to upend itself so that all surviving feet could be properly positioned for escape. But it was like a tortoise which had landed helplessly upon its shell.

Tarzan drove his steel into its thorax, whereupon the monstrosity gave a last flurry of jittering legs and emitted a high-pitched death squeal.

When it settled down, Tarzan became aware of booming laughter. The laughter had been issuing for some moments now, and was rollicking and morbid in its echoes.

Striding over to Dag Dolor, Tarzan demanded, "Why do you laugh at Ramdar?"

"Because you are so ignorant of the forest."

The battle scar that crossed Tarzan's scalp and brow was ordinarily unnoticeable; now it blazed up, red and resentful.

Seeing it spring into life, Dag Dolor suddenly left off laughing, and fell silent. He looked down upon the sword of Ramdar, which was covered with an ichor that was both lividly purple and unpleasantly malodorous.

"Ramdar gave you your freedom and your food. Where is your loyalty?"

"My loyalty is reserved for my jed, the chief of my tribe," he returned in a surly manner. "I do not know his name, but if I should find him, he will have it without question."

The two antagonists stared at one another at great length. Despite Dag Dolor's superior height, his fierce red-eyed regard had difficulty holding the level gaze of Tarzan of the Apes.

The Martian's independent eyes switched between Tarzan's unflinching stare and the burning red scar positioned above it.

"I have not feared you before this moment," he said frankly. "But I fear you now, O Ramdar."

Tarzan said simply, "I asked you where lay your loyalty. You have no jed."

"My loyalty would be to Ramdar, but the sight of you astride the sacred thoat inflames my hatred."

"Explain yourself, Dag Dolor."

"You are as ignorant of thoats as you are of forests," grunted the olive-complected Martian. "Otherwise, you would know that the white thoat is exceedingly rare. Only a green warrior may ride one, and only a jed at that."

Tarzan considered these words. As he did so, the jagged scarlet scar upon his brow started to fade, melting back into the bronze of his high forehead.

Using his short-sword, he turned on his heel and leaped to the broad back of the white thoat, impelling it to turn about smartly until it had completed a full circuit.

After demonstrating his mastery over the creature, Tarzan said simply, "Then Ramdar is your jed now. Be prepared to follow him where he goes, or consign your arms and legs to the bellies of the great white apes of Ramdar."

With those words, Tarzan rode back to fetch his hairless and no doubt ravenous tribe.

Chapter 21

Into the Martian Jungle

THE ALBINO apes of the tribe of Ramdar marched into the gash of a passageway and filed downward into the rockbound basin reluctantly. Tarzan led them astride his magnificent white thoat. His loyal zitidar pulled the chariot along in its dusty wake, its tentacular facial trunks waving about, orange orbs eagerly questing for sights of interest. The surviving shes and balus took up the rear.

The narrow pass was peculiar. It showed every sign of being the result of actions other than natural ones. While indications of erosion were present, suggesting that the cleft was ancient, there were other signs pointing to the possibility that the stony cliff wall had in the past been breached by something massive. Fractured stone, disturbed soil and scattered black boulders marked the unnatural gash. The ape-man read these signs and decided that long, long ago, a force of great size had pushed into the barrier, creating a clear pathway. Whether this was an invading tribe or a migration of great beasts Tarzan could not discern. Centuries of wind and other Martian elements had weathered the passage long ago.

When the tribe broke through into the weaving purple grass, took in the luxurious trees and riotous flowers, and heard the hum of insects, their unease turned into visible nervousness. Their nostrils wrinkled up as their pale ears twitched at the commingled noises of teeming jungle life.

They milled about reluctantly, dropping to their lower four limbs, and ranged about with what was to Tarzan of the Apes astounding reluctance.

Tarzan asked Foad, "Is this the forest Murdank called Desh?"

The gorilla wrinkled his snout and struggled to reply.

"Foad does not know. Only Murdank knows. And Murdank is no more."

Another gorilla offered, "Desh is a word that means forest. It does not mean any particular forest. Just as ape means any ape, and no one ape."

Foad nodded with fang-baring approval. "What does it matter what forest this is? It is a forest. And we are in it."

THAT WAS the consensus among the Tarmanbolgani.

It was plain to see that these gorilla-like creatures knew nothing of jungles or trees. They were creatures of the dead crumbling cities. In Tarzan's eyes, this had debased them as badly as city living does to some Earth men.

Tarzan led them to the sompus tree and climbed it, throwing down the citrus-like fruits to the waiting gorillas.

They caught these juicy fruits reluctantly, fumbled with them, baffled in expression. So Tarzan showed them how to peel and eat them. Mimicking him, they did so, but the expressions on their simian countenances showed that they were not familiar with fruit.

Leaping into an adjoining tree, the ape-man harvested nuts and sent them cascading down to the ground.

Blinking curiously, the Tarmanbolgani took them up and tried to bite them open. They did not seem to be able to distinguish between the hard shells and the sweetmeats within until Tarzan shouted down instructions. Thereupon, they fell to eating properly. A few broke teeth in their confusion.

The nuts seemed to achieve greater favor than the fruit, for the mothers soon passed the liberated sweetmeats to their offspring. A few children tried the fruit, and found it acceptable, perhaps only due to its novelty. These meat-eating gorillas had become so accustomed to devouring ulsios and other animals that the simple pleasures of the jungle were foreign to them.

While they ate and foraged, Tarzan plunged deeper into the jungle, taking to the higher terraces, perpetually on the lookout for whatever strange creatures inhabited this lush forest.

Incredible birds took flight, their plumage distinctly tropical, and Tarzan studied them carefully. None appeared to be threatening.

Scavenging around, the bronzed giant foraged a suitable shaft for a hunting spear and the makings of a bow and arrow set. This proved to be an exceedingly difficult undertaking. Some of the woods were too hard, while others proved too soft. Regrettably, Tarzan's short-sword was not an appropriate tool for cutting wood into lengths that were usable.

The ape-man was forced to discard much of the wood he collected, and forage deeper into the forest.

After some time, Tarzan gave up his futile search and concentrated on fashioning a spear shaft, which proved easier to make.

He carried this back to the chariot, where he sat down and began banging with a stone he scavenged one of the quartz outcroppings that had sufficient mass to be reduced to a spear point. This was difficult, painstaking work, and occupied many hours.

Finally, the jungle lord had a rude spear point, which he affixed to one end of the hardwood shaft by binding it with lengths of banth hide that had been dried in the sun. This, too, seemed unsuitable for prolonged use, but it was satisfactory for the moment.

While Tarzan was so occupied, his ape subjects found spots in the tall grass and sprawled about. Soon they were dozing. Their bellies were full, so life held little of compelling interest for the moment.

Their lack of interest in penetrating the jungle and seeking fresh game continually perplexed the ape-man.

For his part, Dag Dolor displayed more curiosity, disappearing off into the trees, but always returning. He seemed not to know what to do with himself. Not belonging with the apes, who were his mortal enemies, yet showing no desire to flee into the jungle, he wandered away.

During one of his disappearances, Tarzan followed him surreptitiously.

The lumbering green colossus trudged among the forest lanes, meandering about aimlessly. Taking to the trees, Tarzan tracked him by scent spoor as well as through the giant footprints he left behind. The green Martian seemed oblivious of the ape-man's stalking presence.

Came a time when Dag Dolor became more purposeful and began working to the south, breaking a fresh trail.

Sniffing the air, Tarzan detected a fresh odor. It was not pleasant. In fact, it could not truly be termed fresh. For it was foul and disagreeable. It was a carrion odor; of that there could be no mistake.

Dag Dolor trudged toward it, Tarzan following stealthily above and behind the massive Martian, unsuspected.

By this hour, insects became plentiful, but none appeared to be of the pest variety. They did not bother Tarzan, nor did they seem interested in the green Martian as he lumbered forward.

Breaking into a grassy clearing, Dag Dolor came to the origin of the foul smell.

The body of a huge green Martian lay asprawl in the open. His elephantine tusks gleamed in the sun, standing out against the stiff black mask that was his unlovely countenance. His eyes were closed. Yet he showed no other signs of decay, the meat on his massive bones had neither shrunk nor been picked at by scavengers.

The dead Martian wore a leathern harness, to which were buckled various weapons.

Seeing these, Dag Dolor eagerly fell upon them, removed the harness and buckled it about himself, making certain adjustments for his comparatively smaller stature. From its various iron rings depended a long-sword and a smaller blade that appeared to be a fighting dirk, or dagger.

Although far from a hunting knife, it was yet the most serviceable cutting tool the ape-man had so far discovered upon the surface of Barsoom.

As the unsuspecting green Martian secured the harness about himself, Tarzan dropped from the trees and landed directly behind him. The sound of the ape-man's bare feet was soft striking grass, but the green man heard it nonetheless.

Swiftly, Dag Dolor spun, his upper hands suddenly bristling with blades, a long-sword and the dagger. He quickly transferred the latter to his solitary lower left hand, the better to get at his shorter foe.

For a moment the two faced one another, Tarzan's bronzed fists holding the quartz-tipped hunting spear defensively before him.

Showing no fear, the ape-man said, "I will permit you to keep the long-sword provided you surrender the dagger."

"I will surrender neither weapon, O Ramdar."

"Then I will take them from you and leave you with nothing."

A boisterous laugh rolled up from the green Martian's belly, through his elongated torso and out the tusked mouth rising above his throbbing throat.

"Come at me then!" he cried.

IT WAS an unfortunate choice of words, for as the two combatants squared off, something lifted out of the nearest trees. On beating wings, it floated toward the clearing.

His back to the new apparition, Dag Dolor saw it not. He was waving his blades, preparing to sink his steel into his smaller foeman.

But Tarzan, lifting his head, spied the monstrous thing clearly.

In Africa, there exist hornets. This monstrosity was similar to that formidable insect, but the size was closer to that of a bullock. Its otherwise-hairless head was dominated by faceted eyes as large around as a man's skull. It displayed formidable jaws in proportion to these orbs, and from its curled thorax depended a vicious stinger capable of impaling a man—or a hulking green Martian.

Tarzan watched it, and the sound of its beating wings became a strident hum, lifting above the buzzing drone of the lesser insects of the jungle. In its piercing volume, the hum was distressing, and pierced the eardrums.

Dag Dolor was so intent upon his foe that his antenna-like ears took in the sounds, but his brain did not react to them.

Seeing the stupendous hornet of a thing approach, Tarzan took three steps backward, planted his bare feet upon the ground, and prepared to launch his spear from his right shoulder.

At that moment, the hornet's shadow fell over the green Martian with enormous suddenness and Dag Dolor suddenly charged, thinking that Tarzan was about to impale him.

The ape-man's muscular arm snapped forward. The spear whistled through the air, transfixing not the green Martian, but the brown hornet as it was in the act of pouncing upon the doomed Dag Dolor.

The force of Tarzan's cast was decisive. On Earth, he would have achieved his aim, but on Mars his prodigious strength and muscles propelled the pointed weapon deep into the cranium of the looming insect, carrying it backward with a shrill, caustic scream, whereupon the point dropped to the grass, impaling itself into the ground at a perpendicular angle.

Dripping an ichorous fluid, the hornet's heavy body slid down the hardwood shaft to crumple at the grounded spear tip, its frenetic wings suddenly still, its weird death cries trailing into nothingness.

The speed with which everything happened stunned Dag Dolor. The stout shaft had left Tarzan's bronzed fist, and disappeared over the green Martian's charging shoulders before he could react.

Bellowing, the Hortamangani warrior raced toward his unarmed foe. And as he brought his long-sword sweeping backward to take off Tarzan's head, the ape-man jumped to one side, easily evading the whistling blade.

Tarzan sprang again, and was suddenly behind his bewildered antagonist.

Twisting about, Dag Dolor unexpectedly spied the dying hornet. Its size startled him, for his eyes went wide and his forearms momentarily froze, then dropped to his side. His carriage wilted. All of the fight drained out of him.

Ignoring Tarzan, he walked over to the dead insect and stepped around it, making a full circuit of the overgrown insect. The terrible jaws held his attention, but the stinger at the tip of the curling thorax fascinated him for a long time.

Full realization of his brush with a terrible death descended upon the green Martian. Silently, with heavy tread, he stepped over to Tarzan of the Apes, who stood with his muscular bronzed arms folded across his chest, utterly without a trace of fear upon his noble features.

Dag Dolor came to within ten feet and suddenly sank to his knees, whereupon he laid before the bronzed giant's feet the sheathed long-sword and scabbard belt and then, crossing it, added the vicious dagger.

When he found voice, his utterance was a thick rumble of emotion. "Ramdar has saved the life of Dag Dolor. Dag Dolor offers Ramdar his weapons. From this padan henceforth, you are my jed. None other. While your martial skill astounds me, your fierceness is like nothing I've ever seen in any man, red or green. I do not know who or what you are in truth, Ramdar, only that I will follow you to the ends of Barsoom if you would but lead me."

"Well spoken," returned Tarzan. "You may keep your long-sword and your scabbard belt, for I see that you wear it proudly. I will take your dagger."

"My dagger is yours, as is my life and my loyalty. But it is customary for you to return my sword as a sign that you have accepted the fealty offered to you."

"Very well," returned Tarzan, handing the blade back to the kneeling warrior. "I ask one thing of you."

"Name this thing," intoned Dag Dolor, rising to his feet with the scabbard belt in his hand. He buckled this about his waist.

"Since you stand taller than I am, Ramdar asks that you extract his spear from the dead creature behind us."

"It will be done," said Dag Dolor.

Turning about, he marched up to the impaled corpse, and showing scant concern that it might still harbor a shred of twitching life, planted a mighty foot on the dead monstrosity, and attempted to lift free the spear shaft, which became unaccountably stuck.

Unsheathing his sword, the green warrior chopped away at the creature, finally separating the thing from the instrument of its demise.

Carrying this back to Tarzan of the Apes, he laid it upon the ground respectfully, then rose to his full impressive height once more.

"Your bravery trounces me," he stated gravely.

"Follow," said Tarzan, turning his back. Displaying no fear of treachery, the ape-man strode back through the forest toward the entrance where his great white gorillas slept the day away.

Obediently, Dag Dolor followed in his tracks. His hands were empty of weapons, and his heart full of some new emotion, one alien to the ferocious Hortamangani of Barsoom.

Chapter 22

Green Men and Red

THE APES of Ramdar had awoken from their afternoon nap when Tarzan returned. To a man—to use the term advisedly—they were milling about in a state of confusion.

"What is wrong?" he asked one agitated bull.

"We do not like this place."

"Here there is food in plenty," Tarzan told them.

Dag Dolor burst into view, emerging from the trees, and the disgruntled ape pointed in his direction.

"There is no meat. Except for *him*."

Tarzan objected, "Dag Dolor has pledged fealty to me. He will not be eaten. Ramdar insists upon this. Let no other opinion be expressed."

A silent sullenness fell over the gorilla tribe. They exchanged unreadable glances, their simian expressions stiffening.

"Lead us to meat," exhorted another. This ape was Thagg of the maimed hand and missing digit.

"Ramdar will take you to meat. The women and the balus may rest a short period in the jungle. It is not possible to starve. You bulls, take up your war clubs. Follow Ramdar. We will hunt now."

Turning, Tarzan led the way. The gorillas slowly filed after him, moving on all fours and occasionally lifting up on their hind legs to crane their bristled heads around. Forest lanes did not seem to be a thing they were comfortable navigating.

More and more, Tarzan understood that they were creatures of the dead cities and the dried-up oceans. They preferred to sleep in shelters, not upon the open grass nor under sheltering trees, no matter how high they grew.

Wherever they loped, birds took wing. One bull stopped to capture one, biting off its head. Snorting, he expectorated this morsel onto the ground. Then he began stripping the meat with his blunt teeth, but discovered the taste of feathers. He spat out the half-chewed matter, swallowing none of it.

"This is not good meat," he muttered, tossing the carrion away.

As they moved through the trees, Tarzan studied the dagger he had relieved of Dag Dolor. While small in the green Martian's titanic hands, in Tarzan's bronzed fist it had a reassuring heft and weight. The steely blade was not much shorter than Tarzan's lost hunting knife. But it was a stabbing weapon, not a cutting weapon. Still, it bore a double edge, and was exceedingly sharp.

Resolutely, Tarzan collected such wood as he could and started whittling arrow shafts. These were easily collected, and he tucked them into his belt. With the increasing heat of the day, he doffed his banth-hide cloak, going about nearly naked, as was his habit on Earth.

The white gorillas moved cautiously, but when they spied certain insects of size, they fell upon the grubs, much as would the great apes who raised Tarzan when a hairless and helpless balu.

The ape-man sampled these grubs. Their taste was strange, but that did not deter him. He, too, was sick of ulsio. The smell of fresh water drew Tarzan to a jungle pool. Kneeling beside it, he sniffed carefully. He could not decide if the water was safe to drink.

Then a bull lumbered up and without hesitation dipped a great pale paw into the still pool. The bull lapped water from alternating palms until satisfied. Only then did Tarzan drink.

AT ONE point, they rested and the bronzed giant fell to fashioning a bow. This, too, was easily accomplished. Having collected discarded avian feathers for fletching, the ape-man had almost everything he required, but he would need sinew or string to complete the archery set.

Leaving his hunting spear with Dag Dolor, he took the dagger in hand and went searching for a suitable animal. For he was hungry for meat himself.

Far into the forest, Tarzan ranged, and the more he wandered, the more puzzled the ape-man became. Other than birds, there did not seem much game about in these woods. It seemed unnatural.

Once, he spied one of the twelve-legged spiders slipping along a cable-like strand of silk. The thing was hideous beyond description, but he stayed outside of its orbit and was not pursued.

Farther along, he found another arachnid. It had caught in its gauzy ball of a web a fair-sized ulsio. Tarzan was not interested in the meat of the dead animal. No doubt it was infused with the noxious venom of the spider. But it had legs and these legs were governed by tendons and from those tendons Tarzan could make string.

Yet the ape-man had no appetite to take the plunge into the web and make war upon the giant arachnid. He ranged about until he found a rock that he could extract from the soil. It was quite large, about the size of his chest, but Tarzan found that he could pull it free of the moist soil with surprising ease. Carrying this in both arms, he leaped up into a higher tree, lifted the boulder over his black-haired head and let it fly, driving it downward with all of his muscular might.

The tumbling rock crashed through the hazy egg of spider silk, dislodging the ulsio and sending the spider scurrying away, three of its legs fractured and dangling helplessly.

Dropping down, he raced for the dried ulsio corpse and, using his sword, cut off three of the limbs. These he made into a bundle, which Tarzan carried off.

Joining the others, he stripped the legs and harvested the tendons, and began making string by a means he had learned upon the Earth.

With this type of strings, the ape-man affixed the feathers to the blunt ends of the shafts. Scavenging for a tough vine out of which to make a bowstring, Tarzan had a more difficult time. Nothing demonstrated the required properties of strength and elasticity.

Happening upon a length of fallen spider silk which had grown dry and unsticky from age and dirt, Tarzan picked it up. When he tugged at either end, it held firm. This he cut and trimmed, then carefully strung the bow. The latter was not as supple as he would have liked, but it would serve his purposes.

Quickly notching the feathered arrow, he pulled back, then released the missile.

It struck a knot hole in the tree, out of which spewed a cloud of black insects which, from a distance, looked no different than earthly insects. Retrieving the shaft, he noticed that his apes were impressed by the weapon. Apparently, they had never seen a bow and arrow. Perhaps they did not exist upon Barsoom.

Then Dag Dolor ambled up to him and dispelled Tarzan of that false assumption.

"You are a practiced bowman," he rumbled.

"This weapon is known here?" asked Tarzan.

Dag Dolor nodded. "My people do not bother with them, but some of the red men do. But they prefer their blades and pistols."

Tarzan did not understand the Martian word for pistol, but the green man eventually made himself clear. From his description, Martian bullets were not composed of inert metal, but demonstrated explosive qualities.

Tarzan took time to make more arrows, then they continued to explore, seeking to learn how far the jungle extended. The subjects of Ramdar obediently followed their chief. The deeper they plunged into the forest, however, the more unhappy the apes of the Narag tribe became.

Matters took a turn for the worse when they stumbled across other explorers.

Tarzan naturally smelled them before anyone saw them. They gave off the distinctive odor of Hortamangani Martians. The intensity was in a concentration that suggested a small group.

After ordering the others to make camp, the ape-man again took to the trees and cautiously stalked the scent spoor of the others, whoever they might be.

When he came upon them, Tarzan found the hulking party working along a jungle trail in single file. They wore harnesses similar to those that Dag Dolor had harvested from the dead green Martian. These men bristled with weapons as they picked their way forward. Some carried long-swords, and others short-swords. They moved cautiously and warily, often looking about with their uncanny red eyes. But they did not spy Tarzan's sun-bronzed limbs, which were concealed high in the crowns of the fulsome trees.

In all, thirty green Martians comprised the pack. All bulls. Whether explorers or a war party, it was difficult to discern. But the style of their leather harnesses was identical to that of the dead green man whose corpse lay baking in the sun.

Tarzan studied them carefully as they strode between the close-pressing trees. These giants were to a man battle-scarred and maimed, some missing tusks, others ears, fingers and other appendages. There wore bright-colored feathers attached to the metal fillets banding their bald skulls, but many of these plumes were now wilted and forlorn-looking. Every bull clutched a sword, some short and others long. Not a few of these blades were chipped and broken from hard use.

The wary group paused from time to time to partake of the fruit and nuts of various trees. Of these, they ate sparingly, as if conserving their appetites. Their features were gaunt, the flesh on their long bones spare, as though they had not partaken of meat in a long time.

No doubt they hunted meat. So Tarzan followed them without making a sound, stepping from springy tree limb to tree limb, slipping from crown to crown, ever watchful but entirely unseen and unsuspected, at home in his natural element at last.

These fearsome boar-tusked hunters encountered no luck. This was evident from their brutish expressions, although they exchanged not a word with one another. They were uncannily devoid of speech.

Deciding to confront them, Tarzan moved to the west, increased his pace and flashed from branch to branch, swinging in the long-limbed manner of the great apes of Africa. This of course created some little commotion, and it caught the attention of the Martians.

Suddenly, Tarzan leaped straight up out of the trees, describing a breathtaking arc in the burnished sky, ultimately landing several yards before the unprepared leader. The olive-skinned giants naturally recoiled from the suddenness of his appearance.

Once the tusked band recovered from their initial astonishment, they gathered their wits about them and gesticulated in his direction.

TO THE ape-man's surprise, they spoke two words over and over again.

"John Carter! John Carter!"

Tarzan drew his dagger. Muscular legs braced, naked feet planted on the purple grass, he resolutely stood his ground.

Seeing this sign of hostility, the apparent leader unsheathed his gleaming long-sword, stepping forward. He was missing the points of all four tusks, whose blunted and chipped ends only made him more fierce looking. Only one red eye glared, for the other was masked by a bandage made of woven fibre.

"You can only be one man upon Barsoom," he shouted. "John Carter of Helium, Warlord of all Barsoom."

Shaking his head firmly, Tarzan replied, "I am called Ramdar. I know of no one named John Carter."

Consternation mixed with blinking confusion seized the green Martians. They looked at him, and then at one another and fell to arguing among themselves. Tarzan could make out most of the argument.

"Only John Carter could leap so high," one insisted.

Another accused, "You are not red, nor yellow or black. Therefore, you must be John Carter."

"I am not John Carter," insisted Tarzan. "I am Tarzan of the Apes, called Ramdar by those I have befriended."

This puzzled the Hortamangani nomads. Again, they fell into an argument. When it was over, the leader raised his sword once more. As did Tarzan of the Apes. Their blades shone in the streaming sunlight.

"If you are not John Carter, tell me why I should not slay you on the spot," he demanded.

"I do not know the answer to that question. Perhaps you should discover for yourself."

Taking this rough response as a challenge, the green giant took a bold step forward and prepared to give battle.

Holding his ground, Tarzan demanded, "Ramdar does not care to fight you. But if he must, know that Ramdar will be victorious."

The Martian only laughed and continued to advance, a colossal green cyclops boasting fierce broken tusks and four burly upraised arms.

Chapter 23

"He is Made of Bronze"

A S THE fierce-featured Martian closed, Tarzan swiftly drew an arrow and nocked it.

Raising the bow to an acute angle, he aimed high at the monster's shoulder, and let fly. The shaft was small in proportion to the green giant. Its quartz tip drove in and stuck.

Halting at the sudden sting, the Hortamangani warrior turned his head, saw the protruding shaft, red blood leaking out where it had slipped in, and simply laughed uproariously. With the flat of his blade, he swiped at the shaft. It broke off with a snap.

Bleeding profusely from his shoulder, he resumed his advance.

His sword lifted high, he rushed in swinging, as if to cleave the ape-man in two, from crown to groin.

Tarzan aimed at the hilt-gripping fist and sent an arrow through the fleshy part of the forearm, and once again the green giant laughed boisterously, unfazed.

Before they could engage, something stumbled noisily out of the jungle, and suddenly Dag Dolor was standing between Tarzan and his antagonist. Dag Dolor looked at Tarzan and then turned his back on him to face the green giant, who stood three heads higher than he.

"Nurl Jok! Dag Dolor instructs you to lay down your weapon. This bronze man is my jed. I will not permit you to harm him."

Incredulity spread over the heavy features of towering Nurl Jok. His hideous tusked mouth splitting open, he laughed without concern.

"Stand aside, stripling. Your father is dead. I am jed now. Jed of the horde of Churvash Ul."

"I am the only recognized son of Churvash Ul. I challenge you for the right to lead the horde of my father!"

Thereupon, they closed with one another. Their uplifted swords clashed. The long-sword of Nurl Jok was far superior to that of his challenger's blade. Dag Dolor stood a good four feet shorter than the other and was far less heavily muscled. Also, he lacked a lower arm. Yet he gave an excellent account of himself.

Steel clashed, rang, and sparked madly.

Tarzan watched this tableau carefully. He understood that to intervene would not be welcomed. This was a matter of honor. Or such honor as these strange nomads might claim.

Dag Dolor seemed possessed of a fury far beyond his lesser stature. Swiftly, he removed one of his foe's hands, but the other only laughed even as the stump spurted blood.

Contending blades resounded and turned red, as each antagonist found his opening and drew blood.

All around, the green warrior's pack stood in a tense semicircle watching carefully, gaping at the unexpected combat.

"You swear fealty to a puny red man?" taunted Nurl Jok.

Dag Dolor snarled, "He is not a red man. He is Ramdar of Jasoom. He is made of bronze. And I have never encountered a braver or stronger warrior, green or red."

The taller Martian struck again, and once again their blades were weaving glittering webs in the air and shedding sparks resembling leaping spiders.

Stepping back, Nurl Jok raised his long-sword in both hands, preparing to remove the younger man's upper left arm at his shoulder.

But Dag Dolor was wily. He spun about, evading the downsweeping blade twice. Slipping around, he hamstrung his larger opponent.

Grunting in surprise, the other wavered on one foot. The foot went flying away when the short-sword slashed diagonally across the ankle.

With a bellowing war cry, Nurl Jok toppled. The descending short-sword pierced his chest, rupturing his heart. His limbs stiffened, then seemed to collapse. The head lolled dully to the jungle floor.

Lifting himself to his full height, Dag Dolor turned away from his defeated foe and faced the other Martians. He raised his three arms like a maimed green spider of tremendous proportions.

"I claim the right to lead this horde! I reclaim the power and authority of my dead father. I am Dag Dolor, son of Churvash Ul. Who would challenge me?"

Almost a minute transpired, but no words passed among the others. One by one, they stepped forward and placed their swords at Dag Dolor's feet, then retreated, bare-handed.

"We are prepared to follow where you lead us, Dag Dolor," offered one of them.

"So it is done," said Dag Dolor. "Collect your blades."

The green men rushed in to reclaim their weapons, buckling them to their barbaric harnesses.

ONE OF them pointed toward Tarzan and demanded, "What about this pitiful excuse for a red man that you claim to be your jed?"

Dag Dolor turned and faced Tarzan of the Apes.

"Just as you warriors follow me, I will follow Ramdar. There will be no dissent."

But there was. It came from a Hortamangani whose protruding tusks were broken and splintered from past combat. Scars crisscrossed his olive hide.

"How can a jed follow another jed, especially one who is not green?"

"This man has come from Jasoom. We will follow him. He knows the ways of forests, he will lead us out of this one."

The much-scarred green man stepped forward belligerently. "Where would you lead us, Ramdar?"

Tarzan returned his challenge with these unequivocal words:

"Ramdar will lead this horde where he wishes it to go. If you care not to leave your sun-blackened corpse rotting in the grass for scavengers to devour, let there be no argument among you."

"His words are my words," added Dag Dolor, folding the upper pair of burly arms across his olive chest while the third dangled limp-fingered and empty.

And that was the end of that.

Chapter 24

Ramdar the Jeddak

WHEN TARZAN of the Apes reunited with the Tarman-bolgani tribe who followed him as Ramdar, they let out a cacophony of barks, screeches and round-mouthed hooting. For all saw that the bronzed Jasoomian was leading a contingent of armed green nomads.

Being rather dull-witted, they jumped to what was for them a natural conclusion, but one which could not have been further off the mark.

"Behold!" cried Foad. "Ramdar has brought fresh meat."

Fortunate for all concerned, the green men did not understand the grunting language of the great white gorillas. Otherwise, a mutual slaughter would have broken out.

Fearing a misapprehension, Tarzan rushed forward and attempted to intervene.

"These men are not food. They are our new allies. They follow Ramdar, having sworn loyalty to him."

This pronouncement was not greeted with overwhelming enthusiasm.

"We do not need allies," came a surly response. This from Thagg of the maimed finger.

"We are a small tribe," Tarzan pointed out. "As are they. These warriors are the remnants of the horde of Churvash Ul."

Tarzan could hardly refrain from telling the truth in this instance, for the harnesses of the green men bore an identical emblematic device which proclaimed their common identity.

The ape-man saw no point in uttering falsehoods that were self-evident.

"Ramdar calls for peace between the great white apes and the green warriors of the horde of Churvash Ul," he stated.

The green men lumbered up at this point and, seeing the array of pale apes, came to an uncertain halt. Their massive hands plunged for the hilts of their various blades.

Turning to them, Tarzan said, "These are the apes of Ramdar. They will obey him. If they do not, Ramdar will settle them down."

The settling down took over a zode—two Earth hours—during which the great white gorillas of the tribe of Narag waxed surly and combative.

The bull who had bitten off his own finger because Tarzan had broken it was the most recalcitrant of the group. Growling and snarling, Thagg insisted that he would not associate with green man-things.

"Unless it is to consume their raw flesh," he concluded, beating his naked breast.

Tarzan heard him out. He pointed out that they were in a perilous jungle and the greater their numbers, the more assured they were of safe passage to Uxfar.

The statement brought up the unresolved issue of the jungle.

Another ape began insisting that the jungle was a bad place, full of unimaginable terrors, and for the sake of the shes and the balus, it was best to depart immediately.

Since Tarzan had already agreed to this, he simply reaffirmed his intention to march out of the jungle in search of the city of red Martians.

This quieted down the Tarmanbolgani tribe—all except the ornery bull with the missing finger. In his agitation, Thagg dropped to his intermediary fists, hunching his hairless bulk, then lifted himself to his greatest height, throwing out his upper limbs, stretching them, squeezing his fists and waving his great stone bludgeon about. Peeling back his lips, he displayed his gleaming fangs.

He attempted no advance, but the intent was clear—to intimidate the Hortamangani warriors.

For their part, the former horde of Churvash Ul was not so easily cowed. Although the great white gorillas were fearsome in their eyes, they produced sharpened steel blades, whereas the apes brandished only crude clubs.

The green giants, too, lifted their muscular arms, displaying their weapons. A battle impended.

Tarzan ended it by demanding of the bull, "Does Thagg challenge Ramdar for leadership of the tribe?"

"I do!" screamed the other. "I challenge Ramdar!"

"Kreegah!" yelled Tarzan. *"Bundolo!"*

In his fury, he spoke in the tongue of the great apes of Africa. Consequently, Thagg did not comprehend that the ape-man had screamed, "Beware! I kill!" But this did not matter. Tarzan's answer was unmistakable.

SHIFTING HIS war mallet from one hand to another, both laterally and vertically, Thagg prepared to battle the bronzed white ape-man.

All other upraised arms fell. The other gorillas squatted onto their lower limbs and settled down to watch. The burly green men sheathed their swords and did likewise.

Both groups expected a bloody spectacle.

Instead, Tarzan drew his dagger and leaped from a standing position. He sailed up into the face of the threatening Tarman-bolgani, and planted his dagger into his foe's pulsing throat, piercing it, then dropping back with a contemptuous kick to the creature's heaving chest before it could defend itself.

Arterial blood spurted. The simian face froze in shock. Dropping its war club, all four pale hands flew to his heaving chest in a futile attempt to stanch the outpouring of gore. All in vain.

The fury of the doomed took hold of Thagg. His brutish features convulsed and his deep-set eyes grew bloodshot as they fell upon his bronzed antagonist.

Three blood-soaked hands clutching, Thagg lunged downward, intent upon crushing the life out of Tarzan before his own life was over, the other hand clamped over his mortal wound.

The jungle lord calmly sheathed his blade and advanced to meet the bestial, roaring charge.

Batting aside one great paw with contempt, the ape-man drove a bronze fist into Thagg's pulsing nostrils. Propelled by muscles made hard by jungle life and amplified by the Martian gravity, the blow forced the titanic gorilla's head back so hard the snapping of its neck bones could be heard.

Still, Thagg refused to succumb. Stumbling backward two paces, he strove to keep his footing. His groping paws fell away as Tarzan twisted away, landing on his feet. A stunned look replaced the former one of fury. For a moment, as Tarzan watched, one hand on the handle of his dagger, Thagg teetered, his burly bowed legs struggling to hold up his elongated torso.

Then the light went out of his dark orbs. Weakening, the albino beast's knees buckled. He fell forward on his face, whereupon Tarzan of the Apes stepped onto his shuddering back, threw his head high, and gave forth the blood-freezing victory cry of the bull ape.

The speed and effortlessness with which Tarzan had dispatched his lone challenger impressed both sides of assembled antagonists.

After he stepped off the twitching corpse, Tarzan looked about and demanded, "Who else is there to challenge Ramdar?"

The red scar running along his forehead showed that the ape-man's anger had not yet cooled.

The young green man broke the silence with his answer.

"I follow Ramdar!" bellowed Dag Dolor. "My father's horde follows Ramdar. By virtue of his mastery over the savage apes, I proclaim him to be no longer a jed, but jeddak of our combined forces!"

Understanding that the unfamiliar term jeddak was doubtless higher than a jed, Tarzan translated his words into simian speech.

In answer to this, one of the Tarmanbolgani barked, "We are the apes of Ramdar. We will follow Ramdar wherever he goes."

Other apes began barking and calling out their fealty.

"*Ramdar! Ramdar! Ramdar!*" they chanted. "*Ape-lord of Narag tribe!*"

There was no dissent.

The matter settled, Tarzan proclaimed, "Follow Ramdar now. We will hunt for food."

Springing into the higher branches of the trees, Tarzan ranged about, his sensitive nostrils vigilant. He soon smelled something that reminded him of crocodile, but found no pool of water that might be its lair.

Slipping from branch to branch, guided by sense of smell alone, the ape-man followed the creature. Every time he felt he was close to it, his eyes found nothing. Yet a rusting among fallen palm fronds and purple grasses told him that it lay within striking distance.

But where?

BECOMING STILL, Tarzan searched the ground with his eyes. Grasses moved aside, but nothing seemed to push the broad blades apart.

Yet the grass continued twitching and separating.

Was the creature invisible?

A large palm frond lifted up, and the grass ceased its uncanny animation.

Eyes sharpening, Tarzan watched this frond. Gradually, his vision resolved a number of feet that had taken on the color of the surrounding grass, but not perfectly. A foot shifted, turning greenish-yellow to match the sheltering frond.

Then a pair of yellow eyes popped into existence under the shadow of the frond. They fell on him and then vanished utterly, no doubt concealed by closing eyelids that could not be seen.

OBSERVING THE phenomenon closely, the ape-man made out the suggestion of a creature perhaps the size of a very small zebra that went about on multiple legs. He wondered if there existed any four-footed animals on all of Barsoom. Studying this, he recognized that here was a lizard, the first one he had encountered upon this strange planet.

Falling upon it with his dagger, he struck it several times in the throat, and threw the animal over on its plated belly, piercing its heart with a single short downward stroke, finishing it.

In death, the chameleon properties of its cracked hide lost potency and resumed its natural coloration, which was a mottled greenish-gray. It was a lizard, but more like an elongated toad than a crocodile.

The ugly creature was heavy, but Tarzan carried it effortlessly through the trees and flung it down at the feet of the marching green men.

They proclaimed it to be a darseen, and began butchering it.

Disappearing into the trees, Tarzan found another specimen, this one unconcealed, and swiftly dispatched it as before. This carcass he gave to the great white gorillas. Then he shot back into the trees in search of more meat.

The sun was going down by the time the combined horde was properly fed. Even so, game was scarce in this jungle, surprisingly so. The followers of Ramdar had to be content with supplementing their diet with fruit and nuts, which were more plentiful.

During the time that they were eating, Tarzan reclaimed his white thoat, and commanded it and its companions to catch up with his feasting followers. The great chariot trailed behind, dragged by its patient, plodding zitidar.

When Tarzan broke into view, mounted upon the alabaster thoat, the green men stood up, and their swiveling red eyes became strange as they found common orientation, their olive digits leaping up to point excitedly.

One cried out, "Ramdar rides the white thoat of Churvash Ul! Ramdar is truly a jeddak!"

When the zitidar pulled into view, hauling the titanic chariot, the Hortamangani warriors fell upon it, examining its devices, running rough hands along its dusty rails and giving great attention to the beast of burden tethered to it.

"The chariot-throne of Churvash Ul!" another warrior proclaimed.

Dag Dolor imparted, "Ramdar rode out of the dead sea wastes on that very chariot. He rescued me from the cannibal white apes, although I was slow to recognize his greatness. Now I do recognize it."

Those simple words seemed to cement the fealty of the green Martians to Tarzan of the Apes. The jungle lord said no more about it. Instead, he addressed them as one group even though they segregated themselves from one another, the albino gorillas and the olive-skinned nomads not intermingling, switching tongues as necessary.

"Ramdar has reconnoitered the jungle. It appears to be two padans march to the other side of it. To turn back would be to face the sea of moss again and its emptiness. Perhaps the city of red men lies on the other side. We will push in that direction."

One of the boar-faced giants spoke up.

"There is a city in that direction. It is called Uxfar. But it is a city of red men. We will not be welcome there. Nor would it be safe to show ourselves at their gates, given our reduced numbers. We would be slaughtered to the last man." Then, glancing at the other contingent, added, "And ape."

Tarzan considered this.

"To turn back would be folly. We will push ahead, and so circumvent the city."

But in his heart of hearts, the bronzed giant was curious to see the city of living red men. If necessary, he would enter it alone, ahead of his growing horde. For he had not lost sight of his ultimate goal, to escape the planet Mars, if such a thing were, in fact, practical.

THE SUN was preparing to go down. Tarzan considered where they should bed down for the night, given the uncertainties of the jungle, when something passed overhead with a hissing sound that lifted all heads and drew their attention upward.

It looked like a vessel made of aluminum or some similar white metal. It appeared to be traveling in a straight line. Suddenly, it redirected itself and began circling the clearing where the green and white creatures separately congregated.

Tarzan could see that the sky ship was sleek in shape, its lines being boatlike, but he could not perceive any details, nor what type of Barsoomian piloted it.

Deciding instantly to investigate, he ordered his followers to remain at ease. Gathering his steely muscles together, he catapulted himself into the sky, performing an acrobatic feat of vaulting that took him over and above the passing vehicle.

Looking down during the brief interval that he was above the open deck of the ship, Tarzan saw three passengers. They looked like Earth men, except they wore harnesses in lieu of clothes, and their skin was a reddish-copper in hue. Atop their heads, they wore a single upright feather, although one individual sported two. Their size was unremarkable, and nature had blessed them with no extraneous limbs.

These Gamangani Martians spotted him, and rushed about, pointing and shouting. Tarzan could not make out the words, but their expostulations sounded similar to that of the Hortamangani.

Two words stood out; they sounded like an Earth man's name. "John Carter!"

The green men had spoken those words, but Tarzan had not questioned them on their meaning.

Landing, Tarzan stood rigid and watched the craft wheel gracefully in the thin air and descend. It was buoyant in some way that reminded him of an earthly Zeppelin or airship, but it was propelled by some means he could not glean.

No doubt the combined green warriors and great white gorillas had drawn the attention of the passing ship, but now they were intent upon the bronze-skinned ape-man.

The ship seemed to be settling, as if preparing to land. Yet there was a hesitancy about its maneuvering, as if the crew feared landing too close to the followers of Ramdar.

Tarzan decided to make things easier for them. He sprang for the rail, gained it easily, and dropped onto the smooth deck, unafraid.

Looking about, he studied the cockpit and saw that it was mechanical in construction. There were levers, indicator dials, and other controls. At the stern was mounted a large gun of some unfamiliar type.

The feather-decorated Gamangani crew gaped at the apparition of the bronze giant stepping about their deck as if he were a pirate captain who had boarded the vessel with impunity.

They studied him, noting his magnificent physique and his banth-hide breechclout.

One shook off his astonishment and loosened his tongue.

"You are not John Carter!"

Another added, "No, he is not John Carter, although he resembles him somewhat."

"I am Tarzan of the Apes. Why do you mistake me for someone named John Carter?"

Tarzan was told forthrightly, "Of all who dwell upon Barsoom, only John Carter can leap as high as you do. But upon closer inspection, we can see that you are not John Carter. Yet you are not a red man nor a yellow man. What manner of man are you?"

"I am Tarzan of the Apes, as I have told you."

One of the sky sailors pointed beyond the railing and asked, "If you are *Tarzan-of-the-apes,* are those your apes?"

"They follow me."

"And the green men who congregate with them?"

"They, too, Tarzan has conquered. So they follow me. They know me as Ramdar although I am, as I have said, truly called Tarzan of the Apes."

A copper man stepped boldly forward. Unlike the others, he wore two feathers in his simple headdress, signifying his higher rank.

"Where do you come from, *Tarzan-of-the-apes?*"

"I come from the land of Africa, which is a continent on the planet Earth, which the green men call Jasoom."

This statement was met with a grave silence. Then one Gamangani sailor shouted, "Where are you bound, brazen man of Jasoom?"

"Tarzan seeks the city beyond this jungle."

Another demanded, "Do you intend to lead your green men and white apes to the city in question?"

"Such is my intention," Tarzan replied frankly.

"Then you are enemy to the red man and no friend of ours!"

Whereupon the three men drew their weapons. Two brandished short-swords, and another produced a queer pistol and pointed it at Tarzan's bare chest.

The ape-man dodged to one side and then back again as the pistol discharged noisily.

The projectile struck the vessel's rudder and exploded, instantly throwing the airship out of balance. It began to reel and list. One man ran to the controls in a frantic attempt to get it under control.

While another red man redirected the muzzle of his pistol toward Tarzan, the first warrior lunged with his short-sword, seeking a disemboweling stroke. Tarzan disarmed him with a backhanded slap to the flat of the sword and threw him overboard, whereupon he fell to the surface.

The pistol wielder fired again, but by this time Tarzan had jumped from the rail of the crippled vessel, and had dropped from sight.

Thereafter, the remaining crewmen directed their attention to wrestling their wayward craft into obedience. After they did so, they took off, leaving the unfortunate man who fell overboard to his destiny.

Landing safely on the purple grass, Tarzan beheld the incredible sight of his followers, white and green alike, charging madly for a solitary tree that reared high in the sky.

A thrashing amid the branches and serpentine vines told the ape-man that the red Martian had tumbled into the high leafy crown and was caught, struggling there.

The combined horde swarmed the base of the tree before Tarzan could reach it, but the sheer size and unfamiliarity of the trunk evidently defeated them, for their efforts to climb it were in vain. The lowermost branches were just within reach, but they broke off under the immense weight of the would-be climbers.

Drawing up, Tarzan asked, "He lives?"

"Not for long," muttered a green warrior, producing his dagger.

A great gorilla angrily waved a misshapen club and seconded that sentiment with a wordless growl.

"Leave him to me." Without another word, the ape-man leaped into the tree and scrambled up the entwining branches, some of which were draped by the fantastic creepers that boasted wide eyes and flexing hands.

Reaching the spot, Tarzan discerned that the copper-skinned man was broken of body. His mouth was red with his own flowing gore. With each racking cough, it sprayed his clean-shaven jaw.

"You are dying."

The wounded red Martian nodded mutely.

"What is your name?"

"Fal Unnak, First Padwar of the Uxfar Navy."

"Tell me of this John Carter."

"John Carter is the Jeddak of Jeddaks, defender of the red men and ally to some green men, but not all. If you dare show your face in Uxfar, word will reach John Carter and he will slay you and your mongrel horde."

"Does this John Carter live in the city of Uxfar?"

"No, he lives in Helium."

"Where is Helium?"

"I will never tell." Another crimson cough came.

With that, the fine-featured man rolled his head to one side, and his eyes closed in death.

Tarzan left him there.

Now the ape-man was more determined than ever to reach the city of the red Martians.

Chapter 25

The Silent Shape

NIGHT FELL with its usual smothering abruptness. The interval of pitch blackness was mercifully brief. As ever, the Martian night came alive with all its unsurpassed brilliance, once Thuria first appeared, heralding the coming of her cold pursuer, Cluros. The abundant moonlight was here and there intercepted and filtered by the jungle canopy, which seemed to writhe with crawling shadows.

Still, there was light enough to make camp before the lunar orbs concluded their first evening's journey. Tarzan considered it too dangerous to plunge farther into the woodland with the approach of darkness certain to follow the double moonset. On Earth, a different class of predator emerged at night. No doubt the same would be true of this weird jungle of Barsoom.

Hunkering down upon the thick grass, the apes formed a circle around the shes and the juveniles. The zitidar was unhitched from the chariot, and the thoats were permitted to graze upon the cool blades of the scarlet sward, which they did. The green warriors made their own purple nearby.

"We do not associate with apes," explained the one named Jamo Ptannus.

The night's customary coolness did not creep in. Instead, the air remained warm and moist. This was to Tarzan's liking, of course. He declined to don his customary banth-skin cloak.

The others, particularly the great white gorillas, did not much care for this. It was unfamiliar to them. The day was hot and night was cool, and that was the way of things. This was different. It was also, to their minds, unexplained. Particularly did it eat away at their sense of well-being.

"The nights are always warm here," offered Jamo Ptannus. "There is sometimes rain. It, too, is warm. Unnaturally so."

"How long have you dwelt in this jungle?" asked Tarzan.

"Half a solar revolution. We came in through the northern pass. We have yet to find another pass. This strange place is ringed by low hills and peaks at every compass point."

Understanding struck Tarzan. He did not know the Martian word for volcano but he described a terrestrial volcano for the benefit of the Hortamangani, stressing its size and pyrotechnic activity.

Jamo Ptannus nodded heavily. "Such natural formations are rare on Barsoom. But this may be what you call a volcano, and we term a kokurok. But that does not explain the warm air and hot rain. For we rarely see clouds at these latitudes."

Dag Dolor spoke up. "Where is the remainder of my father's horde?"

Jamo Ptannus answered slowly. He flexed his impressive fingers. He made fists, first one, then another and finally all four. It was evident that he was ashamed to divulge his next words.

"We were forty strong when we entered this place. Now we are fewer than thirty. During the time we dwelt here, men would disappear. Some were found the way Nortan Mux was found, an unexplained corpse without evident wounds. What killed him we do not know or understand."

"Your numbers have been dwindling for many moons," questioned Tarzan. "Why did you not escape this jungle?"

"Because we have been hunting the thing that has been killing us."

"According to your account, this unknown thing is well on its way to devouring your horde to the last man. Why do you persist?"

Burly green shoulders lifted and fell in a massive shrug. "We have no women or children left alive. What else would we do with our lives, but avenge our losses?"

Dag Dolor spoke up. "My father would avenge the loss of his people. Not waste his time chasing phantoms."

Jamo Ptannus looked to the great white gorillas scratching themselves and sniffing the moist air. They did not understand a word that was being spoken, of course. Nor did they care.

"We were outnumbered when we were driven out of Vakanor," he declared. "We are even more outnumbered now. Our tribe has no future. We will hunt and slay to the last man."

This appeared to be a species of Martian logic because Dag Dolor made no contrary argument. Instead, he worked his jaw, causing his warthog-shaped tusks to float before his face. His independently mounted eyes went this way and that.

Tarzan asked, "Does any other tribe inhabit this jungle?"

Jamo Ptannus shook his head heavily. "If any do, we have not seen them. But something dwells in this jungle, something mysterious. Our dead are found sometimes with their bones picked clean and looking as if they had died long ago when in truth their corpses would have hardly begun to decay."

"What killed the one lying out on the purple grass?" asked Tarzan.

Jamo Ptannus gave a lopsided shrug and, with his lower hands, plucked at the grass all around him. His ears quivered in a way that reminded the ape-man of the tiny aural organs of Duro, the hippopotamus.

"The same thing that killed the others. What it is we do not know. Only that when we locate it, we will slay the thing without mercy."

Tarzan asked, "You have no inkling of what this thing is, whether man or beast?"

"In my opinion, it is neither man nor beast but something terrible. Some monster from Barsoom's ancient past, possibly. For nothing slays the way this thing kills."

Tarzan considered these words in silence.

"There are beasts in this jungle that are beyond understanding," continued Jamo Ptannus. "Things that do not have names."

"Tell me more," invited Tarzan.

The green warrior pointed to the southeast. "Go in that direction, O Ramdar, and you will find a formation the like of which is unknown upon the face of Barsoom beyond these preserves. It does not look natural. Yet it is not the only one scattered throughout this cursed place."

"What is it called?"

The green man laughed raucously. His mirth was unpleasant to Tarzan's ears.

"We do not know what it is and so we have not given it a name."

"I wish to see this thing with my own eyes."

The giant nomad nodded. "The greater portion of it is the color of polished skeel wood, yet it is not wood. Attached to it is a knob that is black and many faceted. Look for such a thing and you will behold it with your own eyes."

Taking up his hunting spear, Tarzan turned to face Dag Dolor.

"Ramdar leaves you in charge of this horde. I will return when I have satisfied myself as to the nature of this jungle at night. See that no harm befalls any of my followers. For you are now my jedwar."

Dag Dolor stood up and made a two-handed gesture with the palms raised high that Tarzan had learned to be the Martian equivalent of "It will be as you say."

Without another word, the bronzed giant passed into the heart of the jungle, leaving his followers to disport themselves as they wished. Most slept. Others stood watch. They held conversation to a minimum. The white gorillas and the green nomads segregated themselves, having no common speech.

TARZAN OF THE APES first made for the corpse of the fallen green man, which he had found baking in the sun, its olive skin almost black. He was curious as to what had struck him down.

The body was still there. Predators had not consumed any portion of it. This, thought the jungle lord, was unnatural. But he did not know how Hortamangani tasted so far as their appeal as carrion food.

Circling the body, Tarzan used the blunt end of his spear to poke at it. To his surprise, he discovered that many of the bones were broken, fractured and pulverized in some way. This was most passing strange. No jagged bones had stuck out from the flesh. Yet many were broken.

Coming to the massive head, he discovered the skull bones were likewise pulverized. The head still retained its general contours, but Tarzan realized that the supporting structures had lost their original shape.

He could not account for what had done this without also doing external damage. The tusks were still in their sockets. The antenna-like ears were withered, as were the shriveled sightless eyes. These might have been the result of the decay of death.

It was not possible to tell how long the green monster had been deceased. But the smell of putrefaction had not yet commenced. Therefore, it could not have been for very long.

Satisfied that he had learned all that he could, Tarzan pressed on, continuing his strike toward the south, into the heart of the fabulous jungle of unknown trees.

He found the largest tree visible in the immediate vicinity and cast his spear upward so that it impaled its quartz point against a high branch, lodging there for his convenience. Tarzan went up the scratchy bole and sought the highest point in its crown.

There, he found a comfortable perch and peered in all directions. The jungle canopy was still. Winds did not seem to trouble it. Thuria had fallen. Cluros's harsh light filtering down painted the wild foliage as if with a silver brush.

No birds took wing. There did not seem to be anything resembling monkeys in the treetops. The insects slept.

Searching the distant horizon to the south, the ape-man could spy here and there visible peaks. They were not lofty like mountain peaks, but they were shaped like them. They were similar in size and structure to the rocky cliffs through which they had passed in order to enter this weird jungle. Perhaps this area was the surviving caldera of a volcano. If so, hot springs might underlie the jungle floor, which would explain the night heat and the perpetual moisture of the closed atmosphere.

Still, it was only a supposition. Evidence was scarce and circumstantial.

From his vantage point, Tarzan could not descry any formation that resembled polished wood. Retrieving his spear, he sent it on ahead, his muscles propelling it over a half mile, where it described a parabola and landed in the crown of a spreading tree.

There it stood upright, quivering. The distance was great. But Tarzan cleared it with a single mighty leap and landed just short of it. He had become more accustomed to this mode of travel since his inexplicable arrival upon Barsoom, yet the thrill of sailing through the air with impunity had not entirely abated.

Hurling his spear ahead of him, he repeated the tremendous feat.

Finally, he spied it, a broad shape in the moonlight which made it gleam with an unnatural sheen.

Holding onto his spear with one steel-thewed hand, the ape-man landed on the polished surface. He abruptly skidded off. Between its smooth surface and a residue of humid moistness that coated it, it was a slick spot to attempt to alight. Tarzan found himself deposited in the moist soil. He had lost his spear, but soon regained it.

Standing before the monstrous form, for it was much taller than he at its lowest point, he made a cautious circuit of the silent thing.

IN GENERAL, it was the approximate shape of a horseshoe crab. Although there all resemblance fell away into meaninglessness. Semicircular in its circumference, the form was angular in its configurations. One end was higher than the other, which tapered to an abbreviated shape resembling the flat stern of a boat. There was no tail, or other appendage visible. Nor were there signs of external organs governing sight, smell, or hearing.

The thing's color most resembled polished mahogany. Except for the protuberance that stuck up from its highest shoulder at one end. It was as if a black billiard ball had been half sunk into the fantastic shape of moon-shimmered wood. This sphere was not smooth, but nodular in its configuration and brought to mind a medieval mace, but with short, blunted spikes. These nodes, however, were polished and reflected moonlight from many of its gemlike facets.

This black half-sphere reared up some twenty-five feet, while the angular shoulder peaked at twenty and tapered down almost to the ground at its smooth stern.

Examining the thing's base, Tarzan found that it seemed to be sunk into the jungle floor in such a way that an apron of debris confined it and supported the whole. He did not think that the weird thing possessed legs, because he was not cognizant of it as a living being. But it did not appear to have any observable means of locomotion. Nor was there any trail of tracks behind it, assuming the black half sphere constituted its forward end.

The thought came to mind that it could be man-made. But what manner of man would fashion it and for what reason completely escaped Tarzan. It did not display indications of workmanship, nor did it show any signs of age. No cracks suggesting seams marred its unblemished surface. The resemblance to mahogany made the ape-man wonder if it was some weird idol or totem. If so, the thing completely lacked any features apart from its nodular forepart and its seamlessly smooth body.

It did not appear to be a structure, because it lacked doors and windows or any other evidence of habitation.

As to what it was in truth, Tarzan remained baffled. The more he studied it, the greater number of possibilities occurred to him. If he could fit it into his hand, he might classify it as some bizarre form of Martian nut or sweetmeat.

Testing its surface with his spear point, Tarzan could not penetrate it at any point. The blunt end of his spear likewise brought forth nothing more than a deep, hollow echo.

That it appeared to be hollow surprised him. But that realization did not help with the ape-man's understanding. For all intents and purposes, it was a thing beyond his understanding.

Satisfied that he could not penetrate the mystery, Tarzan struck further south. He did not have a definite objective in mind. He only wished to explore.

For if he planned to dwell in this mysterious jungle for any length of time, he would have to understand it as well as he could. And his first order of business was to catalog its sights and smells so that he could differentiate between friend and foe, and discover food.

For the first time in his life, Tarzan found himself in a jungle so foreign to his experience that its myriad smells baffled him, a limitation he was determined to overcome, and eventually eradicate.

Chapter 26

The Unbelievable Thing

RANGING FURTHER into the vast unexplored jungle, Tarzan of the Apes discovered that the deeper he penetrated, the warmer the air became. Deep in the interior, the wild grass shaded from purple to a hue rivaling that of blood.

A cloud of steam appeared to be rising from one point at the midsection of the sunken jungle that showed every indication of being contained within the jagged rim of a volcanic crater so vast its far edge could not be clearly discerned. This cloud continued rising and spreading out. This phenomenon told Tarzan that the lush jungle foliage was fed by its source. Perhaps this excess of moisture explained the scarlet meadows.

Dropping to the ground, the jungle lord moved between trees so tall that their lower branches were thirty feet above his head. At one point, he saw something like an eyeless yellow serpent winding among heavy boughs and warily circumvented that tree, not wishing to have an unpleasant encounter.

Moving cautiously, he came upon another of the stationary formations whose significance eluded him. This was a smaller version of the one he had first encountered. Its general outlines were different in some respects from the other, but not entirely dissimilar. Placing a palm upon one side, he felt its warmth. It was much warmer than the one he encountered before.

As he studied it, Tarzan noticed that the head-high earthwork berm that had surrounded the other specimen was absent. There was also a peculiar odor in the air. He could not place it.

It was unlike anything he had previously encountered on Earth or upon Mars.

The odor caused him to become more alert. But before he could investigate further, the steamy night air suddenly rose in temperature. It became alarmingly hot. His feral senses sharpening, the ape-men turned about, and in the near distance, something was exploding upward.

Moving with extreme celerity, Tarzan sprang into the trees and then rocketed into the sky. He did not know what impended, only that he needed to escape.

But in this regard, flight was not so simple.

Coming to the apex of his soaring vault, Tarzan saw a towering column of water jetting up from a distant clearing in the trees. He knew at once that this was a geyser. It was erupting. The air became suffocatingly hot.

Fortunately, the Martian gravity came to his rescue. Tarzan was pulled downward, disappearing below the spreading foliage.

The super-hot plume reached the crest of its ascension, soon tumbling back down, the pressure of its impelling force subsiding. In weakening, it lost some of its tremendous heat and began pattering the crowns of the surrounding trees with hot rain. Steam swept outward in billowing clouds.

Crouching beneath sheltering fronds, Tarzan let this cover take the brunt of the downpour. It was hot. Scaldingly hot. But not enough to peel the skin off his magnificent body.

The duration of the geyser eruption was perhaps five earthly minutes. A tremendous volume of water was released into the atmosphere, to return and soak into the ground.

It seemed to take a long time before the cascade abated. But that was only because the torrential downpour was so vast.

Roosting birds launched themselves into the sky once the atmospheric phenomenon ceased. Unseen animals voiced peculiar noises. Weird cries rose into the night. Slowly, the troubled jungle fell silent and leaves and palm fronds became once again still.

Climbing back to his feet, Tarzan moved cautiously about. Steaming pools of hot water had formed here and there. He avoided them. Terrific heat rose from each of these pools. The bronzed giant did not care to discover how hot they were to the touch.

Picking his way about, he returned to the strange formation, which was now soaked and exhaling steam from its mahogany carapace.

The application of fresh water did not appear to affect the thing's outer shell. There seemed to be no more to be learned from it, so Tarzan departed and struck north. He did not care to be in the vicinity should the geyser erupt again.

There was no warning sound attending what next happened. What did transpire did so behind Tarzan's back, catching the ape-man by surprise.

He was trotting carefully between the luxurious trees when something stupendous intercepted the starlight and cast a shadow over him. It was long and massive.

Instinct seized Tarzan. He jumped up to the right, seeking the upper branches of the handiest tree. It was well that he did so, for it preserved his life. Something came down upon the spot where he had left behind his naked footprints and smashed the ground with a tremendous thud.

The ground shook. Hot mud splashed. The shaking communicated itself to the trees in which Tarzan had taken shelter. Every branch and leaf shuddered.

Turning, Tarzan beheld a senses-stunning sight.

RISING UP from a crater it had dashed in the mud, a nodular black sphere withdrew. It was attached to a long serpentine neck that boasted annular bands of alternating vermilion and white. This neck was perhaps twenty feet long and terminated in the mahogany shape of the strange formation Tarzan had now twice encountered.

It was a stupefying sight. The nodular head paused, looming over the muddy crater. As if recognizing that the depression was empty, it swayed from side to side only a dozen feet off the ground. Tarzan hung high above this scene. But he saw the weird thing clearly.

What had been a half-orb when partially retracted into the mahogany monster was now revealed to be an ebony globe. And on the forepart of this sphere, a vertical slit had opened up, revealing an eye like that of an enormous owl. The pupil was black, but the surrounding iris was a vermilion oval matching its neck rings.

Not finding its prey, the blunt ebony mace lashed out, displaying anger and frustration. It smashed down like a fleshy bludgeon and beat against surrounding trees, breaking limbs and all but knocking one stout bole off its thick roots.

The muscular strength of the thing was tremendous. Tarzan held onto his perch, and became immobile.

Survival of the jungle was a matter of using one's wits as well as main strength. Tarzan knew better than to challenge the hideous creature, for that is what it plainly was. Instead, he observed the monstrosity in fascinated silence, his hunting spear at the ready, but uncast.

Fear did not seize him. Only innate curiosity. The thing was beyond strange, but it was evidently a creature of some type.

As Tarzan watched, the long neck directed the hammer-like head this way and that. Locating no sign of the ape-man, slowly it withdrew from the trees. Then, the nodular head began to retract.

Like the head of a fantastic tortoise retreating into its shell, the one-eyed cranium slid backward. Soon the globular skull found lodgment in the opening from which it had extended, and became once more a dormant hemisphere. The oblique eye-slit sealed itself up, and in a matter of moments the entirety of the behemoth ceased to resemble a living creature.

What this serpent-necked shell-bodied monstrosity was, Tarzan of the Apes could not decide. But since it appeared to be immobile except for its ability to extend its battering-ram of a skull, Tarzan turned and moved through the trees, this time striking north in an effort to get as far away from it as possible.

Of all the creatures he had so far encountered upon the planet its inhabitants called Barsoom, this had been the most fantastic and disquieting. Only by a combination of its looming shadow and his superbly honed reflexes had the bronzed giant avoided being crushed to a pulp.

It was now apparent what had been striking down the green men of the tribe of Churvash Ul, although it was still a mystery why their outer bodies had not shown other signs of trauma and injury.

Nor was it clear why the creature dispatched its prey in such a devastating manner. He did not seem to possess a mouth with which to eat, although Tarzan had to admit to himself that its single eye was not revealed until it had come to life.

By a combination of running, leaping, climbing and other means, the ape-man rapidly returned to the camp of his followers.

Before he achieved his objective, he came within sight of the body of the deceased green warrior he had earlier examined.

It was no longer there!

Dropping from the concealment of his sheltering tree, Tarzan padded toward that clearing, spear in hand.

Several yards west of the spot where the body had been decaying, he found the Hortamangani's bones. They had been stripped of all flesh. Worse, the picked-clean bones did not look fresh. They were discolored and riddled with holes; it was as if they were worm-eaten. None had been broken in such a way as to gain access to the sweet marrow. But neither did the ape-man smell marrow. The bones had been hollowed out.

Here was a tableau that made the hackles on the back of his neck rise. Barely two zodes had passed since he had examined the body and now it had been stripped of every vestige of life and reduced to a bone pile that might have been moldering for decades.

But a greater horror soon became apparent. These bones were not scattered about or fallen into a disorderly pile. Tarzan saw that the ribs, pelvis bone, arms, and legs were all set in a kind of ceremonial arrangement. Every mortal component seemed to radiate from the central portion. And in its center, set upon a thigh bone that had been driven into the ground like a stake, was balanced the forbidding skull of the green giant.

Whatever manner of creature had devoured the unfortunate Martian, an intelligent species had rearranged its disconnected bones into a macabre pattern that shouted out a silent warning to the uncaring jungle.

Tarzan examined the grass and the dirt around it, but the recent downpour had extended to this reach, obliterating any traces of footprints, manlike or otherwise.

Determining that there was no more to be learned from the grisly cairn of bones, the ape-man continued on his way, determined to reach camp without further misadventure.

PRESSING ON, Tarzan of the Apes returned to camp to find pandemonium.

The great white gorillas were milling about, beating their chests and roaring in a mixture of rage and fear. They were soaked, the bristled hair on their heads plastered down by the brief beating rain.

The zitidar and thoats were likewise agitated, so Tarzan sent his thoughts to them each in his turn, calming them down.

The green nomads were on their feet, clutching their weapons, but they seemed to have better mastery over their emotions than the wild gorilla tribe. Those warriors Tarzan ignored for the moment.

Striding toward the Tarmanbolgani, the jungle lord addressed them in their own clucking tongue, exhorting them to calm down and take control of themselves.

Foad was screeching and shrieking that he had been scalded. But that had not been the case. By the time the geyser water had reached their heads, it was no longer superheated but merely stinging.

"Ramdar commands that you master yourselves."

In time, the agitated apes settled down, roamed about on their lowermost limbs, their knuckles sinking in the muddy ground. They hooted disconsolately.

When all was calm once more, Tarzan addressed his amalgam of a horde, speaking in their separate tongues by turns.

"Ramdar has investigated the jungle. In the center stands a geyser. This is the cause of the heat and the hot rains. If we stay clear of it, it cannot harm us. Furthermore, I have examined the strange formations described to me. They are the author of your troubles. It is a creature of unusual aspect. Its head is like a bludgeon attached to a serpent's body. That is what has dispatched many green warriors ignominiously. I imagine that it consumed them in some strange way."

Dag Dolor lifted his long-sword and proclaimed, "We will slay it, then!"

Tarzan raised a calming hand. "There is more to say. I came upon the bones of the green warrior who lay dead and decaying in the sun. He is a pile of naked bones now."

Jamo Ptannus grunted, "I have told you this. We have found other such bone piles."

"Jamo Ptannus neglected to mention that these bones were arranged in the formation of warning, the empty skull staked to the ground with a thigh bone."

"We do not know who did this," grumbled a green man disconsolately.

"The creature with the serpentine neck and cudgel head could not have done this," Tarzan stated flatly. "For it showed no digits or limbs that I could discover."

The Hortamangani warriors looked uneasy.

"I therefore conclude that another creature or creatures have done this. There is much danger in this jungle, but the most perilous are the things that we do not understand."

Tarzan had been speaking in the tongue of the Hortamangani, but repeating himself for the Tarmanbolgani. One of these latter shouted, "We must leave this accursed jungle. We must find a city suitable for us all!"

Tarzan replied in the gorilla tongue, "And this we will do. Once we determine the swiftest and straightest route to the city of Uxfar."

Repeating himself for the benefit of the green men, Tarzan stood resolute when they began to complain to him that to leave the jungle before slaying and avenging their dead brother would be an insult to their honor.

The jungle lord was considering his rebuttal when the humid night air was split by a piercing shriek. No one in the assembled group was the author of that outcry. It was the speech of neither the great white gorillas nor the green men. It sounded instead like that of a female human.

The shriek came again.

Becoming agitated, the followers of Ramdar reached for their weapons and their eyes swiveled in all directions, seeking the source of the new outburst. The surrounding trees gave up nothing, however.

Taking up his spear, Tarzan said, "Await Ramdar."

Without another word, he melted into the jungle, determined to locate the author of that plaintive cry for help. Perhaps, he thought, it might be a female of the red Martian species. If so, he was anxious to treat with her. Tarzan did not care to be interrupted by unruly Tarmanbolgani, or ferocious green Martians if it came to that.

Chapter 27

Cosooma's Story

AGAIN AND again through the night, the piteous shrieking continued. It became more ragged and less distinct with each repetition. Nevertheless, Tarzan was able to pinpoint the direction whence the cries for aid emanated.

Taking prodigious bounds, landing in clearings where he could and treetops where he must, the ape-man cleared enormous distances until he found himself in the leafy top of a tree overlooking the author of the distress cries.

It was a woman. She was exquisitely formed and wore only a gown garment necessary for the sake of modesty. As seen by the lunar light, the perfect skin of her exposed arms was very white, as if it were composed of shining electrons, or something equally luminous.

Moonlight made her pale skin shine in an ethereal manner. If it were not for the strident sound of her voice, Tarzan might have considered her to be a figment of his imagination, or some jungle phantom.

Here was no woman of the red Martian race, Tarzan was convinced. Her hair, piled high upon her regal head, was a golden hue. Under a high forehead, clear blue eyes shone. They displayed an uncanny opalescence that made them appear unreal, but in an intriguing way.

Briefly, the ape-man observed her from a height. She stood fixed on the jungle trail, which gleamed in an unusual way, as if itself luminous. The young woman was barefoot. She had worn sandals, but these sat nearby. Her outward demeanor was one of agitation. She appeared to wish to rend her garments but instead shook frustrated fists in a strenuous effort to control the futile impulse. Tarzan could see that she was trying to step along the gleaming trail, but it was as if her legs would not obey her.

Again she cried out. But this time her voice was pitifully weak and the cry became an understandable word in the common language shared by red and green Martians alike. "Help!"

Dropping down to the ground, Tarzan approached cautiously. For he knew that in the jungle things are not always what they appear to be.

"What is wrong?"

Hearing this question, she turned, and her face—which had been twisted in anguish—now broke in lines of shock and surprise.

"Oh! Who are you, bronze man? I see you wear no harness, nor do you display devices or the insignia of your rank."

Tarzan decided to keep matters between them simple.

"I am called by my followers Ramdar, jeddak of the combined tribes of Narag and Churvash Ul."

"Cosooma is my name. Please help me, I beg of you—for I am inextricably trapped."

"I see nothing confining you to the spot where you stand."

"I cannot lift the soles of my feet off the ground! I am rooted here."

Tarzan frowned. But he made no move to assist the beauteous one. Not all traps show teeth.

Approaching more closely, he demanded, "What is holding you to the jungle floor?"

"It is the carpet laid by a ghoor."

"I see no carpet, only dirt and some clumps of dead grass."

"The ghoor lays a carpet of his sticky secretions behind him as a snare to the unwary. I am afraid that I am one such unfortunate, for I have inadvertently stepped upon it during the dark period when neither moon sailed the sky. Here I am stuck until the ghoor returns along his track to devour me. If you cannot extricate me from this awful predicament, I am doomed."

Taking up his spear, Tarzan used the chipped quartz point to transfix one of the woman's discarded sandals. Attempting to lift this, he found he could not. The sole of the sandal was stuck to the ground as if by some stubborn glue.

Seeing that this was the way of things, Tarzan transferred the sharp tip of his weapon to the soil around the woman's feet. This he inserted, penetrating the crust. Then he began digging, kneeling in order to slide the flat tip under the woman's bare soles, doing this carefully so as not to injure her by accident.

The soil was strangely hard, like a rock. But it was not stone. It resisted the point of quartz. Only Tarzan's powerful simian muscles enabled him to penetrate it. This did not explain why the woman could not lift her feet, but he concentrated on breaking up the hardened ground.

The bronzed giant did this to one foot, and then the other, until the woman was standing on two clods of dirt that no longer adhered to the surrounding terrain.

"Lift one foot," he commanded.

The woman did so and was amazed to see that her foot came free, although to the bottom still clung heavy clumps.

"Now set that foot down and lift the other."

Cosooma did so successfully. "Oh! I can do this! I am free!"

Driving his spear into the ground to keep it at the ready, Tarzan took a running jump and, springing low, shot across the trail like a human arrow. Gathering up the woman in his strong arms, he carried her to the other side.

His landing was less graceful than he would have liked, but the jungle lord managed to keep his feet and hold onto the woman as well.

"You are a wonder!" she breathed as he set her down on safe ground. "Who are you, bronze one? How came you to this jungle, which the copper men do not visit?"

"Ramdar is a visitor to this land," replied Tarzan. "Is this jungle your home?"

"My home is nearby. We must go there before the ghoor returns."

"Very well. Lead the way. I wish to know more about this ghoor."

As Cosooma led him, Tarzan studied her carefully. She seemed in some way unreal. But that might have been the glamour of the quicksilver moonlight. Her beauty surpassed anything he had ever before beheld—save for his beloved, Jane. It was as if she were the perfect woman. Her radiant eyes, her pale lips, the way her hips swayed as she stepped over roots, arrested his attention.

"I have lived here a very long time," she volunteered.

More than that, Tarzan could not get from her. Cosooma was in a great hurry to reach her home, and he had to increase his pace to keep up with her. In some way the ape-man did not understand, she was very fleet of foot, although she walked at first with some difficulty, as the clumps of loose dirt fell away from the soles of her bare feet.

In due course, the woman broke into a clearing and Tarzan instinctively reached out for one arm, which she elegantly eluded.

For the ever-shifting moonlight showed in the clearing a great shape of mahogany surmounted at one end by a nodular black half-sphere.

"We must avoid that thing," Tarzan cautioned.

"But it is my home," Cosooma said plaintively.

Once more, Tarzan's hackles rose.

"The creature is alive; how could it be your home?" he demanded.

"O, wondrous stranger. It is no longer alive. It is only a shell. My ancestors hollowed it out as a shelter from the elements many, many generations ago. It is very safe to approach."

Unconvinced, Tarzan said, "Prove this to me."

Smiling, the woman continued on, rushing to one side of the shining form.

Cosooma adjusted something with her fingers, then turned to beckon for Tarzan to follow. Swiftly, she disappeared into an aperture that was suddenly there.

The jungle lord hesitated only a moment. Then he followed.

Slipping into the aperture, he found a ladder of lashed sticks that went downward into a reddish glow. When he reached the bottom, he found her waiting for him there.

The air was cool, but also moist. Tarzan found himself standing in an underground chamber. This chamber broke in three directions. Cosooma entered one such space and the ape-man followed cautiously.

The floor had been worn smooth by countless footprints over what must have been multitudinous generations and then overlaid with something resembling limestone. It was smooth.

After taking several turns, they came upon a vaulted tunnel through which flowed an underground river, with stony banks on either side.

Seeing this unexpected waterway coursing along, Tarzan demanded, "Is that water safe to drink?"

"Very safe," assured Cosooma. "For here courses the River Iss."

She said this as if the mere name should impress her companion. But Tarzan disappointed her expectations by not appearing to recognize it.

"You must be thirsty after your ordeal," Tarzan suggested.

"Now that you speak of it, I am."

Kneeling, Cosooma took water up in one spectral hand and drank from her palm delicately.

When she had imbibed her fill, the woman turned and said smilingly, "You see? It is safe!"

Seeing this to be true, the bronzed giant knelt down and cupped his hands, bringing surprisingly cool and refreshing water to his parched lips. He drank his fill, then rose to his feet and turned.

"Where are your people?"

"Alas, they are no more. I am the last of them, the last Orovaran woman of the vanished city of Samabar."

Cosooma hung her head in sadness.

Tarzan told her, "I do not know what an Orovar is, but you are beautiful to look upon."

"If you wish, I can tell you the story of my people."

"Ramdar is interested. But where do you dwell?"

Cosooma gestured with both hands, pointing in the direction of the winding, intersecting warrens. "All of this is my kingdom. What lies in the chambers beyond this point is all that remains of the city of Samabar, which was brought low long before you and I were ever born."

Tarzan scrutinized the black-lined tunnels. They reminded him of lava tubes, passages created beneath African volcanos by flowing magma, which, having drained out, left behind scorched tunnels coated by natural obsidian glass.

"The volcano above created these passages," he stated.

Cosooma shook her auburn hair firmly. "No. You are mistaken. The jungle above is impounded by a crater, yes, but it is not volcanic. In order for you to fully understand, I must tell the sad story of my people."

THEY BEGAN walking along, their bodies limned by the steady scarlet light that seemed to emanate from deeper in the warren.

"Long ago," Cosooma began, "the Orovaran race dominated Barsoom in its wisdom and beauty. We were high-minded people, not like the piratical First Born, whose skin was black, or the yellow-skinned Okarians who inhabit the cold north. Nor were we martially inclined, as was the emerging copper race, which we helped create by interbreeding with the black and yellow men to produce them. Barsoom was beautified by our presence. We built up great cities. We did not make war, except as necessary. This was half a million ords in the past, Ramdar.

"Then the oceans commenced to dry up. The rich atmosphere became thinner and thinner, but remained breathable. This was a slow process. For we Orovars, it was the beginning of a catastrophe. At first, it merely presaged a prolonged mercantile decline. For we were a seafaring race. We traded with other cities and expanded our outreach across the entirety of the face of Barsoom.

"As the seas receded, we simply extended the reach of our wharves and quays and imagined that the planet was entering a new epoch. For all we understood was that the coasts were expanding and we would merely have to adapt to this expansion.

"Upon the spot above our heads was what was once the forest city of Samabar. It was fed in part by the underground River Iss, but in those days it rained often. Our city prospered, despite the fact that it was built upon the shore of a modest inland sea, the Trox, and consequently was the first to retreat, owing to its small size. Forewarned, we adapted to the shrinking waters better than our brothers and sisters in other Orovaran cities, which were built by great oceans, and were wholly dependent upon them.

"Then one terrible day, disaster struck. From interstellar space came a meteor, of great size and terrific force. It struck the city proper like a fist of molten iron. The meteorite was not composed of iron, but some other substance. The city was whelmed, its buildings utterly demolished, the people incinerated and reduced to unrecognizable clinkers. The meteorite created a vast crater where before had stood a city surrounded by forest, one that required no walls.

"Only those who had been traveling outside the city survived. They returned to discover the smoldering crater and everything they ever knew smashed to oblivion. The meteorite's impact had driven it far underground and was still burning. The matter that composed it burned and burned without ceasing, producing liquid ore that filled the subterranean spaces. Our surviving scientists realized it might be thousands of ords before it extinguished itself, if it ever did.

"But all was not lost. Not entirely. For the flowing molten matter that constituted the meteor had carved tunnels under the surface soil, which were warm and habitable. Furthermore, the River Iss passed through this, providing drinking water. Because Samabar was built so far from any other city, the survivors decided to relocate to the underground passages and live there. By that time, the shrinking of the oceans and seas had reached the point where it could no longer be denied that Barsoom was dying. Commerce was dwindling. Sea travel was no longer possible. The green men were on the rise. In their inexorable march across the face of this planet, they sacked city after city. Only the rise of the red men stayed their advance, preventing them from conquering Barsoom from pole to pole.

"All this was long, long ago, Ramdar. Here, untouched by these changes, my ancestors abided in relative peace. But all was not a paradise. The perpetual underground fires gave birth to a geyser that began to erupt and irrigate what was left of the forest, transmuting it into what you see now, an untamed wilderness. New predators rose up. Some appeared to be survivors of creatures that roamed and hunted during prehistoric times. How they came to return, we do not know. It is a mystery."

"Is the ghoor one of these creatures?" demanded Tarzan.

"No. It is not by nature a land animal. The ghoor was originally a foul creature of the ancient ocean floor. When the waters dried up, they attempted to adapt. But most could not adapt. Their carcasses were once found here and there on the dead sea bottoms, but only the hard heads and hollow shells remained. But a few, lured perhaps by the hot moisture they sensed, invaded the jungle, smashing through the protective ring of cliffs, to take up residence there.

"They were few in number and reproduced very slowly. But they could not be easily defeated. It was discovered that when they died, the gigantic internal organ that comprised their living being withered rapidly, leaving behind the shell and the black head, both of which resisted the elements over generations. My ancestors learned to anchor these remains to the ground and set the heads back in place with natural adhesives. These remnants served as shelters from predators, protection from the scalding geyser eruptions, but also as entrance points into the underground network of tunnels."

Tarzan nodded. "I am familiar with an animal that has a soft body and moves slowly on a single pad that secretes mucus, leaving behind a trail of slime. This creature is capable of withdrawing its vulnerable inner body within the shell and thus defeat predators."

"Yes, yes," Cosooma said brightly. "What you are describing is exactly like a ghoor. Only two or three are left. If they can be defeated, the jungle will be a safer place to hunt. Not that it will ever be truly a safe place. Creatures stalk it that are not known to inhabit any other region, whether above the Polodona, or below."

"I do not know this place, Polodona."

"It is the imagined line devised by mapmakers that encircles the middle of Barsoom, dividing it into upper and lower hemispheres."

Then Tarzan understood fully. Polodona was the Barsooomian term for the equator.

The ape-man asked, "I have seen a ghoor extend its terrible head and attempt to crush its prey. How does it devour that prey?"

"It stuns it with a blow, crushing the skull or bones, and while the victim lies helpless, his skin turns blue or black from the terrific bruising. Then it advances, and flows over its prey, crushing it into the soil, pausing while it completely consumes the soft tissues of its victim, leaving only bones. I, myself, had the misfortune to step onto its slime trail, which is almost impossible to foil because it is like glue and hardens the ground beneath, precluding escape. That is another way the ghoor captures prey. For it always moves back and forth along its own trail. I would probably have died of starvation before the ghoor had returned this way, for it creeps along very, very slowly. Although it is a more merciful death than to have been consumed alive, I would have been finished had you not come along, Ramdar."

"The body of a green warrior lies north of this spot," stated Tarzan. "It was black and broken, but not consumed when I first came upon it. No ghoor was nearby. Why is that?"

"Because it moves so slowly, a ghoor will kill even if it is not hungry," replied Cosooma. "It knows that it may return to feast another padan, provided scavengers do not steal the corpse first."

"I have found the bones of one of its victims," pressed Tarzan. "They were arranged in strange patterns. Does the ghoor do that?"

Cosooma shook her auburn head violently. "No, the ghoor does not do that. Something else does that. What it is, I cannot say."

"Not even to the one who saved your life?"

Cosooma averted her radiant eyes. Tarzan expected her to blush, but she did not. In that moment, her beauty was to his eyes unsurpassed. Were it not for his deep love for his earthly mate, the bronzed giant might have felt an upwelling of desire. But he was loyal to those who were loyal to him.

"Perhaps," she said at last, looking him full in the eyes, "this may be divulged to you in time."

"How can the ghoor be defeated?"

"It is very difficult. But it can be done. My ancestors devised a way. To do it requires a long-sword and a bow, as well as suitable arrows."

Tarzan said, "I am impressed that the bow was known here."

"It is uncommon. Only the Orovars employed it of old. It is not a thing favored by the red man or the green man or any other men. Just as their pistols were not the Orovar way." Her eyes glancing toward Tarzan's quiver, she added, "I see that you carry arrows. Are your ancestors Orovars?"

"No," said Tarzan shortly. "But I am practiced with the bow. This one I made myself."

Reaching out to finger it where the cord crossed Tarzan's chest diagonally, Cosooma said, "It is a stout bow. But I have many finer ones at my disposal. Perhaps one of metal would suit you."

"Ramdar would be interested in seeing them," declared Tarzan noncommittally.

"Come then."

Turning, the beautiful Cosooma beckoned him down the passage, leading Tarzan to a sharp turn, around which she swiftly vanished. Picking up his pace, the ape-man followed, hunting spear in hand, his sheathed blades hanging from his metallic belt.

Chapter 28

A Worthy Blade Is Found

FOLLOWING THE ethereal woman, Tarzan was led through myriad passages, all of which were lit indirectly by glowing crimson veins smoldering in the basalt walls reminiscent of burning coal seams, a phenomenon about which he had heard, but had never personally experienced.

Strangely, no smoke or odor was produced by these burning fissures.

Remarking upon this, Tarzan asked, "How can this be? All things that burn are consumed and produce residue."

Cosooma responded, "The meteor, whatever it was, is not like that. Perhaps it is an element, one foreign to this world, as it must be. It burns and burns and burns, and while it diminishes, only light and heat are produced. As pressures build up, water rushing from the river further along is boiled and forced upward. This happens from time to time, but not in any predictable fashion."

The soles of Tarzan's feet became warm and then hot. He disdained sandals or any type of footgear. So the going became unpleasant, but tolerable.

"I am bound for a city of red men that lies beyond this place," he told Cosooma. "Is there a direct way through the jungle that will take me there without having to go around the crater?"

Cosooma paused in her graceful progress, turned, and said simply, "I know of no city in any direction from Samabar. Not inhabited by copper man, nor for that matter, deserted. However,

I have not traveled far from the crater. But to the knowledge of my ancestors, no such city exists. Why do you think one lies close?"

Thinking back to Murdank's telepathic impression of a settlement of many minds, Tarzan forbore to reply directly. Instead, he said, "I have heard tales of such a city. I would meet with these red men, and learn of their science."

"The copper men of today are less advanced scientifically than the Orovars were in their glory days," admitted Cosooma, continuing along. "We developed knowledge they did not. The sailing ship, for example. And other things, such as the atmosphere plants which generate fresh oxygen, without which all races would soon perish."

The way became increasingly hot. Abruptly, Cosooma turned a corner that debouched into a great black-walled chamber. It was in the form of an interior dome, yet the ceiling and the sides were rippled in a way that resembled molten lava that had hardened into glassy obsidian.

Turning, Cosooma proudly proclaimed, "This is the weapons storehouse of ancient Samabar."

Set upon steel pegs that had been pounded into the wall, and arrayed in stout chests and upon polished tables were sufficient arms to provision a formidable military force. Swords of all types, what appeared to be battle axes, bows, arrows, spears—all were evident in profusion.

Going to the nearest table, Tarzan picked up a bow. To his surprise, it was made of hard metal, possibly steel, if steel was a metal produced on Barsoom. Engraved upon it were decorative feathers, making for a sure grip. The winglike weapon was wonderfully strong, but also supple at either limb. The string was also metallic, like piano wire. Plucking it with his strong fingers, the ape-man judged that it would take staunch strength to pull such a cord all the way back.

"Only the strongest of our warriors wielded such a weapon," explained Cosooma. "They were fashioned of such durable metal that if the bow were to fall into the hands of an enemy, he could not use it against us. Since you are not practiced with an Orovar bow, permit me to demonstrate its effectiveness."

Taking up a similar bow, Cosooma nocked a wooden arrow taken from a woven basket, and pulled it back to its greatest extent, then lifted the bow until the barbed metal arrowhead was pointing directly over their heads. She let fly. The bowstring snapped.

The arrow impaled the precise apex of the hardened lava dome and hung there, its feathery fletching standing out.

"I am an accomplished bow-woman," said Cosooma with restrained pride. "It took three thousand revolutions of the sun to develop the muscular strength to wield a bow such as this. If you wish, you may test your strength, but I caution you not to expect very much of your first effort."

Saying nothing, Tarzan accepted an arrow from the woman and studied it. Its shaft was cut of the hardwood Martians called skeel. Its blued point was barbed and its end fletched with varicolored bird feathers.

Nocking it, Tarzan pulled back slowly, and while he was impressed by the bowstring's resistance, his tremendous strength, amplified by the Martian gravity, permitted him to draw back to the bowstring's maximum extent.

An audible gasp came from the woman.

Directing the arrow directly overhead, Tarzan took three steps until he was beneath the still-quivering missile above. He released his arrow. It flew true. His face did not change expression when his shaft bisected the other, splintering the strong wood, and finding lodgment in the lava rock.

Fragments of the woman's arrow fell to the floor, clattering.

"You must be an Orovaran warrior!"

"I am not," said Tarzan, taking up another arrow. This time he turned around and shot the missile out of the chamber to see how far it would fly. It was soon lost from view in the approaching passage. The sound of the metal arrowhead striking an unseen stony outcropping came distinctly back. But it sounded very far away.

This phenomenon told Tarzan of the Apes that with a bow such as this, he could pierce a target a considerable distance away. Removing his makeshift bow, he placed it on the table and filled his banth-hide quiver with barbed shafts after emptying out most of his quartz-tipped ones. A few of these he kept.

The jungle lord did this without asking permission. Cosooma did not raise any objection. With her eyes, she tracked his movements around the chamber with growing appreciation, for his bronze physique was supple and splendid.

Tarzan rummaged among the tables and chests, soon finding what he sought.

Reaching into a chest, he produced a short blue blade that had the recurved style of his father's hunting knife. It was perhaps an inch shorter than the earthly blade. The substance comprising the smooth handle was unknown to him, but it appeared to be polished ivory. Its color and composition reminded him of the tusks of the green giants. He wondered if some long-dead Hortamangani had lost his lower tusk to complete this knife.

The hilt felt comfortable in his right hand. The balance was good. As a fighting blade as well as a hunting weapon, it would serve him well.

Removing his Martian dagger from its sheath, Tarzan inserted the sharp blade in its place. It was a tight fit, but it would stay in place yet slip out rapidly when needed.

Observing this, Cosooma offered, "That blade was forged from an ore extruded from the great meteorite as slag. My ancestors used it to fashion all of the weapons you see all about you, employing for that purpose the fires of the meteor itself as a furnace. It is unlike any metal known on Barsoom, and superior to iron, steel, or any other metal."

The ape-man said nothing. He took up a sword of the same strange bluish metal and cut the air with it several times, noting with still-faced approval the hiss and flutter of the finely wrought blade.

"You are practiced with the long-sword?" asked Cosooma, noting his sure technique.

"A soldier named Paul D'Arnot taught me the art of sword fighting," Tarzan remarked. He continued weaving the air with the glittering weapon, whose leather-bound hilt was studded with diamonds and other brilliants no different than those found on Earth.

Returning the blade to its scabbard, Tarzan asked, "Why were you abroad in the night?"

"Evening is when many creatures sleep. It is safer to pick berries and fruit. And nuts. I do not eat meat."

"You are very strong for someone who does not eat meat."

"Orovaran men and women are trained to be sound of limb, but even stronger of mind. For the mind is considered to be our greatest weapon."

"Do banths roam this jungle?" wondered Tarzan.

"They do not. Banths avoid this place. They are creatures of the seabeds, besides."

Tarzan grunted. It appeared that on Mars, the gorillas and the equivalent to lions had no appetite for forests or jungles.

"I see you wear the hide of a banth about your loins," remarked Cosooma. "Did you slay one?"

"More than one," responded the ape-man.

Cosooma gasped.

"No Orovaran man ever slew a banth in personal combat. What kind of Barsoomian are you, Ramdar?"

INSTEAD OF replying, Tarzan suddenly said, "I must return to my band before dawn breaks. Then we will decide which way to journey."

She rushed up to him, taking one arm in her pale, slender hands. "Let me go with you!"

Tarzan fixed his flinty gaze upon her loveliness. "Why do you wish to accompany me?"

"You are very strong. You are the first man of my type I have seen in a very long time. And… I am lonely."

"Ramdar is on a quest. You will not care to go where Ramdar goes."

"I am just as much a skilled archer as you are a bowman," she returned hotly. There was a lambent light in her eyes now.

Tarzan was unmoved. "I lead a band of green scavengers and savage apes. They are unruly and incorrigible. You would not fit in with them."

Her brows puckered together and fire sprang into her eyes. "Cosooma is not your equal—is that what you are declaring?"

Tarzan said nothing. He did not wish to insult this woman, strong-willed as she was.

Cosooma stamped one bare foot. "I am their superior. Behold!"

She pointed toward the entrance of the lava chamber and Tarzan turned, although he heard nothing untoward.

Entering suddenly, a hulking form loomed. It was a tusked green man. It was not one of the horde of Churvash Ul, but a warrior he had never laid eyes upon before this moment.

The Martian's red eyes blazed in fury. He advanced, waving a long-sword angrily about.

Tarzan reached for his new hunting knife, but before it cleared its sheath, Cosooma had taken up another arrow, and in a breathless second loosened it, striking the green monster in the center of his forehead, sending it careening and stumbling backward, multiple limbs flailing.

The thing fell upon its back, its sword sliding from its dying grasp.

Mildly astonished, Tarzan strode up to the prostrate creature and looked down at it.

It lay still. Unnaturally still. It did not heave its chest nor work its massive jaws in his death agonies. The eyes stared blindly, then slowly closed. It seemed as if its brain had been penetrated its entire length, for only the feathered end of the shaft protruded from its olive-green brow.

"It is dead," he pronounced.

"It never lived," returned Cosooma in a cool tone. There was a trace of mockery in her silken voice, and Tarzan directed his level gaze back at her. She was smiling, her dancing eyes alight.

Laying down her bow, she laughed lightly, as if at some unspoken jest.

"Look again," she said, pointing.

The ape-man turned about. And his eyes widened in a feral way.

For the great green swordsman was no longer asprawl upon the floor! The space stood empty. Even the massive sword was gone.

"Are you a witch?" demanded Tarzan, going to her. "This smacks of sorcery!"

Smiling, Cosooma returned lightly, "Did I not say that the Orovaran people were stronger in mind than in body? Over successive generations, we trained ourselves to master our brains. The ability to project illusions is but part of that mastery. Did you not notice that the creature made no sound in approaching or in falling? Nor did its sword ring upon the floor? Yet so real did it appear that you believed that it was substantial. It was not. I conjured it up from my own imagination. Now I have consigned it to oblivion. For it never was."

Tarzan of the Apes stared at the remarkable woman for some moments.

At length, he said, "If it is your wish to accompany Ramdar, I hereby grant you that wish. But know that Ramdar has a mate who lives far from here. And it is my every intention to reclaim my mate when my quest is concluded."

Cosooma said nothing to that. Smiling, she gathered up arrows and other weapons, including a war spear of hard metal.

Watching this, Tarzan helped himself to the long-sword he had tested, thinking that while it might be longer and heavier than his preference, it boasted a serviceable blade, and weapons were in short supply. He attached the scabbard to his belt, on the opposite hip from his knife.

There were also lengths of rope, made of a tough, resilient matter the jungle lord did not recognize. Wrapping one about his chest meant that he did not have to fashion one of his own out of the purplish Martian grass.

AFTER THEY had filled their hands, Cosooma led the ape-man out to a passageway that wound to the north. As they moved along, they passed an area of intense heat, and Tarzan could see down a long tunnel something burning brightly, something that was almost incandescent.

"That is the heart of the meteor," explained Cosooma. "It has burned for longer than I have been alive, and I have been living for a very long time."

Tarzan evinced no interest in examining the artifact. Instead, he commented, "You appear to be young."

"I have lived almost one thousand ords."

"I do not believe you."

"Then you are a very ignorant fellow. For the Orovaran people, as well as the copper men and the green men, typically live one thousand ords, if they do not succumb to maladies or violent death beforehand."

"If what you say is true," Tarzan pointed out, "you would be approaching the end of your natural life span."

"That is another reason why I wish to accompany you. I have long dwelt beneath this jungle and I would like to see the rest of dying Barsoom before my allotted time runs out."

"What of your people?"

"Sadly, I am the only one left," she said wistfully. "For I have outlived all the others who once inhabited these caverns and passageways."

The ape-man scrutinized the beauteous woman for some minutes. His own expression was unreadable.

Finally, he turned on his heel, saying, "Follow Ramdar."

Chapter 29

Besting the Ghoor

NIGHT WAS not far along when Tarzan and Cosooma exited the void that constituted the empty shell of the dead ghoor, and struck out to the north. A solitary moon transited the sky with amazing speed. It was the lesser satellite, Cluros. Swiftly, it dropped below the horizon, leaving the numberless stars to shed their weak light. Brilliant among them was a steady white speck that did not twinkle and was therefore not a star.

"Behold Cosoom," declared the young woman who claimed to be nearly one thousand years old.

"What of it?" wondered the ape-man, who recognized the luminous object as the planet Venus.

"I was named after that world," she averred. "For its rising attended my hatching. My long-dead parents said that when I broke my shell, I was as radiant as its light. This is a sign. Cosoom will be the lantern that will light our way."

Tarzan did not comment. He had learned from Dag Dolor that of those who walked upright upon Mars, only one species was born alive. All others were hatched in communal incubators. It was no shock to hear that this white woman originated from an egg.

His ever-alert eyes were scanning the surrounding jungle for signs of danger. His sense of smell became filled with unfamiliar odors, which told his brain little.

Pushing to the north, the ape-man broke a fresh trail among the fantastic trees. He bristled with weapons. In addition to his newly acquired knife and the metal bow slung across his chest, he gripped his hunting spear in one hand. The Orovaran longsword bounced heavily at his hip, its scabbard held in place by a stout ring. All this dead weight meant nothing to the ape-man, whose sinewy strength was wonderfully improved by the favorable conditions of Mars.

They encountered trouble only once. Something dropped out of a tree that was as pale as dead flesh. It landed in a pile between them and began gathering itself. It was a great serpentine worm of a thing. Python-like, it formed coils. The monstrosity appeared to be entirely blind, for there were no eyes in evidence.

Turning, Tarzan took in this sight, appraising it by instinct and not experience. Before he could decide whether to kill it or ignore it, Cosooma stepped back and drew a shaft from her quiver.

Eyeless or not, the leprous thing reacted with stupefying speed. Something like a feeler whipped out from the coiled mass to wrap itself around the lower limb of the recurved bow. It yanked.

But Cosooma was strong. She held on tightly.

Seeing this struggle, Tarzan fell upon the creature, his knife jumping into his hand and, for a moment, all pretense of civilization fell away as he drove the blade in again and again, making deep cuts along the vermiform thing's upper regions, snarling and growling like an animal, the battle scar upon his noble brow burning fiercely.

Squirming madly, it bled profusely. The fluid produced was a viscous green. The groping tentacle loosened and dropped away. Cosooma pulled free while Tarzan carved a long rip into the expiring creature's side with a deft swipe of his blade.

Leaving it to writhe in its silent death throes, the pair continued on.

"That was a drulla," explained Cosooma. "They were thought to have become extinct eons ago. Somehow this jungle birthed a new generation of them. Drullas like to wrap their feelers around a victim's throat and squeeze until its prey can no longer take in air."

"I saw no means to eat flesh," countered Tarzan, working his way along.

"The drulla does not eat flesh. It extrudes a barbed siphon that punctures skin and drains the blood. This it does over a long period of time so that the victim lingers helplessly. It is a horrible death."

As they neared the encampment, Tarzan unexpectedly heard a shambling commotion, followed by a crashing through the brush.

A Tarmanbolgani voice lifted up. Not speaking words, but grunting and howling in an extremity of fear.

Tarzan recognized the voice. It was the callow young ape known as Foad. He divested himself of his heaviest weapons, keeping his spear in hand.

Following the sound, the jungle lord crashed out of the trees, and there he beheld in the near distance the gleaming shell of a ghoor.

NOT FAR from the thing was Foad. He had fallen and was trapped in a slick trail of slime from which he could not extricate himself. Only one limb was free, and the angry ape used this to shake a simian fist against the apparent fate to which he had been consigned. His other fists were caught fast, as were his naked knees. All efforts to tear free had resulted in frustration, for his hairless hide was bathed in perspiration and the shock of white bristles atop his head lay flat and matted atop his sloping skull.

Directly in front of him loomed the ghoor. At first, it appeared stationary to Tarzan's eyes. Then he noticed that it was creeping backward now, moving with infinite slowness on the fleshy foot barely visible beneath the smooth protective carapace of its shell, flattening such wild grass as impeded its progress.

Cosooma inserted, "It will crush and consume that ape, resting over him for one zode, until only bones remain."

"I cannot allow this," grunted Tarzan. "How can I kill the ghoor?"

"It takes many men to bring one down, but only if one knows the way. We are but two."

Growling, Tarzan said, "Ramdar is possessed of the strength of many men. Explain what must be done."

Cosooma was aghast. "You would risk your life for that brute?"

"Although he is but a shambling ape, I am the lord of the apes. Quickly! Tell me."

Stepping up, she leaned into his ear and began whispering instructions.

"We must wait until the neck extends. Otherwise, there is nothing we can do. It will extend its head when it is near its prey in order to dash out from him any last resistance. This will take place by daybreak at the latest."

"I cannot wait until daybreak," said Tarzan, withdrawing a skeel shaft from his quiver. Setting it in place, he directed the barbed point at the shell and let fly.

Propelled by his tremendous strength, the missile struck, making a cracking sound and creating a fissure in the hard smooth flank of the thing. It penetrated only a little. Even this much impressed the Orovaran woman.

"No man of my tribe has ever penetrated the shell of a ghoor with a single arrow. Or any number of arrows. Your strength must be beyond that of any man who ever lived before this time."

Tarzan did not reply. Drawing back, he released the second arrow. It split the first, penetrating more deeply. Reacting like a lightning bolt, the fissure extended in both directions. A third missile followed. This split the second shaft, penetrating even further.

This arrested the attention of the creature. The featureless head began to extend, revealing annular neck rings which it extruded with an eerie silence. Tarzan had encountered a creature scientists called an apatosaurus in a subterranean land known as Pellucidar. The muscular neck of that prehistoric beast reminded him of this monster.*

Once it had reached its fullest extension, the oblique eye opened and the head quested about, first directing its attention on the source of its injuries, then it swung about, seeking the author of its troubles with its owlish cyclops eye as big around as a man's chest.

Leaping into the moonlight, Tarzan caught its attention. The head reared back, preparing to strike a bludgeoning blow.

The muscular strength of the neck was prodigious. For it snapped down with blinding speed. Tarzan moved with greater alacrity, however. Leaping high, he cleared the descending black globe, landing on the other side of it.

Stunned by the speed at which his prey had disappeared, the ghoor wavered, at which point both Tarzan and Cosooma commenced unleashing arrows. They struck the root of the neck, which caused the head to flail about in sudden shock.

Tarzan fashioned a loop from his rope and jumped again, this time landing back of the head. He slipped the noose into place. Holding tightly with both hands, the Tarmangani stepped off, and the weight of his muscular body dragged the helpless head downward.

Flashing to a tree, the ape-man secured his end of the rope to a sturdy bough, holding the head in place and preventing it from retracting. Nevertheless, the head stubbornly pulled backward. The rope began to strain. Fibers commenced popping and parting.

During this operation, Cosooma sent more barbed arrows into the root of the neck, one after the other without a single miss. Now six shafts quilled the hollow receiving collar high in front of the massive shell, where the hind portion of the head sat when at rest.

---

* See Tarzan at the Earth's Core *by Edgar Rice Burroughs.*

After recovering his spear, which he had left behind, Tarzan took it up and cast it. It lanced through the air, a long whispering blur. The quartz point split the vermilion eye almost perfectly in twain. The black nodular globe wrenched back, tearing loose the rope anchoring its fat neck.

Now the head began retracting at its maximum speed, whereupon Tarzan took up his discarded Orovaran long-sword and leaped onto the back of the shell, directly behind the muscular neck root. There he set himself.

The speed with which the head withdrew demonstrated that evolution on Mars had given the ghoor the ability to protect itself from harm with great dispatch.

But the gyrating speed of the ghoor was nothing against the fleetness of Tarzan of the Apes.

As explained by Cosooma, the plan of attack was to create a bristling collar of arrows so that the head could not fully retract, whereupon Tarzan was to lop it off at the root.

But the woman's plan did not take into account the tremendous strength of her rescuer.

With a perfect leap, Tarzan gained the neck, ran along its red-and-white banded length. Taking a stance just short of the head, he seized the long-sword in both strong hands. With all his might, he swung the formidable blade once from the left, then, switching tactics, brought the sharp edge in from the right, all but decapitating the creature.

The head was still hanging by a rubbery shred of gristle, whereupon Tarzan dropped his blade, and took a seated position as if riding a horse. Wrapping his strong legs around the ringed column, he lopped the head off with a final cleaving downward stroke of his sharp knife. It sliced through living tissue without resistance.

His feet landed lightly on the ground before the inert head came crashing down.

Dodging aside to avoid the nodular juggernaut, Tarzan reached the woman's side and there they surveyed the death throes of the horrid thing.

The ringed neck remained elevated for almost a minute, as if not realizing that its terminal head was no longer attached. Gradually it drooped, finally settling to ground, where it quivered indefinitely. The main body of the monster resting on its pseudopod foot did not otherwise move. But its infinitely slow locomotion completely ceased, like a slowing ship losing all headway.

An urge to give forth with the victory cry of the bull ape welled up within Tarzan's chest. It was a primal impulse, yet for once he suppressed it, but not without effort. For the cry might mean nothing to the hidden inhabitants of this weird ape-less jungle, and the bronzed giant did not care to draw attention to himself and the others, which might stir even more dangerous foes.

The jagged scar burning on his brow began to fade, a certain sign that the self-control the jungle lord learned in civilization was asserting itself over his bestial natural instincts.

AFTER FIRST wiping off bluish blood against a hairy tree trunk, Tarzan returned his Martian knife to its sheath. He strode up to Foad, demanding, "Why did you desert the encampment?"

"Mercy, O Ramdar! I became hungry and foraged for sompus fruit. Then I became stuck. Only by your intercession do I live."

Tarzan had reclaimed his spear. Lifting it high, he offered the blunt end to the kneeling gorilla. Foad's single free hand reached over, groped, and found the shaft, which he seized firmly.

Tarzan admonished, "Prepare yourself."

"There is nothing you can do for him," interjected Cosooma. "Not unless you dig up the soil all around, which you cannot do without becoming stuck yourself."

Not deigning to reply, the ape-man took hold of the shaft with both hands and set himself. He commenced pulling, while at the same time walking backward. The ape's paw tightened, refusing to let go.

Gradually, inexorably, Foad was hauled from the slime trail and dragged up onto the purple grass, where he began smacking his hands together and attempting to knock off the clinging clods of congealed soil. He did a fair job of this, but a great deal of it remained.

"He will have to bathe if he wishes to remove the slime," suggested Cosooma.

"Apes do not bathe," returned Tarzan.

When he accomplished all that he could, Foad stood up and walked around experimentally. He hunkered down and used all six limbs to go about, knuckle walking because his palms were sticky and encrusted with stony dirt.

"We will return to the encampment now," commanded Tarzan. He had retrieved his sword and was wiping its blade clean of bluish gore against the tall purple grass. Once done, he sheathed it in its scabbard, then took up his spear.

"Ramdar is a mighty ape-lord," grunted Foad. Which for a Tarmanbolgani was the equivalent of profuse thanks and abject gratitude, even if it was expressed in a succession of uncouth barks and grunts.

Chapter 30

BATTLE!

THE CIMMERIAN Martian night still smothered the jungle as Tarzan of the Apes led Foad and the white woman, Cosooma, back to camp.

While the ape-man had grown accustomed to the peculiar smells of the thick woodland, in contrast to the jungles he knew back on Earth, he did not always comprehend the meaning of the odors that caressed his dilated nostrils. They were many and multiform.

Which marked predator and which denoted prey was something he had yet to catalog in his mind. Thus, every new scent might portend danger. Tarzan moved through the jungle accordingly, his eyes never at rest.

A new scent spoor suddenly assailed his nostrils. This was familiar. He had smelled it once before. This was the distinct aroma of the Gamangani, the copper-skinned men of Barsoom.

Tarzan immediately paused, sweeping his spear down and around to block the way.

The others halted. Foad, too, soon smelled the odor.

"It is the stink of red men," he growled.

Then a mechanical whirring smote Tarzan's ears and he glanced upward.

Intercepting the faint starlight was one of the aerial boats controlled by the red Martians. It was descending at an angle, sweeping around shallowly. Its aluminum sides were burnished by the combination of starlight and the brilliant lamp that was the planet Cosoom.

Tarzan told Foad, "It is circling the encampment."

As they watched, crouching low and immobile, they saw a second and then a third boat sweep in. At the stern, spinning propellers drove the craft, producing a faint whirring.

From the nearby camp came a polyglot roar, Tarmanbolgani and Hortamangani alike raising their voices in anger and defiance.

"War!" cried Foad.

"Come!" commanded Tarzan, breaking into a run.

Charging hard, they burst into the encampment where every warrior was on his feet, brandishing the weapon of his choice. They hardly noticed the arrival of Tarzan and Foad, so the unexpected presence of Cosooma was momentarily beneath their notice.

Striding up to Dag Dolor, Tarzan said, "They appear to be scouting."

"They have spied us!"

"Take no hostile action until we understand their intentions."

Jamo Ptannus thrust his tusked face forward. "The intentions of red men are always the same—conquest."

But Tarzan did not see it that way. He was interested in making friends with the red man, that is, if friendship was possible. Again he gave out commands. "Hold your ground! Make no hostile movements. We shall see what they do. Then we will know how to answer in return. Ramdar has spoken."

Neither the white apes nor the green nomads cared for that kind of talk. But they respected their jeddak. They lowered their arms, bringing down their weapons, but only partially so. The apes made a defensive circle around the shes and the balus, lifting their stone mallets of war and jabbering angrily.

The three ships circled warily, dropping several hundred feet with each circuit. The shadowy shapes of Gamangani Martians appeared at the rails. Tarzan spied rifles and revolver-like pistols held at the ready. But no one made an antagonistic move.

This aerial dance continued for several minutes without incident. Then from one of the sky boats a resounding voice called down, "Who is the jed of this horde?"

Tarzan stepped forward and announced, "I am no jed, but jeddak of the great white apes and the green nomads both."

"Are you mad? You wear no harness, nor any metal, yet you proclaim yourself to be a jeddak? You are a low panthan, if you are even that."

"I am Ramdar, leader of the white apes and the green warriors you see surrounding me. I am war chief to one and Ape-lord to the other. Together, they comprise an army of which I am jeddak."

The red man called down. "There has never been a horde upon the face of Barsoom that wedded wild green nomads with savage apes. What manner of man can fuse them together into a single horde?"

Tarzan brought his spear point to his bronzed chest. "Why do you ask that question? You see him before you."

"You are not red nor yellow, but bronze. What are you?"

"I am called Ramdar. More than that you need not know."

"What do you seek, Ramdar?"

"I seek the city of Uxfar."

"That city would be denied to you, jeddak of foul white apes and lawless green nomads."

"Nevertheless, Ramdar intends to march upon that city and meet with its leader."

"What business do you have in Uxfar?"

"I seek—"Tarzan realized that to explain himself fully would only be futile and cause confusion. Then he remembered something. "I seek one who is called John Carter."

"What business do you have with John Carter?"

"The business Ramdar has with John Carter is between John Carter and Ramdar. It is not for other ears."

This announcement was met by silence, broken only by the mechanical sounds of the descending aerial vehicles, pushed along by their steadily beating propellers.

Tarzan folded his arms resolutely and awaited developments.

The bronzed giant had not long to wait.

Again the red man's voice called down. "I have been in radio communication with John Carter. He knows of no jed or jeddak named Ramdar."

"He will know of me when I explain myself. But not before. Tell John Carter I seek to parley with him."

There followed another silence, after which the voice called down, "John Carter has given us leave to take you on board and bring you to Helium, which is his seat of power. He offers safe passage."

"Ramdar declines your invitation. I will not abandon my followers."

"They are not welcome in Helium. Nor are you, if that is your attitude. Prepare to meet your doom."

Suddenly, the near rails were lined with riflemen. They wore simple headdresses decorated with upright feathers. Most spotted single plumes, and a few had two. Evidently, these were indications of their rank.

Without further preamble, muzzle detonations commenced.

Tarzan was not caught off guard. He took up his spear and impaled one of the riflemen before he could get off a shot. Groaning horribly, the man twisted, grasping at the shaft that had transfixed his chest. He fell across the rail and down to his doom.

Two screaming apes fell upon him and tore the unfortunate one limb from limb, then hurled his arms and legs up at the circling ships, where they created more consternation than actual damage.

Tarzan took up the winglike bow, set an arrow in place, and fired upward. The strength of his pull was tremendous. The metal-tipped arrow pierced the keel-plates of the ship and emerged from the deck flooring to the astonishment of all aboard. A second arrow struck the stern, sticking there. The whirring propeller blades froze, blocked by the unbending shaft.

As that ship spiraled out of control, the jungle lord repeated his feat, driving another shaft into another ship.

Behind him, Cosooma also unleashed arrows, red man after red man succumbed to her unerring marksmanship. She seemed not to miss once.

It did not take long for the three ships' captains to realize that they were facing unexpectedly effective opposition.

One vessel went to the rescue of the foundering ship, and took aboard every aerial sailor, living or dead. The other dropped into position for a second fusillade.

Another volley of rifle shots rang out. And when they struck victims, these unfortunates lost limbs when the volatile bullets found their marks.

Dag Dolor shouted above the fray.

"Ramdar, we cannot long withstand radium bullets!"

Tarzan paid him no heed. Racing to the fallen red Martian, he set one foot upon the dead man's back and hauled out his spear, which had survived the fall intact. Stepping clear, he pulled back and sent it whistling skyward once more.

Flying true, it caused terrific damage, piercing another hull. There it hung, dangling but unbroken.

With a carefully calculated leap, Tarzan bolted into the sky, gaining the rail of that wounded vessel. Going among the surprised sailors, he laid them low with bronzed fists that struck flesh and bone like blocks of steel.

The ape-man had no wish to kill anyone unnecessarily. But he would not stand to see his followers blown to smithereens by devastating bullets.

Irresistible fingers seized rifles and pistols, flinging them overboard. He knocked two heads together, stunning the owners, whose senses swam until they collapsed.

Turning to the uniformed captain, Tarzan said, "Tell John Carter that Ramdar is coming to treat with him. Ramdar comes in peace. But he is prepared for war. Tell him this!"

So saying, Tarzan of the Apes sprang for the rail, dropping to the ground, pulling free his jutting spear on the way downward, and landing lightly.

Staggered and disorganized, the two surviving ships broke off and sailed to the southwest.

The Tarmanbolgani and the Hortamangani alike shook their weapons at the sterns of their vanquished enemy, whose propellers beat steadily. One skipped in its rotation, showing that it was crippled.

"The red men flee!" shouted Dag Dolor. "Ramdar has defeated them! Their rifles and pistols are nothing against the might of Ramdar, jeddak of the combined horde."

Satisfied, they fell to tending their wounded, burying their dead and comforting the shes and balus.

Tarzan walked among the fallen and saw that some had died. The shes and the children had been spared, however. None were harmed.

DAWN BROKE more slowly than usual, owing to the high basalt ramparts of the crater rim. The first light peeped over its serrated walls and brought vivid color to the jungle surroundings.

"Attend the words of Ramdar!" he announced. "We will follow those ships to the southwest. They will take us to the city of the red men."

Foad the young white ape spoke up. "Where red men live, there are rifles and pistols. How can we overcome them?"

"Leave that to Ramdar. I will find a way. Now gather together, and we will begin. We will march for Uxfar and not stop until we reach its gates."

There was not a great deal of enthusiasm for that order. Where previously the great white gorillas were eager to sack the city, having tasted its military might, they were now discouraged and disconsolate.

Tarzan gave them time to gather themselves up and face the prospect of another march. The fact that they despised the jungle made the choice easier, but no more appealing.

Escorting Cosooma, Tarzan went to Dag Dolor and said, "I found this Orovar woman living alone in the jungle. She will come with us. She is an expert archer, and I have extended to her my protection."

The young warrior regarded the ethereal woman. "The white woman is your business. But be careful that the apes do not decide to eat her."

The Hortamangani were getting the war chariot of Churvash Ul oriented toward the northern pass through which they had first entered the ledge-bound jungle. The zitidar was hitched into place, and once this was done to Tarzan's satisfaction, he said to Cosooma, "You will ride in the chariot. I will ride beside you upon that white thoat."

Cosooma nodded. "It is good that we brought extra arrows. The chariot can carry them for us."

Stepping onto the chariot bed, which was piled high with foraged fruit, nuts, and berries, she went up on the forward platform, positioning herself so that she could see the way ahead.

"I am eager to look upon the dead sea bottoms again, which I have not beheld since I was a child so long ago, and to enter the city of the red men, hostile as they are. Ramdar, what do you intend to do in Uxfar?"

Now astride the elephantine white thoat, Tarzan turned his noble face to her and said, "The business of Ramdar in Uxfar is for the ruler of Uxfar and no one else."

"If you intend conquest, your legion is too modest."

"Do not concern yourself with the numbers of my followers."

Somewhat haughtily, she retorted, "Then I will not. But it may be that as we march across the dry seabed, our numbers will grow."

"That has been true so far," returned Tarzan. "No doubt it will be true in the future."

As they pushed out of the crater, they came upon a red man who had landed relatively unharmed in a thorny thicket from which he was unable to escape. He was young and appeared sound of limb. His headdress had come off his head and fallen near him.

RUSHING UP to him, Jamo Ptannus reached down and seized him by his black hair, then lay his sharp sword-edge across the pulsing and exposed throat.

"Do you wish me to slay this one, O Ramdar?"

Tarzan asked, "How many feathers does he wear?"

The green warrior spied the fallen headdress.

"Three, O Ramdar. He is an officer."

"Place him in the chariot. Ramdar wishes to learn everything about the red men of Uxfar that he knows."

Looking disappointed, Jamo Ptannus sheathed his sword and took hold of the man by all of his limbs, yanking him forcibly from the imprisoning thorns, then carrying him over to the rolling chariot and throwing him into the back without ceremony or apology.

"Another one for the apes to devour if they become unruly," he grunted.

Hearing this, the unfortunate Gamangani took on an uneasy expression.

"If you do not try to escape," Tarzan told him, "you will not be eaten. Do you understand my words?"

Instead of replying directly, the red man asked, "Are you an Orovaran?"

Pointing to Cosooma standing at the head of the chariot. Tarzan said, "She is an Orovar woman. As for me, I am Ramdar, jeddak of all whom you see around you."

"There has never been a jeddak of such a composite horde."

"Perhaps not upon Barsoom," allowed Tarzan unconcernedly. "But now that I dwell on this world, this has changed for all time."

"You sound like John Carter," mused the Martian. "He, too, united warriors who were previously enemies. The green Tharks follow him, as do my people. But he would never consort with the savage great white apes."

Tarzan said, "There John Carter and I part company. For I was raised up from infancy by apes and learned their language before any other tongue."

At these words, the Gamangani stared at Tarzan in baffled silence. He was still silently staring when the horde flowed out of the meteorite crater and back onto the sea bed surrounding the only jungle dying Mars supported in the present era.

Chapter 31

The Swelling Horde

THE FIRST day of the march to the city of Uxfar was tolerable.

Having left the oppressive heat and humidity of the jungle behind them, the great white gorillas and the green men alike reveled in traversing the dead sea bottoms, which was vastly more to their liking. At least, the olive-skinned Hortamangani preferred it to jungle dwelling. The pale Tarmanbolgani still yearned for a hospitable ruin, but kept their low aspirations to themselves.

During the encampment, they had foraged for fruit and nuts and filled the great chariot with piles of these. It was not meat, but it was sustenance. The green nomads declared that meat was scarce in the jungle, a fact that accounted for their hollow features and gaunt aspect.

Only Cosooma did not complain. Not being an eater of meat, she was content with her lot.

Often during the first day of the southward march, her uncanny eyes went to the commanding figure of Ramdar. Tarzan paid her only the most perfunctory attention. As he rode along on his powerful white thoat, he questioned the red prisoner at length.

"What is your name?" he asked the Gamangani captive.

"I will only say that I am a dwar. No more than that will you extract from me."

Tarzan grunted, "Ramdar was briefly a jedwar. I do not know this word, dwar. Explain yourself."

"How can you be a military man and not know the rank of dwar?"

"In my tribe, we had no rankings other than chief and warrior. I await your answer."

"The leader of one thousand men is called a teedwar. A dwar is one rank beneath him."

Tarzan nodded. It seemed that this man's rank was subordinate to a major, so he must be a captain. Such a man would possess knowledge. The ape-man attempted to mine his brain.

"How far do your sky ships travel?"

The dwar declined to answer.

"Can they reach either moon?"

Silence was all that came back.

"Tell me of John Carter, of whom I have heard," pressed Tarzan.

"There is scarcely a man on Barsoom who does not know of John Carter," returned the red man sharply. "I am beginning to believe that you were indeed raised by apes such as these rabble."

"Those who raised me were not apes such as you see here," said Tarzan calmly. "The Mangani boast only two arms and are dark and shaggy, while the largest of them are not much larger than I stand."

"No such apes exist upon this world."

"I did not say that I was a raised on this world," Tarzan replied calmly.

Foad pulled back into view. Alone among the Tarmanbolgani, he rode a thoat. He did not ride him well, for he did not know how to communicate with his steed telepathically. But the thoat rode with the others of its breed and did not object to the great white gorilla astride it after it had sized the ten-legged beast in its four great arms and thrown him to the ground repeatedly, finally convincing him that resistance was pointless.

Having carried green warriors in the past, the creature bore Foad's tremendous weight without complaint.

The young white gorilla cast his simian gaze upon the Gamangani captive. "I hunger for fresh meat."

Answering in his own language, Tarzan told him, "This man is a valuable prisoner; he will not be eaten. That is my final word."

"And the white woman?"

"She is under the protection of Ramdar. There is no more to be said."

Foad pulled ahead, and the Gamangani regarded Tarzan in abject wonder.

"It sounded as if the two of you were conversing, except that you were not using words but only barks and grunts and other rude sounds."

"I speak the language of the great white apes, which is not like that of the great apes who raised me, but sufficiently similar that I mastered it through practice."

"I do not know whether to believe you or not," confessed the red man.

"Ramdar does not lie."

The stoic Martian's curiosity could not be restrained. "What were you discussing?"

"We were discussing what to do when the fruit runs out. The apes prefer flesh, and I have forbidden them to eat any of my green followers. Your name came up in that regard."

"You would not allow them to eat me, surely."

"Ramdar told Foad that the white woman was under my protection and must not be consumed."

Suppressing a smile, Tarzan said no more. He had not lied, but if the man jumped to an erroneous conclusion, perhaps that would be to the ape-man's advantage.

AS THEY rolled along, Tarzan permitted more than an hour to pass. Then he renewed his line of inquiry.

"Why were your ships in this desolate region?"

"We are scouts. This area is for the greater part unexplored. A decision was made in Helium to map it closely."

"There is more to it than that," suggested Tarzan.

"If this were so," the copper-skinned man allowed, "I would not be permitted to divulge it to an uncouth barbarian such as yourself."

The prisoner fell silent. Tarzan let him be. The soldier did not appear to be lying. Yet he was evasive.

The jungle lord considered all that he had heard. The sky ship had retreated to the southwest. This suggested that the scout ship had come from the city of Uxfar to investigate him. Now Uxfar would know that he was marching toward it. So be it.

Kudu was climbing to the meridian-marking noon, burning like a reddish lantern.

From time to time, the Tarmanbolgani and Hortamangani bulls went to the back of the rolling chariot, and snatched up fruit and nuts to eat and for dispersal among the shes and balus. Whenever the white gorillas did so, they examined the red captive with undisguised interest.

This had an expected effect.

"Am I permitted to eat of this fruit?" asked the prisoner.

Tarzan nodded. "You may eat. But bear this in mind: the sooner these provisions are gone, the sooner my followers will demand meat."

The Gamangani didn't need to hear any more. He ignored the food piled around him and sat in silence, the expression on his copper face unhappy in the extreme.

Tarzan decided to leave the man to his own thoughts.

Turning his attention to Cosooma at the head of the chariot, he asked, "Ramdar has been turning over in his mind the manner in which the green men were reduced to skeletons that had been riddled with pinholes, their moldering bones arranged in disturbing patterns."

Cosooma laughed lightly. "I wondered when you would raise that subject again. It puzzles you, does it not?"

"The disposition of the bones could only have been accomplished by creatures with an intelligent brain and the hands to accomplish their will."

Again, she laughed.

"Will you be satisfied if I tell you half of the story?"

"No," said Tarzan. "But it would be a beginning."

"After the ghoor has squatted upon a corpse-victim, crushing it down with its great weight and dissolving its muscles and other soft tissues, it moves on, leaving the fleshless bones to lie in the sun. There are worms living in the soil, and these will overrun any creature that has died. Emerging from below, they bore through the bones, devour the marrow and disappear back into the soil. They have nothing to do with the rearranging of the bones, except that they eat any connective tissues left behind so that the bones separate after they have concluded their meal."

"Something else rearranged the bones?" suggested Tarzan.

Cosooma's musical laugh returned. "Yes, something else. Something very mysterious."

"I smelled no people dwelling in the forest," said Tarzan. "Nor did I encounter any natives."

"If another race lived in the forest, would you recognize them by their smell?"

The ape-man had to admit that he would not.

"You have made my point for me," smiled Cosooma.

Unable to get anywhere with the woman, Tarzan abandoned the subject.

The conversational silence that followed lasted over an hour. No doubt it was the silence and being a prisoner of such a heterogeneous horde that preyed upon the red Martian's mind. Try as he might to avoid the impulse, he felt himself compelled to initiate conversation.

"Do you intend to sack Uxfar? If so, be advised that your warriors are too few in number."

Cosooma laughed, but did not comment.

Tarzan spoke firmly. "Ramdar intends to treat with John Carter, nothing more."

"You have made war upon John Carter's navy. How can you expect him to welcome you and your unsavory legion?"

Tarzan looked unconcerned. "We will see when we reach the gates of Uxfar."

"You speak with great confidence."

"In my land, I was called Lord of the Jungle."

"And now you ride a ferocious white thoat. A beast reserved for only green jeddaks. You are unlike any man I have ever heard of, save one. With your bronzed skin and your strange ways I would question whether you were indeed born of Barsoom."

"Who is the one you allude to?"

"Warlord John Carter of Helium."

"Is Helium near Uxfar?"

It was now the red prisoner's turn to laugh. That was his only response. Tarzan did not understand why he thought the question humorous.

By the shank of the afternoon, the prisoner's belly would not quit complaining. Without a word, but with careful glances over the high sides of the chariot, he began helping himself to the sompus fruit and a few nuts.

"Our supplies dwindle by the hour," commented Tarzan. His meaning was clear. Still, hunger is a powerful motivator. The prisoner ate his fill, leaving the fate of the meat upon his bones to the next day or possibly the one after that.

They made camp that night and slept upon the moss. Those among the Hortamangani warriors who owned cloaks threw these upon the lichen and slumbered atop the silken garments. The apes sprawled where they would, making uncouth noises in sleep. The prisoner made no move to escape, for Tarzan had wrapped a rope around his throat, and fixed the other end to the chariot rail.

While all slept, the bronzed giant reconnoitered the vicinity.

Taking great leaps, he bounded from here to there, across the nearly featureless sea of moss.

Happening upon a prowling banth, Tarzan crept on his belly and fell upon the unsuspecting beast with savage suddenness. With his Martian knife, he slew it with two quick strokes that pierced its heart and opened up the throat. The banth never made a sound. It knew not what felled it.

Wiping the gleaming blade upon the yellowish hide, he returned it to its sheath and then lifted the beast with only a little effort.

The awkward size of the ten-legged creature made it difficult to convey back to camp. Several times Tarzan had to set it down before hoisting up the carcass again and carrying it to the chariot. Once, he flung it ahead of him like a stupendous rag doll, breaking its neck in the process, and leaping after it.

He landed more heavily than normal near the back of the chariot, and dropped the dead animal to the mossy carpet.

Only the prisoner woke up, no doubt because he understandably slept lightly. He saw the bronze man he knew as Ramdar depositing a full-grown banth scarcely four yards distant.

Sitting up, he blinked his eyes rapidly, as if rejecting the sight.

"A banth! How did you slay it?"

Tarzan patted the sheathed knife at his hip.

The prisoner grunted. "To kill a banth with a long-sword would be a feat worthy of John Carter. Yet you used only a knife? How can this be?"

"For Ramdar, this is how he obtains fresh meat. I will butcher this animal in the morning. You have won a reprieve, at least until this carcass is exhausted."

"I confess that I am relieved," admitted the warrior. "But more than being relieved, I am astonished. How did you bear that beast single-handed?"

"It was difficult," confessed Tarzan. "But it was accomplished."

The red Martian stared at the bronzed white man and noticed that the breechclout that he wore around his loins was banth hide. He had noted this before but had not considered it significant. Now he believed it to be very significant.

"You have conquered banths before?"

"Only five or six."

"Whether to believe you or otherwise," admitted the red prisoner, "is a question I ask myself often."

Reaching into the chariot's open back, Tarzan found the banth skin that he used for sleeping, and picked it up.

"This is the skin of the first banth I slew."

After that had sunk into his brain, the red Martian said sincerely, "I now believe that John Carter would be very interested in treating with you. But your numbers are too modest to sue for entry into Uxfar. We will all be slain before we reach its gates. Of that I am certain."

ON THE morn, the campground awoke to the sound of Tarzan butchering the banth. Great enthusiasm came from the gathering horde. To enjoy their first meal of meat since leaving the forest of Desh made every simian mouth slaver.

Knowing that the green nomads had eaten little meat during their jungle exploration, and seeking to instill in the four-armed creatures an impulse toward gratitude, the ape-man fed them first.

No gratitude was expressed, but Jamo Ptannus grunted, "We have never before eaten banth meat."

"It is scarce," agreed Tarzan.

"No green man known to me has ever vanquished one—although many have tried," the other said, chewing the raw meat methodically.

This the bronzed giant took as an expression of admiration, which he decided was more important than gratitude.

As the horde noisily broke its fast, Tarzan issued commands.

"Once our bellies are full, we will move on."

Jamo Ptannus asked, "How many haads to Uxfar?"

Tarzan glanced toward his prisoner for an answer to that question. But the red man firmed up his lips and looked away.

At that, Dag Dolor marched over and pointed his sword at the man's throat. He pressed it slowly into the Adam's apple.

"Ramdar demands an answer, calot!"

"It is too far, and your numbers are too few."

Sitting nearby, Cosooma laughed.

Soon, the horde was again on the march. The red warrior saw that the group was extremely well organized, although they kept apart from one another. Sight of such an organized horde made his scalp creep and the coppery skin of his bare arms prickle.

THE DAY was not far along when seven sky ships hove into view.

Seeing this, the red man broke out in a pleased grin. No doubt he anticipated an early rescue.

"Each ship has a complement of thirty men," he informed Tarzan. "You are far outnumbered. Surrender is your only sensible option."

Dismounting his white thoat, Tarzan did not reply. He was scanning the approaching ships.

They drew closer, dropping lower with each passing mile. It appeared that the horde of Ramdar would shortly be overwhelmed by air.

Unexpectedly, however, the ships turned around, breaking for the west.

The red Martian's expectant expression collapsed.

"I do not understand this behavior! They had the advantage. Now they flee."

Cosooma said gravely, "The copper men saw that they were outnumbered."

Both Tarzan and the red prisoner looked to the woman as if she had gone mad.

Then laughing, Cosooma half-turned and pointed behind her.

Striding in a majestic procession across the dead sea bottom was a mighty army of combined red, green and yellow men and great white gorillas. Most were afoot. But there were many splendidly caparisoned warriors mounted on thoats of appropriate sizes. Gleaming chariots led the formidable array.

The red warrior looked at this impressive phalanx with disbelieving eyes. Even Tarzan's expression registered uncharacteristic astonishment.

The trailing army had produced no sound, raised no dust yet looked as real as any armed force that had ever marched into battle.

Tarzan glanced toward Cosooma. "Your doing?"

Smiling mischievously, Cosooma raised one hand and snapped her fingers.

Instantly, the martial array disappeared from view. No trace of it remained.

So quickly did this seeming miracle transpire that the Hortamangani and the Tarmanbolgani leading the way failed to notice that for a brief period of time their numbers had swelled into an overwhelming force that would intimidate any city standing on the face of Barsoom.

The red Martian remarked, "An army with no substance may intimidate air scouts, but you cannot penetrate the city gates with phantoms, no matter how impressively arrayed."

Cosooma smiled, her opalescent eyes twinkling.

"What I can make visible with my thoughts," she said confidently, "I may make palpable as skeel with practice. By the time we reach Uxfar, you will hear the thunder of the legion of Ramdar and Cosooma."

The red Martian looked to Tarzan. In a sincere voice, he said, "I surrender my former skepticism. If you make it to Uxfar, you may well penetrate the gates of the city. Beyond that, however, I would not venture a guess as to your ultimate fate, for no mercy will be shown to you."

"Ramdar only wishes to return to his home jungle. Only that and nothing more. But no man or beast will stand in his way until he does so."

Chapter 32

John Carter's Account Commences

MY NAME is John Carter, formerly Captain Jack Carter of the Confederate Army. That much of my earthly life I do remember. My childhood I can no longer recall. I assume that I had one, yet when I search backward in my memory, I have always been about thirty years in age. I cannot account for this. But there the matter stands. A man's memory is his only certain record of his past existence and mine is faulty in that respect.

As for my present existence, it is as far removed from that of Captain Carter as the life of an Arctic polar bear is removed from that of an Australian kangaroo. So many ords have passed that I no longer think of my natal planet as the Earth, but as Jasoom, inasmuch as I have abandoned speaking English.

In my last earthly incarnation, I was a proud son of Virginia. I cannot say to you that I was Virginia born, for I recall nothing of my earliest existence. After the Civil War, which concluded so regrettably for my side, I could not bear to return to a fallen Richmond and so became a penniless wanderer, an exile from my beloved Virginia, which would never again be the same sweet place.

For some years, I was content with the life of a footloose soldier of fortune. It was in Arizona while prospecting for gold in an effort to reclaim my lost wealth that I seemingly expired while under siege from a band of murderous Apaches. That they never took my scalp I cannot explain either. But I passed from the Earth in some manner equally inexplicable.

How I came to dwell on Barsoom baffles me to this day. It would seem that I died, but instead of going on to my reward, whatever that might have entailed, I was transported to the Red Planet, where I progressed from naked stranger to once again becoming a rootless soldier of fortune, or panthan. This journey culminated in my achieving the rank of Prince of the House of Tardos Mors, and Warlord of Mars. It was a long and arduous march, but at the end of it my ultimate reward was to unite the red and some green men of this planet in peace and to wed the incomparable Dejah Thoris, by whom I had two splendid children, Carthoris and Tara.

Here in the Twin Cities of Helium, I rule with my consort, with my children at my side. And here I begin my tale....

A period of peace had fallen over the Heliumetic Empire. With no wars or conflicts in the offing, I instructed Kantos Kan, Overlord of the Heliumetic Navy, to undertake mapping the vast unexplored territory that lay below the equator between Korad and Bantoom and extending south into the dead Sea of Tjanath and nearly to the green capital city of Warhoon. Little is known of this tract of desolation. It had never been mapped. Much of it was the mosslike vegetation such as covered the other dried sea bottoms. Green nomads were presumed to roam it, as did the great white apes, both of whom had been spied from the air. Ruined cities left over from the epoch of the nearly extinct Orovars dotted the landscape. That much was known, but little more.

Therefore, I decided that this largest unexplored territory of Barsoom deserved a better understanding.

This project proceeded without immediate incident. Then aerial scouts sent from the red city of Uxfar reported to their jeddak, Sud Sorovon, a strange encounter with a small horde that was a mixture of green nomads and great white apes. Nothing like this had ever been reported in the history of Barsoom as it survives to this era. As ferocious as the warlike green men were, the great white apes were far more savage, brutes without an understandable language, boasting only stone clubs for weapons. Since time immemorial, they were mortal enemies of the red men, having nothing to do with one another except during their perpetual but intermittent warfare.

Kantos Kan came to me with the first report.

"Kaor, John Carter. This motley band appears to be marching out of a forest unknown to our cartographers."

"It staggers the imagination that two savage and perpetually hostile nomadic tribes would join forces."

"There is more to it than that. They appear to be led by a man. He is not white, nor yellow nor black. The hue of his skin is bronze."

"Could there be a hitherto unknown race of bronze men inhabiting the unmapped lands of the south?"

Kantos Kan shook his head. "More likely he is an Orovar, some of whom survive from their era. His skin appears white, like yours, and like yours, the Barsoomian sun exerts its bronzing influence."

"The Orovar people were a high race," I reminded him. "It is unlikely that any of them would sink to barbarism, cavorting with apes and green men."

"Unlikely, but perhaps not impossible. This bronze jedwar has beaten off the scout ship, which subsequently crashed in the desert. But not before we received an incomplete radio report. I request permission to investigate further."

"I grant you that permission," I told Kantos Kan, dismissing him.

Less than a week later, he was ushered back into my presence and gave his report.

"The scouting party has located the strange bronze man, John Carter. He is leading his horde in the direction of Uxfar. We have made contact with him. He claims to be a jeddak calling himself Ramdar, and wishes to treat with you."

"Inform this Ramdar that I offer free passage to Helium if he comes alone and of his own free will."

"I will do as you say."

Kantos Kan was not gone very long. He returned to report that my invitation had been declined.

"A battle has broken out, John Carter. This Ramdar is a bowman of great skill. His arrows have crippled Uxfar ships. But there is more. He is a prodigious leaper. From the ground, he bolted into the sky, landing on the deck of one of our cruisers, laying out the crew with his bronzed fists. His message to you is that he is marching on Uxfar and that he comes in peace, but is prepared for war."

"It is a march of many padans to Uxfar," I told Kantos Kan. "Any danger this Ramdar presents is not immediate. Assemble a squadron of three cruisers. We will go to meet him and take his measure."

"There is more."

"Speak."

"This Ramdar has captured a prisoner. It is Hadron of Hastor."

This unwelcome intelligence took me aback. Tan Hadron of Hastor was one of the finest officers in my service. He fought valiantly by my side on more than one occasion.[*] He was presently on detached duty to the Jeddak of Uxfar, Sud Sorovon, aiding his aerial cartographers.

"We will rescue him, of course. And quickly."

FLYING THE proud colors of Helium, our cruisers lifted off and swung east toward Korad, beyond which lay the last position of the strange horde led by the unknown jeddak, Ramdar.

Buoyed by tanks containing the Eighth Ray, the squadron swept through the thin air with impressive speed, pushed along by steadily whirring stern propellers, and guided by a compass mechanism which regulated their course. The helmsmen needed only to watch for difficulties en route and be prepared to assume control to avoid unforeseen obstacles.

In the lead ship, I stood by the radio receiver attired in my cloak and harness, with my long-sword at my hip. Word reached

---

[*] See A Fighting Man of Mars *by Edgar Rice Burroughs.*

me that the Jeddak of Uxfar had dispatched a portion of his modest fleet. I saw no reason to dissuade him, so I encouraged him in this course of action.

"Sud Sorovon, I bid you to observe this horde and take no action at this time. My ships will presently arrive."

"As you say, John Carter."

The transmission went silent.

As we raced toward the equatorial zone, I considered all that I had heard.

Until my initial adventure upon Barsoom, no red man had ever made peace with the green men of Mars. Now it appeared that another had come along to rival my remarkable accomplishment. It was most passing strange to contemplate. To my mind, the most disturbing portion was the apparent alliance between a nomadic green horde and a tribe of savage apes. Reports had reached me of scattered ape tribes which appeared to be gaining intelligence and were wearing makeshift harnesses of banth hide in emulation of the civilized races they encountered. But none of these reports told of apes speaking an understandable language or carrying weapons any more advanced than stone clubs. That apes and green men could hold congress together baffled me, frankly. I was determined to learn the secret of this bronze jeddak calling himself Ramdar, for it boded ill for the cessation of hostilities that was temporarily the condition of civilized Barsoom.

Soon enough, we were speeding over the expanse of yellowish vegetation that marked so much of Mars's desolate and desiccated surface. Not for the first time, I pondered the days long before this era, when the white-skinned Orovar empire had sailed what are now mere dead depressions, but were once formally surging oceans.

But for the remnants of those lost and evaporated bodies of water, I might never believe such an epoch had existed upon dying Barsoom. But the histories did not lie.

Could this Ramdar be an Orovaran, his skin bronzed by nomadic dwelling? It was the most logical explanation that came to mind. Yet somehow it failed to satisfy me. The man's hair was as black as a red Martian's, not blond or auburn as were pure-blooded Orovarans. There was more to this unpleasant prospect of a dangerous new alliance among barbaric tribes. I had striven mightily in my period on the Red Planet to bring peace to Barsoom. This unexpected alliance offered a fresh threat. Civilizations had risen and fallen upon Mars in the past. I would not permit the Heliumetic Empire to fall to barbarians, not so long as there was life left in me.

As the zodes wore on, I paced the deck, considering the matter from all angles. I concluded that I lacked sufficient intelligence to draw firm conclusions. The nagging feeling that there was more to the rise of Ramdar continued to haunt me. But I could not put my finger on it with any conviction.

Casting my concerns aside, I studied the horizon.

Kantos Kan came up to me, reporting, "John Carter, we have a transmission from the commander in chief of the Uxfar fleet, Vam Dirasun. You must hear this for yourself."

Turning up the radio receiver, I instructed the other party to speak.

"John Carter, I must report to you that I have dispatched the Uxfar fleet, and that it has been forced to turn around."

"Have you been attacked?"

"No. But by some miracle the amalgamated horde has swelled to six times its reported size. It now comprises half of a dar—five hundred strong. I myself just counted twenty-five war chariots, as well as dozens of thoats strong enough to carry green men. Some of these thoats are being ridden by apes!"

"Apes?" I gasped. "Apes do not ride thoats."

"The apes of Ramdar ride thoats. I beheld this with my own eyes."

I asked, "From where do these new recruits hail?"

"I cannot say. The horde is running through an uninhabited basin. It would seem to be impossible that they could acquire these numbers, but they have."

"If you have seen this with your own eyes, I must believe you."

"I have seen this with my own eyes," returned Vam Dirasun, "yet I can scarcely believe the words forming in my mouth. But I swear to you that this is true. Knowing that the smaller horde had driven off three ships, I concluded that this larger horde posed too great a risk to my modest fleet. So I turned around, to await orders from Uxfar."

"What does your jeddak tell you?"

"Sud Sorovon instructed me to take further orders from no less than John Carter, Warlord of Barsoom."

"Very well. Stand off from the horde at a safe distance. I will join you directly."

"There was one more thing, O Prince. I hesitate to say it aloud."

"Hesitate no longer."

"The bronze jeddak named Ramdar rides a white thoat. It is not one of our tame thoats. This wild specimen is large enough to carry a green man."

"You saw this clearly?" I demanded.

"I swear by my first ancestor that my words are unalloyed."

"Once again I am forced to believe you, Vam Dirasun. Await my coming."

Switching off the receiver, I turned to Kantos Kan.

"No red man can ride a royal white thoat reserved for a green jeddak," I imparted.

"No red man," agreed the overlord. "But with your great strength and agility, you could manage it."

"Perhaps. But I would not care to make the attempt. Green men are often brutal in the treatment of their thoats. This makes them tremendously difficult to master. How could this Ramdar accomplish such a physical feat? It defies logic."

"May I suggest that be the first question you ask Ramdar after you capture him?"

"I am anxious to do so. How long until we make contact with the horde?"

"Less than one zode."

"Then this barbarous company should become visible very soon."

WHEN THE size of the army of Ramdar became apparent, it bid fair to take my breath away.

I have seen many strange sights upon the face of Barsoom in my time. The therns of the southern pole. The atmosphere plant that supplies oxygen to this dying planet. The hideous Kaldanes of Bantoom.

Those sights naturally would have startled a man born upon the Earth. To most Barsoomians, however, they would have been only as striking as encountering one of the great white apes. But even a Barsoomian would have dropped his jaw and stuck out his eyes in wonder at the army trooping along the ocherous moss.

It was as Vam Dirasun had reported. Five hundred strong, if not more. This bizarre complement consisted of great white apes and green men marching in unison, divided into two wings, each flank consisting of approximately fifty warriors each. The green men strode on the right while the great white apes marched on the left flank. Straggling behind them were female apes with their children. They appeared to be disciplined and highly organized. Such a thing seemed impossible to one who knew the ways of both races. They lacked a common tongue. So I looked to the individual riding in the lead for my answer to this riddle.

Putting a field glass on him, I saw that he was tall and muscular in comparison to the average red man, thewed like a heroic bronze statue. He wore a cloak of glossy banth hide. An apron of the same material depended from a metallic belt. Yet he wore no harness, no metal, no trappings.

From this strange belt hung a sword in its leather scabbard. I could not see it clearly, but the hilt was strangely fashioned.

It was not the hilt of any sword forged by a red man of any city in my experience.

Athwart his magnificent chest was a bow, and across his back a quiver packed with arrows. Of all the races that ever dwelt upon Barsoom, only the present-day inhabitants of Lothar and the Orovars of old were bowmen, both of which are pale-skinned. Neither the red nor green Martians employed them in war, only for sport.

I studied his face, expecting to see brutality. Instead, I beheld nobility. His wild hair was black like my own, but his eyes showed undeniable intelligence. His features demonstrated a sharp determination mixed with a noble cast. I looked in vain for any scarlet scar that would justify him going by the name of Ramdar. I saw none.

His Herculean physique was startling in its wiry musculature, the exposed skin was the bronze of a white man who had dwelt in the elements for most of his days. Yet I could not tell whether his skin was naturally bronze, or if this was the result of the beating sun.

He rode upon a magnificent white thoat the way a native mahout of India might sit upon an elephant, straddling the withers just behind the elongated head, his naked legs apart. The thoat appeared to be entirely under his control, showing no signs of rebellion.

Passing the glass to Kantos Kan, I asked, "What do you make of him?"

After studying Ramdar for some minutes, he replied, "I make nothing good of him. Any man who can fuse green nomads together with wild apes is a menace to the natural order on Barsoom."

"I cannot disagree with you, Kantos Kan. But I would like to know this man's story. I imagine it to be remarkable."

"If you intend to take him prisoner, you must attack with great speed and dispatch. For if you drop into their midst, you will swiftly be overwhelmed."

I considered the fellow's words for some minutes, and then made my decision.

"Order on my behalf the fleet of Uxfar to withdraw to a safe distance. Circle our ships around the horde, also at a safe distance. We will inveigle them into thinking that we do not intend to attack."

"It will be done as you say."

"When I feel the time is right," I added, "I will introduce myself to Ramdar."

Kantos Kan smiled tightly. "I do not doubt, John Carter, that it will be a memorable introduction, one this war chieftain without harness will never forget."

I studied the troubling horde again before replying.

"I suspect that neither of us will soon forget what is about to transpire."

Turning on his heel, Kantos Kan gave the order to his helmsman and the lead cruiser swung about, the others trailing in its wake.

The sun was a few zodes yet from setting. I knew that I must make my move before darkness fell, for while darkness is the friend of surprise, it is the enemy of well-laid plans.

Chapter 33

Face to Face

I ALLOWED a full zode to pass before I gave my instructions to Kantos Kan.

It lacked another zode until sunset, which I determined to be sufficient time to accomplish my aims. They were very simple. To parley with Ramdar, and to take him prisoner, if necessary.

But first I must inveigle him into thinking I meant him no harm.

"Swing about slowly, Kantos Kan. Carefully settle ahead of the horde. When we are almost to the ground, I will alight. Then return to the air and await my signal."

This was done. I went to the rail in preparation to step off. I could easily have leapt to the ground from the deck and landed safely. But I feared that such a bold maneuver would be seen as threatening. Before I made any overt move, I wished to take the measure of Ramdar.

The craft settled, its weapons stowed out of sight. When the keel ground into the cushioning moss, I stepped off lightly and strode unafraid toward the advancing horde.

A rumble came from them, voices rising in concern. I could make out no words, but the cacophony was a disturbing mixture of green men cursing and pale apes growling. Despite my steely will, I could feel my skin crawl. I could not shake off the conviction that apes and men should not share common cause. It was against natural law. It was as if a grizzly bear had begun courting a cougar.

My hands open, my sword banging against my side, I advanced unhurriedly. Pragmatically, I had left my radium pistol behind.

Meeting the gaze of Ramdar, I felt something electrical course through me. It was as if I was being regarded by a wild animal, not a man. There was something distinctly feral about the way the fellow's eyes pierced me.

The trooping horde neither sped up nor slowed down in its coordinated cadence. It continued along at its steady and unhurried pace.

Ramdar regarded me with eyes that were entirely without fear. And why should they not be? The man commanded an army of giants. He had nothing to fear from one individual. Or so I imagined he believed.

When I had traversed half the distance between us, I halted. Lifting one hand, I showed that it was empty of arms.

"Kaor!" I greeted him firmly. "Are you the one who calls himself Ramdar?"

"Who are you?"

"I am the one you seek. John Carter, Prince of the House of Tardos Mors, Jeddak of Jeddaks and Warlord of all Barsoom."

Hearing these words, Ramdar slipped from the withers of his thoat and padded forward on bare feet.

I noted the confident swing of his carriage, the apparent strength of his limbs and an uncanny sensation I could not identify. Ramdar was in the shape of a well-proportioned man of indeterminate age, but there was something about him that did not square with outward appearances. Despite his near nakedness, he radiated a subtle but unmistakable sense of primitive majesty.

He strode up to me until we faced one another. Ramdar stood taller than I by the merest margin, and I am six feet, two inches in height. Yet something about his presence made me feel as if I were standing before a much larger man. His animal vitality was a palpable thing, and not merely a feature of his mighty muscles and rolling sinews. His gaze was intelligent, yet somehow also apart from ordinary human emotions. The cast of his sun-darkened features was stern, the gray of his eyes a darker shade than my own. Momentarily, I had the queer feeling of facing someone who might have been an ancestor stepping forth from the forgotten past. I shook off this unaccountable feeling.

My attention went to his garments. They struck me as barbaric. His crude metallic belt displayed the workmanship of the green men, a scavenged armband stripped of all gems and brilliants. His banth-skin apron reminded me of the tales of the great white apes who affected harnesses of similar hides.

Yet Ramdar appeared extremely comfortable in his skin. When my eyes went to the hilt of his sword, I did not recognize its ornate design.

I addressed him formally. "You wear no harness, no metal, nor any insignia of rank, Ramdar. Are you a panthan?"

"I am called by my followers, Ramdar, jeddak of the combined tribes of Narag and Vakanor."

"You mouth that declaration as if you were the Jeddak of all Jeddaks," I responded tersely. For his failure to repeat the universal salutation of Barsoom, "kaor," offended me.

The fellow's bronzed countenance twitched and I sense that he took exception to my hot words, for the words he hurled back at me were hotter still.

"I am also known as Tarzan of the Apes."

"Do you intend to make war on Uxfar, *Tarzan-of-the-apes?*"

"Only if Uxfar does not welcome me. I come in peace."

By this time, the horde had ground to a halt of its own volition. A thousand eyes were staring at me with undisguised malevolence.

"Whether Uxfar personally welcomes you or not, Sud Sorovon will not stand for you bringing a barbarian horde to his gates. Nor will I."

"The horde of Ramdar goes where it will," he returned, folding his muscular arms haughtily.

"Are you called Ramdar or *Tarzan-of-the-apes?* Make up your mind."

"Tarzan is my true name. Ramdar is the name the white apes conferred upon me during my time as jedwar among them."

HIS WORDS were so sincerely expressed, I did not know what to make of them. It was as if he were a caricature of a Martian fighting man, one taught to ape the red men by the tremendous four-armed brutes who befriended him.

The power to read the minds of Martians belongs to me alone of all inhabitants of Barsoom. Yet when I attempted to penetrate to this man's thoughts, I encountered a barrier, or block. I could not peer into his mind or read his brain-waves. Nor did I understand why. Could he be more akin to ape than man? The inchoate thoughts of the great white apes also confounded me.

"Regardless of the status you hold among apes and nomads," I told the stern fellow, "I must insist that you accompany me, if we are to avoid unnecessary bloodshed."

He stood his ground, arms folded resolutely. "I refuse this."

"And I also ask that the red man who is your captive be surrendered to me. Hadron of Hastor is one of my warriors. His safety is my responsibility."

"And if Tarzan refuses?"

"Tarzan should think twice about refusing," I warned.

Our exchange became more heated and from the chariot whose design I did not recognize, a woman's head popped up. She was a fair-skinned beauty, and her marvelously coiffed hair was golden-blonde in color. I confess that she was the most radiant woman I had seen on the face of Barsoom since my first meeting with my beloved Dejah Thoris. There was something about her features that arrested my attention. I could hardly tear my eyes away from her. Her bearing was regal, and for a moment I wondered if she were also a prisoner.

"Is that woman your consort?"

"Cosooma follows Ramdar."

This declaration confused me; did this strange man not know his own name?

"She is an Orovar woman," I declared. "But you do not appear to be an Orovar, despite your bronzed skin. Nor is the cast of your features consonant with the white men of Lothar."

"I am Tarzan, Lord of the Jungle. I have questions for John Carter."

I smiled thinly. "John Carter has questions for you. If you will accompany me to my cruiser, I will convey you to Uxfar, where we will discuss your concerns. But your horde must remain behind until our business is concluded."

"Tarzan is interested in this discussion. But I will not abandon my horde. The questions I have for you must be answered here and now."

There was something about the man's manner that was fast getting under my skin. He was dressed in the most barbaric fashion, yet he carried himself as if he were supreme among jeddaks. This offended me to the depths of my soul.

"And the business that I have with you cannot be conducted out in the open," I returned stiffly. "You must come with me, Ramdar. I guarantee you safe conduct as long as you surrender your blade and promise to take no violent action against my forces or myself."

The sounds of our loud voices clashing must have reached the ears of the halted horde. From one of the leading great apes came an impatient progression of growls and barks.

Turning his head, Ramdar responded in kind. The syllables emerging from his mouth were not couched in any language I could imagine. They were the utterances of a wild animal.

The great white ape subsided, settling back onto his four lower limbs, wrinkling his snout in disgust.

"You speak the tongue of the great white apes?" I inquired.

"Apes raised me," he said flatly.

"Remarkable. The great white apes reared you to manhood?"

"Not these Tarmanbolgani. Other apes. Now I grow impatient."

In that moment I saw the long scar upon his forehead spring to life, like a smoldering fork of lightning. This was my chief warning that the impatient warrior was becoming agitated.

Thinking that he was on the verge of growing violent, my hand drifted to the hilt of my blade by instinct. I did not mean to draw it, only to prepare for the possibility.

Before I could withdraw my hand, Ramdar's fingers sought the hilt of his blade and it whisked from its leather, flying into view. To my surprise, it was not his long-sword, but a mere knife. Yet the blue blade was long and finely wrought, perhaps half the length of a short-sword.

No longer having a choice in the matter, I drew my own steel. And there we stood, just feet apart, blades poised in the air.

"I do not intend for a duel, Ramdar," I assured him.

"Then you should not have seized your weapon."

"It is not proper for a warrior to fight another with a superior weapon. I must refuse. Or you must draw your long-sword."

"Fear not, John Carter. My knife will be sufficient against your sword."

He advanced two paces, weapon poised for a disemboweling stroke.

"Very well," I said, resigning myself to the inevitable. "If we must fight, kindly permit me to sheathe my sword and draw my dagger instead."

"Tarzan does not wish to fight you. I only seek—"

But it was too late. I consider myself the greatest living swordsman upon Barsoom and at the sight of the threatening blade lifted before me, I could not do otherwise but defend myself. Perhaps a small part of my thinking was I did not recognize the bluish metal from which Ramdar's peculiar weapon was forged. I was interested in seeing how well his steel would stand up to mine.

I was not long in learning this unhappy fact.

I lunged, driving my blade before me, confident in my prowess. My aim was simply to disarm him, then appeal to his more rational side, assuming this vandal possessed any such.

I quickly learned that my martial skills were meaningless.

Our blades made brief, rasping contact, sparked off one another, and with a growl, Ramdar swept his knife around, and with a resounding clang, broke off my blade at the guard with a single blow that staggered me.

It was an unbelievable sight. His speed was demonic in its ferocity. In that moment, I could not tell if it was the might of his right arm or the strength of his blade that rendered my weapon useless. I barely registered the sound of my steel falling to the ground, unbloodied.

Staring at the blunted hilt, I realized the shocking truth. Throwing away the maimed weapon, I took a step backward.

"You are strong," I told him.

"I am Tarzan," he rejoined, as if that explained all.

I had not brought my pistol, nor would I have turned it against a swordsman. Such would have been against my honor, and the common military etiquette of Barsoom.

The point of his blade whipped up to rest beneath my chin.

With that gesture, no doubt this fellow thought he had an advantage over me. He did not know my strength, nor the power of my muscles in the Martian atmosphere.

Endeavoring once again to lull him into a false sense of confidence, I remarked, "It's a pity you broke my blade. I would like to see what manner of swordsman you truly are."

Instead of responding, Ramdar asked, "The ships you fly. Do any of them leave the atmosphere?"

"Why do you ask?"

"Answer at once!" And the point of his curious blade pressed deeper into my larynx.

I made my move then. With the palm of my hand, I struck the flat of his knife. To my astonishment, the weapon did not go flying. True, it shifted several inches, but it did not leave his grasp. The bronzed arm held firm, as if it were truly forged of the metal it so closely resembled.

Abruptly, he dropped his blade, took hold of my harness and then shook me the way a terrier shakes a rat.

It pains me to write these words. But his might was not the might of a normal Barsoomian, nor that of any Earth man. It was the unbridled strength of an animal. It surpassed my own, which is paramount among men on this warring world. Momentarily, I was helpless in his fierce clutch. In a flash of a moment, I believed that Ramdar was in truth raised by apes. But I could not understand how they conferred their titanic strength into his comparatively puny physique.

I tore myself loose from his grasp with an effort, losing a portion of my harness as I did so. This angered me. This much-scarred barbarian was manhandling the Warlord of Mars as if he were a mere panthan.

Making a fist, I drove it in the direction of his chin. My knuckles made contact, rocking his head back. But then a bronze fist connected with my forehead, and I found myself tumbling through the air like an acrobat who had lost control of his performance, to land in a stretch of moss that was made the worse for my scraping along it.

Growling in the most ferocious manner, he charged after me.

"You are no Orovar!" I told him. "You are not a man. You are a beast!"

I decided to take the advantage. I leaped into the air, thinking to impress him, and perhaps to knock sense into him.

My leap took me twenty feet upward, but Ramdar followed me, arcing over my head, grabbing my hair on the way down and pulling me back to the ground.

It was a staggering feat of agility. I felt as though I had fallen into the hands of one of the great white apes, who could use and abuse me at their will, owing to their titanic size and overwhelming muscular strength.

Yet this Ramdar was no more robust than I!

I slammed back into the ground, this beast-man landing astride me, perfectly upright on his unshod feet.

A naked foot pressed down upon my breast bone, holding me to the ground. It seemed to be an ordinary foot, but when Ramdar exerted pressure, I could feel my rib cage crackle and the breath squeeze out of my lungs.

"Whence do you hail?" I gasped.

If he heard me, he did not deign to reply. The burning scar on his brow was alive now as his eyes blazed down upon me. He no longer resembled a semi-civilized man but a savage brute whose bloodlust has been aroused.

Taking hold of his ankle, I attempted to twist his foot off of my pounding heart. And in that, I succeeded only slightly.

"Come!" he snarled. "Answer my question. Do the ships of this planet leave this atmosphere for other worlds?"

"Why do you ask?"

"Answer!"

I do not know what I would have done next, but the unexpected happened.

A fight broke out among the horde.

Ramdar's head swiveled around, momentarily distracted.

IN THAT moment, I gathered up all of my strength, and launched myself off the soft moss.

Together, we shot into the thin atmosphere of Barsoom. I did not have the strength nor the leverage to push us very far into the atmosphere, but it was sufficient to disentangle myself from this powerful barbarian.

Being more prepared, I landed first, and then sprang to one side. In doing so, I spied the cause of the commotion.

It was Hadron of Hastor. He had turned upon one of his captors and relieved him of his short-sword. Unfortunately, the weapon had belonged to a green man and required the brave padwar to employ both hands to wield it.

This he managed to do with some success, lopping the hand off the wrist of the enraged green man who was attempting to recapture him. That worthy backed away, his wrist-stump spurting blood.

Wielding the sword again, Tan Hadron used it to smash his fetters, and broke free of the confines of the chariot, where he had been lying out of sight.

"John Carter," he called. "Take this!"

He attempted to throw the sword, but it was too heavy to go far. Nevertheless I leaped forward, and in two bounds, captured it. It was not a very wieldy weapon, but my terrific strength permitted me to manage it. Taking it in both hands, I jumped back into the fray.

One jump, two jumps and then three, I cleared the horde, which was now milling about, attempting to flow in my direction.

Landing well ahead of them, I faced Ramdar, who rushed in to meet me.

There I stood my ground, and took up the ponderous short-sword in both hands. To someone of my size, it was more like wielding an axe than a sword. But I reasoned it was sufficient to meet the coming charge.

For in racing to meet me, Ramdar ignored his fallen knife. From its scabbard whisked his long-sword. Once again, our weapons were not equal, but I reasoned that I was battling a foe who, in his ignorance of civilized customs, had forced my hand. Therefore, I felt no dishonor.

When we collided, our blades clashed and smashed against each other, striking sparks, ringing, but not bending.

My opponent was a fair swordsman. It was clear to me that he had some training in the past, despite his barbaric trappings. But he did not possess my skill. But neither did I wield a blade consummate with my martial training.

And so we stood there, hacking and slashing, stamping our feet in half circles, beating at each other's steel, attempting to win out, but succeeding only in making an infernal racket that was matched by the shouting and hooting of the watching horde.

I will admit that I held my ground against Ramdar's superior steel and strength, but only due to my determination and greater skill. My broad blade was more than strong enough to stand up to his strange weapon, whose constitution I began to suspect was not common steel.

Minutes passed. Neither one of us gained ground, although we gave the effort all of our might and main.

I could see the red scar on Ramdar's brow burning more brightly with each passing moment. And a strange respect for him grew in my breast. I did not know what manner of man he was, but Ramdar was both determined and fearless. Moreover, his fighting heart reminded me more of a wild animal than a human being.

On this world, the green men are considered the most ferocious fighters of all. Ramdar put them all to shame with the sheer ferocity of his fighting skills. That they were not as polished as mine was entirely beside the point. Blow after blow we traded, yet neither one of us yielded.

I do not know how long we contended. It felt like the beginning of an eternity. I was beginning to tire, yet my savage opponent showed no signs of fatigue. From where could he have obtained his animal strength?

As I struggled to continue to hold my ground, the fight was taken away from me.

The abbreviated twilight of Barsoom commenced without my taking notice, so engrossed in personal combat was I at that moment.

Seeing my growing plight, and realizing that the abrupt curtain of night was soon to fall, Kantos Kan ordered the cruisers to come to my aid.

Dropping from the sky, they skimmed low to the ground. From the rails, sailors commenced firing at the cheering horde with their radium rifles.

Pandemonium was thus created.

Radium bullets detonated, blowing apart apes and green men alike, sending up cascades of severed limbs and spurting fountains of gore.

A careening cruiser swept in at almost ground level, and a grappling hook and line was lowered. Tan Hadron seized the hook and affixed it to his harness. By this means, the crew attempted to haul him aboard. As he was in the act of being pulled by his harness onto one deck, a green man charged in and executed a mad upward lunge, severing the cable. Tan Hadron fell back onto the mossy carpet, whereupon the cruiser was forced to seek loftier skies, gun crew firing from the stern.

Seeing his horde come apart in pandemonium and confusion, Ramdar made a sound that I could only describe as animal-like, and he smashed aside the great blade in my hands, tearing the hilt from my two-handed grasp in such a way as to numb my fingers and make it impossible for me to recover the weapon, much less wield it to advantage.

Recognizing the hopelessness of my situation and knowing that I could get nowhere with my ferocious opponent, I executed a mighty leap and cleared Ramdar's head, landing fifty feet behind him, then bolting into the sky once more in the direction of the cruiser manned by Kantos Kan.

I confess I landed there with less grace than was normally my wont. But I was off-balance, my fingers numb, and I had been through an ordeal the like of which I had never experienced previous to this encounter.

Two warriors rushed to help me to my feet, but I shook them off.

"Your orders, John Carter?" asked Kantos Kan.

The blackest night I could ever imagine clamped down at that rueful moment. And I knew that no force at my disposal could give succor to Tan Hadron.

"Order the ships to withdraw to a safe distance," I said tersely. "We have lost the initiative. Now we must contemplate new tactics if we are to block the advance of this unnatural horde."

The order was given to cease fire, and the cruisers turned about to rendezvous with the small fleet of Uxfar.

I did not know what I would do next. But I did understand one thing. Ramdar's horde may possess superior might. But I was a military man, one with a sure grasp of strategy and tactics. I was confident that I could win out over this super-barbarian once I applied the disciplined power of my civilized brain.

Chapter 34

Council of War

IT WAS my firm intention to rendezvous with the Uxfar ships and organize another attack. I could not leave Tan Hadron in their rude clutches.

But as our squadron sped through the arid darkness, my cruiser began losing altitude.

The helmsman looked up from his controls and declared, "It is the starboard buoyancy tank."

Taking hold of a deck rope, I affixed one end to a stout iron ring on my harness and the other to the starboard gunwale. Dropping overboard, I lowered myself until I discovered the cause of the problem.

It was an arrow. It had pierced the carborundum aluminum hull and penetrated the starboard ray tank.

I took hold of the shaft and found that it was fashioned of wood. It appeared to be skeel, but the fletching was a kind of feather unfamiliar to me. I could not place the species of bird that produced it. The arrowhead was likewise unique. I did not recognize the metal from which it was fashioned, and it was barbed in a style new to me. This puzzled me. Orovars had used steel for their arrowheads. This metal displayed the same bluish sheen as had the blade of Ramdar.

Extracting it by main strength, I tucked the thing into my harness and removed from my array a temporary patch that adhered itself to the pierced hull plate. This would stanch the leak, but the cruiser would not be fully airworthy until the tank was replenished.

Scrambling back aboard, I showed the arrow to Kantos Kan by the illumination of our running lights.

"I do not recognize this blue metal," he mused.

"Nor do I," I offered.

Kantos Kan fingered it thoughtfully, "Could this strange man be from another world, such as Jasoom?"

"This is a metal not found upon the Earth," I declared. "If Ramdar hails from another planet, I would not venture a guess as to which one it might be. But it cannot be Jasoom. Men of Jasoom are not like half-wild animals. Nor can I imagine a white man being raised by apes. Ramdar also speaks the common tongue of Barsoom, which puzzles me greatly. "

"Whoever he is, Ramdar possesses strength and agility far exceeding your own. He is therefore a formidable opponent."

I could not gainsay that, for we had experienced the truth of it firsthand. I knew that if I encountered Ramdar again in combat, I would be hard put to defeat him unless armed with a sword such as his. The likelihood of that seemed remote to me.

As Thuria made the first of her thrice-nightly visits, we rendezvoused with the Uxfar ships.

Reluctantly, I gave the signal to abandon further offensive action, ordering all craft to return to the city of Uxfar.

"There we will lay plans for tomorrow," I told Kantos Kan. "No doubt the horde will sleep tonight and advance not a haad further. The city is not in immediate danger."

"What of Tan Hadron of Hastor?"

"If Ramdar planned to slay him, he would be dead already. As much as it galls me to leave him behind, his rescue must await the dawn."

These instructions were transmitted to Vam Dirasun in the other flagship vessel.

Together, every ship fell in line behind ours and swept west toward distant Uxfar.

Long did I ponder the significance of the arrowhead composed of no recognizable Barsoomian metal. Whence had this bronze man come? How had he arrived upon Barsoom? And why was he so interested in whether Martian ships could fly into outer space?

The answer to these questions began to become obvious. Clearly, Ramdar hailed from some other world. No doubt he wished to return to it. At the same time, he had carved out an existence upon Barsoom that threatened its very foundations.

I resolved to defeat him by any means at my disposal. His unholy horde was a threat to all, one which I could not countenance. This Ramdar was intelligent yet bestial. My thoughts went to accounts I had read of the Mongol conqueror, Genghis Khan. An intelligent, even learned man, he swept across the known world of his time, laying waste to cities, putting them to the torch and sacking them of their riches and their women.

When I thought of Ramdar, I imagined someone like Genghis Khan. Had he worn an eyepatch, the barbaric fellow would have passed for a lawless pirate upon my home world. He appeared to be part brigand, but one with miraculous abilities, not the least of which was the ability to communicate with the great white apes, with whom social intercourse had never previously been achieved.

As I pondered the riddle of Ramdar, an idea grew in my brain. It seemed fanciful at first, but as I dwelt upon it, I wondered if the old adage of fighting fire with fire might not apply to the problem of the barbarian horde trudging toward Uxfar.

Going to the radio sending set, I transmitted a message to Helium.

It was my hope for that message to commence the start of the solution to the entire problem.

WE ARRIVED at Uxfar well before dawn. Jeddak Sud Sorovon greeted us personally. We placed both hands on one another's shoulders, smiling warmly.

Uxfar had been an outpost city at the edge of the unexplored territory in the Western hemisphere of Barsoom. Under its previous ruler, it had kept to itself. But when Sorovon Ojar passed away due to old age, his son Sud Sorovon made entreaties to the House of Tardos Mors to be accepted into the Greater Heliumetic Empire.

I had met with Sud Sorovon and found him to be wise beyond his years, and farseeing. An alliance was swiftly arranged. The first test of this alliance came when I instructed Kantos Kan to map the great unexplored territory. Inasmuch as Uxfar lay in the westernmost edge of that great unknown space, I invited Sud Sorovon to participate.

This endeavor he undertook with great enthusiasm. It was also in the interest of Uxfar. Situated northeast of the horde of Warhoon, and not knowing what threats might exist in the opposite direction, Sud Sorovon was keen to know what the vast unmapped expanse harbored, for good or for ill. Now that Uxfar was under the protection of Greater Helium, he felt it would be prudent to penetrate into those wilds.

Repairing to Sud Sorovon's palace, Kantos Kan and I gave a full report of our encounter with the growing horde of Ramdar.

The young jeddak listened intently and without interrupting, the sign of an intelligent man.

"You believe that Ramdar hails from another world?" he declared.

"It would explain his tremendous strength and superior agility," I replied. "As for the tale of being raised by apes, perhaps there is some truth to it, provided that Ramdar came to Barsoom as a child, an orphan of the universe."

"So you do not think he hails from Jasoom?"

I shook my head firmly. "While he resembles a Jasoomian in some respects, I cannot imagine that the Earth gave birth to him. While there exist savages upon Jasoom, this man is some combination of man and animal unheard of on my birth planet."

Changing the subject, I asked, "Bring me your most current map of the great unexplored territory. I wish to see what you have discovered while we plot our future response to this new threat."

The map that was brought by slaves of the retinue of Sud Sorovon was so large it could not fit atop the apartment's spacious ersite table. So we laid it upon the patio floor and sat all around it, reading the map by bright moonlight.

The cartographers had rendered it by hand, and while great portions of the unexplored area lay blank, they included elements inscribed that were unfamiliar to me, who had overflown that unknown desert several times.

Tapping one element, Sud Sorovon said, "This crater encompasses a forest quite different from any other, for it is warm even at night."

Due to Barsoom's declining vitality, forests were rare on the Red Planet. All but the one in the center of Greater Helium had sprung up around the equator. This crater lay far south of that line.

Sud Sorovon went on, "Trees grow in this forest that we do not recognize. No doubt there are other creatures that might be strange to us. This feature was discovered at the same time as the barbarian horde."

"Do you think that the forest harbored these nomads?" I asked.

"It is a reasonable supposition. But so far unproven. What do you think, John Carter?"

"I agree that it is reasonable. And I wonder if this is the spot upon which Ramdar landed upon Barsoom. He asked about atmosphere ships; perhaps he landed here in something like one."

"If so, that ship wreckage would be found in the woods."

I agreed, saying, "Tomorrow, dispatch a scout to that forest and see if you can discover any remnants of such a craft. If you are successful, bring back a sample of the alien metal with which Ramdar's sword and arrows are fashioned."

"Consider it done," declared Sud Sorovon.

My attention went to a broad ovoid patch that the cartographers had painted white. It lay far from any known spot.

"What is this odd desert?" I inquired.

"Something never before seen upon Barsoom, John Carter. It is the remnant of a great lake. After this body of water had dried up, a layer of salt remained in the basin that once harbored the impoundment. I propose to you that we name it after my late father, Lake Ojar, for he was a salty fellow, as you know."

"A lake of salt? The salt will have value."

"Exactly. I propose to claim it in the name of Uxfar, and to mine the salt jointly with Helium. For it is otherwise useless. Nothing grows there. Not even lichen. No hunger-ravaged banth would enter this cursed zone. It is but a bald crust of salt baking in the sun, upon which nothing could survive. And so vast that should anyone attempt to cross it, whether on foot or by thoat, they could not possibly survive the passage."

I studied the white patch for some moments in silence; for a fresh idea was brewing in my mind.

Tapping the dead spot with one finger, I transferred that digit to a spot where I believed that the barbarian horde was bedded down for the night, north of the 20th parallel.

"If Ramdar's horde can be driven south," I said, "and forced onto the dead lake bed, we can deprive his forces of all nourishment, and all hope of escape."

"A good idea, John Carter. How do you propose to do that?"

I answered swiftly, for the idea that was forming in my mind joined with the scheme already pending.

"Before I arrived here," I said, "I dispatched a radio message to Helium, requesting the aid of one who might help us stand against Ramdar."

"Do you mean Tars Tarkas, the great Thark?"

Shaking my head, I said, "I considered sending for Tars Tarkas, since we are contending with a horde composed of green men, in part. But the person I sent for is not a Thark, but one with special talents that are not fully understood by me. But I believe them to be useful in the battle to come. And if I am correct about the plan now forming in my brain, she will be essential to our success."

Sud Sorovon looked at me with puzzled mien.

"She?"

"A trusted friend I have known since my wandering days upon the face of Barsoom, before I achieved my present rank."

Sud Sorovon looked intrigued. A slow smile tugged at the corners of his firm lips.

"I greatly look forward to be presented to this formidable warrior whose name I expect you will divulge before the evening is over."

"Her name," I informed him, "is Thuvia of Ptarth, now a Princess of Helium."

Chapter 35

THE DREADNOUGHT

THERE WAS no landing stage large enough to accommodate the *Dejah Thoris* when she hove into the night sky over the outpost city of Uxfar. The largest battleship in the fleet of Helium, the *Dejah Thoris* was classed as a dreadnought. It had taken many years to construct her, but she had never yet gone into battle.

When her keel was first laid, it had been suggested that she be called the *Dotar Sojat,* after the name by which I was known when I was first upon Barsoom, and a captive of the green Tharks then led by Lorqas Ptomel. The cognomen was bestowed upon me after I had slain two of their fierce warriors in combat, one named Dotar and the other Sojat. In the years since, I have had occasion to employ it as an alias when secrecy required. I was somewhat loath to see the name emblazoned on the bows of a ship, yet honored as well, for the great vessel was to fly the honored colors of Helium.

Over Kantos Kan's mild objections, I had renamed her *Dejah Thoris,* pointing out that, like the princess I had won and wed, she was incomparable. There was no dissent, and so she was launched under that proud name.

A servant in the retinue of Sud Sorovon awoke me with word of the vessel's arrival.

Throwing off my sleeping silks and furs, I drew on my harness and accoutrements and went down to the scarlet sward before the palace where the dreadnought was settling into place.

She was a magnificent vessel, bristling with cannon, more than equal to any single city's aerial complement. I had undertaken to have her built not so much for battle, but as a deterrent to conflict. My reasoning was that a ship so formidable would deter any aggressive nation from waging war against any city allied to the Heliumetic Empire. She had not been in service long enough to prove or disprove my theory, but I had great confidence in the *Dejah Thoris*, whether in war or in peace.

But it was not her large complement of fighting men and her armament that caused me to summon her to Uxfar. Rather, it was the passenger she conveyed.

Thuvia of Ptarth was regal in her bearing as she stepped off of the fantail. I knew her well. And why shouldn't I? She had wed my son, Carthoris, and resided with him in Helium. How strange it was to think that, when I first encountered her as a lowly slave, one day we would both belong to the royal family of Greater Helium or that years later, she would lay the egg from which hatched my first grandchild. A finer daughter-in-law imagination could not conjure.

"Kaor, John Carter," she greeted. "I have come as you bid me to."

"And I am grateful that you did not hesitate. A great danger faces Uxfar, if not all of Barsoom. Follow me and I will relate to you the details."

Escorted by a contingent of guards from the *Dejah Thoris*, we repaired to the palace and found a room comfortable enough to accommodate us as I explained the issue facing me. Kantos Kan joined us.

I told Thuvia of the barbarian Ramdar and his amalgamated horde. Going into great detail and sparing her no particulars, I intrigued her in a recitation that brought audible gasps from her lips.

So rapt was she held by my words that Thuvia barely interrupted the trend of my narrative.

Only when I had concluded did she speak.

"This Ramdar converses with apes?"

I nodded. "They appear to do his bidding and are loyal to him, just as are this wild tribe of green warriors whose metal is unknown to me."

"There are many rootless bands of green men tramping the dead sea bottoms," Thuvia remarked. "I see nothing remarkable about these nomads."

"Roaming by themselves, I would tend to agree. But under the command of Ramdar and coexisting with the great white apes, they represent a strange new development in the evolution of Barsoomian culture."

"Putting aside the matter of Ramdar's origins," Thuvia continued, "what would you have me do?"

"Do you remember when we first met? You were a prisoner of the unholy Therns in the Golden Cliffs of the Valley Dor."

Repressing a shudder that caused her bare red shoulders to shiver, she replied, "Could I ever forget those horrid days? I had foolishly taken the last pilgrimage down the River Iss, and instead of reaching paradise, I found myself a slave of the so-called Holy Therns. You rescued me from that hellish life. I can never thank you enough, John Carter."*

"But you have," I returned graciously. "You succored me in your own turn, through your mastery of the savage banths. It is that subtle skill that impels me to seek your assistance in this hour of impending peril."

"Please explain."

"Just as Ramdar has mastery over the great white apes, you possess power over the banths that roam the dead sea bottoms. You know their secret language, and they become compliant in your presence."

"I have never explained how I came to acquire it," Thuvia commented. She smiled knowingly. "Nor will I now, for I scarcely comprehend it myself. Now what would you have me do?"

---

* *See* The Gods of Mars *by Edgar Rice Burroughs.*

THE SUN was in the act of rising. Light streamed through the windows of the high chamber in which we conferred, making artificial illumination unnecessary.

"The *Dejah Thoris* is fitted with barracks sufficient to carry a full umak of cavalry into battle, along with iron-barred stalls for their war thoats. And while ten thousand mounted soldiers might defeat the horde of Ramdar, for reasons of my own, I do not wish to destroy him and his ragtag freebooters, but instead bring them to heel and discover their secrets."

Thuvia's perfect eyebrows knitted together in perplexity.

"I fail to comprehend, John Carter. Please enlighten me."

"With the *Dejah Thoris*," I explained, "it is possible to range over the dead sea bottoms in search of roaming banths. Finding them, you could speak to them in their subtle language and invite them aboard."

Thuvia's dark brows shot upward. My suggestion astonished her. That much was plain.

"Such a scheme as you outline can be accomplished, of course. But it will take several padans to execute. How many banths do you propose that I lure into the stalls reserved for cavalry thoats aboard your dreadnought?"

"As many as practical. For the horde moves slowly but steadily toward Uxfar. I propose to unleash your banths into the teeth of this horde, driving it back and then southward if it is possible to do so."

"I have never before attempted to control so many wild creatures at the same time," Thuvia remarked.

"This is understandable," I reassured her. "I propose that this mission be accomplished in several stages. First, to drive the horde back, or at least to bring them to a halt. Secondly, to push them to the south."

"Why to the south?"

"In the hope that they fall into a snare from which there is no escape."

Thuvia nodded thoughtfully. "Of course I am prepared to execute your wishes. When shall we begin?"

"Immediately," I replied. "The sun is rising, and the banths are no doubt stirring from their midnight slumber. It will be easier to spy them from the air by daylight. And while at the moment we are not pressed for time, neither do we have a xat to waste. The present status of Tan Hadron is uppermost in my mind. It is my hope to scatter the horde and to rescue him in the confusion."

"No doubt he will have many tales to tell," suggested Thuvia.

"This, too, is part of my plan. The more I can learn of Ramdar, the more wisdom I can apply to his ultimate disposition."

"Ramdar sounds too dangerous to be permitted to live."

"While I am inclined to agree with you, Thuvia of Ptarth, that decision must await sufficient intelligence to justify his execution. If Ramdar can be captured alive, I will convey him back to Helium for trial."

"You are a wise and just ruler," declared Thuvia. "It was a wondrous day when Fate deposited you upon the dead sea bottoms of Barsoom, to commence your rise to power and authority."

Modesty forbade me from answering her directly. Instead, I directed, "If you are rested from your voyage, I should like to start immediately."

"I am eager to begin."

With that, we departed to say our farewells to Sud Sorovon of Uxfar, for we did not know when we would return.

Chapter 36

The Hunt

WE SET out at once in the *Dejah Thoris*. The reddish sun of Barsoom was rising into the empty sky of early morning, its warming rays suffusing the thin atmosphere and driving away the evening chill.

The operation as I planned it was deceptively simple. We would scour the dead sea bottoms for prowling banths, and then set down wherever we found them. After which, Thuvia would work her sorcery. I could scarcely think of it as anything other than a mystical art. Although I had seen her perform this feat before, I never fully understood it.

As she had explained it once before, when young, Thuvia had been thrown into a pit of wild banths. And instead of being devoured alive, a mere morsel for the ravenous flesh-eaters, they had fallen under her spell. It was uncanny, inexplicable. Yet I had beheld it with my own eyes, and my life preserved as a result.

After we spied a specimen of the tawny yellow, largely hairless beasts, I bid Kantos Kan to set us down at a near distance. This was done.

"There is no need for you to follow," suggested Thuvia as she exited through a loading port in the lowermost deck, corresponding to the orlop deck on a sailing vessel, on the port side of the massive ship.

"I know," I told her. "But it would be unchivalrous not to accompany you into danger. Not to mention what my son,

Carthoris, would say to me if harm befell his beloved wife while under my protection."

Thuvia laughed lightly. "I would agree with you, if there existed any danger. There does not. I will bring this banth back as tame as a cub."

The Barsoomian banth cub is no more tame than an Egyptian cobra viper, and is large as a fully grown cougar, but I had told Thuvia about Virginian house cats. No doubt that is what she meant.

Exiting the landed craft, she stepped out upon the ochre moss, and walked gracefully and unafraid in the direction of the skulking banth. It was crawling along nearly on its belly, emitting low, disquieting moans.

It is the way of these ferocious semi-feline creatures to sneak up on their prey and then erupt with the most bloodcurdling and awful roars. Invariably, this transfixed any hapless prey, whether it be a red man, a green man, or a thoat, all of which they devour with relish.

Catching the approaching woman's scent, the fierce banth turned its glaring green eyes in her direction and reared up with its dark mane bristling. Opening a ravenous mouth, it gave forth with one of its terrible senses-freezing roars.

Thuvia's features were as unmoved as the cold face of Thuria, the nearer moon. I watched from the main deck rail to which I had prudently retreated, my hand on the butt of my radium pistol in the event something went wrong.

But nothing went amiss. Forward she stepped, serene and without fear, her beautiful features composed.

The banth went into a crouching position, setting its five pairs of legs and preparing to spring. Before the brute could uncoil its sturdy muscles, Thuvia commenced singing in a contralto voice very much unlike her usual speaking tone.

It was neither a lullaby nor a love song, nor was it a martial hymn. Rather, it was a singsong cadence that did not contain words as I understood them. There was a purring quality to her singing. It carried for a respectable distance through the thin morning air.

In the act of preparing to pounce, the banth hesitated as these melodic sounds reached attuned ears.

What transpired next was remarkable, and as mystifying as the laws of nature.

Hearing these sounds, the creature began to subside. Its long tail no longer lashed behind it. In the emerald fury of its eyes, the avid eagerness for red meat that lurked deep within also expired.

Instead of springing and tearing off the head of the unarmed woman, the banth crept out from its hollow, and padded softly toward the crooning beauty.

Still singing, Thuvia glided to a halt while the banth approached her in a supplicant manner.

This was not a full-grown banth, yet it towered over her. Nevertheless, it began purring throatily and rolled around in the moss, permitting her to insert slim, coppery fingers into its bristling mane, caressing its ears and soothing its savage disposition.

Now she spoke to the beast in a purring tone. Once satisfied that she had the creature's absolute obedience, Thuvia turned and beckoned for it to follow.

I raced down into the hold, where a thoat stall stood open.

Although I trusted to Thuvia's mastery over the fierce species, I did not trust a banth not to launch in the direction of any stranger it met. Ordering two crewmen to seek concealment, I watched from the top of a spiral companionway where I could remain out of direct view of the beast, which docilely followed Thuvia into the cavernous hold.

Speaking soothing words, she invited the banth onto the lowermost deck and then to the open cage. It padded inside. Unhurriedly, she closed the iron-barred gate, casually locking it.

The banth appeared to be slightly taken aback, although that is a difficult thing to say about such creatures. Their yawning mouths with the rows of needle-sharp teeth stretching back behind the ears could hardly be mistaken for a grin. Certainly not a grin of pleasure. It more resembled the toothy smile of a hungry crocodile. But the bewitched beast voiced no objection. It settled down to await its mistress's pleasure.

Departing with a final word of assurance, Thuvia ascended the companionway ramp and joined me on the middle deck.

"You must have been a witch in some previous existence," I declared.

Smiling, Thuvia suggested that we seek more specimens. Climbing to the top deck, I ordered the helmsman to again take to the skies.

Banth often hunt alone, but they can also be found stalking prey in small packs. We were fortunate that morning. We happened across two packs, one consisting of four males, and the other a female accompanied by two juveniles. It did not matter their age or their sex. Once Thuvia approached them, they melted before her soothing song.

Once all eight of the terrible creatures were squatting placidly behind iron bars, I gave the command to seek the horde of Ramdar.

Through the cold night, the ship drove onward. Thuvia retired to her cabin, while I stood watch on deck.

DURING THE journey east, a lookout noticed something in the distance.

Rushing to me, he cried, "John Carter! It is a man leaping through the air!"

This could only be Ramdar the barbarian.

"Turn the ship in his direction," I directed.

The *Dejah Thoris* swung majestically northeast. Striding toward the bow, I put a field glass to the horizon.

It was indeed the bronze-skinned demon. He was hurtling prodigiously from place to place, clearing distances that far exceeded my own prowess as a leaper through the Martian atmosphere. Surely, I thought, he would soon spy us. But his attention was fixed upon the undulating ground, not on the skies above and beyond him.

I felt a momentary chill seeing him drop onto the moss and then flinging himself back into the sky. Once again, the fellow's animal vitality struck me as beyond anything I had ever encountered in man or beast. He seemed intent upon some particular goal, but as I watched, he began to hop in differing directions, as if seeking something.

It soon dawned upon me that Ramdar was not after a particular fixed spot, but that he was hunting.

With difficulty, I kept my glass upon him as the *Dejah Thoris* beat steadily in his direction.

I saw that he carried no pistol, nor a long-sword. Neither was his quiver of arrows at his back. Instead, suspended from his belt was what appeared to be his strange hunting knife. That was all.

Then I spied something yellow and glossy against the vegetable yellow of the boundless moss.

A banth! The solitary creature was moving from the hollow to a rise from which it could spy any wandering prey and pounce without warning.

Ramdar clearly noticed this movement, for he dropped to the ground, set himself and sprang in a new direction. In two prodigious leaps, he cleared the space between himself and the hunting creature.

What transpired next did not entirely surprise me. Nevertheless, it was one of the most shocking sights I had ever beheld on the face of Barsoom.

Dropping from the sky, Ramdar fell upon the beast before the creature could become aware of danger descending upon him.

Ramdar landed behind the unsuspecting banth, and without hesitation mounted the elongated creature's back. Dropping into a seated position, both legs clamping and enwrapping feline ribs, he drew his knife and began to draw blood.

Had I not beheld this with my own eyes, I would scarcely have believed the tale if told by another.

Twisting and turning, the banth attempted to snap an arm off its tormentor, but Ramdar proved too strong for it. His blade plunged in again, becoming encrimsoned, and the lunging needle-teeth could not seize any part of him.

Up until this moment, I had not suspected the muscular strength of Ramdar. Truly, he was a masterful individual. I had no doubt that he could be the equal to any white ape or green Martian he battled in hand-to-hand combat. The unfortunate banth bucked like a bronco, twisting and attempting to roll over in an effort to crush the bronze-skinned savage tormenting it with impunity.

Nothing worked. Every effort was for naught. Weakening, the banth began to thrash about with less and less force until it slowly and agonizingly keeled over, having lost control over nerves and muscles.

Leaping off the tottering brute, Ramdar landed at a safe distance. There, he let it complete its dying.

Then he placed a naked foot on its hairless flank and threw his head back in a defiant gesture. Even at the distance of half a haad, I could hear the weird cry he gave.

The banth had a reputation of having the most terrible roar of any Barsoomian beast. Ramdar's fierce cry was not so loud, yet it demonstrated a carrying quality that staggered me, for it resounded in the thin atmosphere.

That it was a cry of triumph, I had no doubt. But it was scarcely the utterance of a human being. Nor was it the roar of a great white ape, although perhaps the sounds were allied in savagery. The red blood pouring through my veins wanted to congeal into ice, so fierce was that weird utterance.

At my side, Thuvia and Kantos Kan went equally pale.

It was Thuvia who voiced the thought that was in my brain but had yet to reach my tongue.

"That creature is no civilized man. He is a wild beast!"

Before Kantos Kan could order the helmsman to overhaul conqueror and conquered, Ramdar wiped his blade off on the banth's bristling mane, sheathed it and then, displaying physical strength beyond imagination, seized the banth by one heavy forepaw, and sprang up into the sky, taking the limp monster with him.

Here I confess to wondering if I were suffering from a hallucination. But the others saw it, too.

It was not that Ramdar did not struggle with his burden; he did not leap so high as before, nor did he land so gracefully. Twice in succession, he dropped the dead brute upon landing, only to gather it up again and seek the skies once more.

Very quickly, the man and his conquest receded from sight. South they went, toward the waiting horde. And I knew that in his way Ramdar the unbelievable was bringing to his army its morning breakfast.

Kantos Kan looked to me questioningly. "What are your orders, John Carter?"

I did not hesitate, responding, "Ramdar may be able to defeat a single banth. But I have no doubt that if we set our ferocious cargo upon them, the horde will scatter. We will see then what we might accomplish."

Majestically, The *Dejah Thoris* beat on, driving south.

Chapter 37

Engagement from the Air

After Tarzan of the Apes had distributed the banth meat to his horde, an equal share among them, he repaired to his chariot-throne to consider matters as they stood.

Self-reflection was not a dominant trait in the ape-man's mental makeup. He had been raised an ape, and carried into adulthood all the traits that went with such a raucous and primitive life. Food, shelter, and other such simple creature comforts were his primary concern.

He did not engage in much reflection as an adult, even after he had discovered his legacy—that he was a peer of England. Self-criticism was also something in which he rarely indulged.

Tarzan had committed mistakes in his storied life, as has any man or animal. These mistakes he acknowledged, then put behind him. If they could be reversed or repaired, he did so. But in nature most mistakes conveyed the unfortunate quality of permanence. Many were fatal.

As he cut his banth meat into raw steaks, the ape-man considered that he had made a mistake in treating with John Carter. He had not wanted to sound mad to the man, so he had not explained himself. In spite of his earthly sounding name, John Carter evidently belonged to a Barsoomian civilization. If it were anything like civilizations on far-distant Earth, it would no doubt build prisons and insane asylums, and similar such accommodations.

Tarzan did not care to be consigned to either. So he avoided addressing the matter directly and had gotten to the point of his dilemma.

Now, he realized that he had done so precipitously.

Weeks of dwelling among the naked white gorillas, and then their Martian opposites, the barbaric Horta-men, had steadily stripped the veneer of civilization from him. Among the great apes of Africa, the ape-man regularly reverted to the primitive. But even during the wild revels of the Dum-Dum ceremonies of the tribe of Kerchak, Tarzan always remembered that he was as much a Tarmangani born as he was Mangani-raised.

Leading a band of uncouth Tarmanbolgani had made him take on some of their less desirable traits and mannerisms. This had been unfortunate. He had been abrupt with John Carter when he should have been polished.

All of these recriminations journeyed through the ape-man's thoughtful brain as he devoured his breakfast, enjoying the taste of banth blood as much as the texture of the meat. More so, for the texture was strange while the blood was good and salty. He felt his strength gaining, his dark mood restored by the satisfying rawness of fresh meat.

Keeping her distance, Cosooma watched him carefully.

Tarzan glanced her way. The look on her pale face was impassive, but her luminous eyes told him that she had never encountered a man such as himself. Certainly not one who ate raw meat with undisguised relish.

Finishing his breakfast, wiping his hands on a carpet of moss and scouring his face with a clump of the springy stuff he ripped free, the ape-man stood up and padded over to the copper-skinned prisoner, whose name was unclear to him.

"Have you eaten?" he asked.

"I am not hungry."

"If you fear to deprive my tribe of their nourishment, fear no more. For, as you can see, they are eating. Their stomachs will be satisfied until I can find more meat. You should eat your share."

"I do not eat banth," the captive replied.

"There are nuts in plenty. I will bring you some." Tarzan turned away.

The ape-man returned a moment later with a double handful of nuts. He laid them on the moss before the prisoner and then sat down with him.

"Come, come. Eat. And while you do so, tell me your name."

The strapping red prisoner stared at the pile of food a long time before he took up the first nuts. They cracked easily under his strong fingers, and he began to eat.

"It will do you no good to conceal your name, and knowing it might make conversation more interesting," stated the ape-man.

"I will tell you my name, but it will mean nothing to you. I will not tell you my rank."

"Tell me your name, then."

"I am Tan Hadron of Hastor."

"I am happy to know your name. Tell me, do you know John Carter?"

"I decline to say. But everyone on Barsoom knows of John Carter. We call him the Warlord. John Carter is the Jeddak of Jeddaks."

Tarzan nodded. "How did this John Carter arrive at such an exalted position on Barsoom?"

"He battled his way up to his present status. When he first came here, he was an O Mad."

"I do not know that term."

Tan Hadron shrugged. "It will do no harm to tell you. An O Mad is a man with no name."

"Strange. Did his parents not give him a name at birth?"

"I cannot answer that question, for I did not attend the birth of John Carter. But know that he will not rest until he has rescued me from durance vile."

"He may not need to."

The red Martian looked up from his meager breakfast.

"Your meaning is not clear."

"Ramdar is considering sending you back to John Carter with a message, one of peace," advised Tarzan.

"You have already made war upon John Carter. Do you expect mercy?"

"You think highly of John Carter, do you not?"

"He is the greatest swordsman upon Barsoom, possibly the greatest warrior who ever lived on Barsoom."

"I can see that in his nature."

Seeming to forget his breakfast, Tan Hadron said earnestly, "John Carter is a Prince of Helium and the Empire of Helium. By temperament, he is kind. Yet he has waged many just wars and he has won them all. Thus, we refer to him as the Warlord. No other name is necessary for those who know of him."

"John Carter is not like you. His skin was almost as pale as an Orovaran, but displaying the tan of an outdoorsman. Do such as he rule the red men?"

"You must remember to ask that of the Warlord when next you meet," said Tan Hadron in a dry tone of voice. "But be quick with your question ere John Carter drive his blade into your entrails before you finish speaking."

Tarzan examined the man's harness, and noted various items and devices. A stout iron ring depended from one leather strap. He had noticed such rings on the harnesses of the sailors of the sky ships. Another item was a round mirror. He could see no purpose in it. But he recalled that other sailors also sported mirrors on their harnesses.

Tarzan contemplated sending this prisoner back to John Carter and suing for peace in the hope that it would advance the ape-man's cause. But he could not leave his horde at the mercy of the red Martians. Not after having led them this far across the trackless dried-up sea bottoms.

This represented a quandary for Tarzan. His chief objective was to find a way home, if such a thing were possible. But he had acquired adherents, and even if they were strange to his eyes, they were warriors and deserved the respect normally accorded to brave men.

As Tarzan considered the prospect of setting his captive free, an excited rumble rose up among the two components of his composite horde.

Looking up, the ape-man saw Tarmanbolgani and Hortamangani alike rising to their feet, suggestive of weird many-armed towers that gesticulated wildly.

Dag Dolor came stamping over, waving his surviving arms, pointing with his upper right hand in the direction of northeast.

"Ramdar! Behold, a great ship!"

Standing up, Tarzan looked to the north and beheld the sight. It was a stupendous airship, greater than any he had previously encountered.

On Earth, it might have been mistaken for a great Zeppelin. But this sky ship was greater still in size and impressiveness, and it displayed the open deck of the lesser Martian ships.

Bristling with weapons, it bore down upon the encampment.

Gore-smeared mouths began setting up a polyglot shouting. No one doubted but that this was a warship bearing down upon them with hostile intent.

Rushing to his throne-chariot, Tarzan took up his mighty metal bow and slung his quiver of arrows across his neck and back. Leaping up to the driver's platform of the chariot, he bounded two more steps until he stood upon the highest point of the great Martian mastodon's dorsal ridge.

Drawing a single arrow, he fitted it to the steely bowstring.

Watching him, Cosooma spoke up. "Your shaft will never reach that ship, for the distance is too great."

Face inscrutable, Tarzan drew back the bowstring to its greatest extent until the wings were bent almost double, and every cord and tendon in his neck and bronzed arms stood out strikingly. He let go, releasing the arrow.

The missile flew along in a shallow arc, embedding its metallic point in the blunt bow of the ship.

Few among the horde possessed the visual acuity to recognize that the arrowhead found its mark. But among them was Cosooma.

"Impossible!" she exclaimed.

Notching another arrow, Tarzan said, "Not for Ramdar of the Apes."

The second arrow strained backward, and the muscles along Tarzan's bare arms once again grew rigid, taut tendons sticking out dramatically.

When the arrow was released, it found lodgment beside the other.

The approaching air monster continued beating onward, and the sound of its whirling propellers began to cut through the dry Martian atmosphere.

Cosooma frowned. "Do you hope to bring it down with mere arrows?"

Notching a third shaft, Tarzan shook his head. "I am giving fair warning to all aboard that vessel that I will defend my horde."

The third missile struck close to the other two, forming a peculiar decoration.

All along the forepart of the ship, heads and shoulders crowded the bow rails, swords lifting into view, catching the rising rays of the sun.

"It would appear that you have stirred their ire," intoned Cosooma.

"Worse," interjected Tan Hadron. "You have aroused the wrath of John Carter."

SEEING THAT his arrows had not dissuaded the approaching sky ship, Tarzan lowered his bow and turned, saying, "Then I will go to meet this Warlord who has impressed you so."

But before the ape-man could divest himself of his quiver and take flight, the Gargantuan ship suddenly altered course, shifting to port, and presenting its starboard side toward the encamped horde.

Tarzan watched it carefully as the starboard rail came into view. It was lined with swordsmen with their blades raised high. But that was not what impressed him most. Stout cannon muzzles were pointed in his direction.

Tan Hadron spoke up. "The ship is not yet in range, Ramdar, but it will be soon. Allow me to suggest that you surrender now or face utter destruction."

Tarzan said nothing. He had dropped his bow and quiver of arrows to the bed of the chariot-throne and returned to the back of the three-eyed beast of burden which was rarely detached from it.

Leg muscles coiling in order to spring into the sky, Tarzan did not hesitate. But before he could launch himself, the great ship began settling toward the ground, still well out of cannon range.

Hesitating, the ape-man turned his head and demanded, "What is he doing?"

Tan Hadron's coppery face was puzzled. He shielded his dark eyes with a hand, and ventured at last, "The ship appears to be landing."

Dag Dolor spoke up. "We may expect cavalry to be dispatched at any moment."

Great propellers falling still, the ship settled onto the cushioning ochre moss, its flat keel so broad it acted as an elongated landing foot.

A great hatch opened, consisting of two doors that slid apart.

From within the cavern of its lowermost hold, there came a sound that was metallic. A series of clangs, like dropped iron bells. The meaning of these sounds was not immediately apparent, but as all eyes fixed upon the darkness of the open hold, a pair of bulging green eyes materialized.

For only a moment, they glared, Then, with a tremendous roar, the owner of the green orbs sprung out. *It was a wild banth!* And it was not alone.

With startling abruptness, the cargo hold disgorged banth after banth. They charged out. Fixing their glare upon the watching green men and great white gorillas, they tore madly in their direction, seeking fresh meat.

Buckling on his sword, Tarzan charged forward to meet them. His speed was striking. When he had cleared many yards, he sprang skyward. After only three successive bounds, he dropped down into their midst.

There were but eight of them. All were caught by surprise—but their surprise did not last long. They broke off their headlong charge. Twisting their long bodies about, they sought the flesh of this interloper who had dropped out of the scarlet sky. Their roars were terrible.

Drawing his sword, Tarzan lopped off the head of the first attacker. Its body continued its charge, trampling its own tumbling head, and collapsing before the decapitated beast reached its intended prey.

Tarzan turned—just in time to meet the spring of another ravenous banth.

Ducking under its flashing claws, Tarzan came up beneath it, disemboweling the beast with a sideways stroke. With the flat of his blade, he smashed the mortally wounded creature to one side, knocking it into a howling fellow.

Leaping ahead of another attacker, Tarzan twisted in midair and came down upon its tawny back. Taking the sword in both hands, the ape-man split its skull longitudinally with another downward cleaving stroke.

The creature collapsed on its many feet. Not even its tail twitched in death. It was utterly conquered.

Tarzan stood upon the bizarre corpse, and unmindful of the danger gathering about him, threw back his black-haired head and gave forth with the weird victory cry of the bull ape. The sound caused the remaining banths to fall silent in something akin to awe, and then shrink back in consternation, their tails sliding under their hindmost legs.

Stepping off the creature, Tarzan addressed the cowed survivors.

"You crave Tarzan's muscle-meat, come and take your share if you can! But I covet my life more than you do! And I will cleave the flesh attached to your bones before you can sink your yellow fangs into my own flesh!"

The hungry creatures, of course, did not understand any word the ape-man spoke. But they understood his tone. It was one of defiance. Nor did they doubt his prowess. It could be countenanced that some of these creatures were man-eaters. They were accustomed to getting their way when they seized human beings in their ravenous jaws.

Instinctively, they understood that this bronze-skinned creature was not soft, nor easily conquered.

From the high rail of the great sky ship, a strange purring song wafted out. Tarzan had never heard such a sound before. But he soon realized it was a woman and she was singing in an enthralling way.

Scanning the gleaming rail, his gray eyes soon fell upon her. She stood next to John Carter. With her dark hair piled high upon her head, she resembled royalty such as he had encountered upon two earthly continents. From her open mouth, the singing continued to issue forth.

The flattened ears of the surviving banths perked up at this sound. Slowly, reluctantly, almost servilely, they fell into a retreat, withdrawing back within the open cargo hold as if summoned by the uncanny song.

Tarzan let them go. The banths he had laid low were sufficient to feed his horde for now. He picked up the nearest corpse without effort. Struggling with its shifting and ungainly body, he took hold of one massive paw and sprang once more into the sky, intent upon delivering the beast to his hungry warriors.

Behind him, a cannon opened up, coughing a screaming shell that exploded behind him, tearing apart the moss upon which he had stood but a moment before.

Leaping to the left, the ape-man landed, then shot south.

Another shell erupted—but failed to strike its mark, landing to one side.

Soon, the bronzed giant was out of range of the powerful weapon.

The cannon then opened up on the banth corpses, disgorging multiple shells in close succession, tearing them into bloody rags and creating crimson showers that painted portions of moss the livid color of Martian grass.

Arriving at his encampment, Tarzan was greeted as a conquering hero.

"They have destroyed the other banths," greeted Dag Dolor.

"Crushed flesh is still meat and may be eaten," stated Jamo Ptannus.

Carefully, Tarzan set down his burden, turned and stared back.

The majestic sky battleship was returning to the upper atmosphere, but this time it swung away, presenting her speeding propellers to them.

"They retreat," grunted Dag Dolor.

Addressing Tan Hadron, Tarzan said sternly, "Your Warlord is not so brave as your praise makes him out to be."

"John Carter never gives up."

"And Ramdar never surrenders."

"I fear the day when you clash again," intoned Tan Hadron.

"And well you should."

Chapter 38

STRATEGY

IT DID not gall me to order the *Dejah Thoris* to break away and head northward after our starboard cannon had pounded the slain banth corpses into an inedible ruin.

In truth, I had not expected to stampede the horde of Ramdar during our first foray. My intention was to test their reactions, the better to understand how the barbarian thought.

I had not anticipated him rushing ahead to intercept the banths, destroying them utterly. Nor did I figure that he would turn my onslaught into an opportunity to feed his subjects.

Turning to Thuvia, I remarked, "We will require many more banths to accomplish our aim."

"This Ramdar is prodigiously strong. All three of his arrows pierced the bow at a distance I would have thought impossible."

I nodded somberly. "Without question, his strength exceeds my own. However, I cannot entirely conceive how. Increasingly, he does not appear to be a man born on Barsoom. Of that, I am becoming convinced."

Thuvia said, "Locate more banths, John Carter. I will take care of the rest. This Ramdar cannot fight them all at once. He and his legion will be overwhelmed, provided sufficient numbers can be mustered."

Kantos Kan, Overlord of the Heliumetic Navy, stood beside us, absorbing every word.

Addressing me, he offered, "John Carter, if we unleash an army of banths, surely this barbarian horde will be overrun. If overrun, they will be consumed to the last man. At the same time, Tan Hadron will be devoured as well. He must be rescued before that hour."

I turned to him and laid one hand upon his shoulder. "Let it be clearly understood between us, Kantos Kan, I will not allow Tan Hadron to remain a captive much longer. I will lay plans for his rescue. Of that, you may be assured. But for now, we must prosecute our war against the composite horde according to our plan."

With that, I sought the radio transmitter with which I would communicate with Helium, the better to effect my goal of succoring Tan Hadron.

Soon, I was in communication with my son, Carthoris. I did not need to explain the situation of Tan Hadron. He was well aware of it.

"I have a mission for you," I began.

"You have but to say the words and I will execute them to the letter."

No finer son could have been born on Earth or Barsoom. I knew that I only had to explain my needs and Carthoris would see that they were executed to the letter.

"Take a fast one-man flier," I directed. "I want you to visit an old friend and ask of him a favor. I do not doubt but that he will grant it. Now, listen closely, my son. The life of Tan Hadron depends upon your perfect understanding of my wants…."

Chapter 39

The Loyalty of Tarzan

THE HORDE of Ramdar was on the march once again. Tarzan led them directly to the churned-up soil and the deep shell-craters where the dead banths had been blasted asunder.

Much of the meat was inedible, but great gobs of it were still good. The shattered bones revealed the sweet marrow within.

Pointing to these remnants, the ape-man commanded, "Fill your bellies. But keep order while you eat. Let there be no fighting among you."

There was no fighting, as such. Among his uncouth legion, shoving and scuffling did not count as fighting.

Tarzan let his green men and albino gorillas eat their fill, knowing that their breakfast had been sufficient, but they would need fuller bellies to continue on to Uxfar, an unknown number of haads to the southwest.

Tarzan had deposited Tan Hadron in the back of his chariot, and went to speak with him there.

"Tell me of the great ship," he demanded.

"I know nothing of it, never having beheld it before today."

"What is its range?"

"I told you, I do not know."

"Tell me what I wish to know, and I will consider releasing you into the custody of John Carter."

Tan Hadron made a preliminary noise of contempt. "I would be a fool to believe a barbarian who consorts with apes."

"Ramdar tells you the truth. Answer him."

The ferocity of the man's words made the Martian flinch in spite of himself.

"The truth is that I have never seen such a ship before," he admitted grudgingly. "How can I tell you about it under those circumstances?"

Dag Dolor lumbered up to listen to the conversation in silence. He folded his upper arms across his broad chest, the surviving lower hand resting upon the ornate hilt of his sword.

Tarzan continued in an earnest tone. "I promise that I will not allow you to be eaten if you tell me what you know."

"The promise of a barbarian carries a value that is unknown to me," said Tan Hadron with thin diplomacy.

Tarzan abandoned his line of questioning. Instead, he said, "A ship of that size might be forceful enough to escape the atmosphere of Barsoom and travel to other worlds."

"What is your interest in other worlds?" countered Tan Hadron.

"Ramdar is tired of Barsoom. Another world would be more to his liking."

Interest caused Tan Hadron's dark eyebrows to quirk upward.

"Do you have another world in mind, or have you no preference?"

Tarzan said nothing. This conversation was not proceeding down a trail he cared to travel.

Turning to go, he said, "You will not be eaten. You have the promise of Ramdar. Remember this."

Tarzan next sought Cosooma, who had drifted away from the meat-eaters.

"A copper-skinned woman controls the banths," he told her. "She does this through song. Tell me about women who do this."

Cosooma's pale face looked blank.

"I have never heard of such a woman," she stated. "Of course, I have traveled very little upon the face of Barsoom over the course of my one thousand ords. Why do you think such women exist?"

"I spied a woman summoning the banths back into the great sky ship, and her song demonstrated the quality of a purring entreaty."

"A woman who speaks to wild banths in the way you converse with great white apes seems quite rare," Cosooma returned tartly. "Perhaps you should fetch her. Perhaps you will fall in love, and possibly marry."

"Tarzan already has a mate. He does not need another."

Hearing these words, Cosooma's entrancing face fell.

"If you have a mate, where does she dwell?"

"Far from here. But I will be reunited with her, if it is possible to do so."

"And if this is not possible?"

"Then Tarzan will die upon Barsoom alone—but not until his time comes."

TURNING, THE ape-man went among his horde, who were devouring such scraps as had not already been seized and consumed. The gorillas particularly dug around the blasted soil, picking up bone shards, licking the blood off them and sucking out the marrow, which they particularly relished.

Cosooma followed, but at a respectful distance. She did not trust the green men and specifically did not care to be in the vicinity of the great white apes, whom she saw as no better than savage beasts.

Tarzan had given her only perfunctory attention up until now. Cosooma wanted more. Consequently, she threw off her regal reserve in an attempt to bare her hungry heart to this magnificent bronze-skinned warrior.

"Ramdar, do you not find Cosooma very beautiful to behold?"

"Cosooma is unquestionably beautiful. But Tarzan is pledged to another."

"Another who is not here. If you cannot be reunited with your beloved, would Cosooma of Samabar not be a worthy mate for you?"

"Cosooma is very beautiful," admitted Tarzan. "Perhaps the most beautiful woman I had ever beheld. I do not understand why I feel this, for prior to this time, I have never recognized a woman to be more fair than my mate, Jane."

Cosooma brightened. But then her face fell. For that was all that Tarzan ventured. His expression became grim, his mouth thin-lipped.

She continued, "When I was younger, I was considered the most beautiful woman of my race. Men sought me, implored my parents for my hand."

Tarzan said, "I do not doubt this. You are beautiful still. But I belong to another."

"I am not only beautiful, but I do not age outwardly. Any woman you would ever know will eventually grow old and wrinkled. Youth always withers. She will become unattractive, perhaps ugly. Would you not want a flower that never faded?"

Tarzan said nothing to that. His thoughts appeared to be elsewhere.

"What are you thinking, Ramdar?"

The ape-man was a long time in replying.

"I am thinking," he said at last, "that if I am to feed my horde I will need many, many banths. More than I can hunt over the course of the suns and moons that stretch ahead. A woman who can summon banths with her voice would ensure the success of my plan to reach Uxfar."

"You propose to kidnap this woman?"

"If I must. But I prefer to barter the red captive for the woman whom the banths obey. Perhaps John Carter would agree to such a trade."

"Perhaps he would," Cosooma allowed. "But I would not trust him. Any more than he should trust you. You are both prodigious warriors. Barsoom may not be large enough to contain the both of you."

Tarzan said nothing to that. He did not doubt that there was some truth in the woman's words. But he had a single immediate goal in mind. To reach Uxfar. To achieve that goal, he would undertake any risk, dare any danger, and seize any opportunity that presented itself.

While the most beautiful woman in all of Barsoom hovered hungrily behind him, the thoughts of Tarzan of the Apes were upon only one she.

Jane Clayton, his mate. All other examples of womankind meant nothing to him. He had found her and won her and lost her and regained her time and time again. To live without her was unthinkable. To abide upon Barsoom any longer than what absolute necessity required was intolerable.

Tarzan would go home or die. He was fatalist enough to understand that no other choice mattered to him. The ape-man would sacrifice anything but life itself to reach the jungles of Africa again. But until he knew that there existed a trail home through the empty spaces between the planets, he would remain loyal to his horde and all who were attached to it.

This was the mind of Tarzan of the Apes.

Chapter 40

Warhoons

FOR THREE days and two nights the horde of Ramdar marched toward Uxfar, somewhere beyond the featureless horizon.

During these days, Tarzan of the Apes collected banths, and kept his warriors marching. These were days of boredom—and anticipation. Banths were growing scarce. It became increasingly difficult to feed apes and men equally.

On the third night, after the Tarmanbolgani and Hortamangani had bedded down in separate spaces, Tarzan went to Tan Hadron and spoke to him quietly.

"John Carter has not returned in three padans."

The copper-skinned captive said simply, "The Warlord is an intelligent man. He saw the way you dispatched those banths. And how your ragtag army consumed them to the last shred of meat and bone. He knows that if he sends more your way, you will only turn them into food."

Tarzan evinced the merest knife-edge smile.

"John Carter has switched tactics. He hopes to starve Ramdar and his horde. But I am a hunter. I know where to locate meat. We will reach Uxfar before we starve."

Tan Hadron looked around the limitless sea of moss that served as an extended bed for the horde of Ramdar.

"Your horde has shrunk with the rising of the moons."

This was true. For no sooner had Thuria climbed into view and Cosooma retired to her chariot-throne bed and lay down her golden head to sleep, than the greater portion of the army simply faded away.

Tarzan had gotten used to it, as had the horde. Since the navy of John Carter had not returned by night, it did not matter. Cosooma needed to conserve her mental strength.

Tan Hadron remarked casually, "That woman cannot sustain her illusions interminably. It is aging her. Anyone can see this."

Tarzan shrugged negligently. "She only has to keep up her illusions until we reach the gates of Uxfar."

"It will be your undoing, if you reach those gates. No doubt Sud Sorovon is waiting for you with his defenders, and inasmuch as Helium is pledged to his defense, the army of the Warlord will support him."

Tarzan did not reply to this. What he would encounter at the gates of Uxfar did not concern him on this night. Nor would it concern him on the coming day. It was his way to live one padan at a time and only plan so far ahead as necessity demanded. The ways of the jungle abided deeply in him—even if no jungle surrounded the ape-man at the present moment.

Abruptly, Tarzan said, "I cannot trade you to John Carter if he does not return."

"Perhaps John Carter awaits you in Uxfar, Ramdar."

The conversation lapsed for some moments. Tarzan was scanning the horizon all about with his sharp eyes. There was no wind. When there was a wind, it was soft and blew so steadily as to be unnoticeable. The silence of the Martian night was an experience so absolute that it was nearly unnerving.

Tarzan heard nothing in this breathless hush. In the jungles of Africa, approaching danger sent its warning messages ahead. The rustling of branches. The snapping of fallen twigs. Certain animal sounds. But here there was nothing. If banths or men trod the ochre moss, no discernible sound was created by their footfalls.

It was not the sound of feet that caught Tarzan's attention, however. His jungle-honed senses had detected something else.

Seeing the ape-man's sudden attitude of attention, Tan Hadron started to speak, but Tarzan cut off his question with a sharp sweeping gesture.

Tarzan saw nothing in the direction his ears told him something moved. But before long, the sound swelled and became many sounds, and he began to recognize them.

The creak of harness leather. The clanking and clinking of accoutrements. Soon the smell of sweat came to him. Not the sweat of red Martians such as Tan Hadron. This was the musk of great green man-boars tramping through the night.

Buckling on his sword, the ape-man started off in the direction of the approaching party. Tarzan did not leap into the air, not wishing to attract attention. He simply walked forward, shoulders squared, all his jungle senses alert, prepared to meet danger or comradeship, whichever offered itself to him.

The hurtling moons made the tiny shadows in the crevices of the moss crawl and writhe as if alive.

Tarzan advanced several hundred yards before he could descry the approaching party. It was a war party of green men. They came on foot, except for one who was astride a giant thoat. He rode in the lead, the others spread out in tramping wings on either side. The party numbered some thirty warriors. But such warriors!

In the shifting moonlight, Tarzan could see that they were the dregs of the dried ocean floor. Some were missing hands and limbs, eyes and fingers. Many of these Hortamangani lacked one tusk and some had lost both, their shattered stumps gleaming like ivory shards.

The leader lacked none of these things. He still owned all of his limbs, both of his Horta-like tusks, and his round, disconnected eyes shone scarlet in the moonlight. He alone appeared whole.

Circling his bald crown, a fillet of gold supported a single white plume that drooped as if weary of traveling.

Tarzan walked until they could see him, then he came to a halt with his arms folded. There he waited, patient and unafraid in his posture. The ape-man wanted these men to see him, to know that he saw them. He did not intend to offer challenge or offense. He would wait to see their demeanor.

The huge jeddak spied him immediately, showing no outward concern. Across the withers of his mount was balanced a war lance, approximately forty feet in length and shod in metal for its entire impressive length.

Lifting a pale olive hand in a fist, he signaled for his much-battered party to halt. Then, riding forward, he brought his impressive slate thoat to a halt, and spoke.

"Hail and greetings! Do I behold Ramdar, of whom I have heard much?"

"I am called Ramdar."

A booming laugh came from the barrel chest of this green chieftain. The plume of royal distinction on his forehead waved with his shaking.

"Perhaps you have heard of me. I am Dak Kova, Jeddak of the Warhoons."

"Ramdar has never heard of you, Dak Kova."

Spreading one arm around and behind him and then the other in the opposite direction, the green Martian said, "Behold the remnants of my horde. They were defeated by John Carter. I have heard of you, O Ramdar. I wish to join in common cause with you. For the red men have decimated my horde, and I offer my sword and the swords of my warriors in return for your leadership and protection."

Tarzan heard these words and considered them. He was not intent upon making war, but war was being waged against him. Numbers would give him a greater advantage, especially since the greater portion of his legion was entirely imaginary, and the product of a woman's waking will.

"Ramdar accepts your offer, Dak Kova. Camp here for the night. At dawn, I will prepare my horde for your arrival. Then you may join us."

"Let it be so."

Before turning to address his war party, the green Martian asked, "I have never encountered a man of your color upon Barsoom. From what land do you hail?"

"Africa."

"I have never heard of it."

"That is because it is far from here."

Turning, Tarzan made his way back to his encampment. He was not followed.

WHEN HE reached the spot, Tarzan went directly to Dag Dolor, rousing him from sleep.

With one hand flying to his sword hilt, he halted. "What is it, Ramdar?"

"A war party of green men has come. They camp to the southwest. Their jeddak calls himself Dak Kova. Have you heard of him?"

"I have, O Ramdar. He was a jed among the Warhoons until the day he challenged and slew his jeddak, Bar Comas."

"Dak Kova claims to have been defeated by John Carter, his horde reduced to a handful of survivors. They appear to have gotten the worst of their encounter."

Dag Dolor grunted, "Most warriors who challenge John Carter end up receiving the worst portion of the battle. John Carter is a mighty man upon Barsoom."

"I have given Dak Kova permission to join our horde with the dawn. Finish your sleep. I will stay and watch. In the morning, prepare your men for the coming of Dak Kova and his Warhoons."

"It will be as you command, O Ramdar."

Lying down on his cloak, Dag Dolor went back to sleep.

Pretending to sleep upon his own cloak, Tan Hadron had heard every word. The conversation had interested him greatly. He did not know what to make of this new development, only that it would be useful to know in the future.

The fame of Ramdar appeared to be spreading around this portion of Barsoom. If the coming of Dak Kova meant anything, it implied that other adherents would be drawn to the horde that marched upon Uxfar.

If this continued, reasoned Tan Hadron, the ranks of Ramdar might conceivably swell in truth to a force rivaling its apparent illusory size.

For the first time, the red captive commenced to worry about the future of Uxfar.

"Where," he whispered to himself, "is the Warlord? What could be keeping him?"

Chapter 41

The Old Egg

ALTHOUGH I was then unaware of it, at the moment that Tan Hadron wondered about his Warlord, I had departed from my dreadnought in a speedy scout flier, along with a detachment of hand-picked men.

Chief among them was Vor Daj, young padwar in the retinue of my personal guard. Hor Vastus, an officer in the Heliumetic Navy, accompanied us. There were two others, Fak Dur and Nal Usk, both trustworthy sailors in my service.

I had decided to investigate the crater from which the mysterious Ramdar had seemingly emerged. It would take some time for Kantos Kan to locate prowling banths and for Thuvia to lure them aboard the *Dejah Thoris*. My presence was not necessary for the successful completion of that operation.

"It is my intention to discover the source of the metal from which Ramdar's sword was forged," I told Hor Vastus.

He nodded in agreement. "When you meet again in combat, it will be good to wield a blade that is the equal of that barbarian's knife."

"No sword will lend to my sword arm strength equivalent to that of Ramdar in muscular might," I advised. "But our blades will be equal. I can only hope that my fighting prowess, along with my swordsmanship, will prove to be the decisive edge."

Vor Daj chimed in. "John Carter has never been bested in all the ords he has dwelt upon Barsoom."

"Never bested by a Barsoomian," I corrected. "Ramdar may hail from some other world."

The flier swept down upon the luxurious jungle, from which billows of steam arose in its center. Details of the spot were difficult to discern beneath the hurtling moons, which threw shadows shifting this way and that with each passing moment, making it seem as if contradictory winds were stirring the tree tops.

The night was hot and humid, far more so than any other portion of Barsoom I had ever before encountered. This wild place was far different from the Kaolian Forest, which is the largest known survival of ancient woodland on Barsoom.

We set down in a lush purple clearing and stepped out, our swords drawn.

"Seek any signs of naked footprints," I instructed my men. "There may be a crashed ship, if Ramdar arrived in such a contrivance."

I did not inform them that the scout party I had dispatched previously to seek such a ship had reported no sign of any vessel of the sort. But this jungle was so vast and difficult to penetrate on foot that I could not assume that their failure to uncover an interplanetary craft meant that it did not in fact exist.

We fanned out. Almost immediately, Vor Daj encountered something resembling a serpent, but without a discernible head. Confronting it, he did not hesitate. His swift sword clove it in two. Both ends squirmed and flopped upon the jungle floor, extruding strangely colored blood a brighter hue of green than any green man.

IT WAS Hor Vastus who came upon the great egg.

It lay in a shallow crater of gathered ferns and twigs, resting not upon its side. The object sat on its round end, tapering to a blunt point at its apex. The dust of decades, if not centuries, lay upon it. Whatever creature had laid it had been tremendous in size, but evidently had not returned to finish hatching its brood.

Summoned by his low whistle, I drew up and scrutinized the egg. Not a single crack showed in its shell. Its original color might have been white or perhaps a light gray. Now it was dirty gray. Placing one palm against its side, I detected no warmth other than what would be expected in such a humid locality.

"I have never beheld such an egg," gasped young Vor Daj, who arrived in response to the summoning whistle.

"It may be a malagor egg," suggested Hor Vastus.

"Should we destroy it?" asked Vor Daj.

I studied the object as I considered the question. "Perhaps it could be salvaged and studied by our scientists. We will come back for it later."

Again, we fanned out. Nal Usk accompanied me. Before long, we came upon footprints leading to a great mahogany form that was like nothing I had ever before seen; a polished thing so large and imposing that it rivaled a zitidar. Its immobility struck me as unnatural. Yet it did not appear to be living. Its shape in profile reminded me of a Gargantuan leather shoe, being higher at one end than the other.

Some of the footprints were unshod, and I thought of Ramdar.

Could this thing be a ship of some kind? I wondered.

Investigating, I made a circuit of the still form, and found an aperture that led downward into the puzzling structure.

Leaving Nal Usk to stand guard, I entered into the innards of the thing, picking my way by aid of a radium flashlight. Swiftly recognizing by its ribbed interior walls that it had been hollowed out, and perhaps once lived, I climbed down a makeshift ladder and found myself in a warren of intersecting transverse tunnels.

Water ran steadily, and the fresh smell of it came to my nostrils. An underground waterway!

"The River Iss," I whispered. It must be, for only one such watercourse survived on the face of modern Barsoom. It wound its prodigious course for a significant way to the Lost Sea of Korus and the legendary Valley Dor, to which Barsoomians of all races once went when their allotted span of one thousand ords had expired—until I stamped out the foul false religion that fed their delusion.*

---

* See The Gods of Mars *by Edgar Rice Burroughs.*

Down that river many Martians of different colors have journeyed in their final days, only to discover stark horror instead of the promised afterlife. Shrugging off the horrid memories of the Valley Dor, which I had encountered firsthand upon my second journey to Mars, I continued my explorations.

It appeared that a race of men had once dwelt here beneath the steaming jungle. I wasted no time in exploring, for I swiftly found a great vaulted room containing a wealth of swords, arrows, and lances resting upon shelves and in elaborate chests.

The sight of it impressed me deeply. These were weapons sized for a red Martian, not a green warrior. They were splendid in their workmanship and excellent in the keenness of their edges. The shimmering blue metal appeared to be identical to that of Ramdar's blade.

Going among these weapons, I picked up one and then the other, and never once set down a blade that did not bring a thrill to my fighting soul.

There were too many to carry away, so I selected a handful of the best and bore them back to the ladder and up to the surface.

I peered about. Of young Nal Usk, there was no sign!

With my radium light, I sought his footprints, but the ground was disturbed in such a way that the tracks of our arrival had been obliterated. I could not make out what had churned the soil in such a bizarre manner, but it would be meaningless to follow the trail of upheaval without reinforcements, since the broadness of the disturbance suggested something of overwhelming size.

Momentarily, I paused by the mahogany form, whistled once and then twice again, and waited for my detachment to arrive.

No response came. I signaled again. Again there was no reply, by whistle or by arrival of men.

Laying down my burden of blades, I selected the one that most appealed to the swordsman in me, and with that firmly in hand, went in search of my missing detachment.

Chapter 42

The Replenished Horde

THE CAMP roused at the first red crack of the dawn. They did so with surprising quietness. Nothing like a cock crowed. Barsoom awoke as it always did, from a smothering hush to a sunlit one.

Within the hour, the tattered remnants of the horde of Dak Kova drew up to the encampment outskirts, halting there.

"Hail, Ramdar!" greeted the green jeddak.

Dismounting from his thoat, he stepped forward and lay his sword at Ramdar's naked feet.

Tarzan lifted it and returned it to him, declining to buckle it on, indifferent to that portion of the Barsoomian custom.

That settled, the other green Martians repeated the custom until all blades had been offered and returned.

Only then did Ramdar present Dag Dolor and his green warriors to the new arrivals. This was done without excessive ceremony.

"Dak Kova is proud to lend his strength to the growing horde of Ramdar," said the burly chieftain. "I willingly surrender my rank and title. No longer will I proclaim myself to be Jeddak of the Warhoons of the north. Henceforth, Dak Kova is but a jed under the command of Ramdar."

Dag Dolor said nothing. He stared at the other wordlessly, as if appraising him as a potential foe or rival.

They studied one another at length, the two olive-skinned chieftains and their warriors. Few words were spoken. Dag

Dolor had previously explained that the green men of different tribes, although belonging to one race, were not united in any manner. Perpetual war existed among the hordes. Alliances were rare, and fragile in duration. This ceaseless state of conflict was being set aside for the greater good of the exalted horde of Ramdar.

As Dag Dolor had explained, "The green men of different tribes do not normally associate with one another, except to slaughter each other. That is the way of the green race."

Tarzan announced to all, "Those who follow Ramdar must respect all others who follow Ramdar. If the green warriors of Vakanor and the great white apes of the Narag tribe can make peace, then the horde of Dag Dolor and the Warhoons of Dak Kova can find common cause."

There was no dissent. Neither was there enthusiasm. The two tribes of green men glared at one another, but that was the natural state of their fiery orbs. Even after all these weeks on Barsoom, Tarzan sometimes found their red regard disconcerting.

Off by themselves, the hairless white gorillas observed the new arrivals, but paid them little heed. They were busy scratching themselves and rousing the shes and the balus.

There was a little meat left over from the previous day's hunt, so those still hungry helped themselves to the dwindling nuts and other edibles. The slovenly gorillas fed their women and children first, and if necessary, went without.

As the green men of Dak Kova wandered about the camp, keeping clear of the great white gorillas whom they plainly feared and respected, their leader came upon Tan Hadron in irons.

"What is this, O Ramdar?"

Tarzan explained, "A prisoner. He belongs to the navy of John Carter. I am considering returning him to John Carter as a gesture of goodwill."

The green chieftain looked askance at his new jeddak. "What would that accomplish? Better to feed him to the white apes before they become ungovernably hungry."

"Ramdar has not yet made his decision," returned Tarzan flatly. "But John Carter has something Ramdar desires in return."

"What is that?"

"A woman," replied Tarzan.

Hearing these words, the plumed jed shook with uproarious laugher. He seemed to find the notion amusing. His men also laughed boisterously, their broken tusks gleaming red in the smoldering light of dawn.

Tan Hadron was staring at the laughing green man strangely.

The green jed stared back with frank challenge in his eyes.

"Do you not recognize Dak Kova when you lay eyes upon him, puny red man?"

"I have never before laid eyes upon Dak Kova," replied the captive.

"Then be grateful to the gods of your people. For were you not under the protection of Ramdar, I would remove your head with a single swipe of my blade. Then I would present your head to my men as a plaything. Perhaps one of them would like to wear your hairy scalp to keep his skull warm."

Turning his back scornfully upon the captive, the green jed went next to Dag Dolor and engaged him in conversation.

"What city did you call home?"

"Vakanor."

"I have never heard of it."

"It lies to the north, below the 10th parallel. My father was Churvash Ul, Jed of Vakanor."

"I have never heard of Churvash Ul," said the green man contemptuously. "Know you of Dak Kova?"

"Dak Kova is said to command the Warhoons of the north."

"I am he. Tell me of the battle in which you lost your arm?"

Dag Dolor said frankly, "I did not lose my arm in battle. My father's horde was ejected from Vakanor. I did not escape with him, but fell captive to the ape-lord Murdank, who gleefully consumed my limb. Murdank would have consumed the entirety of me had it not been for the bronze jed, who rescued me."

Dak Kova laughed boisterously as if he found the idea of a fellow green man losing his arm to a hungry ape humorous.

Dag Dolor noticed the other warriors foraging about, with missing limbs such as himself.

"What calamity befell your warriors?"

"John Carter befell them."

Dag Dolor glared contemptuously. "Ramdar is mightier than John Carter. Stronger. More forceful. If John Carter returns, Ramdar will destroy him utterly."

His red gaze shifting about, the green chieftain said, "I will believe this when I see it."

"You doubt the power of Ramdar?" challenged Dag Dolor.

"Dak Kova would not be here if he doubted the power of Ramdar. Dak Kova needs only to see the power of Ramdar with his own eyes to be fully convinced of his worthiness to ride a white thoat."

"Then take care to keep your warriors away from the great white apes," returned Dag Dolor. "The sight of so many men with missing limbs will give them ideas that you would not find appetizing. We are out of meat. Count on Ramdar to supply fresh banth meat. But if he runs out of banth to catch, there is no telling how these unruly apes will behave."

The green jed dropped a heavy hand to the pommel of his sheathed sword and said, "I have slain many apes. I would not fear to slay more."

"Ramdar values his apes more than he values his green warriors. He speaks their tongue. He claims to have been raised by apes. Do not cross his apes unless you wish to cross Ramdar himself. Then more than your limbs will be at risk. He will take your head off with one swipe of his superlative blade."

"I hear your words, and mark them appropriately."

Turning, the green jed continued his investigations of the camp.

HE DISCOVERED Cosooma by accident.

"I have never seen a woman of your color," he remarked. "Nor any woman possessing hair like shining gold."

"Nor will you ever again," returned Cosooma coldly. She walked off without another word, having no interest in speech with any green warrior, whom she plainly considered beneath her station.

Having freshened up, the woman from Samabar consumed a small quantity of nuts, sat down in the back of the chariot, and closed her uncanny eyes. She was quite a long time in her meditation, but when the ethereal Cosooma rose, she did so with a strange inner fire. Her eyes were freshly luminous.

All around, the imaginary warriors who had faded after sunset were restored to their splendor. Thoats. Chariots. Green men and red. And others. The hues of their skin and animals were supernaturally vivid, and virtually lustrous.

The Warhoons were taken entirely by surprise to behold the materialization of such a splendid legion all about them, and they backed up until they formed a protective circle, their blades lifted high.

Tarzan strode up to them and stated, "This is the doing of the white woman, Cosooma. Her ability to materialize warriors who are not real is one of the reasons I permit her to accompany us."

"This staggers me," admitted the green chieftain, blocky jaw hanging down in awe, his formidable tusks askew.

"You will become accustomed to it, if you follow Ramdar."

"Dak Kova will never get used to sorcery. But if you say the word, my hordesmen and myself will do what we can to adjust to this miracle."

Tarzan told them, "They disappear with the coming of night. They will not trouble your sleep."

Then he stepped over to his impressive white thoat, mounting it as he would an elephant of Africa. Lifting one bronzed arm, he proclaimed that it was again time to march.

The horde of Ramdar organized itself with impressive speed. The great white gorillas arrayed themselves on his right, all green men mustering on the left.

The army of illusion taking up the rear, Ramdar led them westward, toward Uxfar.

During the organization of this procession, the red glare of the green jed and the dark gaze of the coppery captive encountered one another—then turned away as if shrinking from each other's regard, much in the manner of old enemies who did not care to acknowledge the other's existence....

Chapter 43

THE EGG OPENS

I DID not fear to follow the swath of disturbed ground that led away from the weird mahogany structure that overlaid the underground chambers from which I had emerged into the ever-changing moonlight.

If something had carried off Nal Usk, I was determined to deal with it forthwith. It made no difference if it were man or monster; I would rescue my warrior, if rescue were possible. If not, I would summarily avenge him.

The trail wound through the jungle, disturbing the purple grass, crushing it almost completely in a broad band more than a dozen feet wide. Stout branches were broken, warning that the unknown creature possessed masterful strength.

The trampled trail debouched from the woods to the dusty gray egg that stood in its ancient nest, still whole and unbroken, standing on its thicker end, which served as a natural base.

Halting before it, I looked about the nest. The trail stopped here. Some of the debris that surrounded the egg showed signs of being pushed about. Yet the egg remained intact.

It was a mystery.

Stepping back from it, I whistled anew.

In short order, the tramp of feet amid the underbrush turned my attention to the east.

Hor Vastus strode up, accompanied by the sailor, Fak Dur.

"I came as rapidly as possible," declared Hor Vastus. "What is wrong, John Carter?"

"I discovered the source of the exotic blade carried by Ramdar, but that is not of great moment. I found the shell of a great dead creature, which concealed the way into a warren of tunnels. Nal Usk stood guard while I explored below ground. There I found many fabulous swords, all forged from an unknown metal. When I emerged, Nal Usk was gone. I followed this fresh disturbance to this spot."

I lifted my newly acquired blade and we surrounded the great egg.

Hor Vastus reported, "There is no sign that it has broken open."

"Perhaps it is not an egg," suggested Fak Dur.

"Of course it is an egg. Probably the egg of a malagor—even though they are considered to be extinct."

That was my belief, as well. The malagor was a great bird, according to the ancients of Barsoom. No such bird has been seen since our arrival, nor had one been reported by the scouts of Uxfar. Inasmuch as the malagor is approximately the size of the legendary Arabian Roc, and therefore a giant among birds, I could scarcely accept that this was a malagor egg that had never hatched. But I could not otherwise explain the phenomenon of Nal Usk's inexplicable disappearance.

"Surely, Nal Usk is not within that egg," murmured Hor Vastus.

"These tracks suggest otherwise," I told him.

"Are these tracks?"

"Something large and powerful trampled this ground," I pointed out.

KNEELING, I examined the ground closely. For the first time, I detected a pattern in the disturbed soil. This pattern suggested that the creature—if it was a creature—employed a means of locomotion that was unlike anything I could imagine. It seemed to tear up the ground as it moved. Amid these disturbances were impressions suggesting myriad distinct and separate elements, all uniform in size and spacing. They brought to mind a carpet of bristles, all pressing themselves into the soil in unison, tearing it up as it crept along. I knew of nothing living on Earth or Barsoom that moved in such a disorderly manner.

"Stand back," I commanded.

Lifting my blade, I took the hilt by both hands and prepared to crack open the egg-shaped thing.

I swept my blade back and forth before me, building up momentum as I advanced, for I intended to make a shallow sideways cut. Not knowing what lay within, I did not care to pierce the shell too deeply.

On a backward swipe, the tip of my blade slashed a horizontal line midway up the gray object's vertical axis, as the egg stood on one end.

Stepping back, I braced myself for any reaction.

This came swiftly. The top of the egg lifted, revealing a seam that was nearly perfect, as if cut by a keen blade. Something caused the top to topple backward, revealing the unexpected.

To all appearances, the egg was entirely empty!

The edge reared three heads taller than any of us; therefore we could not peer into it from where we stood watching.

Hor Vastus stepped forward with the obvious intention of doing exactly that.

Wishing to exercise caution, I waved for him to hold back.

Then an indescribable thing unfolded itself from deep within the egg, pushing into view. I did not have a name for it, at first. I could not call the brown-colored extensions that lifted up tentacles, for they were triangular in shape, but as they revealed themselves, they groped and crept about in the manner of octopus tentacles.

These fleshy protrusions were broad and flat, while their undersides bristled with innumerable writhing extensions that were alive. Tubes of some sort, I realized.

Two of these triangular extrusions waved at us, warningly.

Stepping forward, I pierced the nearest with my blade, and the maimed thing hastily withdrew. Yet another flopped out, reaching in the direction of Hor Vastus.

While this was transpiring, I heard muffled sounds of a man in distress.

Since the commotion seemed to be coming from within the egg, I deduced that Nal Usk lay within. Determined to release him, I commenced hacking at the retreating tentacle. It was tough, but my blade's edge sliced through its writhing brown flesh easily.

Hor Vastus and the other man, Fak Dur, began cutting and slicing, steadily degrading the tentacle nearest to them. This brought another triangular arm flopping outward, seeking to defend itself from the egg's high rim.

In the middle of this tumult, I detected a new sound. Although muffled, it was a crack of noise, its sharpness somewhat smothered. No sooner had it sounded than the muffled man's outcries ceased altogether.

Sensing what this meant, I redoubled my efforts—*and out of the egg spilled the angry thing in its squirming entirety.*

Although maimed by our effective bladework, it quickly became evident to me what the creature was. My Barsoomian comrades had not the advantage of having once dwelt upon Earth, so the monster was to them a groping horror without a name.

For the great creature was some species of starfish. No doubt it ranged the silty ocean beds when Mars was young. Now it was a fugitive that dwelled in an empty malagor egg it had appropriated as a clever shelter.

Hacking and slashing, we fought the flailing abomination, removing the soft, blunt tips of each writhing limb, even at the risk of our lives.

It was silent throughout—perhaps blind as well. For it quested and clutched about, using its disintegrating triangular arms with little success. Each time a segment was lopped off, it attempted to crawl away upon its tubelike feet. Having no independent self-awareness, these fugitive portions were summarily stabbed into submission.

One tried to climb my right leg, but a sideways swipe of my sword lopped it off. Landing on its smooth side, it simply curled up, its tubular wriggling feet unable to gain traction.

Seeing that we were making headway, I advanced toward the much-reduced thing, which by now had completely evacuated its shelter egg. Spreading out its full length upon the ground, it showed itself to be larger than the interior of the egg would allow. No doubt it was adept at curling its seven radial arms into its hiding place, taking up as little volume as possible. Only two arms were extended now. The remaining five had been hacked to mere stumps that quivered helplessly.

Stepping onto the writhing brown mass, I ignored the upcurling arms and brought my sword point forcefully down with both hands, inserting the sharp tip into the central point of its aboral surface.

A thin squeal emerged from deep within its being. Then the wildly flopping arms began to waver and settle until all animation ceased.

We stood our ground and watched it expire.

When we were satisfied that it lived no more, we took stock of ourselves. None of us were injured—although my brave comrades were pale with horror.

"On Jasoom, this would be called a starfish," I explained. "They are harmless to men, but never reach such a stupendous size in our oceans."

This explanation made little impression upon Hor Vastus and the other men. Their exertions had taken some of their breath away.

Rushing to the edge of the open egg, I peered downward into its void.

My heart sank.

Huddled at the bottom of the empty space lay Nal Usk. He was dead. I could see from the shape of his head that his skull was fractured. And I knew what the sudden cracking noise had been.

Reaching in, I lifted up the body and bore it out, laying it upon the freshly churned-up ground.

I told my aggrieved men, "The great starfish carried Nal Usk away, intending perhaps to consume him at its leisure. When we threatened it, the creature crushed his skull with irresistible muscular contractions. On Jasoom, a starfish will attach itself to a clam and by exerting its awful arms, fracture its shell in order to get at the living meat within."

My explanation was insufficient, for my warriors did not know what a clam was, but that did not matter.

A moment later, Vor Daj trotted up, attracted by the commotion.

"What has happened here, John Carter?"

"A tragedy," I explained. "We will speak of it no more. I have found the blade I sought. There are others, if any of you wish to claim them."

No one volunteered. They preferred the trusted blades of Barsoomian steel that they knew so well.

"We will take the body of Nal Usk back to the flier," I said. "I have satisfied myself that the blade of Ramdar was not forged upon another world. How this man came to be upon Barsoom, I do not yet know. But I will not waste time searching for a ship that might not exist."

Having spoken of my intentions, I directed my men to lift up the fallen sailor, Nal Usk. Together, we bore his cold clay back to the flier in silence.

Chapter 44

The Hunger March

THE DAY proved to be the longest that the composite legion of Ramdar had faced so far.

Hunger gnawed steadily at their bellies. Tarzan had scavenged only a single banth and a dozen ratlike ulsios from the surrounding terrain. He divided these among his horde, and almost immediately the warriors of Dag Dolor and the Warhoon remnants commenced squabbling over the spoils.

Jamo Ptannus and a Warhoon hordesman drew daggers and stood on the point of gutting one another.

Tarzan interceded by taking away the portion designated for the green men, saying sternly, "When you have disciplined your men, you will eat. Not before."

The daggers were put away amid red glares all around.

The disjointed carcass went into the back of the lead war chariot, displacing Cosooma, who resented it mightily. She climbed onto the driver's platform and sat there looking pale and tired. Her luminous eyes appeared to have dimmed, and her overall appearance had lost some of its ethereal glamour.

Spurned by her leader, the sole survivor of Samabar had slowly sunk into silence, turning her haughty back upon Ramdar whenever opportunity arose.

The store of nuts far diminished, the future appeared bleak.

After a pause to rest, the march resumed.

The green men having fallen into a muted sullenness, Tarzan took their cowed mood to be satisfactory proof of their obedience and began distributing joints of meat among them, riding to each jed atop his alabaster thoat, forcing them to eat on the march.

Even with this, there was insufficient food for the green warriors. They bore the insult of their hunger in stoic silence. But the red hotness of their eyes grew increasingly belligerent.

"They will turn on you," warned Tan Hadron, shackled in the back of the now-empty chariot throne, which he had reclaimed after the meat was removed. Previously, he had been forced to trudge behind it, pulled along by his chains.

Riding beside the zitidar, Tarzan pulled back and said, "I understand how to maintain discipline. If not, I am not afraid to slay the unruly."

That was all Tarzan said about it. But concern for the future began to vex him—although he quickly pushed all dark thoughts aside. Only the way ahead mattered.

AN HOUR beyond midday, with Kudu the sun streaming a reddish light upon all, Tarzan's far-seeing eyes noticed something on the eastern horizon, directly behind them.

Perhaps it was the soft whirring of great propellers that alerted him. Yet there was no wind to carry that distant sound. Possibly it was that innate and indefinable sense the ape-man shared with all wild creatures that warned of approaching danger. For he turned his head without reason and, before anyone else of his band, detected the great ship following them with his jungle-honed eyes and ears.

Pointing back, Tarzan called out to his tramping legion, "Behold!"

Tan Hadron twisted his head around and watched the sky with restrained anticipation. He saw nothing for a time.

Finally, the pursuing warship hove into view, bristling with armament. It was flying low to the ground in order to avoid being sighted. Now it began to lift skyward, abandoning the advantage of a stealthy approach.

"Continue marching forward," Tarzan called out.

"It is the great warship of John Carter," advised Tan Hadron. "He will certainly soon begin shelling you at the rear. What will you do then, Ramdar? Your forces are hungry. The greater portion of them do not even exist. Surrender would be a wise consideration."

"Ramdar does not surrender."

Turning his obedient thoat around by thought command alone, the ape-man began moving among his horde, beginning with the great gorillas and then infiltrating the green warriors, exhorting them to keep marching.

Dag Dolor warned him, "The ship will surely overhaul us before long, O Ramdar. We have not the strength to run for very much longer."

Tarzan fixed him with his steely gaze, saying, "Warriors who follow Ramdar do not run. They stay their course. Advise your men to do the same."

Riding to the hordesmen of Dak Kova, Tarzan repeated his orders.

The Warhoon jed replied, "If John Carter commands that vessel, as you say, I fear for our future."

"Fear for John Carter instead. Ramdar is mightier than he will ever be."

At those bold words, the green nomad laughed so hard that his golden fillet almost fell off his hairless skull.

"Your audacity does not cease to astound me, O Ramdar. Perhaps in another life you were a green warrior such as myself. Why else would you be so fearless?"

Out of the corner of his eye, Tarzan caught a brief flash. But when he looked toward it, he saw nothing. It came from the direction of his war chariot. He decided it was only the sun reflecting off the mirror dangling from the harness of Tan Hadron. This phenomenon had happened before. The ape-man took no further notice of it.

His eyes returning to the approaching ship, an idea formed in his brain.

Noticing the change of expression on Tarzan's stern features, Dag Dolor spoke up, "What are you thinking, O Ramdar?"

"I am thinking that the hold of that ship is filled with banths. For I smell their musk, yet none are within sight. No doubt they are confined by cages."

"Do you expect them to be unleashed upon us?"

"Not if John Carter is as wise as his reputation boasts."

"Of what value are those banths if he dares not unleash them so that we may eat them?"

"Perhaps," Tarzan said slowly, "they can be liberated to our advantage."

His wide-spaced red eyes shifting back and forth between the great sky vessel and his bronze-skinned jeddak, Dag Dolor inquired, "Do you propose to liberate them?"

INSTEAD OF replying, Tarzan turned his alabaster thoat about, and charged to the rear, the animal's eight legs stampeding with increasing vigor as he picked up speed.

Making certain that his sword was firmly in its scabbard and his knife in its sheath, Tarzan stood up on the back of the thumping animal, and launched himself, using the thoat's momentum to propel him forward.

His leap was prodigious. The ape-man sailed through the air, coming down hard on both feet, his sturdy leg muscles cushioning his landing.

Again he sprang, and again, Tarzan cleared the space between him and the mighty sky vessel until he was sailing high over its open deck.

His arrival was not unexpected. The sun had made his bronze skin gleam, painting him as a distinct target. A dozen swords were raised to receive him.

Tarzan landed in their midst, and his sword leapt from its scabbard.

They rushed in from all sides, making very little noise, other than the tramp of their sandal-shod feet upon the skeel-wood deck.

No blade touched Tarzan of the Apes. His sword point jumped here and there, blocking and lunging, sliding and banging, his mighty sword arm proving irresistible to the red men and their ordinary blades backed by mere human strength.

Amid the clamor of rasping and clanging metal, sturdy steel blades broke at the guard, leaving their wielders stunned and stark of eye. Other swords jumped from nervous fingers to go tumbling over the gunwales. Not a man who stepped in to engage the furiously parrying interloper managed to hold onto his weapon. It was astounding.

Tarzan moved about the deck with impunity, knocking down all attackers with the flat of his blade, tripping others, kicking their blades away from clutching hands, yet drawing little or no blood, and demanding, "Where is the woman who sings?"

"You will never take her!" shouted a man who wore a uniform of command.

"Who are you?"

"Kantos Kan, Overlord of the Navy of Helium."

"Where is John Carter?" demanded Tarzan.

When no one replied, Tarzan said, "Tell John Carter that I offer the red prisoner in exchange for the woman who can sing to banths. I will not harm her. Tell him this!"

Then Tarzan vaulted the rail, his seemingly impervious sword once more sheathed.

The ape-man did not leap off the ship, but instead clambered down with simian speed and agility until he came to the great double doors on the lower side of the ship's broad hull. He found the edge of one corner, and smashed it in with a bronzed fist. It broke readily. Hanging by one steel-strong hand, he pulled out his Samabaran knife and used it to pry the door open; it swung wide.

Sunlight entering the dark hold brought the growling and snarling of caged banths to his ears.

Working his way down, unafraid of the height and confident in his sure grip, the ape-man swung into the hole, landing on his feet.

There he beheld a row of cages, each one containing a captive banth. From the shadowy iron-barred interior, rows of emerald eyes glared at him hungrily.

The ape-man gave them a similar return stare.

"You see me as meat!" he taunted. "I hold you in the same low esteem!"

Whirling, Tarzan smashed the remaining door outward, whereupon it broke free of its hinges and went tumbling down to the cushioning moss far below.

Then, turning his attention upon the cages, the ape-man smashed the locks with his sword, one after the other as the thunder of shod feet stormed along the main deck and down the spiral companionway that led below.

Tarzan paid those urgent sounds no heed. He smashed each lock in turn, its components unable to stand up to the miraculous Samabaran sword against which forged steel was no more than brittle iron.

Throwing open the cages one at a time, the ape-man slew each banth in its roaring, snarling turn, then effortlessly flung its bleeding carcass out the open hatchway.

The shuffling approach of shod feet grew louder. Shouts of men reached him.

Having no more time to release and slay, Tarzan fell to opening cage doors and reached in, pulling out the cowering banths by their tails and flinging them alive out into the open air, whereupon they plummeted to their doom, howling in fury.

He had not gained dubious freedom for the last three banths when armed sailors swept down and attempted to engage him.

Laughing wildly, the ape-man unleashed a dark-maned banth. It came out of its cage roaring. Tarzan evaded the snapping mouth nimbly, then booted it in his tawny hindquarters, sending the confused beast galloping in the direction of the approaching swordsmen.

Common sense overtook righteous anger, and the copper-skinned swordsmen who had almost reached the foot of the companionway reversed course and attempted a contentious retreat, becoming entangled of blade and limb.

Falling on the rearmost of them, the banth began ripping one red man apart with claws and teeth. Defending swords swiftly plunged into the creature's vitals, and it was soon rendered asunder in a violent welter of gore.

By the time the Martian sailors had reached the lowermost hold, Tarzan had swung out the open hatchway, and swiftly climbed back onto the deck, which was deserted but for a skeletal crew that eyed him in awestricken bewilderment.

Running along the gleaming starboard rail, the ape-man soon reached the ship's stern, swung over the side. Holding on with one hand, he dropped his sword into the main stern propeller.

The miraculous blade was caught by the whirling blades. The propeller flew apart, leaving the unharmed weapon to fall back to ground, whereupon it bounced once on the soft moss.

Flying pieces of propeller banged and dented its still spinning and churning companions. The silent electrical motors began laboring.

SATISFIED THAT he had crippled the great ship in part, Tarzan dropped to the ground, landing on his feet, and rushed to reclaim his weapon.

As the mighty battleship began listing and drifting aimlessly, the victory cry of the great apes once more resounded through the cloudless skies of Barsoom.

From John Carter, there was no reply. The stupendous dreadnought remained silent.

Chapter 45

Damage Report

WHEN I learned of the calamity that had befallen the proud dreadnought, *Dejah Thoris*, I could not contain my ire.

"How could one man have done so much damage?"

Over the flier's radio receiver, Kantos Kan responded without apology. *"Ramdar is a demon, John Carter. He could have slain us all but did not do so. Instead, he simply taught us a harsh lesson. The wounded will all survive, but we lost one man, Omal Le, to an escaped banth."*

"What lesson did you take from his attack?"

"That he is stronger than we imagined. Ramdar is all but invincible. He beat us back as if we were children. Our swords might as well have been sticks of sorapus wood! When you arrive, you will find a litter of broken swords we picked off the deck and made into a sorry pile at our stern."

"The sword of Ramdar is superior to our finest steel," I stated. "Continue your report, Kantos Kan."

The overlord went on. *"Ramdar demanded possession of Thuvia of Ptarth. She was belowdecks at the time, and Ramdar did not bother searching for her. Instead, he released almost every banth and flung them overboard as if they were mere soraks. It was almost beyond belief. This demon is like nothing Barsoom has ever before witnessed."*

"Hold off from the horde a safe distance," I ordered, "lest Ramdar attack again. But keep it in sight. If you are able to do so safely, pummel all escaped banths with your deck cannon, so as to make them unpalatable."

"*There is more, John Carter. Ramdar has offered to trade Tan Hadron for Thuvia. Of course, this is an impossible exchange.*"

"Tan Hadron will be ransomed ere long. Be confident of that."

"*I have no doubt on that score,*" returned Kantos Kan. "*Tan Hadron was able to send us a message via heliographic signal. Alas, we did not receive all of it.*"

"Tell me."

"*Tan Hadron informs us that Ramdar desires to depart from Barsoom. He also asserted that the barbarian horde is not what it seems to be. We did not receive all of that part of the message, so we do not know what that portion means.*"

"Await the arrival of my flier," I told him. "I will rendezvous with the *Dejah Thoris* as swiftly as I am able."

TRUE TO my word, I soon reached the vessel and inspected her from my circling flier before landing upon the deck.

Just as Kantos Kan had told me, the damage to hull and stern propellers was considerable. This Ramdar was a superman. Worse, he was what the overlord claimed him to be—a demon.

Surveying the damage, and taking Kantos Kan's report, I asked, "How well can the ship navigate?"

"One buoyancy tank appears to be leaking, but very slowly. She is not quite crippled, for two of her great propellers still turn freely. But she lacks full headway and will not maneuver as she should."

"We will catch up with the horde, harry it with cannon and so commence driving Ramdar southward."

"Toward the great salt expanse?"

I nodded firmly. "Ramdar has only sufficient provisions to keep his horde marching another padan or two. We will provide him with the motivation to alter course toward his destruction."

"As you command, John Carter."

I sought out Thuvia in her private quarters, belowdecks.

After I knocked, she bid me to enter.

"John Carter," she greeted, coming to her feet. "Ramdar is truly a demon from another world. A terrible planet, no doubt, and not one as civilized as Barsoom."

I imparted stiffly, "Ramdar has offered to trade Tan Hadron for you. This will not be permitted, of course, but it tells me that the barbarian is struggling to feed his growing horde."

"Just as I have been struggling to lure wild banths onto this ship," returned Thuvia. "Unfortunately, they have become very difficult to find. Now that we have lost the latest supply, I fear that we will be unable to capture sufficient numbers for our future needs."

"I will devise another plan," I told Thuvia. "One that will not require so many banths. Especially since Ramdar has a distressing habit of eating any that come his way."

"I have watched this horde from afar. It still grows."

"I expected this. As time passes, you will learn that the increasing strength of the horde of Ramdar will prove to be its very undoing."

"How can this be?"

"Firstly, more mouths to feed means hunger and hardship for all. Secondly, I have dispatched Carthoris on a secret mission. If he has succeeded, Ramdar is in for a very rude surprise—one that I will not reveal to you at this time."

Thuvia eyed me with understandable concern. "Lest I become this barbarian's prisoner, John Carter?"

"You will never fall into the hands of this bronze-skinned brigand, I promise you. My son, Carthoris, would never forgive me if you did. Remain in your quarters. Once darkness falls, a speedy flier will return you to Helium. For your work here is done and there is no longer any need to tarry at such great personal risk to yourself."

"As you wish, John Carter."

Thus reassured, I left Thuvia to join Kantos Kan on deck. The sound of cannon fire had just commenced. The steady thunder meant that Ramdar would not feed upon the hard work of my ship and crew, and gain strength therefrom.

Chapter 46

Secret Signals

THE BOOMING of cannon commenced just as Tarzan of the Apes was exhorting his horde to reverse course and march in the direction where more than a dozen banths were strewn inert in death over the carpet of moss, waiting to be claimed.

"They are pulverizing your food again," suggested Tan Hadron, lifting his shackles emphatically.

"We will scavenge what we can," stated Tarzan indifferently.

"And you will charge into cannon fire, inasmuch as John Carter will foresee your intention."

"His ship is damaged," returned Tarzan. "Perhaps I will destroy it this time."

"Sue for peace, Ramdar. You are a mighty jedwar. The Warlord is a just ruler; he will permit you to live. As for your horde, you must consider it to be a doomed legion."

Tarzan wore his quiver of arrows across his broad back so that the feather-fletched ends lifted above his right shoulder. His bow stuck up over the opposite shoulder, held in place by its metallic string, which pressed diagonally across his mighty chest, denting the bronzed skin.

Removing the bow with his left hand, he extracted an arrow with his right, and stood up on the back of the alabaster thoat, who jarred to an instant halt the moment the ape-man's brain projected his desire into its receptive brain.

Tarzan could spy the cannon pointed downward; a gunnery officer of some kind was directing the gunner to fire punishing bursts of shells into the ground below. Banth carcasses exploded at intervals, spraying bits of bone and viscera everywhere about, painting the moss-like vegetation scarlet.

Aiming steadily across a distance no other archer could have dared, the jungle lord released his arrow. Through the thin atmosphere of Mars it flew, lodging in the unprotected skull of the gunner, who pitched backward and out of view.

The officer recoiled in surprise. The second arrow transfixed him in the throat. His hands came up, clutching, but there was nothing he could do. After half a turn, he lurched behind the gleaming rail so far away.

Without hesitation, another gunner took the place of the first, and the cannon barrel shifted ponderously downward. Aiming along a flat plane, the new gunner fired in the direction of the horde.

In rapid succession, three shells landed, falling far short. Shredded moss and lichen cascaded harmlessly downward amid clumps of rust-red soil.

Tarzan dispatched the second gunner with a missile through an exposed shoulder. The man reeled away, clutching the protruding shaft, his coppery features twisting in agony.

When a third would-be gunner raced for the now-empty position, Tarzan dropped him with another far-flying arrow. It cut across the top of the man's close-cropped scalp, creating a fresh part.

Both hands attempting to stanch the blood soaking up through his hair, the red sailor flung himself below the protective bulwark of the vessel's gunwale.

A silence fell. No one attempted to man the cannon that sat on its swivel mount, gray smoke curling up from its massive barrel, which swung slowly and aimlessly about.

Dag Dolor strode up and asked, "O Ramdar, what would you have your warriors do now?"

"We will fetch our next meal. Leave it to Ramdar to suppress all opposition."

No hesitation showed in the faces of the green men and albino gorillas alike. Onward they marched, a unified force motivated by the determination of their jeddak, as much as by the necessity to eat.

Tan Hadron spoke up. "Consider that you are marching into a trap, Ramdar."

"If I am," returned Tarzan, "why would a man such as yourself warn me?"

"I have watched you for several padans now. Ramdar, you are brave. You may be half-animal, but you are a warrior born. I did not understand how such as you came to be, but you have my respect. If you surrender yourself, I am sure I can communicate my observations to the Warlord of Warlords, and John Carter will show you a just mercy. All considerations rightfully due to a warrior of your stature will be accorded you."

Tarzan offered nothing in response to that. His expression appeared to be one of indifference, but in truth he took the words seriously.

If Tan Hadron represented the kind of soldier who followed John Carter, then perhaps the Warlord was deserving of respect as well. But at this moment, John Carter was at war with the horde of Ramdar. The ape-man's personal objectives were subordinate to his responsibilities toward those who followed him.

The horde rolled on, largely silent and equally unyielding in its aims. Only the war-chariot of Ramdar rumbled with each revolution of its high wheels.

Watching the strange barbarian, Tan Hadron came to realize that no response was forthcoming. He was a puzzle, this bronze-skinned brigand. Tan Hadron could not fathom him. So he ceased to try.

As they marched forward, Tad Hadron saw that the stricken dreadnought was turning about. But this time, it was not intent upon flight. It began beating toward the approaching horde.

A frown came over Tan Hadron's coppery brow.

It would have been sound tactics to retreat and permit the horde to fall upon the scattering of dead banths and then attack with cannon. Yet the Warlord appeared to have an altogether different objective in mind.

What could it be?

Tan Hadron could not conceive of John Carter's present strategy. But he had confidence in the Warlord's tactics.

SO INTENT was he upon watching the maneuvering warship that the red prisoner did not realize that the green jed calling himself Dak Kova had shifted over upon his own thoat and was pacing the war chariot on the opposite side from where Ramdar rode, commanding and unafraid upon his impressive white thoat.

A low voice growled, "Greetings, Tan Hadron of Hastor."

His head swiveling about, the red Martian beheld the great green chieftain riding along, his war lance balanced across his tremendous thighs. Suspicious, Tan Hadron asked him in a low tone, "What do you want of me, Dak Kova?"

"Understanding."

"Speak then."

"I am a spy sent by John Carter. At the appropriate moment, I will release you from your fetters. But you must seek escape."

"Lend me a sword and I will seek battle, not flight."

A grin twisted the green jed's long-tusked mouth.

"I would loan you my lance, but you would break your back attempting to lift it."

"Free me and I will locate a worthy sword."

"Hear the words of your Warlord through my lips. When the opportunity arises, you will escape and not fight. For there is a plan. And you must play your part."

"It galls me to hear these words. If what you say is true, I have no choice but to obey."

"You have no choice but to obey," returned the green man. "Otherwise, you may perish with the horde of Ramdar, which is destined to be slaughtered to the last man."

Lifting his head and looking around, Tan Hadron saw the horde arrayed all around, both real and illusionary. His eyes fell on golden-haired Cosooma, seated on the platform ahead of him, apparently oblivious to their conversation.

"The white woman and Ramdar should be spared."

"That will be up to John Carter, and no other. Remember my words. Your life will depend upon them."

The green jed drifted back to his men, his slate thoat turning about.

Taking care not to be noticed, Tan Hadron removed the mirror from his harness and used it to capture the reddish rays of the sun. By carefully tilting the polished surface, he produced reflective signals which he trusted someone from the approaching ship would discern.

After a few minutes, an answering flash came. It told that his message had been received. But little more than that.

Tan Hadron was not disappointed. He understood that transmitting a longer heliographic response would invite suspicion to fall upon him.

Restoring his signal mirror to its leather strap, he sat back to await developments, which promised to be decisive.

Chapter 47

"Instructions are Confirmed"

I WILL admit that the marksmanship of the barbarian Ramdar staggered me.

Archers were not commonly found on Barsoom. But the skill of this bronzed giant was superlative in all ways. The strength with which he delivered his shafts was unsurpassed. They had penetrated the previously impervious cannon shields of forandus metal. Equally noteworthy was the preternaturally keen vision that permitted him to aim at such a daunting distance, well out of bowshot for an ordinary warrior. No one born upon Barsoom could equal such a feat. Of that, I was certain.

Seeing the gunners fall from the starboard rear cannon, I ordered Kantos Kan to leave off all gunnery.

"I will lose no more men to this super-barbarian's powers."

"As you wish, John Carter."

"Turn the ship about, and we will meet Ramdar and his mad horde."

Kantos Kan nodded. "And if he breaks into retreat, we will pursue him."

"He will not retreat," I assured Kantos Kan. "He knows that his horde will soon starve if he does not avail himself of fresh meat. He must feed it. But he cannot defeat us."

Listing to port, the great dreadnought came about, while sailors worked to locate the small but steady leak from one of the buoyancy tanks. The surviving working propellers drove the craft sluggishly, but eventually, she turned her nose toward the advancing force.

I turned my field glass upon Ramdar and observed him astride his giant thoat—a massive beast only a green man could fully control. A strange thrill coursed through my blood at sight of him. Despite his barbaric trappings, which included a cloak of banth hide, his weird horde followed him without hesitation, riding into the teeth of the mightiest warship ever to sail the skies of Barsoom.

"What motivates him?" I wondered.

Ramdar remained an unfathomable mystery to me. And that made me all the more determined to bring him to book. If I were forced to slay him, I would prefer that it would not be before I wrested from him the story of his life. I had thought I was unique among Barsoomians, but Ramdar's story promised to rival my own, if not surpass it.

As I studied Ramdar's grim face, a flash of light appeared behind him, and to his right. It was coming from the war chariot and began spelling out a message. I had no doubt this communication came from Tan Hadron, still a captive.

It said: "Know that Ramdar seeks to claim the dead banths. From Dak Kova, a green jed in your service, I have received instructions to escape at earliest opportunity. Please confirm."

Taking my own signal mirror in hand, I replied in kind.

"Instructions are confirmed."

The *Dejah Thoris* beat on steadily. I knew that my plan was working.

Before long, Kantos Kan drew up and reported, "John Carter, we are over the field of dead banths."

"All stop," I ordered. "Hold this position. Let Ramdar and his forces come to us."

"As you wish, John Carter."

My hand drifted to the hilt of my strange new sword. If Ramdar were the leader I judged him to be, he would come ahead and face me man to man. I could not predict the outcome of that confrontation, only that I was ready for it.

The dreadnought slid to a slow halt, its straining propellers falling silent. It cast a stupendous shadow over the field of slain banths.

Again, I lifted the glass and watched the impassive features of the barbarian. He seemed unperturbed by my bold maneuver. That made me all the more eager to confront him once more.

Chapter 48

Parley of Peril

WHEN THE stupendous sky ship drew to a quiet stop, Tarzan of the Apes called for his horde to pull up short. Less than the earthly equivalent of one mile separated them. Tarzan watched in silence.

To claim the dead banths would be to march into the teeth of the mighty airship's armament, which could easily turn about and bring its punishing deck-mounted rail cannon to bear upon them.

So long as its blunt bow faced them, it was impossible for Tarzan to pick off the sailors manning the cannons, for the bulk of them were stationed on either side and at the stern.

Cosooma called out, "O Ramdar, what will you do now?"

Tarzan did not hesitate in his reply.

Urging his white thoat forward, he said, "I will face John Carter."

"But if you are slain, what will become of Cosooma?"

Without looking back, Tarzan said, "Cosooma has lived for one thousand ords without Ramdar. Perhaps you will find a way to live for another thousand ords without Ramdar."

"Your words are cold. You are heartless!"

"John Carter is said to be a man of rectitude. If you must surrender to him, I am sure he will show you mercy."

"Go to your death, O Ramdar, if that is your wish."

If Tarzan of the Apes heard her, he did not reply.

The striking alabaster thoat padded across the ochre moss, making almost no sound other than its labored breathing.

It had crossed less than half of the space between the two opposing forces when down from the high rail jumped John Carter, to land upon the mossy carpet. In his right hand flashed a long-sword.

Tarzan saw that this blade was of the same shimmering blue metal that comprised his own weapons. The grimmest of grins touched the ape-man's sun-bronzed countenance. "Here is a man who learns from his mistakes," he told himself.

Riding steadily, Tarzan brought his thoat to a halt and then dismounted. Not twenty feet separated the two men.

As he approached John Carter, he did not draw either blade swinging from his hips.

"I wish to speak with you, man to man," he stated.

"Are you a man?" countered John Carter.

"I was not born from an egg, and so count myself as one."

"I do not believe that you are an ape, as you claim."

"Enough!" said Tarzan. "I claim this meat all about us. Withdraw your ship, so that my warriors may feast."

"I offer you a trade, Ramdar. You may have these banths, but first you must return Tan Hadron of Hastor."

Tarzan shook his head stubbornly. "I will trade Hadron for the woman whom the banths obey."

"Thuvia of Ptarth is married to my son, Carthoris. She will not be surrendered."

His bronze hand going to the hilt of his sword, Tarzan pulled it free and said, "Then we must fight."

"Before you die, tell me this, Ramdar. From what world do you hail?"

Before Tarzan could reply, the sun slipped to the horizon and the thin atmosphere became suffused with crimson light.

Two bright blades lifted and caught that harsh light as Tarzan and John Carter advanced upon one another.

But before they could clash, a commotion arose up behind the ape-man. Yells, curses, followed by the clamor of blades smashing into one another. What began as an outburst swelled into a furious uproar.

Turning his head, Tarzan saw the chieftain calling himself Dak Kova in the act of driving his formidable war lance into the warriors of Dag Dolor. One was quickly skewered, and expired, waving helpless hands that clutched now-useless weapons.

At the forefront of the war chariot, Cosooma stood up, lifting her magnificent bow in one hand. An arrow was swiftly fitted to it.

She called out in warning, "Ramdar! We are betrayed!"

The arrow flew.

His eyes fixed upon Tarzan, John Carter did not see the approaching missile until it was too late. It struck him on the left shoulder, turning him half around with the force of its flight.

Seeing this, Tarzan stepped in and smashed his blade against that of his foeman.

Although injured, John Carter gave a creditable account of himself. Contending blades thrust and parried; sparks flew off alien blue metal. A clamorous din arose.

The first minute of combat proved indecisive. John Carter wove a glittering net of flashing bladework. Tarzan easily feinted and blocked every stroke, but his skill was not as great as that of the white-skinned Martian, whose sword point continually sought an opening in the ape-man's more careful guard.

John Carter pressed his skill and daring, forcing the other onto the defensive, lest he be skewered.

But the greater strength of Tarzan could not be brooked. There was no penetrating his guard, for his reflexes were preternatural in their instinctual alacrity. Each time John Carter executed a deft, flashing attack, the bronzed swordsman's superior strength and reflexes blocked it without effort.

The battle raged for not very long. The shaft in John Carter's left shoulder bled profusely with every passing second; his strength began to ebb, his superb reflexes slowing.

Knowing that victory was nearly at hand, but not wishing to harm the other, Tarzan brought the flat of his sword against the other's exposed temple, knocking him senseless. Onto the moss he fell, stunned and momentarily helpless.

His opponent vanquished, the jungle lord stepped back. Turning to face the noisy disarray that had befallen his well-organized horde, Tarzan spied a red warrior approaching.

It was Tan Hadron, no longer a prisoner.

"Where is your honor, barbarian?" he raged. "Having your woman striking first and then taking advantage of a worthy foe?"

Tarzan said harshly, "I gave no such order."

But Tan Hadron heard him not. He snatched up the fallen blade of John Carter and prepared to engage.

Tarzan told him, "I have no wish to slay you, red man."

"Then you will die!"

The copper Martian's blade flashed in the dying rays of the sun, seeking Tarzan's vitals.

Tarzan blocked it, then swept up his sword arm. To Tan Hadron's immense surprise, his own blade leaped upward, leaving his stung fingers, unable to hold onto the hilt, which was slippery with gore.

Stepping in, Tarzan knocked him aside with the flat of his blade, and caught the descending sword in his free hand.

Sprawled upon the moss, Tan Hadron looked up to see the bronze barbarian wielding two superlative swords, one in each fist.

"Do your worst!" he shouted. "If you slay us, you will be slaying your betters."

"Ramdar only slays those who deserve death," intoned Tarzan, sheathing his own blade and dropping that of John Carter at the senseless Warlord's feet.

"Tell John Carter that Tarzan of the Apes returns his sword, and gives him his life. This token of respect will not be offered again."

Then, turning without another word, the ape-man took to the sky, hurtling back toward his disorganized horde, intent upon settling what appeared to be a bloody mutiny taking place.

Chapter 49

Freed

STANDING UPON the back of the chariot-throne of Ramdar, the better to see the impending battle between John Carter and the barbarian of bronze, Tan Hadron took little heed to what was transpiring around him.

The horde had halted, waiting expectantly.

As the barbaric assemblage watched, the green jed who claimed to be Dak Kova moved among his tribe, whispering to them. They began drifting about, taking positions adjacent to the other green men.

The sun was going down. They waited for the moment in which the light would begin to fail.

No one suspected treachery, and so they shifted about, unchallenged.

All eyes stayed fixed on the bronzed figure of Ramdar as he dismounted from his white thoat, no less so were the eyes of Tan Hadron, who knew that the next few minutes would be decisive.

So the red captive did not see the tall green jed wearing a plumed fillet slip up behind him, and carefully unsheathe his sword.

Reaching down, he took hold of the man, spun him around and broke the chains binding his hands with his blade, crying, "Go! It has begun!"

If Tan Hadron was inclined to hesitate, a swift push from an olive-green hand knocked him out of his spell. He sprang into action. Jumping over the chariot-rail, he broke into a run, racing toward John Carter and his hovering warship. No one challenged him. No one even noticed his flight, for they were already embroiled in other matters.

At scattered points among the horde, the green nomads of Warhoon turned upon other green warriors, driving their blades into unsuspecting bodies.

Dag Dolor lost his upper left arm to a descending blade. Before he realized he had been attacked, the heavy limb dropped to his feet, fingers clutching. His upper right hand found the hilt of his long-sword, which purred from its scabbard, its steel catching the light as it did so.

Whirling to confront his attacker, the maimed warrior saw that it was a three-armed Warhoon swordsman and cried, "You have signed your death warrant!"

The other laughed. "It is you who are bleeding profusely. Fight or lie down and die. The outcome will be the same either way."

Dag Dolor struck. His enemy was taller than he, but that did not matter. He chopped off the man's lowermost left hand, and then bisected his sword arm at the elbow, forcing blade and forearm to drop to the moss.

"Die, traitor!" he yelled, driving the point of his blade into the other's breastbone, splitting it with a distinct crack.

Fights broke out among the hordesmen, and in the milling conflict, hardly anyone noticed that Cosooma raised her bow and drove a whistling shaft into the shoulder of John Carter.

Looking about for another foe, Dag Dolor spied the supposed Dak Kova and rushed over to challenge him.

Hearing the swift approach of labored breathing, the green chieftain turned about and beheld the smaller warrior charging onward with bloody sword lifting.

Throwing back his head, he laughed raucously.

"Do you think to best me, armless one?"

"Prepare to die, Warhoon!"

Lifting his sword, the green man hurled back, "I am not of Warhoon. I am a Thark!"

"I do not care what tribe claims you! Death will be your lot."

But before Dag Dolor could engage his towering foe, the loss of blood from his fresh stump took its toll. Stumbling, he lost all headway. He collapsed into the dirt, gripping his sword tightly. For he knew that to lose the weapon meant instant, ignominious death.

The Thark stepped up to him, placed a heavy green foot on his sword wrist, holding it down. He was preparing to deliver a death blow when another green warrior of the horde of Churvash Ul entered the fray.

It was Jamo Ptannus, whose greater maturity made him the Thark's equal in height and size.

Soon their blades were clashing, razor edges that rasped against one another. Dag Dolor lay insensate on the moss, oblivious to all that was going on around him, for pandemonium had overtaken the horde of Ramdar.

Seeing the green warriors disintegrate into conflict, some of the great white gorillas pounced upon the fallen, taking up severed limbs, greedily devouring the still-warm flesh; other bulls swept up the bloody spoils of war and brought them back to the hungry women and children.

The remote Martian sun set on this welter of destruction, sudden darkness blanketing all.

Chapter 50

Betrayal

DARKNESS SMOTHERED the dead sea bottoms below the Barsoomian equator when the muscular bronze form of Tarzan of the Apes dropped down in the midst of his furiously fighting horde.

Neither misshapen moon had yet risen, yet the keen eyes of the bronzed giant could discern by faint starlight that the two green hordes had fallen into chaos. He did not doubt the loyalty of the horde of Churvash Ul, so he did not hesitate to bring his sword to bear against the green warriors of Dak Kova, supposed Jeddak of Warhoon.

Discovering one of the latter in violent conflict with another green man, Tarzan interceded and broke the back of the foeman with a leaping kick that shattered his spine.

The olive-skinned warrior collapsed, all four arms threshing about, frenzied fingers tearing up the moss, but unable to rise again.

The size of these green men was formidable, but the might of Tarzan of the Apes was more formidable still.

After sheathing his sword, he plucked arrow after arrow out of his quiver, and, with unerring aim, dispatched as many as he could impale with barbed shafts that struck with the speed of lightning bolts. Here and there, a missile struck a jugular vein or impaled a beating heart, and that green Martian was struck down. Where the man-sized shafts buried themselves in gigantic muscles, they failed to retard the ape-man's foes, bringing only stinging annoyance.

In the dark, amid the clamor and confusion, Tarzan concentrated on settling raging individual battles before more of his warriors fell. When he could, the jungle lord aimed for the weird red eyes, splitting them and producing immediate blindness and consternation. After that, loyal swords decided matters in swift order.

Over the din of battle, Cosooma's voice lifted.

"Ramdar! Hear me! Dak Kova is not who he says he is! He is an enemy! A tool of John Carter!"

Before the ape-man could respond, the boisterous voice of the supposed Dak Kova bellowed out, "Where are you, Ramdar? Come and face my steel!"

"I am here!" shouted Tarzan, flipping onto the back of his white thoat, so as to stand head and shoulders above the fray.

The green jed spied him almost at once. He was in the act of parrying a thrust from Jamo Ptannus's long-sword. Beating back the other with a sudden surge of fury, he tripped Jamo Ptannus, who went down. A lethal blow would have followed, but the momentary victor turned about and charged away. He hastily mounted his thoat, while Tarzan brought his own massive steed around.

Swords raised, they came at one another like earthly knights of old prepared to joust.

The colossal green warrior seemingly had the advantage in height, as well as in the more massive size and weight of his blade, but he soon discovered that this advantage was negligible.

As the charging mounts pounded toward one another, Tarzan stood up, balancing on naked feet, and lifted his sword high, intent upon decapitating the other.

Here, they were unevenly matched. The green chieftain's sword had a greater reach than Tarzan's, but it still was forged of mere Barsoomian steel.

Grinning fiercely, the jed shouted, "I bring you a message from John Carter. And that message is death!"

The gruesome grin adorning the green warrior's face collapsed when Tarzan's superior sword swept around and broke the larger blade in twain, sending its upper length tumbling away.

The pounding thoats went charging past one another, neither foeman having yet drawn blood.

Staring in consternation at his dismembered blade, the green warrior angrily flung it aside and took up his forty-foot lance, setting it before him with one hand while he steadied his body with his remaining hands on the neck and withers of the laboring mount.

The opposing thoats came about again, lined up anew, and began racing toward one another, padded feet trampling soft moss already slick with gore.

If Tarzan feared the great lance, it was not in his expression.

The green warrior shouted, *"Know before you die that my name is not Dak Kova. But Tars Tarkas the Thark!"*

"That name means nothing to Tarzan of the Apes."

"Nor does yours! Let, then, one of us die under his true name!"

Tarzan dropped back into a seated position, and when the two animals were on the verge of colliding, he sprang from his mount and executed a high arching somersault in the air.

The bouncing lance, driving for the spot he had vacated, passed over the white thoat's spine, scoring it, but not deeply. A howl of pain arose in response. Then the two animals collided with a terrible sound, followed by cries of pain and despair. Both animals were stunned by the thunderous impact.

Flung from his war thoat, Tars Tarkas held onto his bloodied lance. As his wounded mount slowly sank to the moss, it lurched to one side, its skull crushed, broad nostrils gushing gore.

Dropping down from the sky, Tarzan fell upon the lance. He chopped the weapon in twain, leaving only a broken stump protruding from the ponderous handle.

Once more, the great green Thark lifted high a weapon to his goggling red eyes, and the snarl coming from his gaping mouth was one of anger and frustration.

"What manner of warrior are you?" he bellowed.

"I am *Tarzan-of-the-Apes,* jeddak of the tribe of Narag and the horde of Vakanor both."

Tars Tarkas clambered to his feet. He spread out all four arms, showing empty hands.

"As you can see, I am temporarily bereft of weapons."

"I am not," said Tarzan coldly. "Order your warriors to halt, or I will remove all four of your arms and feed them to my apes."

"I believe you, *Tarzan-of-the-apes.*"

Lifting his voice, the green jed began calling for his warriors to cease fighting.

It was some minutes before the last of the fighting died down, but at last it did. Many green limbs had fallen to the ochre moss, to be collected by foraging gorillas. This, as much as the sound of Tars Tarkas's voice, brought a halt to the bloody proceedings.

Tarzan addressed his beaten foe. "Go back to John Carter. Tell him he is to leave the horde of Ramdar alone."

"Your horde is decimated. What will you do, *Tarzan-of-the-apes?*"

"That is for Tarzan to decide. Now go!"

Tars Tarkas said, "I will carry back to John Carter any other message you care to impart."

"Tell John Carter if he does not retreat, I will fall upon his great ship and destroy it with my invincible blade. Do not delay."

"Rest assured that the great Warlord will know those words. But I cannot promise what he will do about them."

"You will have to wake him up before you can learn," countered Tarzan.

And while the great white gorillas of Ramdar consumed the severed limbs of many newly maimed green men, Tars Tarkas took his ragtag warriors and departed the vicinity unmolested, for the fighting had exhausted all participants.

A PROFOUND quiet fell over the horde. Tarzan looked about. His warriors were spent, their numbers greatly thinned. He left them to husband their ebbing strength. For he had no words for them at present.

He found Cosooma huddled in the back of the great war chariot, uninjured but shaking with something more akin to anger than fear.

"Are we defeated?" she asked imploringly.

"Not as long as I live."

Lifting her head, she looked around and laid stricken eyes on the carnage strewn all about. The sight of savage white apes consuming the remains of the fallen caused her to turn ghostly pale.

"How will you control your horde now? They have fallen into cannibalism."

"My Tarmanbolgani will obey me. And the green warriors are loyal to Dag Dolor, who, in turn, is loyal to Ramdar."

But Dag Dolor was nowhere to be seen.

Ranging among the feasting and the fallen, Tarzan found Jamo Ptannus, whose glossy green torso was raw with open sword cuts, none of which appeared mortal.

"Where is Dag Dolor?" he demanded.

Jamo Ptannus pointed to a pile of corpses with his encrimsoned short-sword.

"There. Know that if he does not survive the night, Jamo Ptannus stands ready to be your jedwar."

THE APE-MAN followed the compass point the sword indicated.

There he discovered a young green warrior sprawled on the gore-smeared moss, his left shoulder a jelly of coagulated blood.

It was Dag Dolor. His red eyes were half-shut, and his great chest heaved with the exertions of respiration.

Taking up fistfuls of moss, Tarzan used this to stanch the blood, and then lifted the ponderous green man, carrying him back to the war chariot of his dead father.

When this was done, the ape-man looked to the west and saw that the great warship had dropped onto the carpet of moss and was collecting the defeated horde of Tars Tarkas through the main cargo hatch.

John Carter could not be seen, nor was Tan Hadron visible. There was no doubt in the jungle lord's mind that both men had been collected and brought aboard deck.

Tarzan had not anticipated how the conflict would unfold, so naturally he failed to foresee its actual conclusion.

Before long the all-powerful ship lifted into the sky, and its dwindling running lights showed that it was slowly backing away. But after a while, it paused again, holding in place, stationed as if waiting.

Tarzan moved among his hordesmen, separating the great white gorillas from the dispirited green men. When he had cuffed them apart through his irresistible strength alone, he announced, "We will camp here for the night. Those of you with meat, finish eating. Then sleep. Ramdar will stand guard. If the enemy ship moves closer, I will deal with it. But in the morning, we will resume our march."

Jamo Ptannus asked, "The apes have eaten. But what about us?"

"You may butcher the thoats that have fallen. I will gather what banths I can from the dead scatterings so that we will have meat for tomorrow. Maintain discipline. Do not falter. Uxfar cannot be much farther."

"The city will be prepared for us."

"John Carter believed that he was prepared for Ramdar. But you can see that he was not. Do as I say."

And that was the conclusion of the argument.

Chapter 51

"I Still Live"

WHEN I awoke, at first I did not know where I lay. Before I recognized the glow of radium lamps dispersing the darkness of the windowless chamber in which I found myself, my sword hand instinctively went for the hilt of my blade. But it was not there. Nor was my scabbard. I lay upon a ship's berth. My head ached. I discovered a bandage encircling my brow. When I moved my other arm, that shoulder throbbed. Remembering the arrow that had pieced me there, I saw that it had been removed and the wound dressed.

"I still live," I breathed.

As I attempted to rise, a gentle hand stayed me.

"Do not be alarmed, John Carter. You are safe aboard ship. For this is the *Dejah Thoris*."

Turning my head, I recognized the warm face of Thuvia smiling down on me. On either side of her hovered other equally familiar faces, Kantos Kan among them. Beside him stood Tan Hadron, looking gaunt but vital. Last but not least, towering over all, was my great good comrade of long standing, Tars Tarkas, Jeddak of Thark. His tusked grin was the most reassuring expression of all, for he was my first true Barsoomian friend.

"Kaor, John Carter," greeted Kantos Kan. "Welcome back."

"Did Ramdar get the best of me?" I demanded, sitting up.

"Do not be embarrassed," Tars Tarkas assured me. "Ramdar got the better of me, as well. Truly he is a warrior beyond the common panthan who tramps the face of Barsoom."

"He lives?"

"He does," inserted Tan Hadron. "But his horde has been greatly reduced. Even now they struggle among themselves, the white apes consuming the bodies of the fallen green men."

I laughed in spite of the gruesome image conjured up in my brain.

"I imagine that will do no good for the morale of this Ramdar," I remarked grimly.

Studying my limbs, I found them to be whole and relatively undamaged. Only my skull and shoulder pained me. I stood up, and found myself to be unimpaired of leg.

Thuvia imparted, "It was fortunate, John Carter, that the arrowhead that pierced your shoulder was neither barbed nor poisoned. You will heal in time, or so the ship's doctor assures me."

"More fortunate, I conceive, that Ramdar did not launch that missile. Otherwise, I would been permanently crippled."

Tars Tarkas spoke up. "Ramdar revealed to me his true name, John Carter. He called himself *Tarzan-of-the-apes*."

"He told me the same, Tars Tarkas. That strange name means nothing to me."

"Nor to me, John Carter. I have never seen the like of him, although in some ways he reminds me of you. He has great fighting spirit."

Kantos Kan declared, "Say the word, John Carter, and we will pound this barbarian and his followers into dust with our cannon, ending the menace once and for all."

I shook my head firmly.

"You may grind his horde into the moss, Kantos Kan, but so long as Ramdar himself lives, he has the ability to destroy us. We must further weaken him."

Kantos Kan said, "Reinforcements are coming. The forces of Ramdar will not reach the gates of Uxfar. We will drive them south toward the great salt remnant of Lake Ojar. And there, on its parched face, they will perish of thirst, if they do not surrender first."

"There seems to be no avoiding it," I said, buckling on my sword. "But before Ramdar dies, I wish to engage him one more time."

"Why must you, John Carter?" asked Tars Tarkas, his red eyes staring.

"For one reason and one reason alone," I declared. "While Ramdar lives, I can no longer consider myself the greatest swordsman on all Barsoom."

And Tars Tarkas laughed boisterously. "Well spoken!"

MY SHOULDER wound freshly dressed, I passed the night laying my plans.

First, I saw to it that Thuvia of Ptath was spirited away by my trusted aide, Vor Daj. Not until the flier was safely launched and lost from my view did I breathe a sigh of relief. Once this was accomplished, a tremendous weight was lifted from my shoulders. For, despite my assurances to my beloved daughter-in-law, deep inside I understood that if the forceful brigand penetrated the lower decks of my ship, it would be difficult to stay his demonic strength.

From Tan Hadron, I learned all I could of Ramdar. Of particular interest was the white woman, Cosooma. The fact that she could cast illusions reminded me of another old friend, the bowman, Kar Komak of Lothar. His was a strange story, for he was not hatched of an egg laid by a woman. No, Kar Komak was a warrior birthed in the imagination of Tario, jeddak of the white-skinned Lotharians of ancient seafaring Barsoom. Conjured up repeatedly to do battle, he eventually attained a type of reality that made him as solid of sinew as any fighting man.*

"Is Cosooma a Lotharian?" I asked him.

---

* See Thuvia, Maid of Mars *by Edgar Rice Burroughs.*

"She is not, John Carter. Her city was called Samabar, until a great meteor crushed it utterly, driving her people underground. She claims that she is the last of her kind."

"No doubt she is an Orovar woman, then, of which some few survive into this era."

"It would seem," continued Tan Hadron, "that the blue blade Ramdar wields was forged from the metallic meteorite that fell from the sky long, long ago."

I nodded. "No wonder I do not recognize its metal. It is fortunate that I have gained a blade of similar composition, for the sword of Ramdar appears to be otherwise invincible."

"It is not only his sword that is formidable," Tan Hadron cautioned me. "His strength is beyond yours. Even armed with a blade of comparable metal, besting him in combat smacks of the impossible."

"Impossible or not," I returned, "any man can be defeated in battle. First we will crush his horde, and then we will deal with Ramdar. Now that I comprehend that his fantastic forces are, in part, illusory, I can lay my plans accordingly. For the threat is not growing as I feared."

Tan Hadron asserted, "I am convinced that Ramdar hails from another world. His thews are like his skin—bronze. And he questioned me as to whether the science of Helium has created ships capable of traversing the outer dark of space. I believe that he seeks a way home."

"Unfortunately, our scientists have never achieved such a thing. Therefore, Ramdar is a castaway, marooned upon Barsoom. As such, he becomes our problem. He claims to have been fathered by apes. He is too savage to be allowed to run free and threaten civilization."

"I must tell you that this man impresses me, John Carter. He averred that he did not command Cosooma to pierce you with her arrow in order to gain undue advantage in combat. And when you lay helpless and insensate upon the ground, Ramdar could have slain you, but did not, sheathing his sword and dropping your own blade into the ground."

"What do you make of him, Tan Hadron?"

"Ramdar is wild, more savage than the green nomads and low apes he commands. Yet there is a spark in him that stirs a grudging respect in me. He bid me to inform you that having returned your sword and spared your life, he is not inclined to do so again. I do not think you can capture him alive, as you desire."

"Having twice tasted defeat at his hands, Tan Hadron, I am of a mind to believe you. If Ramdar prefers death to capture, that will be his choice. But it will not be mine."

Chapter 52

Reinforcements

TARZAN EXPENDED considerable care and bush skill slipping out into the night and across the plains of endless moss, dragging back the carcasses of the banths, those which survived intact from the shelling of the previous day.

Not leaping into the air as was his usual custom for fear of attracting attention and gunfire, the ape-man accomplished his tireless work under the ever-shifting shadows of Barsoom's mismatched moons, Thuria and Cluros. Consequently, he slept but little.

Over the course of his unusual life, Tarzan had slept in the finest beds in England as well as in the hard crotches of Africa's towering trees. He was comfortable in either.

During his sojourns upon Mars, he had become accustomed to sleeping on the spongy moss and lichen of the extinct sea floor. While it was sufficient in many respects, and even more comfortable than a too-soft mattress and feather-filled pillow, the ape-man yet pined for the high, reassuring boughs of jungle trees. Such were his earliest beds, when he was but a hairless balu of the tribe of Kerchak, and the ones he most favored.

After sleeping for a few hours, Tarzan awoke with the dawn and crept among his tattered horde. First, he went to the great white gorillas, and admonished them for eating the remains of the maimed green warriors.

"Severed limbs are of no use to those who lost them," grunted Foad defensively.

"Should we starve while fresh meat decomposes?" added another ape. This was a large bull named Druk, who had lost one eye in combat. The eyelid was now shut.

"This must stop," Tarzan told them in their own grunting language. "Going forth, we will eat only banths and whatever else can be scavenged."

The Tarmanbolgani complained that they were weary of the march and only yearned for the comforts of a city. This was a growing sentiment among them.

"It does not have to be a city alive with men," muttered Druk. "A ruin such as Vakanor would suffice."

"Uxfar is the nearest city," returned Tarzan. "No doubt we are only a padan or two's march from its gates. We will continue in that direction."

There was grumbling and barking complaints, intermixed with muttered skepticism that the place ever existed, but no one directly challenged the will of Ramdar.

Tarzan left them to jabber and mutter among themselves.

It was more difficult to make peace among the surviving green men. Dag Dolor still slept, his grievous wound having sapped his energy. Tarzan addressed the others.

"Ramdar promises that the apes of Ramdar will confine themselves to eating banth meat from this padan forward. What transpired last night could not be avoided. We will continue the trek to Uxfar. And I will protect you from the forces of John Carter."

"John Carter is allied with Tars Tarkas, the great Thark," Jamo Ptannus said flatly.

"I do not know him."

"Tars Tarkas is the Jeddak of the Tharks. Perhaps the greatest among green men, for he long ago made an alliance with John Carter and the Heliumetic Empire. Together, they keep the peace on Barsoom, by word or sword, whenever it suits them."

Tarzan stated, "Tars Tarkas fell back against the might of Ramdar. His horde has been driven back to John Carter in defeat. Do not fear Tars Tarkas."

Thus was the matter settled for the moment.

Later, Tarzan went to Cosooma. "When we reach Uxfar, arrangements will be made for you to dwell there in comfort."

"Do you already consider yourself to be the Jed of Uxfar, without ever having laid eyes upon its towers?" she asked sullenly.

"Arrangements will be made for you," repeated Tarzan. "Let there be no more talk about this."

The ethereally pale woman of Samabar sneered, "I follow you and trek across the arid face of Barsoom, and you discard me at the first city you come to?"

Tarzan was unsparing with his words. "It is my expectation to return to my homeland, if it is possible to do so. You cannot come to Jasoom. You would not like it there."

Having unburdened himself of his opinion, Tarzan turned away. Laying a slim hand on one bronzed arm, Cosooma stopped him.

"O Ramdar, was it not clever of me to strike John Carter with an arrow once I realized that you were betrayed by the false jed, Dak Kova?"

"It was not clever," Tarzan retorted. "It was spite. And it shamed Ramdar in the eyes of the copper men. For I fight my own battles."

Cosooma's mood swiftly changed. "Ingrate!" Seeing no alteration in the bronzed warrior's impassive regard, her voice softened. "I have never divulged to you what rearranged the bones of the dead in the jungles of Desh. Would you like to know the answer now?"

"Speak."

"Cosooma did that."

"For what purpose?" asked Tarzan, genuinely interested.

"To frighten anyone who entered the jungle, for I dwelt there alone. And while I craved companionship, I did not care to be taken by any man, green or copper. In truth, I have not craved the companionship of a man until I met one who was neither of those colors. The only man who interests me is the hard hue of bronze. Will you not consider that if you cannot return home, Cosooma would be a worthy mate to you?"

"I will not consider any alternative to returning home," replied Tarzan quietly. "But I acknowledge you to be one of the most beautiful women I have ever beheld. I cannot foresee what may or may not happen if there is no certain trail to my home jungle. Do not ask me this again. If the matter needs to be raised again, it is I who will raise it."

"Your indifference is a dagger in my heart," Cosooma said, turning away.

"I am not indifferent to you," responded Tarzan. "I am loyal to those who are loyal to me. My true mate has ever been loyal to me. And if I ever hold her in my arms again, it will be as if you and I had never met."

"Is kindness not in your heart?"

"I am Tarzan of the Apes. The only kindness I knew in growing up was given by my mother, Kala, who—if she beheld me now, among the terrible Tarmanbolgani and the Hortamangani warriors of many arms—would undoubtedly consider me to be lost and ill-fortuned."

"An ape would demonstrate more heart than you, heartless one!"

Tarzan did not deign to respond to that. He strode off.

Lying back in the shelter of the chariot-throne of Ramdar, Cosooma closed her eyes and attempted to conjure up her imaginary army.

Her elaborate phantoms were slow in coming. When they did materialize, they were fewer in number and lacked the color and clarity that had attended previous incarnations.

"If I knew what your mate looked like," she spoke aloud, "I would conjure up her likeness, if only to see if your cold heart was capable of melting. But then my own heart would break. And what good would that do?"

Already out of range of her voice, Tarzan could not reply.

Mustering the horde took longer than usual, but at last Tarzan got his forces organized, and they spread out in much-depleted wings on either side of him. They started pushing southwest, in which direction they believed Uxfar to stand.

Tarzan rode atop his great alabaster thoat, which moved sluggishly, a consequence of its collision with the war thoat of Dak Kova. It had survived, but the other had not. The lance wound across its spine had begun closing, but the lumbering beast struggled to plod ahead.

BEHIND THEM, the great sky ship of John Carter followed at a decorous pace. It did not attack. Nor did it close with the wounded stragglers of the horde.

Before many hours had passed, the skies before them began to fill with other, less impressive ships, flying colors that they did not recognize. Still, their size rivaled that of the sea-going warships of Earth, Tarzan saw.

Cosooma stood up in the perpetually rumbling war chariot, and exclaimed, "Behold, Ramdar! This must be the sky fleet of Uxfar!"

"We will continue our push," proclaimed Tarzan.

No one turned aside. Both wings continued plodding along.

Soon, the approaching fleet settled to the moss, and great hatch doors opened in the sides of their hulls. Instead of fierce banths, however, red men mounted on slate-skinned thoats appropriate to their size disembarked.

They began tramping toward the leading skirmish line of the horde.

Behind them, the great war vessel of John Carter swung about slowly and ponderously. The starboard cannon batteries began firing, their explosive shells falling far short.

Consternation seized the horde. The green men yanked their blades from scabbards. The apes jabbered excitedly, brandishing their crude war hammers skyward.

Rousing from his sleep due to the calamitous noise, Dag Dolor sat up and demanded, "O Ramdar, has disaster befallen us?"

Seeing the way to Uxfar blocked by mounted cavalry, and harried at his rear, Ramdar shouted out orders.

"Turn south! We will swing around the cavalry. As for the cannons, if they find our range, Ramdar will deal with them. At present, they are wasting their ammunition. They do not have sufficient reach to strike us."

This was repeated for the benefit of the great white gorillas who had begun milling about in confusion and fear, circling to protect their helpless charges, the shes and the balus.

Slowly, reluctantly, the surviving horde of Ramdar turned to the south.

The cavalry also shifted southward, but did not charge. Nor did the great airship, whose cannon detonated intermittently. Her shells continued to fall far short of their target.

Turning his head toward John Carter's flagship, Tarzan of the Apes suspected that this was deliberate, and intended to force them south.

Having no other choice in the matter, the ape-man decided that south is where he would go. He was resourceful and confident enough in his own abilities that he believed that if it were possible to turn the tables on his enemies, Fate would present him with such an opportunity.

Yet he felt a pang in his heart. For his keen sense of smell had begun to detect distant odors, such as prepared foods, flowers and other unmistakable scents denoting civilization.

Uxfar, then, was not far distant. No doubt another day's journey would reveal her proud towers. But the unseen city would have to wait.

Tarzan said nothing of this to his followers. Now was not the time for arguments or dissension… not if the horde of Ramdar was to survive….

Chapter 53

OJAR IS REACHED

FOR TWO padans, we pushed and harried the discouraged horde of Ramdar south. And for two padans, they marched doggedly, growing increasingly tired and hungry.

The bronze-skinned warrior was not so easily discouraged, however. Ranging about the dead sea bottom, he scavenged banths, which he defeated with a savage ferocity that impressed even Tars Tarkas. For disdaining his sword, he employed only his knife.

Standing beside me at the port rail, where we watched the astounding performance, the great Thark asked me, "Why do you permit him to feed his horde, John Carter?"

"For one reason only. So that they retain the strength to reach the salt Lake of Ojar, where they are certain to meet their doom. If I force Ramdar into starvation before that time, he will turn on us and wreak tremendous damage. See how effortlessly he carries a half-grown banth over his head as he jumps from point to point?"

Ramdar seemed almost to fly, so great were his leaps.

Standing beside us, Kantos Kan remarked, "This barbarian is tireless."

"No one is tireless forever," I assured him. "By the time the remnants of the horde reach the salt crust, much of the fight will have gone out of them. There will be dissent, unrest among the great white apes and the green nomads. If they choose to make a stand at the edge of the lake bed, we will have a fight. But if they elect to brave its expanse, it will be his certain destruction."

"That is a wise plan, John Carter," stated Kantos Kan. "I do not see how it can fail."

Tars Tarkas laughed mirthlessly. "No military plan is ever achieved without flaw or risk. This great scab upon the face of Barsoom has never been explored. Who knows what will be discovered there? I would not underestimate this man, *Tarzan-of-the-apes*, or whatever his true name is."

"I will not, Tars Tarkas," I said firmly. "On Barsoom there is a saying very much like one I knew upon Jasoom. And that is, an army marches on three legs, one of which is its stomach. Without food, Ramdar and his horde will soon be crippled."

And so we continued to stalk them, harrying their rear with an occasional shell and letting them hear the steady thunder of the cavalry of Uxfar following behind them, out of reach of Ramdar's far-traveling arrows.

The sun was going down when they came to the verge of the vast white crust.

We watched them through our field glasses. Understandably, the barbaric horde pulled up short, not certain what they faced. For there was no similar feature elsewhere upon Barsoom. Since Lake Ojar was previously unmapped, they could not guess at its true size.

Apparently, they held council as twilight melted into darkness. I would have directed radium searchlights on them, but I did not want to provoke Ramdar, for I knew he could gain our deck in a series of prodigious leaps and wreak havoc upon us. I was counting on his loyalty to his horde not to desert them, nor to incite our mighty cannon.

My judgment proved correct. After half a zode of consultation, the faint sounds of creaking harness leather and the low rumble of Ramdar's war chariot told me that the horde had resumed the trek south. They had entered the great salt desolation. I doubted that any of their number would ever depart it alive—unless it was under my authority and in chains.

Chapter 54

Crossing the Crust

WHEN THEY came to it, the horde of Ramdar hesitated to enter the great pale patch that lay like an unhealed scab upon the face of the dead sea bottom. The hairless gorillas were particularly afraid. They hunkered down stubbornly.

One-eyed Druk spoke for them all when he said, "We have never seen a wilderness such as this. It is as if this part of Barsoom had died. There is no moss or lichen. No water. There is nothing. Just a desert of barren white crust."

Tarzan addressed him from his chariot-throne. He stood on the forward rail so everyone could see him. There, in the dying light of the sun, his bronze skin appeared molten. He wore his cloak of banth skin.

"On the world from which I come," he declaimed, "there are places like this, places where lakes have dried up, leaving only salt. I cannot tell how large this one may be. But if it has not completely dried out, there will be water in the center, perhaps other things we can eat, such as fish."

Cosooma asked, "What if the water is too salty to drink, Ramdar?"

"We will not know this until we come to it," stated Tarzan.

"Nothing grows here," she said. "What am I to eat when the last nuts run out?"

"If we turn back, they will train their guns on us. It will be a slaughter. I cannot have that. We will dare this lakebed of salt."

A green Martian spoke up, asking, "What if we do not find food?"

"We will slaughter the remaining thoats and, if necessary, the zitidar. Ramdar has spoken. We must march while the sun is down and we are not subject to the copper men's cannon fire."

And so they resumed their march, the orange-eyed zitidar continuing his plodding course, the mouth of its lowermost trunk investigating the ground, but finding no sustenance. Tarzan dropped down to his customary place in the chariot, on the high driver's platform. Behind him lay piles of moss he had torn up from the dead sea bottom as forage for the animals.

Standing behind him in the vehicle bed, Cosooma said, "Dag Dolor still sleeps."

Beside the woman, the maimed green Martian lay heavily, his wounds bound tightly and no longer bleeding.

Tarzan stared down upon him. "Rest will do him good. When he is well again, he will be fit enough to fight if need be. In the meanwhile, a sleeping man requires no food."

Under the speeding moons, the horde marched until their energy began to flag, and soon Tarzan permitted them to make camp. Making two separate groups, and keeping far apart from one another, the terrible Tarmanbolgani and Hortamangani fell into a deep slumber in which no pangs of hunger disturbed them.

Tarzan slept, too, making a bed of his banth-skin cloak. He knew that he would need his strength in the days to come.

DAWN BROUGHT sudden illumination.

With the first touch of solar rays upon his bronzed features, Tarzan sprang to his feet. The camp was rousing. The jungle lord gave his hordesmen time to get themselves organized for the push ahead.

With a mighty leap, Tarzan soared upward. He had but one objective. And that was to reconnoiter this weird zone of salt by daylight.

His first landing was difficult, for the salt crust abraded the soles of his feet. But he soon saw that for all around, there lay nothing but white desolation. It was of such a harshness as to make the endless dead sea bottoms seem inviting by comparison.

Another leap produced the same bleak prospect. It was impossible to say in which direction the salt petered out. The flatness of the baked surface was deceptive. Martian sunlight made the broken crust shimmer, blurring distant details. The ape-man could not gauge how many sun's march it would be until substantially different terrain was encountered.

The great warship of John Carter hung far to the north. It had not advanced overnight. Nor was there any sign of the pursuing Martian cavalry. Evidently they had not entered the zone of encrusted ground, for their thoats were dependent on the moisture found in the roots of the moss for sustenance.

The ape-man said nothing as he returned. Grimly, he went about his horde, mustering them to their feet and exhorting them to again push south.

"What did you see?" Cosooma breathed, once the chariot-throne resumed rolling along, hauled by the mastodonian zitidar whose eye-stalks now drooped wearily. Beside it, the alabaster thoat staggered along, eyes glazed in pain, a small mountain in motion.

"I did not see Uxfar. Nor are we pursued by cavalry. For now, we are safe."

"Safe to march to our deaths," she muttered darkly.

"That remains to be seen," commented Tarzan.

The climbing sun began shedding rays upon the great white scab that were less red. The flat salt surface became warmer, acting like a crude mirror, making them squint to keep out the harsh reflected solar rays.

The first day's trek was uneventful. Dag Dolor still slept. The grumbling was kept to a minimum. There were no fights.

But as the afternoon wore on, something appeared in the sky in the direction toward which they were marching, something translucently violet in hue and impossible to discern in the harsh salt-reflected sunlight.

No one noticed it at first. Not even Tarzan. For it was utterly silent.

Wavering, it dropped downward, then approached patiently not four feet above the shimmering ground. Due to the blinding glare of the terrain, it was not noticed until it attracted the attention of an observant green man. He yelled out in warning, pointing with his war spear.

It was a solitary denjuru. Its stingers swiftly enwrapped an unwary green warrior, who began to scream while simultaneously drawing his sword. He slashed out at his attacker, and such was his maddened fury that he inadvertently lopped off one of his own hands, creating a pool of gore in the bleached salt.

The tall green man did not seem to notice. Stump spurting scarlet, he charged about, hacking, and slashing thin air. Not comprehending what he was fighting, the warrior flailed uselessly, for the oblate thing had attached itself to his broad olive back.

Attracted by the commotion, Tarzan drew his own blade and came bounding toward the stricken Martian.

He struck only once, impaling the thing, which deflated like a violet balloon.

It was too late. The tottering green warrior began puffing out and expanding, gases filling interstices in his hulking body, and lifting him off the ground.

Helpless, all six limbs gyrating, he rose to his inevitable doom.

Knowing what was to come and understanding the effect it would have upon his demoralized and hungry horde, Tarzan vaulted upward and removed the man's head with a single decapitating swipe of his sword.

The hairless head tumbled back to the ground first, the body only after the gases had begun leaking out. It landed with a sad finality.

While the hairless white gorillas shrank from the sight, the green nomads gathered around Tarzan, setting their backs to him, repeating the word, "Denjuru! Denjuru!" and scanning the skies for more of the things, their swords raised defensively.

No more fluttered into view. But the persistent glare made it difficult to see with certainty. The green men hesitated to break their combative stance.

THE APE-MAN explained, "I know the odor of their lairs. I cannot smell any scent spoor. That one may have been but a scout."

Some of the bolder green warriors gathered around the dead violet bladder of a monstrosity, poking it with the points of their blades.

Jamo Ptannus asked, "Can one be safely eaten?"

"I do not know," admitted Tarzan. "But I would not take the risk. It is full of poison."

Reluctantly, the green men left the dead denjuru, and they continued their hungry march.

"Watch the skies," warned Tarzan from his chariot. "Where there is one, there could be others. For their nests harbor large colonies. They slay in the manner you just beheld. The only defense is to kill them before they attach themselves to your body."

No one could have questioned the bravery of the green Martians, but as they trudged along, their blood-red eyes became haunted with something that looked like the beginnings of fear. Their jaws hung slack with thirst and hunger, their great tusks gleaming dully in their parched mouths.

They tramped along until the sun went down. Only then did they seek rest. No one had eaten all day, but neither had any warrior complained.

"Sleep!" commanded the ape-man. "I will stand guard. If any denjuru return, Ramdar will deal with them. Sleep secure in that knowledge. I have spoken."

The horde slept, untroubled by nightmares or the hurtling moons of Barsoom, whose wayward beams painted the endless salt with stark light, etching the cracked and broken ground deeply.

Patrolling the perimeter, Tarzan of the Apes passed the night in silent contemplation. He did not permit himself to fear, nor would he allow himself to despair. But on this night, he felt as if the Earth were farther away than ever before.

Chapter 55

Food from Nowhere

WITH THE new dawn, the horde of Ramdar was slow to rouse from their uneasy slumber. No one cared to awaken to an empty stomach. But slowly they did bestir themselves.

Tarzan went among them and saw that two of the balus had perished overnight. Their mothers, upon discovering this unhappy fact, became inconsolable. The bulls, in turn, grew solemn. They lacked the energy to complain.

Recognizing the gravity of the situation, the ape-man went to the green horde and addressed Dag Dolor, who had regained sufficient strength that he was sitting up in the back of the chariot-throne of his father.

Tarzan said, "We must slay the last of the thoats, so that we have strength for the march ahead."

"To slay a white thoat is to admit defeat, O Ramdar."

The other green warriors joined in that sentiment.

"The white thoat is sacred," stated Jamo Ptannus. "To slay him is sacrilege. To eat him is worse."

Dag Dolor pleaded, "Ramdar, you must slay the zitidar instead. He will provide more meat. Spare the thoat so that you may ride tall as our jeddak. If you do otherwise, you will lose esteem in the eyes of your green followers."

Tarzan recognized the truth of their words. He could not dissuade them, but neither would he permit the zitidar to be eaten if there was a chance to salvage it. He knew that if he were reduced to walking on foot with the towering Tarmanbolgani and the terrible Hortamangani, he would lose status in their eyes. They might turn on him.

"Remain here," he told them. "I will search for food."

Taking to the clear skies, the jungle lord hurtled southward. Yet everywhere he ranged, the blinding glare of the salt expanse defeated his vision. Tarzan could see little beyond several haads.

Landing hard, he considered his prospects. The thoats and the zitidar would soon falter and perish, having no moss or lichen to feed upon. The way ahead was unknown. The future appeared hopeless. There was no trail or track to follow. Only a hot, shimmering crust. The ape-man noted that if this were the equatorial sun of Africa, the ground would become impossible to traverse. Barsoom's weaker sun merely made the ground uncomfortably warm under his naked feet.

When he returned to his horde, Tarzan was afoot. For every time he landed on the salt, it tore up the bottoms of his feet, and he knew he could not afford such repeated injuries. If he were to continue reconnoitering, he would need protection.

Ignoring the others, the bronzed giant went to Cosooma, who sat in the back of the chariot-throne whose high sides concealed her from avid eyes. "I do not see any hope."

"Why do you tell me?" she replied thinly.

"You are the only one who is not suffering."

"Look more closely, Ramdar. Do you not see the lines in my face, the hollows in which my once-beautiful eyes now sit? Do you not notice me aging before your very eyes? Or are you oblivious to these things as much as you are blind to my beauty?"

Tarzan peered through the ever-present glare.

He saw that indeed there were lines in Cosooma's soft face that were not present before. The haunting luminosity of her eyes had also faded. But this had not been readily apparent in the glare of day.

"I do not wish to surrender to the forces of John Carter," he said at last. "Nor will I push my followers to certain doom.

Perhaps Tan Hadron was correct. If I surrender myself, mercy may be shown to the rest, white and green alike."

"Why should the Warlord show you mercy? You have twice despoiled his great warship, the pride of his navy. And defeated him at every turn."

"But now it is I who stand on the precipice of defeat."

Heaving a great sigh, Cosooma said, "I have conceived an idea."

"What is it?"

"The illusions I create. They have some measure of substance. The longer I focus on them, the more real they become. With sufficient effort, I could make the apes and the fierce warriors believe that thoats created from my imagination could be eaten."

Tarzan frowned. Something like incredulity crossed his impassive features.

"I do not believe you. The mind cannot create meat that may be eaten."

"Or I can create the illusion that you have returned with as many banths as necessary," she continued urgently. "You could feed them the banths. They would not question that illusion."

"But it would not fill their bellies."

"If I create the illusion that their bellies are full," she returned haughtily, "they would believe their stomachs. And so have the strength to march another padan. Perhaps two."

Tarzan considered the woman's words. At last, he said, "If you believe that you can accomplish this miracle, Ramdar will welcome this respite."

"I am willing to do so, Ramdar. But is Ramdar willing to give Cosooma what she desires?"

"What is it you desire?"

Her voice became imploring. "Your heart. Nothing less. Will you give it to me? Will you give it to me without reservation? Will you take me into your arms with the entirety of your being?"

Tarzan shook his noble head. "No, I cannot. For the heart of Tarzan belongs to another. I have told you that."

"You will throw all of our lives away out of manly pride?"

"Not pride," returned Tarzan. "Love. Honor. Loyalty. These are the virtues that matter. Do what you will. But if I am forced to butcher the zitidar, you will have to walk instead of riding the chariot. Or you will have to be left behind."

With those words, the ape-man turned his back upon the woman of Samabar and walked away.

Cosooma glared at him. The hard look in her eyes verged upon hatred. But soon that rising emotion melted. She looked about from her perch on the war chariot and saw the hungry white apes and the disconsolate green men foraging aimlessly for food on the cracked ground. And she knew that before the day grew long, they would be turning upon one another in an orgy of mutual cannibalism.

"Ramdar!" she called. "I will create banths. But you must lead them to foster the illusion that they exist. I will need a zode in which to conjure them up. For they must smell and taste like banth."

Tarzan nodded. "I will keep the peace until you do this."

Then Cosooma lay down under the rays of the climbing sun and shut her eyes.

A zode passed. During that time, Tarzan checked the faltering zitidar, and attempted to reassure it. The brute's orange eyes were growing dull. A definite feeling of unease showed in the way its eye-stalks lifted and roved about, vainly seeking the familiar ochre moss that represented sustenance.

The bundles of that plentiful growth carried in the chariot had been parceled out to the surviving animals. But the last moist ration had been consumed and now there was no more.

The thoats were milling about, digging their snouts into the cracks in the salt. But these were proving to be barren of any growth. Where moisture was discovered, it was scant and too salty for the creature's tastes.

This boded badly for finding potable water deeper in the heart of the evaporated lake. Tarzan began to consider turning about before it was too late to save the animals.

COSOOMA'S VOICE broke the silence that dominated the Barsoomian day.

"O Ramdar! Behold!"

Spying the woman pointing to the west, the jungle lord sought the source of her excitement. He spied it instantly.

A tawny banth emerged out of the surrounding glare, jaws slavering. Seeing the beast, Tarzan took out his short-sword and cried out so that all could hear him, *"Kreegah! Bundolo!"*

Neither the apish nor green followers understood those warning words, but Tarzan stepped up without fear and charged the creature from its flank. The ape-man drove his blade into the banth's sinuous side. To his surprise, it gave out a deathly roar, and rolled over on its side without further resistance.

Stepping back, the jungle lord saw that his blade was smeared with gore. He had felt the sharp point slip into the creature's ribs, and this seemed somehow real.

Raising his voice, he shouted, "Come! There is food."

The green men fell upon the dead banth first, for they were closer. Their blades swept in and rendered the inert thing with slashing blows that separated meat from bones, casting the steaming organs aside for later. Soon, they were eating the hot meat, disdaining the raw bones.

The ape-man carried the bones to the jabbering gorillas, who relished the marrow. Foad and Druk fought briefly over the spoils. Druk cuffed Foad, who bared his yellowish fangs, but the argument ceased in a diminishing succession of growling and snarling.

While that miracle was transpiring, two more banths appeared. That they materialized from nowhere was not noticed by the gorging horde. Tarzan made quick work of them. He had expected to play-act a charade, but the tawny creatures appeared to possess some semblance of substance.

As he distributed fresh gouts of meat to the gathering gorillas, he tasted of one. His tongue believed that it was real and when the warm meat slid down his throat, his empty belly received it gratefully.

Tarzan decided not to question this welcome sensation. For as much as anyone, he needed nourishment for the day ahead.

While the ravenous throng feasted, the ape-man went to Cosooma and said, "You have Tarzan's gratitude."

Her eyes pierced him with their hunger. "Cosooma wants more."

Tarzan ignored the statement. "You have no more food of your own. You must eat meat."

She turned her head away from his outstretched palm and the red mass that sat upon it. "I have never eaten meat. The thought is repugnant to me."

"How can you maintain your strength if you do not eat?"

"When I regain my energy, I will attempt to create the illusion of nuts and berries. This is what I will eat."

"Why did you not think of this before?"

Cosooma said sadly, "Because I know that these nuts and berries will be an illusion. I will taste them on my tongue, but my belly will know better. I do not know if they will sustain me."

"While you are discovering this, I must find a way forward. But to do so, I will need to protect my feet."

Scrounging around in the back of the great chariot, Tarzan of the Apes found scraps of banth hide and with long straps of harness leather that had been scavenged off the bodies of the Horta-men's corpses, tied them tightly around his feet.

Thus protected from further injury, he charged into the cloudless sky. This time, the jungle lord was gone for several hours.

THESE HOURS were discouraging. Between the perpetual glare and the vastness of the great salt desert, he could see nothing other than more of the same. A flat depressing anti-oasis of shimmering heat and desolation.

But during his explorations, his keen nostrils picked up an odor. It smelled of old wood, among other things.

Redirecting his course, Tarzan bounded toward that distant conglomeration of smells.

What he found all but staggered him.

Deep in the heart of the great salty scar, sunk into the ground, was a sight Tarzan never expected to see.

A sailing ship!

Or rather, a shipwreck. Reaching it, the ape-man saw that it baked in the sun, and had probably been baking for centuries as Martians reckoned time.

It was as large as an earthly caravel of the past. Her sails were long gone and the naked masts were leaning drunkenly. From the forward portion of the bridge, a great octagonal porthole stared ahead like the empty eye socket of a wooden Cyclops, while along the lower superstructure's sides a row of portholes consisting of alternating triangles showed. The hull was half submerged in the salt, and as Tarzan landed on the deck, the stiff planks beneath his feet groaned under his weight.

The ship's timbers had been bleached almost white. It was a ghost ship. As Tarzan moved along with care, lest the rotted wood under his feet give way, he realized it must have been submerged in water long, long ago. When the water evaporated, it had been uncovered. And so it remained.

The realization disheartened him.

For he knew and understood that this expanse was not formerly a salt lake, but a remnant of an inland sea. That meant that it was vaster than he had imagined.

Finding his way down into the lower decks, the ape-man discovered the cargo hold. There were casks and chests strewn about. The skeel wood had stood the test of time. Most were intact.

Taking a short-sword, he plunged the point into one cask, and was rewarded by a trickle of clear water.

Replacing his sword, he cupped his hands and brought a measure of the water to his face. Sniffing it uncovered no disagreeable odors. Carefully, he tasted the cool liquid. It was slightly pungent to the taste, but otherwise appeared to be undiluted water, and therefore potable.

Tarzan drank his fill. And then tipped the cask over so it would no longer leak.

Returning to deck, the ape-man made sure his makeshift banth-hide foot coverings remained in place. Soon, he was leaping back in the direction of his waiting horde.

The journey to this forlorn place would be a matter of one padan. The horde was yet strong enough to undertake that harsh trek. And once they reached the shipwreck, they would have shelter and water. That would be sufficient to calm their nerves and give Tarzan of the Apes time to plan for the future, whatever it might be.

For the jungle lord was no more of a mind to turn back and surrender his faltering forces to the unknown mercies of John Carter and his army of Gamangani warriors. He would press on.

Chapter 56

The Spectral Hulk

IT TOOK more than a padan to reach the shipwreck in the heart of the crusty salt patch. Night was upon them when they sighted it at last. The dome of stars showed the outline of the hulls and surviving masts. But only Tarzan could see it clearly.

Although they lost another balu during the march, the horde of Ramdar arrived in optimistic spirits. Tarzan had explained his discovery, and the prospect of fresh water had heartened every follower.

As they approached the wreck leaning in the salt, Thuria rose, shedding her lunar light, transforming the pale cracked ground beneath their plodding feet into a shining pool of reflected light.

Abruptly, everyone could see clearly.

Sight of the bleached masts and broken timbers of the old ship painted pale by moonlight caused the terrible Tarmanbolgani and the tusked Hortamangani to hesitate.

When the second moon arose, Cluros's shifting shadows made the wreck seem to come alive, as if spectral fingers were caressing it.

The haunting sight had a disquieting effect upon everyone.

"I have never beheld such a vessel," stated Dag Dolor, who had recovered sufficiently to trudge along with the others. "Such an ancient hulk must be haunted."

From his chariot, Tarzan asked him, "Do green warriors believe in ghosts?"

"We believe in the dead. And we know that some are restless, and roam freely. Nor may they be slain by steel."

"I discovered no ghosts. Only water. We will take shelter in that ship and make our stand there."

Slowly, reluctantly, the diminished horde advanced. The chariot continued to rumble and the surviving thoats and zitidar plodded forward, their parched tongues hanging from open mouths. The animals had lost weight, and continually fretted for lack of forage. Tarzan did not know how to placate them, but for the hope that Cosooma could conjure up the illusion of moss and lichen. But he knew at least that he could water them soon.

Soon enough, they reached the shipwreck. There they began climbing onto the deck, using breaks and chinks in the hull for hand and toe holds.

While they were doing this, Tarzan slipped below, going directly to the main cargo hold, carrying out heavy casks two at a time perched atop his broad shoulders, and bringing them out onto the deck.

Great porcelain jars had survived the ravages of time and immersion. These the apes salvaged for drinking cups. He also discovered bowls of similar glazed material. Carefully, he measured out rations of water. These were passed around.

At Tarzan's command, Dag Dolor and Jamo Ptannus conveyed bowls of water to the animals standing forlornly below, with the result that their bestial orbs were rekindled with the spark of renewed life.

The simian shes and the balus were carried up to the leaning deck and they drank as well. They crowded at the stern, which they indicated with firm gestures and upraised cudgels constituted their territory.

The ship was of a size to accommodate the red Martians, so the lower decks could not be penetrated by the hordesmen, who were curious if food could be found in the hold.

The ape-man assured them this was not the case.

COSOOMA DREW Tarzan aside and said, "This is a merchant ship of old seafaring Samabar, such as plied the shallow sea of Trox, the first to dwindle to nothing during the long planetary drought. The words inscribed on the bow are in the written language of my people. This vessel is named *The Shaggador*. The name means *'The Sojourner.'*"

Tarzan nodded. "The green warriors and the apes cannot go below, except where there are breaks in the deck and holes in the hull sufficient to admit them. You must stay below, where you will be safe. They have water for now. And the animals can still be slaughtered for meat when their bellies awaken to the reality of your illusions. If this is in truth an inland sea, the march to the old sea bottoms may be greater than the sustaining power of your illusions is strong."

"John Carter can lay siege to us here, if he chooses to do so."

"We have shelter. We will see what tomorrow brings. While I live, I continue to hope."

With that, Tarzan went below and sought restful sleep on his banth-skin cloak. Cosooma followed him down a companionway, and she laid her sleeping cloak in the same cabin, but a respectful distance away.

Sleep did not come to her easily. There was a gnawing in her stomach. It would not go away. That alone did not keep her awake. She knew that the great white apes would not hesitate to make a meal of her should they ever turn against their bronze-skinned jeddak.

In the middle of the night, Cosooma slipped over to the slumbering warrior and roused him from his sleep.

"What is it?" asked Tarzan, snapping awake in an instant.

"Promise me that you will not let the great white apes who follow you make of me a meal."

"As long as I live, I will not permit this."

"I give you my gratitude and make this offer in return. If I should perish, you may consume as much of my flesh as will sustain you. I would prefer this if it would keep me out of the stomachs of the terrible white apes."

"I will neither eat you nor allow you to be consumed," said Tarzan. "Go back to sleep."

Cosooma returned to her warm sleeping silks, but rest was slow in coming. She feared the break of day. And the long struggle ahead. For she could see no way out of their awful predicament.

Chapter 57

PLANS

THE *DEJAH THORIS* had not followed the horde of Ramdar over the course of the two padans of marching. I had decided upon this course of action after conferring with Kantos Kan and the others, who agreed with my reasoning.

I decreed that we would permit Ramdar and his nomads to penetrate deeper into the great Salt Lake of Ojar and suffer the privations that would inevitably result.

During this time, I laid plans.

Ordering the dreadnought to land on the dead sea bottom, we undertook necessary repairs and took on fresh troops. The banth cages were fixed and secured once more. From the supporting ships of Uxfar, we accepted elements of cavalry, warriors and thoats alike.

I watched operations from the rail with my companions. All went smoothly. The soldiers of Uxfar took their orders well. Vam Dirasun, commander-in-chief of the Uxfar Navy, was in charge of this transfer operation.

Tars Tarkas told me, "I begin to conceive the wisdom of your battle plan, John Carter. You will let them exhaust themselves and then deploy fresh cavalry into their midst."

"It is my hope to surround them and force a surrender. They will be out in the open, without shelter or cover."

But like all battle plans, this one ran into difficulties before it could be implemented.

In the middle of the night, a scout flier returned. Hadron of Hastor piloted it.

As he disembarked from the landing stage, we greeted him warmly, pleased that he had come out of his captivity with such spirit that he had volunteered to scout the unnatural horde as it navigated the barren lake of salt.

"Strange news, John Carter," he greeted.

"What is it?"

"Lake Ojar will have to be renamed. For it is not a lakebed at all, but the floor of an inland sea of ancient times. The horde has found a relic of those days. Sunk into the salt is an ancient sailing ship, a broken hulk now. They have taken shelter there."

"We can lay siege to a shipwreck as readily as we can an open encampment," I told him. "Thank you for your efforts, Tan Hadron. We will let them abide there until the dawn. No doubt hunger will keep them awake, further exhausting their will to fight. Then we will surround the ship. If they surrender, we will take them aboard. But if they choose not to surrender, so be it. I have spoken."

The last of the cavalry thoats had been brought aboard and secured in the iron cages below. I turned to Kantos Kan and said, "When you are ready, we will push into the dead sea of salt. I expect that by the time the sun once more sets, we will have this unpleasant matter completely in hand."

The Overlord of the Navy of Helium smiled confidently. "How could it be otherwise? This Ramdar is but a barbarian, and you are the Warlord of Warlords."

Chapter 58

Siege

THE HORDE woke up hungrier than when they had gone to sleep. This would have been a natural consequence of the passing of hours, but in fact, their sleeping minds had shaken off the illusion of having eaten.

Half starved, the great white gorillas started foraging for something to eat, some of them tearing up planks and chewing on the ancient dry wood. It proved impossible to chew. The taste was understandably bitter as well. So they spat it out.

They had slept on the raised back deck, while the green warriors had taken up residence in the bow and the midships, out of understandable concern that the hungry apes would encroach upon their territory with ravenous intent.

Upon awakening, the two elements of the horde of Ramdar eyed one another warily, the great white gorillas seeing the green men as potential breakfast, while, recognizing their precarious position, the latter grasped for the hilts of their swords.

Dag Dolor turned to his nearest shipmate and said, "I have never eaten the flesh of an ape."

Jamo Ptannus remarked, "Can it taste worse than banth?"

The hairless albino gorillas did not understand the tongue of the green nomads, and so could not object to this frank discussion as to their possible future. But mistrustful looks were exchanged, and the apes gathered up their crude war clubs, holding them at the ready.

Fortuitously, Tarzan of the Apes emerged from below, perceived what impended, and placed himself between the belligerent forces.

"We are hungry," shouted Foad, who spoke for the gorillas.

Replying in their own language, Tarzan told them, "Ramdar will locate food."

Foad struck the rotting deck with his war club and said, "We will eat now. Not later. Slaughter the thoats. We will devour them."

One-eyed Druk echoed his hairless comrade. "Thoat meat is good," he jabbered. "It will give us strength."

"I will do this," said Tarzan. Turning to the green warriors, he said, "We will eat the thoats, except for the white one. He will be spared."

This was done under the reproachful orange eyes of the zitidar, which may have suspected its own fate was nearing.

Possessing sound limbs, Jamo Ptannus employed a war hatchet to decapitate the first thoat while his fellows used their long-swords to rend the beast once the head fell to the crust, turning it crimson as grass.

The great gorillas did not wait for their share. Howling, they fell on a great slate thoat which had begun to stampede away at the hideous sight of the butchering of its companion. This unfortunate creature they tore limb from limb. The remaining apes descended on the carcass, and used their terrible fangs to rip out large chunks of still-living meat, which they gobbled down greedily.

TARZAN STOOD guard over his alabaster war steed. No one challenged him.

There was sufficient thoat meat to dull the worst of their hunger pangs. And while the two factions broke their fast, Tarzan went below and foraged, confident that the white thoat would not be molested.

Cosooma met him and asked, "What transpires above?"

"They are eating. But their stomachs will require more than can be provided. The zitidar must be next."

"We are trapped here, are we not?"

Tarzan did not reply. He pushed his way below, searching every cabin and warren in the sagging, gloomy ship, Cosooma following.

Ranging about, he found nothing of great interest, certainly nothing that could be foraged for food or any other necessity. The salt water that had immersed the ship so long ago had also degraded a great deal of the structure of the old hulk.

In the lowermost deck, Tarzan found a spot in the forward hold where the keel had rotted away. It was too dark to see much, but by dint of sunlight streaming through the chinks in the decrepit hull, he saw what appeared to be a crude tunnel leading down into the seabed.

His nose told him that something unpleasant lurked down there. He did not immediately recognize the smell, for some of it belonged to the ancient sea.

Grasping Cosooma by her arm, he urged, "Come quickly."

"What is it?"

"I do not like the smell. It reminds me of denjurus."

They went up a companionway that consisted of a spiral ramp and soon emerged out on the broken, sun-whitened deck under the shadow of one leaning mast.

"Perhaps whatever is down there died long ago," suggested Cosooma. "For it smelled of great age."

"I must fill that hole regardless. While the others eat, I will gather rubble for this purpose."

The sun was by this time well above the featureless horizon. The glare of day had returned, making it all but impossible to see beyond the immediate environment of the tumbledown shipwreck.

Therefore, Tarzan could not perceive the far horizon in any direction. Hot sunlight produced a constant glare that made his eyes ache.

To his ears, over the sounds of communal eating, came a distant whirring. He knew that sound. It smote his ears with grim familiarity.

"John Carter," he told Cosooma tightly. "He approaches."

Going below, the bronzed giant gathered up his longbow and arrow and returned to deck. Removing his long-sword from its scabbard, he lifted it skyward and proclaimed, "Take arms! The warship of John Carter approaches!"

The horde broke off its eating, and a defiant roar welled up from more than a dozen massive throats.

Turning to Cosooma, Tarzan asked, "Can you create warriors?"

She nodded bravely. "I will surround the ship with a fresh legion."

"Do this."

Closing her opalescent blue eyes, Cosooma concentrated with all her might.

All about the shipwreck, one by one they commenced to materialize. Green men and red men and great white gorillas, all resplendent in their harnesses and barbaric accoutrements. But they lacked distinctiveness. Their hues were pale and wan. They resembled ghosts clinging to life.

Tarzan said, "I can see through them."

"Give me more time," pleaded Cosooma. "Oh, if only I had real food in my belly and strength in my brain. I could conjure up an army that would intimidate all of Barsoom."

But Cosooma of Samabar lacked the will to produce perfect warriors. Instead of being surrounded by a protective legion, *The Shaggador* appeared to be ringed by an army of forlorn phantasms.

Then, through the terrific glare, the bow of the *Dejah Thoris* broke through, a terrible sight.

But that was not the thing that made the combined horde of Ramdar utter sounds of consternation and fear.

Out of the glare off the rotting port rail of the foundered hulk stepped a line of cavalry, proud copper soldiers mounted on slate thoats, wearing the devices of Helium and Uxfar—although the forces of Ramdar did not know that.

Moving steadily, they closed in until it became abundantly clear that *The Shaggador* was surrounded on all sides by fresh red Martian troops, a legion forming an unbroken ring whose war thoats stood shoulder to shoulder.

They came to a halt, the red cavalry sitting on their war steeds, their swords still sheathed in their scabbards, radium pistols holstered at their hips, stoically awaiting orders from the Warlord of Barsoom with hard dark eyes set in their fixed countenances.

Beside Tarzan, Cosooma breathed, "O Ramdar. We are lost."

Instead of answering, the ape-man rushed to the bow of the ancient ship, threw back his head and in angry defiance gave the warning cry of the great apes of Africa, prolonging the angry syllables so that none could fail to hear them.

"*Kreegah!*"

Chapter 59

The Revelation

AS THE terrible call rang out over the vast desiccated inland sea of salt, I could hardly repress a shiver. I had heard that prolonged yell before, yet it chilled me in a way I could not express. Beside it, the war cries of the Apache brave and the terrifying Rebel yell of my days as a Confederate officer were only the pitiful mewling of infants.

Standing at the starboard rail with me, Tars Tarkas rumbled, "John Carter, I have heard many fierce war cries and worse things in my life. But that sound freezes my very blood."

"Do not fear, Tars Tarkas," I assured him. "Ramdar and his abominable horde are entirely surrounded. He will surrender or he will die. There is no other alternative left to him."

"Will you not fight him?"

"Truly, I ache to clash blades with him again. If for no better reason than to avenge the arrow wound that makes my shoulder ache."

Grasping the hilt of his long-sword, Tars Tarkas offered a fierce grin and said, "We will send him back to Africa, wherever that is."

When I heard these words, I was taken aback, as if struck a blow.

Turning to my friend, I asked, "What did you say?"

The great Thark looked down on me, and his tusked grin would have put a demon to shame. "We will send him back to the land of Africa, from which he said he hails."

"Africa? Africa is a continent on Jasoom!"

The Jeddak of Thark laughed without concern. "Then this barbarian hails from Jasoom. What of it? *Tarzan-of-the-apes* must be defeated, regardless of his origins."

This news stunned me. Hitherto, I had assumed that Ramdar had come from some unknown world where apes ran wild. For he claimed to have been reared by them.

Addressing Tars Tarkas, I asked, "Did he tell you that his true name was *Tarzan-of-the-apes?*"

"He did, John Carter."

Tan Hadron was with us. "John Carter, he told me otherwise. He said his name was 'Tarzan of the Apes.' He did so when you lay insensate, after having been whelmed by his sword. He was very angry. This was when he commanded me to inform you that having spared your life, he was of no mind to repeat the favor."

Now I was truly amazed. For unlike Tars Tarkas, Tan Hadron had uttered three words in English, a language he did not know: Of the Apes. The Thark had used the Barsoomian words that meant "of-the-apes." *Ko-do-raku.*

I repeated the name, Tarzan of the Apes, enunciating the syllables separately as they are spoken in American English, and without the heavy Thark accents.

"Did he say it like that?" I asked eagerly.

"Yes, John Carter, he did," replied Tan Hadron. "Just as you spoke those very words."

"In his anger," I explained, "he lapsed into his native tongue. Ramdar was proclaiming that his name is Tarzan and that he belongs to the apes."

"Does he not?" grunted Tars Tarkas unconcernedly. "For he travels with a tribe of the brutes."

"Tarzan is of Jasoom, my friend. I would not have believed it, for he is unlike any Earth man I have ever imagined. This alters my thinking. If he comes from my natal planet, I must strive to capture him alive."

"How would you do that, John Carter, when he has shown you that he is masterful beyond reason?"

"I do not know, but I must find a way. I must learn his story."

But Fate had another plan.

For a strangely feathered arrow stuck the gunwale, not one safad below us.

And down on the salt plain, the phantom legion of Ramdar advanced toward the encircling cavalry of Uxfar.

"We are under attack, John Carter!" announced Kantos Kan gravely from the ship's controls. "What are your orders?"

Chapter 60

The Battle of *The Shaggador*

TARZAN OF THE APES stood on the bow of the shipwreck, *Shaggador*. He loosed his first arrow, and his far-seeing vision told him that the shaft had struck the *Dejah Thoris* just below the starboard rail, where John Carter and his officers were assembled, barely an inch from where the Warlord rested one hand.

The ape-man could have split John Carter's skull with his arrow. But he had no immediate desire to do so. His intention was to warn the crew that they were vulnerable and exposed to his arrows.

Limping to his side, Dag Dolor cautioned, "He will attack now." He held a sword and a dagger in his surviving fists.

"Perhaps my arrows will dissuade him," said Tarzan, nocking another and pulling back with all his steel-thewed muscular might. The shaft flew a great distance. This time it struck the long rail, lodging there.

The giant green warrior who had called himself Dak Kova threw up all four arms in surprise as he stepped back from the unexpected strike.

"They will now move into cannon range," warned Dag Dolor.

Tarzan growled, "Then I will clear the decks of their gunners, as I did once before."

Cosooma drew near, took stock of their predicament, and resignedly took up her bow and quiver of arrows, saying, "Here we may die. But I am prepared to sell my life dearly."

In the act of extracting another arrow from his quiver, Tarzan turned to her and asked, "Can your ghost legion fight?"

"If I will them to do so."

"If you will them to fight, can they win?"

Cosooma shook her head sadly. "I can compel them forward, but I cannot control them individually. They own only a kind of half-life. It will be all I can do to keep them clothed in substance. Even now you see that they are but shadows of their former selves."

"If the cavalry advances," Tarzan instructed, "have your legion meet them. Even if they fall before the copper men's swords, they are not truly real and therefore cannot be counted as casualties."

"I will do as you say, Ramdar. But I do not know what the outcome will be."

Tarzan nodded. Redirecting his nocked arrow, he pointed it at one of the mounted soldiers who stood patiently waiting for orders.

The man saw him and did not flinch.

"These red men are brave," muttered Tarzan.

"They will charge into our teeth, O Ramdar," warned Jamo Ptannus, sword in hand. "And if necessary, they will die for John Carter, for he is the greatest warrior Barsoom has ever known, even though his skin is not red like theirs."

Tarzan turned his attention back to the rail of the great warship looming just out of cannon shot. Slowly, it turned and began to beat toward them.

Its proud bow protecting the crew on its deck, the immense vessel approached steadily through the thin air of the dying planet.

The round bows were reinforced, and while cannon were mounted openly on either side, their crews were protected by movable shields, which had been attached to protect them from Tarzan's formidable Samabaran arrows.

Aiming carefully, Tarzan sent a shaft toward one of the cannon, and while it pierced the metallic shield, it did no damage, merely lodging there.

Creeping closer, the craft seemed to float rather than fly. And then the starboard cannon erupted, unleashing three successive shells. They struck *The Shaggador's* stern, blasting it asunder and killing five apes who had been hunkering down there. Among the casualties was old one-eyed Druk, who was blown apart in a violent shower of alabaster limbs.

The surviving gorillas became wild, and began pounding the deck with their war clubs, jabbering and screaming madly.

They howled in bestial rage, crying out for their mighty Ape-lord to protect them.

Rushing to Jamo Ptannus, who carried a war spear taller than himself, Tarzan plucked it from his olive fingers and rushed forward with it.

Bringing the impossibly long spear back over his shoulder, the bronzed giant let fly as he sprinted.

The spear flew a distance so great that apes and green men alike were mesmerized by the sight of it traversing space. It seemed impossible that the tremendous shaft could clear the entire distance to the stupendous sky ship. But it did.

It pierced one cannon shield and penetrated deep into the inner mechanism, destroying it. The devastating weapon fell silent, its crew deserting it in shock and surprise.

Dozens of fists lifted in raucous approval, both green and white. Cheers and roars of defiance resounded, carrying to the decks of the dreadnought, *Dejah Thoris*.

TURNING TO Cosooma, Tarzan said swiftly, "Unleash your phantoms. I will lead them."

"No, Ramdar, it is madness. Do not go! Do not leave me to the green warriors and the terrible apes."

Savagely, the ape-man told her, "Stay! Dag Dolor will guard you." Turning to the green man, he exhorted, "Do this. Protect Cosooma with your life. I will turn back the copper men."

So saying, the jungle lord vaulted over the rail and into his chariot-throne, where his greater store of arrows lay. The zitidar pulled forward, but sluggishly, its massive strength far depleted.

Lopsidedly brandishing his blades in his surviving arms, Dag Dolor called to his fellow hordesmen and shouted, "Seek shelter below! Ramdar will succor us. Hurry!"

The green men were loathe to do this. They wanted to fight. But sight of the advancing ghost legion successfully slowed the encroaching red soldiers, which swiftly reformed into a phalanx in order to engage them where they could.

Dag Dolor cried, "We must prepare to defend the ship against boarders. Follow me!"

Reluctantly, clutching their swords, the green warriors shouldered below, knocking aside door frames, enlarging them so they could negotiate their way below. They were forced to crawl along, the old hulk's ceilings being too low for their towering height. Their intention was to fortify a position belowdecks, one that could be defended against superior numbers.

But in the act of smashing open space in which to do this, a horrible smell assailed their slit nostrils. Through chinks in the moldering hull, harsh sunlight disclosed something moving silently from the lowermost portion of the vessel.

Something that fluttered and displayed a translucent violet coloration....

AT THE demolished stern, the great gorillas were tumbling overboard. Mad with fury, they stampeded toward the encircling cavalry, in the opposite compass direction from which Ramdar charged.

A slaughter swiftly ensued.

The red men, reluctant to use their pistols when confronting crude war clubs, urged their thoats forward, and were soon charging. Their steel was naked and raised high. Into the thick of the great white gorillas they smashed.

Their first contact was a howling hurricane of flailing swords and blunt war hammers. Pale white limbs and hands jumped off fresh-cut stumps, as the enraged gorillas dashed in the skulls of red man and slate thoat alike.

This only added to the cavalry's resolve. They fought back with a ferocity that was equal to that of the apes, but tempered with intelligence. Their merciless steel plunged into yielding apish vitals.

Turning their raging thoats around, some soldiers stood up on their backs, and decapitated the charging apes with slashing swords whose shiny steel soon ran crimson with gore.

Outnumbered, the gorillas had no chance. Although they felled many foes, they were soon groaning and bellowing in their death agonies. The survivors turned, retreating toward the ancient ship, the only shelter left to them.

Tarzan of the Apes was unaware of this slaughter transpiring on the opposite side of *The Shaggador*. As the wild-eyed zitidar pulled his chariot forward, on either side of him the phantom army formed two spreading wings. It swept around and behind to encompass the entirety of the ancient wreck, but their numbers were painfully thin.

The jungle lord began unloosing fresh arrows at the advancing cavalry. Every arrow struck true. Men fell from their mounts, metal-bladed missiles sticking from their unprotected necks. The thoats, which were striding forward in a measured cadence, now broke and ran.

Leaping off his chariot, Tarzan rushed to meet them, his gleaming Samabaran sword in hand.

No one could stand against him. No blade was strong enough to turn his metal. No hand was vigorous enough to withstand his pummeling blows. Red men commenced to fall from their steeds, and although they carried radium pistols in holsters, no one availed themselves of those deadly guns.

Tarzan knew they would not. His talks with Tan Hadron had informed him that red Martians do not lift superior weapons against inferior arms. And so the guns remained holstered. Only swords were lifted. And no steel blade was as strong as the invincible sword of Ramdar of the Apes.

All around him the phantoms fought, but they were weak, and were soon beaten back, their proud pennants dropping.

Returning to ground from a soaring jump, Tarzan looked about and saw the state of Cosooma's legion. Many were staggering about, wounded. Some fell to the salty crust, where they faded away, a little at a time.

The phantoms had slowed the cavalry—but that was all. They could not be held back.

Over Tarzan's head, another succession of shells whistled, detonating in a drumbeat amidships *The Shaggador*. For the great sky ship had turned about, presenting fresh cannon, which came into action.

Seeing that the shipwreck was coming apart with every detonation, Tarzan grasped his sword hilt more firmly, ran several paces and threw himself into the thin atmosphere.

As he cleared the space between the battle and the great dreadnought of the sky, he once again gave forth the warning cry of the bull apes of Africa.

"*Kreegah! Bundolo!*"

Chapter 61

Confrontation

"THE OUTER ring of defenders is pulling back, John Carter," reported Kantos Kan.

"Order the helmsman to come about," I told him. "Prepare to resume shelling. Where is *Tarzan-of-the-apes?*"

"He has driven his chariot into the cavalry and is making a good account of himself. The bronzed demon is proving unstoppable. He slays with a ferocity that rivals that of the great white apes."

"Would that we could take him alive. Continue shelling the hulk. Destroy the horde to the last man. If any survive, we will deal with them accordingly."

"At once, John Carter," said Kantos Kan, saluting.

Addressing Tan Hadron, I said, "Let us go to a flier. I will take on Tarzan myself."

"He has beaten you twice before. And you are yet freshly wounded."

"It may yet be that he will best me for a third time, Tan Hadron. But I will defend my ship and we will see who is the greatest warrior on Barsoom."

Grimly, we moved to the stern landing stage where a speedy flier had been hoisted onto the deck. But we never reached it.

For, dropping out of the sky, plummeted the demon himself.

His body gleamed with perspiration, and here and there was caked with salt. About his waist gleamed a crude metal belt supporting an apron of banth hide. As always, he wore no harness. But in one sinewy hand was gripped his terrible blue sword.

"Stand back, Tan Hadron," I said, stepping forward to meet my bronze nemesis, my blade purring from its scabbard. I silently thanked the Eternal Mystery that the barbarian's arrow had pieced my left shoulder; otherwise, I would be all but helpless against his blade.

Addressing the bronze devil, I said, "We meet once more, Ramdar—or should I say Tarzan of the Apes? If you have come for Thuvia of Ptarth, I have sent her home in anticipation of your return."

"I have no use for a woman who can summon banths in a place where no banths roam," he growled. "Tarzan warned you that when next we clashed, I would not spare your life."

Our marvelous blades, nearly perfectly matched, almost touched one another. The moment of truth had come.

"I AM told you hail from Africa," I challenged.

Instead of replying, Tarzan advanced, his gray eyes terrible, the red scar that gave him his nomad name erupted on his brow, a livid lightning mark.

I thought I was mentally and physically prepared for the combat that I faced. Looking into the savage eyes of this barbarian, I felt a momentary pang of unease.

Then his blade was sweeping toward me. My guard was sufficient to withstand the first thrust, but the broad blade of Tarzan danced like a magical thing and licked through, its tip scraping the proud insignia of Helium upon my harness.

Startled, I stepped back, assuming a fresh stance. My blade engaged once more. Weaving a bluish web of metal before me, I advanced. The blur I created seemed to baffle my foe, for he had difficulty following my sword point.

In that moment of dazzlement, I struck—my blade leaping high and above his guard.

A black lock of hair leapt from his head, and I drew back before my opponent could react. His gaze went to the errant lock floating down like a dark tuft of feather.

Laughing, I exclaimed, "You did not expect that, did you? Not for nothing am I proclaimed the greatest swordsman on two worlds!"

Tarzan of the Apes was not impressed by my boast. The terrible scar on his brow grew further inflamed. No humor, no respect for a worthy foe, showed in his gray eyes. There was only a kind of feral madness.

I set myself, prepared in mind as well as body. For the moment of truth had arrived.

The battle proved short. It was stunning in its brevity, for I had steeled myself for a protracted struggle, a contest the like of which I had never before faced.

Two equally matched swords clashed, locked, and then in a manner that transpired so rapidly I could not perceive it, Tarzan's chopping sword smashed my own blade from my strong fingers.

As before, I was helpless to stand up to the barbarian's superhuman strength. But I had no opportunity to absorb the magnitude of my defeat.

A fist that felt like a block of bronze struck me full in the chest, knocking me back. I went down, momentarily stunned.

And a naked foot stepped onto my chest, besmirching my devices, pressing down with irresistible force. I could feel my rib cartilage crackling under the immense pressure. My hands went to the man's ankle and attempted to wrest him free. But I could not. Strong as I was under the Martian gravity, this bronze-skinned beast-man was stronger still.

His sword point found my throat and pressed downward. Merciless eyes bored into my own.

"What do you know of Africa?" he demanded hotly.

"I have never visited the Dark Continent, but I have heard of it. What do you know about the Earth, Tarzan of the Apes?" I pronounced his name in proper English, not employing the

Barsoomian words signifying *of-the-apes*. But he did not seem to notice this.

"I come from Africa, which is on the Earth."

The sword point dug in further. And I was helpless to remove it. To do so would be to risk slicing my fingers off.

I could hear the pounding of feet all around me—my loyal sailors coming to my rescue. But I feared they would not be in time.

I then said the fateful words that no doubt spared my life.

"I am John Carter of Virginia, late of the Confederate army."

I spoke in English. And the savage barbarian recognized them! His steely eyes reflected a wild surprise. Quickly, he mastered his emotions.

The blade withdrew. Powerful fingers reached down, grasped my harness straps and pulled me to my feet as if I were no more than a child.

"How did you come to Barsoom?" he demanded, the point of his blade floating before my face.

I spoke frankly. "I died. I was translated here, I do not completely understand how. But here I stand. I still live."

This information seemed to stagger the bronze-skinned Hercules. For he released me and stepped backward. The wild look on his metallic features appeared to melt.

To my left, Tars Tarkas stepped around, sword and dagger in his massive hands. To my right, Tan Hadron had his blade poised to strike. Both were prepared to make short work of my foe.

"Stand fast!" I told them.

Addressing Tarzan, I said, "You call yourself Tarzan of the Apes. Is that your name upon the Earth?"

The bronzed barbarian did not reply immediately. He seemed dazed.

But his gray eyes came back into focus. He looked at me frankly and said, "My parents named me John Clayton. I was orphaned when an infant and abducted by a tribe of great apes. I grew to be one of them. They called me Tarzan, which in their language means White Skin."

We spoke in English, so the others did not understand us. Respectfully, they held their distance, their expressions baffled.

"How did you come to Barsoom, John Clayton?"

"I do not know. I was struck down by a thunderbolt. When I awoke, I was here."

"Then it would seem as if you are 'dead,' just as I am," I declared.

A thread of anger colored his response. "How can this be? I am solid. I have flesh. My bones are whole. I hunger and thirst and so I eat and drink. I am still alive."

"I cannot account for what has happened to either of us, Tarzan. That is the truth. Only the Eternal Mystery may know the answer."

Tarzan looked about as if the enormity of his situation was only now sinking in. He shook his shaggy head, as if to clear it. I did not think that there was anything vulnerable about the man, but now I saw that there was. He believed himself to be marooned upon Barsoom, and it became plain to me that his questions about spaceships meant that he yearned to return to his former life in impossibly distant Africa.

I attempted to read the man's mind. But, as before, it was futile. It remained impenetrable to my thoughts. I did not understand this, but there was no gainsaying it. Whatever the composition of Tarzan's half-feral mental processes, their secrets were denied to me.

As if reading my own mind, he suddenly looked at me with a clearer gaze.

"You rule the greatest empire on this planet. Tell me, do your scientists build ships that can cross interplanetary space?"

Sadly, I shook my head, "Alas, no. There are scientists who are working on the problem, but we have not yet solved it. So if you are desirous of returning to Earth, no ship of this world can accommodate you. And for that, you have my sincere sympathy, Tarzan of the Apes."

Whatever machinery comprised the mind of Tarzan, it was not slow to understand the hard reality of my words.

Lowering his sword slightly, the bronzed giant said woodenly, "Then I am trapped here. Stranded for life."

Before I could reply, a series of cries came from the shipwreck, which had been battered most severely, and was now smoldering.

I could hear a single word repeated plainly. But I did not understand it.

"Denjurus! Denjurus!"

Looking back, Tarzan snapped, "I must go! My horde needs me."

I had been about to ask the fellow to surrender, thinking he was defeated in his own mind by the certain knowledge that he was a castaway on an unfamiliar world.

But Tarzan surprised me. His dynamic muscles came to life with an animal vitality. Without another word, he stepped to the rail and sprang ahead of the glittering swords of Tars Tarkas and Tan Hadron.

To them, I said, "Remain here. Cease all shelling. I intend to follow Tarzan."

"He will slay you, John Carter," warned Tars Tarkas.

"I do not think he will slay his fellow Earth man. I am the only one who speaks his native language and understands his present predicament."

With that, I sprang for the flier, and took off alone. I did not know what I was going to do. But I was interested in knowing what was meant by the word "denjurus." For the voices of the fierce green warriors who cried out that word did so with a combination of anger and dread. Green men were not readily cowed. I knew that something terrible was afoot.

Chapter 62

The Secret of Cosooma

TARZAN OF THE APES reached the ghostly shipwreck before I could overhaul him in my flier. His ability to cover distance far exceeded that of my own. If in fact he had been reared by apes, they had lent him a good measure of their tremendous muscular strength.

Landing ahead of the skirmish line of mounted soldiers, I stepped from my flier and spoke to Vam Dirasun, who personally commanded the Fifth Utan of Uxfar cavalry. "Hold your lines. Do not advance. Await my instructions."

"Yes, John Carter," replied the commander-in-chief of the Navy of Uxfar. Turning his animal around, he ordered them back.

I took to the air again, this time without my flier, and was soon thankful for my sandals, for the sun-baked salt crust made for rough landings.

Gaining the deck of the shipwreck, I saw that the stern deck had been demolished and was ablaze. But the wood, cured by centuries of wind and sand, had partially petrified, and the ship was in no danger of burning away.

Agitated green men milled about the deck, their swords raised. Some pointed them down into the old hulk's hold.

I spied Tarzan accosting a green man whose insignia I did not recognize and who lacked two of his arms. Their loud conversation was easy to follow.

"We tried to retreat to the lowermost deck, O Ramdar, and attempted to conceal ourselves there. Six apes followed us down. But they soon rushed out, howling and screaming. For deep within lies a nest of denjurus. They are escaping and exploring the holds. I lost a warrior, the first who encountered one. So I ordered my men back to open air. We must abandon this ship, Ramdar, or we are lost."

"Take your warriors and go!" Ramdar told them. "I will deal with the denjurus."

"If we go," another green man complained, "the cavalry will fall upon us and we will be cut to pieces."

Stepping forward, I announced myself. "I am John Carter. I will give you safe passage off the ship. You have my word that my forces will not attack you. But you must yield to me first. Surrender your horde, Tarzan of the Apes. It cannot be allowed to tramp the dead sea bottoms and threaten our cities."

Tarzan looked as if he were in no mood to surrender. The scar on his bronzed forehead was livid.

"What will become of my horde if we do this?" he hurled back, taking a posture of defiance.

"We will turn the green men loose wherever they wish and restore the surviving apes to the dead sea bottoms. But you must accompany me to the city of Helium. Not as a prisoner, but as my honored guest."

"Do not trust him, Ramdar," warned the maimed warrior. "He will put you to the sword."

Switching to English, I said, "I give you my word as a gentleman of Virginia that I will do no such thing."

These words seemed to have an impact all out of proportion to the force with which I gave them.

Tarzan turned to his maimed lieutenant. "Go, Dag Dolor. It will be as he says. There will be no more killing. Where is Cosooma?"

"Below. She refuses to come out. I do not know why. She has locked herself in a cabin."

Turning to me, Tarzan said, "I must find the woman."

"I will go with you."

"It is dangerous. The hold is full of denjurus."

I was on the point of asking what the exotic word meant, when out of a ragged rent in the deck boards came something I had never before beheld during my long years fighting across the barren face of Barsoom.

It was a fat bloated thing, violet in color, with frilly edges that acted as wings. Tentacles trailed down from it. And to my earthly eyes, it reminded me of a jellyfish, although very different in many respects.

Seeing this, one of the green men gave out a yell and charged it, bursting the creature with the sharp edge of his sword, releasing a viscous internal fluid.

It fell to the deck, but then another one emerged and then another, floating toward us.

The two violet things surrounded the green man, attaching themselves to him, whereupon he went into a frenzy of convulsions as they stung and stung and his body swelled up and began to float upward into the sky, his sword dropping from fingers that I assumed to be lifeless, or very nearly so.

"I have never seen such creatures," I told Tarzan.

"I must find the woman," he said, disappearing down a companionway.

Fully cognizant of the danger into which he plunged, I followed him, heedless of the risk.

If this bronzed barbarian was willing to brave these creatures in order to protect his woman, I could show no less a degree of chivalry.

Together, we plunged into the hold, and worked our way through the rotted corridors of the decrepit old ship. I employed a radium light to show the way through the close darkness.

Tarzan soon encountered one of the violet things, and his blade swept up to impale it to the petrified roof. It expired quickly, becoming limp. Extracting his blade, he scraped the thing off and continued on.

More of the floating creatures materialized. I felt something flutter behind me and turned. From around the corner, two more approached. My blade licked out, and I accounted for one without effort, but the second swept around and behind me. I could feel its sinewy tentacles scraping the nape of my neck.

The blade of Tarzan came sweeping in, knocked it aside. He stepped on the obscene thing. It perished with a sound like a bursting bladder.

"Thank you," I said, and we went on.

"Cosooma! Where are you?" he shouted.

The cracked voice of a woman came, hardly distinguishable.

"Do not seek me, Ramdar! I am prepared to die."

"I will not let you die. For you are of my horde, and I will find you."

The woman did not answer.

We moved among the corridors, and I could sense the great age of the ship which dated from the time of the vast surging oceans of Barsoom. The smells were overpowering and unrecognizable.

When we found the cabin to which the woman had retreated, we could see why she had done so. For the gloomy corridor outside of the shut doorway was choked with the violet denjurus, clustering there like a hive of earthly bees.

Pausing at the turn in the gloomy passage, Tarzan swept back one mighty arm and kept me from advancing farther.

"There are many of them," he said, pushing me back around the corner and craning his head forward.

"How many?"

"Seven. They hover in front of the closed door. No doubt they were aware of Cosooma and are seeking a way in."

"They are seven and we are but two, but our sword arms are strong and our blades greater than any forged of steel."

"You saw the denjurus, and how they kill."

"I did." Stepping in front of him, I drew my radium pistol, and aimed it.

Four shots I fired, and four violet monstrosities were blown apart. Three fled. Tarzan raced after them, impaling one and then coming back to join me at the door.

I put my hand on the knob and threw it open.

Upon a pallet on the floor lay the white-skinned woman. Her gown was ragged and caked with dust and salt, and she looked as if she had awakened from a slumber as long as the life of the shipwreck. Her hair was a lustrous white.

"Do not look upon me!" she shrieked, pale fingers flying to her face.

"Do not be afraid," I returned. "I am John Carter. You are under my protection."

"Do not let Ramdar behold me," she moaned. "I beg of you!"

But it was too late. Tarzan stepped into the room. And I could see in his penetrating gray eyes a hint of wonder.

The Orovar woman Cosooma turned her face away from him and buried it in her withered and gnarled hands.

Tarzan demanded. "What has happened to you, Cosooma?"

"Nothing," she moaned. "Nothing has happened to me. I told you that I have lived one thousand ords. But I lied. I have lived much, much longer than that. So long that I have aged. For I have had the terrible misfortune of having outlived all other people of destroyed Samabar, the last of whom perished centuries before this era. Now you see me as I truly am. For the Cosooma you beheld was an illusion, a figment of my imagination. And having expended my remaining energy upon the phantom legion I created to defend us, I have lost my ability to maintain the illusion of my youth. I am sapped of all my power, bereft of my remaining strength. This thing I have done for you, O ungrateful stone-hearted Ramdar."

Shoulders sagging, she sobbed wordlessly. Her despair was palpable.

"Now you will never desire Cosooma," she moaned piteously. "You will not even wish to look upon her...."

I did not understand all that was transpiring, but what Tarzan did next filled me with sympathy.

Sheathing his sword, he stepped forward and gently lifted the ancient woman in his arms, intoning, "You will come with me, Cosooma. You will be safe. I will find a place for you in this dying world. Just as I must find a place for myself, another castaway here...."

Burying her white head in his naked bronze torso, the woman wept in bitter silence.

Together, we made our way onto the smoldering deck, where I lifted my sword and proclaimed that the battle of the shipwreck was concluded.

"All hostilities will now cease! We will take aboard the survivors and their animals."

The combined cavalry of Helium and Uxfar heard me clearly. Vam Dirasun raised his sword in assent.

TURNING TO Tarzan of the Apes, I advised, "Now I must ask you to surrender your sword and knife as a gesture of good will."

"Tarzan never surrenders his weapons," he said firmly.

I ignored the breach of military decorum. "Then how do I know that you will conduct yourself accordingly aboard my ship as an honored guest from my home planet?"

"Because I give you my word as a peer of England."

I could scarcely credit my ears.

"What do you mean by that?" I demanded.

"My full name and title is John Clayton, Lord Greystoke. I am a peer of England, a viscount."

"In that case," I returned graciously, "you may retain your sword as long as it remains sheathed."

"It will remain sheathed as long as it is not needed," he said flatly. "But if danger comes, I will not hesitate to raise it against any enemy."

"I am satisfied with that. Come, Clayton—or should I call you Lord Greystoke?"

"I am Tarzan of the Apes, Lord of the Jungle, and a friend to John Carter of Virginia, if he remains a true friend to Tarzan."

To my immense relief, that appeared to resolve our remaining differences.

Chapter 63

Amnesty

THE *SHAGGADOR* was quickly evacuated. The ancient wood of her decks continued to burn, and so the old hulk was slowly consumed, taking with it the underground nest of denjurus.

A few of the violet monstrosities escaped the collapsing hold. They were dispatched with expert shots from long-barreled radium rifles. Tars Tarkas brought down many from the deck of the *Dejah Thoris,* his boisterous laughter booming across the salty wastes whenever a fluttering denjuru exploded in midair, producing a brief rain of viscous fluid.

Soon, all was peaceful again.

Once we gathered up our dead and wounded, and Vam Dirasun had taken the cavalry aboard his ships, the disposition of the shattered horde of Ramdar became my immediate concern.

The *Dejah Thoris* had landed on the great salt crust. And at my suggestion, the surviving great apes, along with their disconsolate females and young, were taken aboard and secured in the lowermost hold.

Tarzan of the Apes first spoke to them in their grunting language. Reluctantly, and only after repeated rough reassurances, they took their places in the iron-barred cages where formerly wild banths had been kept. The war chariot and its exhausted zitidar were also brought on board. Tarzan mentally commanded the brute to trudge his ponderous way aboard, its round orange eyes whipping about, marveling at the cavernous interior of the great ship.

There were no untoward incidents. The surviving apes were thoroughly beaten in body and in spirit. At Tarzan's suggestion, we made a pile of their stone clubs and crude war hammers and left them where they could be seen, along with the promise that they could reclaim them once they were set free.

After that, we journeyed to a place in the dead sea bottoms where the cartographers of Uxfar had discovered the remnants of a crumbling city of ancient times. The ruin was deserted. So we set down on its verge and the cage doors were opened. Tarzan led the apes out the open hatchway and onto familiar comforting moss and bid them farewell.

I did not understand a word that was spoken, but it seemed to me that their parting was less than amicable. The discouraged apes collected their stone cudgels, trudged into the city and soon vanished from our sight.

Returning to the ship, Tarzan stated, "I was their Ape-lord. Now Foad leads the tribe of Narag."

"You do not act as if you will miss them," I observed.

"The Tarmanbolgani are not true apes, but strange gorillas lacking hair. I am glad that my association with them has come to an end. For they were lazy and uncouth in their ways."

As the dreadnought lifted back into the sky, we joined Tars Tarkas on the open deck. He had taken the green men in hand. Only a handful of survivors remained. Of them, the warrior called Dag Dolor was speaking to the great Thark.

We walked into their earnest conversation. Tars Tarkas turned to me and said, "I have offered these warriors an opportunity to become Tharks, but they have declined."

Addressing Tarzan, Dag Dolor said simply, "My father, Churvash Ul, led the horde of Vakanor. To Vakanor, I wish to be returned."

Hearing this, Tarzan looked to me. "This is my desire as well." Then, without waiting for my reply, he said, "Dag Dolor, I return to you the white thoat, along with the war chariot and zitidar that belonged to your father. These will be yours, along with the gratitude of Ramdar for serving him so well and faithfully through such hardships."

The maimed and much-battered green man placed two surviving hands on the bronze warrior's strong shoulders. His red orbs expressed an emotion I have seen in but a few of his kind. Gratitude.

"Without you, O Ramdar, I would have been eaten by the great white apes. It is I who am grateful to you. Although I am a green man, I will always remember my bronze jeddak."

It took half a padan, but we found the ruin of Vakanor, and there we released the ragtag green nomads and all of the accoutrements that belonged to them.

The parting was curt and without further sentiment. But at last, the war chariot rumbled through the city gates, and so that episode was concluded as well.

WE FLEW directly to Helium, where, with the sun burnishing the scarlet tower of Greater Helium, the *Dejah Thoris* received a hero's welcome.

We disembarked, and as we escorted him up the Avenue of Hope, Tarzan of the Apes was greeted with a mixture of awe and wonder, for all of the populace had heard of him. Inasmuch as he wore no harness, many looked at him askance, for even by Barsoomian standards he was practically naked.

It was our custom to take a captive to the Hall of Righteousness for judgment. But in this instance, trying Tarzan would have impossible, even if I had not granted him amnesty for his past actions, which I now understood to be the product of a series of unfortunate misunderstandings. The masterful bronzed warrior would never submit himself to such an indignity and imprisoning him would have been pointless. No dungeon could have withstood his animal strength.

"You are a guest in my palace," I informed him. "I must introduce you to my wife, Dejah Thoris, Princess of Helium, and our family."

This was done. My family marveled at him, for he was a splendid physical specimen of manhood. When Thuvia was introduced to him, there was an understandable tension, but they soon grew accustomed to one another, and that palpable feeling of unease evaporated.

The ancient Orovar woman, Cosooma, was given a quarters of her own, to which she retreated and refused to come out. But she accepted the food that was served her and we left her in peace, for she shunned all company and companionship.

Tarzan showed himself to be fully capable of adjusting to civilization, for over the course of the next several days, he began to comport himself in a manner befitting a British lord. Although we could not get him to wear harness or sandals, he willingly replaced his banth-hide apron with a loincloth and cloak made of the finest silks. And while he preferred raw meat to cooked food, he did not decline the latter.

To my surprise, he ceased to wear his wonderful Samabaran sword, but kept his fighting knife, explaining that he was not a swordsman by nature, but a hunter.

This impressed me deeply, for I feared no swordsman born on Earth or Barsoom. But Tarzan had earned my unqualified respect in his handling of the blade.

My family and I were enthralled and often horrified by Tarzan's accounts of his life and exploits in Africa, London, Paris, and places unknown to me, particularly the lost land of Pal-ul-don in Africa. In his sometimes reticent manner, he managed to convey the complexities of being an individual of noble birth who through a freak of Fate—the shipwreck of his parents—survived by dint of an inner fire brought out by a tribe of African apes who took him in hand. Reflecting on the shifting fortunes of John Clayton, Lord Greystoke, I felt as if my own destiny were not so strange after all.

Tarzan of the Apes showed understandable interest in the city and its ways. But always he seemed remote. We got along well, except in one respect. Discovering that we kept slaves, he expressed a muted but unmistakable disapproval of the time-honored practice. Nothing I said could convince him that this was a Barsoomian custom established centuries before my arrival, and that I long ago came to understand that nothing could be done about it.

The matter was soon disposed of, and not raised again.

Outwardly polite, he visited the forest that stood in a valley of Greater Helium. This he found to his liking, for he quickly took to the trees, exploring them by walking along such branches that would support his weight. When he found the generous crotch of a sorapus tree, he stretched out upon it, and stared off into the sky as if I were no longer present. I could tell that this was a poor substitute for the African jungle. Even though I could not read his actual thoughts, I could sense the workings of his mind.

"Are you hungry for your homeland?" I called up.

"And for my beloved wife, Jane, my son, Jack, and all of my friends."

"In that, you are different from me, Tarzan. For I was without close family when I first came to Barsoom. I discovered my family here. I found my true home upon this dying world. My life is in Helium now. Until you came along, I had hardly spoken English in many years."

"Tarzan will never feel at home on Barsoom. He is at home in the jungle. Nowhere else."

"We have greater forests here. But not many. Perhaps we can make accommodations for you in the Kaolian forest, or in the wild jungle you call Desh, if that is what you prefer."

"I prefer to go home," Tarzan said simply. "But tonight, I will sleep in this tree."

He was fixed in his thinking, and so I did not press him on the point. But after a time, I came to a new form of thinking.

ONE MORNING, I greeted Tarzan as he walked around the palace grounds, sunk deep within himself. My faithful calot, Woola, had taken a liking to him and was following close behind. But the bronzed giant paid him little heed.

"I have sent for someone whom I would like you to meet," I declared.

Tarzan looked at me.

"His name is Kar Komak," I explained. "Like you, he is a consummate bowman. Unlike you, he was never born of woman or egg. Instead, he was created long ago by the mind of the jeddak ruling the city of Lothar."

A flicker of intrigue came into Tarzan's eyes. "This man is like the phantoms of Cosooma?"

I nodded in confirmation. "Unlike them, he has taken on material substance. He will not fade. I sent for him because I believe Kar Komak to be an appropriate person to take charge of the woman, Cosooma, for they belong to the same race of ancient white Martians."

"I agree with your thinking. She may not live very long, but she deserves to be among her kind."

"But there was another reason, Tarzan. Kar Komak is an accomplished etherealist, one who holds that the power of the mind is superior to the reality of substance. That means he also possesses the ability to create substance from thought alone. It is an amazing skill, and in years gone by he has taught me some of his art.

"I had not told you this as yet because I did not care to raise your hopes. But after my advent on Mars, I have on more than one occasion returned to the Earth. Not through my own efforts but through circumstances I did not clearly understand. In all cases, I returned to my former body, which became reanimated once my spirit was restored to it."

The normally impassive features of Tarzan of the Apes suddenly acquired a spark of renewed lift. The vaguely haunted look in his eyes cleared.

"You are saying it is possible to return to my body."

"Possibly. But I must point out that I had made provisions for my cold corpse to be placed in a mausoleum, and left undisturbed. No autopsy was performed, or injury done to it. Thus I was able to reclaim it. In your case, we do not know the state of your body. Perhaps it was destroyed. Possibly it has been buried and now exists in the state of decay, in which case I doubt very much you would wish to reclaim it."

"I understand," said Tarzan.

"Even so," I continued, "Kar Komak bequeathed to me the secret of traversing space and bringing along with me my trappings and weapons. Like you, I arrived upon Barsoom as naked as the day I was born. Seldom have I returned to Earth, for I have left all terrestrial matters behind me. I have never before divulged to any other being, red or green, the secret of translating between worlds. But I am prepared to divulge it to you so that you may return to Jasoom, your rightful home. That is, if you are prepared to take the risk that I have outlined to you."

Tarzan did not hesitate in his reply. Looking me directly in the eye, he said with deep sincerity, "To be reunited with my beloved Jane and my family, I would dare any peril in the universe."

Then, in the Martian manner that I taught him, Tarzan of the Apes placed both strong hands upon my shoulders. I did him the courtesy of doing the same.

"So be it," I said. "When you are ready, I will show you how to cross the trackless space between Barsoom and Jasoom."

No more was said about it until Kar Komak arrived and took possession of Cosooma. Another padan passed while Tarzan of the Apes dwelt in his unspoken thoughts, making peace with his fearful choice and the consequences entailed.

That morning, as the sun rose, I found him on the balcony watching the solar orb, his only connection to the world he knew.

At my approach, he turned and said simply, "Tarzan is ready."

"Are you ready to die?"

He shook his head in a way I considered to be at once stubborn and fatalistic.

"I am still alive. And I will remain so as long as I am able."

"Well spoken. Come. Let me teach you the way, so that you will find the path homeward to whatever your destiny may be. But I cannot promise you that you will be able to transport your sword and knife with you."

"Only one knife holds meaning for me. It belonged to my human father, whom I never knew. My Martian blades are yours to keep, John Carter."

WITH THAT, he removed his short blade from its scabbard and handed it to me without ceremony.

"I am honored, Tarzan of the Apes," I told him sincerely.

"I ask only one other thing of you, John Carter."

"What is that?"

"If your scientists ever learn to communicate with Earth, tell them that Tarzan of the Apes once walked among your people. Word will reach my family. This way, if I fail to return to Africa, they or their descendants will know of my fate."

I had not apprised my guest of recent scientific developments concerning the Gridley Wave, which had led to limited contact with the Earth, for I deemed this knowledge contrary to John Clayton's resolve, not to mention his peace of mind. To hear earthly voices again across millions of unforgiving miles might do more harm than good to his psychology.

I was to learn to my astonishment that the radio device's inventor, the American Jason Gridley, had shared an adventure with Tarzan in recent years.* Had I known this, I might have decided otherwise than I did. But my thinking at the time was that if my new friend failed to escape Barsoom, I could offer

---

* *See* Tarzan at the Earth's Core *by Edgar Rice Burroughs.*

the solace of communication with the Earth until the end of his Barsoomian days as consolation.

Placing my hands on his shoulders, I spoke from my heart.

"I have known you as an indomitable foe and a superlative friend, Tarzan. I cannot envision you failing in any endeavor you undertake. But I will do as you say, for though I may never acknowledge you to be the greatest swordsman ever to tramp the face of Barsoom, I truly consider you the mightiest hunter of two worlds...."

For the first time since I encountered him, Tarzan of the Apes managed a smile. It was a welcome smile full of civilized humanity....

Chapter 64

Vengeance

WHO CAN say what is in the mind of a wild animal? Through the long days, Jad-bal-ja the Golden Lion stood guard over the shallow earthen grave that encompassed the lifeless body of Tarzan of the Apes.

Standing sentry, the magnificent black-maned lion left his post only to seek water and hunt for food. Following each successful kill, he dragged the warm carcass back to the grave site and ate watchfully while Kudu the sun and Goro the moon made their daily rounds in the sky.

No one came to the grave, although less than a moon had passed since the body had been laid in the clay. Still, Jad-bal-ja did not abandon his master even though all sense and all reason, whether instinctual or otherwise, would indicate that no hope for resurrection existed.

It was night when the soil started shifting. The moon was full. And in the night sky, the red eye of Mars looked down, although the Golden Lion knew nothing of the planet and would have cared even less had he possessed knowledge of it, which burned so many millions of miles away from Africa.

Jad-bal-ja slumbered as the soil first heaved upward. His sleep was not broken. Then a strong hand, as bronze as metal, broke the soil.

Only then did one yellow-green eye open. And then the other. Abruptly Jad-bal-ja sat up, and padded forward, a low growl arising in his throat.

Stepping up to the groping fingers, the mighty feline used his paws to dig, but kept his terrible claws retracted.

Soon, a black-haired head was excavated, then a second hand. Gray eyes opened, shedding dry earth.

Together, Tarzan of the Apes and his faithful Golden Lion pushed aside the soil so that the ape-man could sit up. His gaze took in his surroundings. His magnificent head rotated from side to side. His powerful chest expanded as his nostrils took in fresh air, filling dormant lungs.

The air smelled sweet to him, for this was the humid night air of Africa. Looking skyward, he beheld for the first time in long weeks the full luminous splendor of Goro, the only moon he loved.

Using his hands for leverage, Tarzan pushed himself up, freed his legs and was soon standing, whole and intact.

Purring deeply, the Golden Lion paced around him, rubbing his whiskers against Tarzan's dirt-caked legs.

"Faithful Jad-bal-ja," murmured the ape-man, "you did not once leave my side, did you?"

Jad-bal-ja continued his joyous pacing, purring with growing excitement, for his master had returned. That he had returned from the dead did not unduly impress the Golden Lion. Jad-bal-ja had complete faith in Tarzan of the Apes, whom he revered as the rightful Lord of the Jungle.

Looking down at his limbs, Tarzan saw that he wore his antelope-skin G-string, but his knife and scabbard were missing. His fingers went to his muscular neck. Gone, too, was the gold locket, which held the pictures of his human mother and father, whom he did not remember.

"So Sobito is a thief, among his other faults," growled the ape-man.

Grasping Jad-bal-ja by his black mane, Tarzan knelt and put his mouth to one feline ear. "Find Sobito. Lead Tarzan to the black witch doctor."

Jad-bal-ja understood. Tail swinging, he turned about, and started moving through the jungle trails.

The Tarmangani took to the upper terraces of the treetops, the better to track his hunting lion. Together they moved through the night with practiced stealth, making impressive time.

Tarzan paused only once, and that was to drink from a gurgling jungle stream. He would have washed the dirt from his limbs, but the familiar moon was full and would paint his bronze limbs, revealing them to watchful eyes. Time enough to bathe later. He resumed his silent hunt.

The fact that he was empty-handed mattered to the ape-man not at all. He would find Sobito. And he would mete out his terrible brand of jungle justice.

SOBITO SQUATTED high in the sheltering crown of a towering camphorwood tree, cataloging his herbs and trinkets. Around his hips looped a rude leather belt holding up the scabbard containing Tarzan's knife. At the bottom of the sheath was nestled the precious kingo root, with which he had called down the thunderous wrath of his storm god, Meriki, who had struck down the former Lord of the Jungle. This talisman Sobito considered to be his greatest juju. Around his neck was the golden locket of Tarzan. He felt satisfied, all but invincible. Life was good.

The wily old witch doctor did not see the black-maned lion slip up from the dense woods below and behind him. Nor had he heard any rustle of leaves telling of a stalking predator.

Sobito only glanced downward when a night breeze brought to his nose the unmistakable smell of lion.

Through a break in a close-by grove, he spied the greenish eyes of the Golden Lion, Jad-bal-ja. And he knew fear.

Scrambling to gather up his treasures, Sobito failed to detect a wide loop of woven grass cast upward to snag a bough far above his head until the noose tightened, shaking the leafy limb.

He stared up in surprise, half expecting to see his terrible nemesis in the upper terraces. But Tarzan was dead. Sobito had buried him. Then who—?

A stern voice in the night said coldly, "Tarzan lives, wicked one. And because Tarzan lives, Sobito must face punishment."

At the sound of that familiar voice, the old witch doctor's nerve became unstrung.

"Who speaks? A ghost?"

"Tarzan is no ghost."

Looking about frantically, Sobito could discern no source for that stern voice. Then it resumed speaking.

"Take hold of the rope, Sobito. Climb down and face Tarzan of the Apes."

"I refuse."

"Do not make Tarzan climb up to get you. Tarzan is angry."

"Your words are not hot. They sound cold. You may be Tarzan in truth, but you are only a powerless ghost."

"My words are cold because my anger is cold. Come down. You are an old man, Sobito. Although Tarzan is sorely tempted to wring your treacherous neck, he will not do so. That would be too merciful for what you have done to the Lord of the Jungle. Tarzan will take you back to your bamboo cage, where you will live out your remaining days in abject misery. Now come. Tarzan is impatient."

Reaching for the handle of his stolen hunting knife, Sobito plucked it out and flung it to the grass below.

"Take this and be gone."

"Throw down the locket as well."

Sobito hesitated. But finally he removed the gold chain and dropped it.

"Is the ghost of Tarzan satisfied now?" he quavered.

"Face me, Sobito. Or Tarzan will send his lion up to fetch you. If you were not so scrawny, Jad-bal-ja might be tempted to eat you. But if you cooperate, I will command him not to do so. Tarzan promises this."

The old witch doctor searched the ground below, but descried nothing of his phantom tormentor. But when his frightened eyes fell upon the patch of sward where the knife and gold locket had fallen, they were no longer there....

Desperation seized Sobito now. Reaching into the empty knife sheath, he plucked out the gnarled kingo root. Once his withered fingers gripped it, a renewed courage flowed into his craven heart.

Lifting the juju talisman above his head, Sobito cried out, "I cast you out of this world before. I will cast you out again!"

"Come down, Sobito, lest you fall and break your neck. Tarzan will not complain if you do. But he does not wish to be cheated out of his just revenge."

Sobito's lips writhed as he commenced his chant—a plea to his great thunder god, Meriki.

The night sky above was no longer clear. A mackerel cloud bank had rolled in, threatening to obscure Goro the moon. There was no smell in the air that foretold of rain. No freshening wind, no grumble of thunder. Only silence.

Yet—those lowering gray clouds soon gave forth with an answer. A distant rumble, long and low, like a prowling animal approaching.

The wily old sorcerer lifted his deep voice in triumph. "Do you hear, ghost of Tarzan? The god of Sobito is gathering his strength. He will smite you if you do not take your lion and go."

"I have given you my last warning," intoned Tarzan, stepping out of the shadows and into a silvery bath of moonlight which illuminated a jagged scar on his bronzed brow. This was now a crimson vein pulsing with raw anger. "Come down now."

Sobito did not answer. Instead, there came a crack, and a white-hot sear of lightning flashed down to detonate the crown of the great camphorwood tree.

Fire erupted among the exploding branches, black smoke uncoiling from the ignited wood.

Out of the shattered treetop rolled a charred thing that had once been a spiteful old man. It landed at the base of the tree, illuminated by the fitful, crackling fires above, inert and smoking as a rumble of thunder appeared to move on….

Having felt the hairs on his naked body rise—a familiar warning sensation that presaged a coming lightning bolt—Tarzan had retreated into the brush, Jad-bal-ja having surrendered to the same primal instinct when his luxurious mane responded in kind.

When they emerged, Jad-bal-ja reached the body first. He sniffed it curiously, then recoiled, cooked meat not being to his taste.

Tarzan looked down at the smoldering husk. Then he placed one naked foot on the old witch doctor's scorched skull. Throwing back his head, he gave forth the victory cry of the great bull ape, a sound that had been feared throughout the jungle for as long as Sobito had lived. It would continue to be heard long after his carcass had been devoured by such scavengers who did not disdain roasted flesh.

The jungle lord spoke up, his tone devoid of emotion. "Tarzan has been cheated of his vengeance, but he does not mind. Sobito's angry god has turned his fury upon the one who abused his influence. Meriki may be a god of wrath, but he is no mere witch doctor's servant."

Jad-bal-ja growled deep in his throat, as if voicing agreement.

"I wonder where the spirit of Sobito has gone?" mused the ape-man, glancing about. His gray eyes went to a break in the mackerel sky, where red Mars burned distantly. "Perhaps it will awaken upon Barsoom. If so, Sobito's wicked magic will avail him little against the ravenous banths of the mossy sea bottoms."

Giving the massive lion a firm pat on the top of his head, the ape-man said, "Come, Jad-bal-ja. It is time to go home. Jane and Jack are waiting. No doubt they are wondering what has kept

Tarzan of the Apes so long from their side. Perhaps we will one day tell them. Right now I think it is better not to."

Then Tarzan melted into the brush, unseen and unheard, joined by Jad-bal-ja on the trail.

And so the stealthy pair slipped into the night, and were unchallenged as they trekked their contented way homeward. For the jungle both feared and respected them as lords.

About the Author

WILL MURRAY

WILL MURRAY was first exposed to Tarzan of the Apes when his father took him to see *Tarzan's Greatest Adventure* in 1959. He was too young to read and therefore too immature to understand what he was watching. But something must have stuck. He watched a lot of Tarzan movies during the following years.

A decade later, Murray read *The Gods of Mars,* and became a fan of the works of Tarzan creator Edgar Rice Burroughs. After finishing the Mars series, he jumped to the Venus books and then Tarzan. These books not only opened up for him the many worlds of Edgar Rice Burroughs but also the greater universe of pulp fiction, where he continues to reside today.

Fifty years later, Murray inaugurated a revival of Tarzan in book form with his 2015 novel, *Tarzan: Return to Pal-ul-don,* which led to *King Kong vs. Tarzan* and the present epic, *Tarzan, Conqueror of Mars.* Like many other authors, he credits his writing career to the imagination of Edgar Rice Burroughs.

Will Tarzan of the Apes return to Barsoom? Only time will tell....

About the Artist

ROMAS KUKALIS

ROMAS BRANDT KUKALIS is an award-winning artist specializing in fantasy and science-fiction subjects.

A graduate of the Paier College of Art, Romas immediately plunged into the world a professional art, executing his first commission within three weeks of entering the field. Hundreds of covers followed. He is specially known for painting covers to the Marion Zimmer Bradley's Darkover books, Anne McCaffrey's Rowan series and K.A. Applegate's Animorphs Chronicles.

Expanding beyond book covers, the artist professionally known as Romas has created and executed original designs for product development units of Hasbro Toys, the Bradford Exchange and the Franklin Mint. He has contributed to numerous role-playing games, such as cards for *Magic: The Gathering*, as well as computer game and audio CD packages, including character art for the Harry Potter style guide for Universal Studios.

With his wife, writer/illustrator Allison Barrows, Romas recently collaborated on the five-book graphic novel series, *Dangerous Gambles*, as well as *Renegade*. They are presently working on a new graphic novel project, *Superego*.

Tarzan, Conqueror of Mars is the artist's first contribution to the Wild Adventures series. About his wraparound cover, he says, "It is a very great honor to be depicting this iconic character, and humbling to follow the many fine artists who have done so.

"To properly place such a monumental figure as Tarzan in this painting, I first set out to create the environment. A nighttime sky was suggested by the author early on and I started with that. Because I was using acrylic paints that dry very quickly, I mixed the main pigments and saved them in containers. Once I had the full complement of colors ready, I transferred the paint to a palette, picked up five or six large brushes and rapidly laid the paint, softening and blending the night background. I did the same thing for the middle-ground flat plain. Next, I spattered the stars and added the moons, Thuria and Cluros. The background atmosphere was now mostly complete, so I created the petrified sea galleon on the flat plain to achieve a ghostly quality. I followed with the Martian moss and then the white and green characters. That accomplished, it was time to introduce the heroic Tarzan figure, which I stylized slightly to give him his otherworldly majesty. To do this, I borrowed colors surrounding him and included them in his figure, solidly positioning him in the Martian setting. The entire process, from sketches to finish, took about five to six weeks. I heartfully thank Will Murray, Henry G. Franke III, and Edgar Rice Burroughs, Inc., for inviting me to work on this wonderful project. A special thanks to Joe DeVito."

About the Patron

HENRY G. FRANKE III

HENRY FRANKE is the Editor of The Burroughs Bibliophiles, the non-profit literary society devoted to the life and works of Edgar Rice Burroughs. He is only the third editor of the Bibliophiles' *The Burroughs Bulletin* since it was first published in 1947.

Henry was the Contributing Editor and penned the introductions for IDW Publishing's Library of American Comics archival series reprinting Russ Manning's Tarzan daily and Sunday newspaper comic strips. Volume 1 won the 2014 Eisner Award for Best Archival Collection—Strips. He also wrote book introductions for IDW's *Tarzan: 1929* daily strip reprints and for *Tarzan and the Adventurers,* the fifth volume in Titan Books' *Complete Burne Hogarth Comic Strip Library.* He is in demand as a speaker on Edgar Rice Burroughs and his creations, having made presentations at PulpFest, the Mid-Atlantic Nostalgia Convention, and various ERB fan conventions. He is serving for the third time as the Official Editor of the Edgar Rice Burroughs Amateur Press Association (ERBapa).

From 1977 to 2009, Henry served in the U.S. Army.

Henry specializes in collecting art inspired by Burroughs' stories. "I am pleased to be a part of the creation of Romas Kukalis' painting for the cover of *Tarzan, Conqueror of Mars,*" he says. "For decades, fans of Tarzan and Barsoom have waited for an authorized novel about the ape-man on Mars. Not only is Romas' painting an exquisite work of art, it helps bring to life this matchless story of Tarzan's adventure on the Red Planet."

About

Edgar Rice Burroughs, Inc.

FOUNDED IN 1923 by Edgar Rice Burroughs, as one of the first authors to incorporate himself, Edgar Rice Burroughs, Inc., holds numerous trademarks and the rights to all literary works of the author still protected by copyright, including stories of Tarzan of the Apes and John Carter of Mars. The company has overseen every adaptation of his literary works in film, television, radio, publishing, theatrical stage productions, licensing and merchandising. The company is still a very active enterprise and manages and licenses the vast archive of Mr. Burroughs' literary works, fictional characters and corresponding artworks that have grown for over a century. The company continues to be owned by the Burroughs family and remains headquartered in Tarzana, California, the town named after the Tarzana Ranch Mr. Burroughs purchased there in 1918 which led to the town's future development.

www.edgarriceburroughs.com
www.tarzan.com

KING KONG VS. TARZAN

Available at AdventuresInBronze.com

DOC SAVAGE
SKULL ISLAND

The Man of Bronze meets the 8th Wonder of the World is a historic matchup untold for 80 years! Before the world knew them, King Kong and Doc Savage faced off in Will Murray's monumental new novel.

$24.95 softcover
$39.95 hardcover
$5.99 ebook

THE WILD ADVENTURES OF THE SPIDER *by* **WILL MURRAY**

THE SPIDER
MASTER OF MEN!

The DOOM LEGION

TARZAN

BOOK SERIES #1

TARZAN Return to Pal-ul-don

By Will Murray

Tarzan returns in an all-new story by Doc Savage scribe Will Murray! With the African continent engulfed by World War II, John Clayton enlists in the RAF and plunges into the Land of Man in this exciting sequel to "Tarzan the Terrible."

Hardcover edition includes Gary Buckingham's "Tarzan and the Secret of Katanga."

Available from adventuresinbronze.com
and ERBurroughs.com/Store

www.EdgarRiceBurroughs.com

THE ARGOSY LIBRARY

SERIES 7 INCLUDES:

* BRAND * TUTTLE * BECHDOLT *
HORN * McCULLEY * ROSCOE *
* HALL & FLINT *
* BEYER * McCALL *
* MONTGOMERY *

THE BEST FICTION FROM THE FRANK A. MUNSEY LINE

THE ARGOSY LIBRARY

1. GENIUS JONES by Lester Dent
2. WHEN TIGERS ARE HUNTING: THE COMPLETE ADVENTURES OF CORDIE, SOLDIER OF FORTUNE, VOLUME 1 by W. Wirt
3. THE SWORDSMAN OF MARS by Otis Adelbert Kline
4. THE SHERLOCK OF SAGELAND: THE COMPLETE TALES OF SHERIFF HENRY, VOLUME 1 by W.C. Tuttle
5. GONE NORTH by Charles Alden Seltzer
6. THE MASKED MASTER MIND by George F. Worts
7. BALATA by Fred MacIsaac
8. BRETWALDA by Philip Ketchum
9. DRAFT OF ETERNITY by Victor Rousseau
10. FOUR CORNERS, VOLUME 1 by Theodore Roscoe
11. CHAMPION OF LOST CAUSES by Max Brand
12. THE SCARLET BLADE: THE RAKEHELLY ADVENTURES OF CLEVE AND D'ENTREVILLE, VOLUME 1 by Murray R. Montgomery
13. DOAN AND CARSTAIRS: THEIR COMPLETE CASES by Norbert Davis
14. THE KING WHO CAME BACK by Fred MacIsaac
15. BLOOD RITUAL: THE ADVENTURES OF SCARLET AND BRADSHAW, VOLUME 1 by Theodore Roscoe
16. THE CITY OF STOLEN LIVES: THE ADVENTURES OF PETER THE BRAZEN, VOLUME 1 by Loring Brent
17. THE RADIO GUN-RUNNERS by Ralph Milne Farley
18. SABOTAGE by Cleve F. Adams
19. THE COMPLETE CABALISTIC CASES OF SEMI DUAL, THE OCCULT DETECTOR, VOLUME 2: 1912–13 by J.U. Giesy and Junius B. Smith
20. SOUTH OF FIFTY-THREE by Jack Bechdolt
21. TARZAN AND THE JEWELS OF OPAR by Edgar Rice Burroughs
22. CLOVELLY by Max Brand
23. WAR LORD OF MANY SWORDSMEN: THE ADVENTURES OF NORCOSS, VOLUME 1 by W. Wirt
24. ALIAS THE NIGHT WIND by Varick Vanardy

THE ARGOSY LIBRARY

25. THE BLUE FIRE PEARL: THE COMPLETE ADVENTURES OF SINGAPORE SAMMY, VOLUME 1 by George F. Worts
26. THE MOON POOL & THE CONQUEST OF THE MOON POOL by Abraham Merritt
27. THE GUN-BRAND by James B. Hendryx
28. JAN OF THE JUNGLE by Otis Adelbert Kline
29. MINIONS OF THE MOON by William Gray Beyer
30. DRINK WE DEEP by Arthur Leo Zagat
31. THE VENGEANCE OF THE WAH FU TONG: THE COMPLETE CASES OF JIGGER MASTERS, VOLUME 1 by Anthony M. Rud
32. THE RUBY OF SURATAN SINGH: THE ADVENTURES OF SCARLET AND BRADSHAW, VOLUME 2 by Theodore Roscoe
33. THE SHERIFF OF TONTO TOWN: THE COMPLETE TALES OF SHERIFF HENRY, VOLUME 2 by W.C. Tuttle
34. THE DARKNESS AT WINDON MANOR by Max Brand
35. THE FLYING LEGION by George Allan England
36. THE GOLDEN CAT: THE ADVENTURES OF PETER THE BRAZEN, VOLUME 3 by Loring Brent
37. THE RADIO MENACE by Ralph Milne Farley
38. THE APES OF DEVIL'S ISLAND by John Cunningham
39. THE OPPOSING VENUS: THE COMPLETE CABALISTIC CASES OF SEMI DUAL, THE OCCULT DETECTOR by J.U. Giesy and Junius B. Smith
40. THE EXPLOITS OF BEAU QUICKSILVER by Florence M. Pettee
41. ERIC OF THE STRONG HEART by Victor Rousseau
42. MURDER ON THE HIGH SEAS AND THE DIAMOND BULLET: THE COMPLETE CASES OF GILLIAN HAZELTINE by George F. Worts
43. THE WOMAN OF THE PYRAMID AND OTHER TALES: THE PERLEY POORE SHEEHAN OMNIBUS, VOLUME 1 by Perley Poore Sheehan
44. A COLUMBUS OF SPACE AND THE MOON METAL: THE GARRETT P. SERVISS OMNIBUS, VOLUME 1 by Garrett P. Serviss
45. THE BLACK TIDE: THE COMPLETE ADVENTURES OF BELLOW BILL WILLIAMS, VOLUME 1 by Ralph R. Perry
46. THE NINE RED GODS DECIDE: THE COMPLETE ADVENTURES OF CORDIE, SOLDIER OF FORTUNE, VOLUME 2 by W. Wirt
47. A GRAVE MUST BE DEEP! by Theodore Roscoe

THE ARGOSY LIBRARY

48. THE AMERICAN by Max Brand
49. THE COMPLETE ADVENTURES OF KOYALA, VOLUME 1 by John Charles Beecham
50. THE CULT MURDERS by Alan Forsyth
51. THE COMPLETE CASES OF THE MONGOOSE by Johnston McCulley
52. THE GIRL AND THE PEOPLE OF THE GOLDEN ATOM by Ray Cummings
53. THE GRAY DRAGON: THE ADVENTURES OF PETER THE BRAZEN, VOLUME 2 by Loring Brent
54. THE GOLDEN CITY by Ralph Milne Farley
55. THE HOUSE OF INVISIBLE BONDAGE: THE COMPLETE CABALISTIC CASES OF SEMI DUAL, THE OCCULT DETECTOR by J.U. Giesy and Junius B. Smith
56. THE SCRAP OF LACE: THE COMPLETE CASES OF MADAME STOREY, VOLUME 1 by Hulbert Footner
57. TOWER OF DEATH: THE ADVENTURES OF SCARLET AND BRADSHAW, VOLUME 3 by Theodore Roscoe
58. THE DEVIL-TREE OF EL DORADO by Frank Aubrey
59. THE FIREBRAND: THE COMPLETE ADVENTURES OF TIZZO, VOLUME 1 by Max Brand
60. MARCHING SANDS AND THE CARAVAN OF THE DEAD: THE HAROLD LAMB OMNIBUS by Harold Lamb
61. KINGDOM COME by Martin McCall
62. HENRY RIDES THE DANGER TRAIL: THE COMPLETE TALES OF SHERIFF HENRY, VOLUME 3 by W.C. Tuttle
63. Z IS FOR ZOMBIE by Theodore Roscoe
64. THE BAIT AND THE TRAP: THE COMPLETE ADVENTURES OF TIZZO, VOLUME 2 by Max Brand
65. MINIONS OF MARS by William Gray Beyer
66. SWORDS IN EXILE: THE RAKEHELLY ADVENTURES OF CLEVE AND D'ENTREVILLE, VOLUME 2 by Murray R. Montgomery
67. MEN WITH NO MASTER: THE COMPLETE ADVENTURES OF ROBIN THE BOMBARDIER by Roy de S. Horn
68. THE TORCH by Jack Bechdolt
69. KING OF CHAOS AND OTHER ADVENTURES: THE JOHNSTON MCCULLEY OMNIBUS by Johnston McCulley
70. THE BLIND SPOT by Austin Hall & Homer Eon Flint

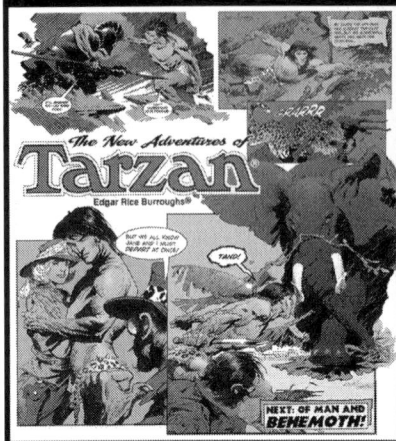

EDGAR RICE BURROUGHS AUTHORIZED LIBRARY™

COLLECT EVERY VOLUME!

For the first time ever, the Edgar Rice Burroughs Authorized Library presents the complete literary works of the Master of Adventure in handsome uniform editions. Published by the company founded by Burroughs himself in 1923, each volume of the Authorized Library is packed with extras and rarities not to be found in any other edition. From cover art and frontispieces by legendary artist Joe Jusko to forewords and afterwords by today's authorities and luminaries to a treasure trove of bonus materials mined from the company's extensive archives in Tarzana, California, the Edgar Rice Burroughs Authorized Library will take you on a journey of wonder and imagination you will never forget.

Don't miss a single volume! Sign up for email updates at ERBurroughs.com to keep apprised of all 80-plus editions of the Authorized Library as they become available.

1. TARZAN OF THE APES
2. THE RETURN OF TARZAN
3. THE BEASTS OF TARZAN
4. THE SON OF TARZAN
5. TARZAN AND THE JEWELS OF OPAR
6. JUNGLE TALES OF TARZAN
7. TARZAN THE UNTAMED
8. TARZAN THE TERRIBLE
9. TARZAN AND THE GOLDEN LION
10. TARZAN AND THE ANT MEN
11. TARZAN LORD OF THE JUNGLE
12. TARZAN AND THE LOST EMPIRE
13. TARZAN AT THE EARTH'S CORE
14. TARZAN THE INVINCIBLE
15. TARZAN TRIUMPHANT
16. TARZAN AND THE CITY OF GOLD
17. TARZAN AND THE LION MEN
18. TARZAN AND THE LEOPARD MEN
19. TARZAN'S QUEST
20. TARZAN THE MAGNIFICENT
21. TARZAN AND THE FORBIDDEN CITY
22. TARZAN AND THE FOREIGN LEGION
23. TARZAN AND THE MADMAN
24. TARZAN AND THE CASTAWAYS

THE JOURNEY BEGINS AT ERBURROUGHS.COM

© Edgar Rice Burroughs, Inc. All rights reserved. Edgar Rice Burroughs®, Edgar Rice Burroughs Authorized Library™, Tarzan®, and Tarzan of the Apes™ owned by Edgar Rice Burroughs, Inc. The Doodad symbol and all logos are trademarks of Edgar Rice Burroughs, Inc.

ENTER THE EDGAR RICE BURROUGHS UNIVERSE

When a mysterious force catapults inventor Jason Gridley and his protégé Victory Harben from their home in Pellucidar, separating them and flinging them across space and time, they embark on a grand tour of strange, wondrous worlds. As their search for one another leads them to the realms of Amtor, Barsoom, and other worlds even more distant and outlandish, Jason and Victory will meet heroes and heroines of unparalleled courage and ability: Carson Napier, Tarzan, John Carter, and more. With the help of their intrepid allies, Jason and Victory will uncover a plot both insidious and unthinkable—one that threatens to tear apart the very fabric of the universe!

CARSON OF VENUS: THE EDGE OF ALL WORLDS
by Matt Betts

TARZAN: BATTLE FOR PELLUCIDAR
by Win Scott Eckert

JOHN CARTER OF MARS: GODS OF THE FORGOTTEN
by Geary Gravel

VICTORY HARBEN: FIRES OF HALOS
by Christopher Paul Carey

THE FIRST UNIVERSE OF ITS KIND

A century before the term "crossover" became a buzzword in popular culture, Edgar Rice Burroughs created the first expansive, fully cohesive literary universe. Coexisting in this vast cosmos was a pantheon of immortal heroes and heroines—Tarzan of the Apes®, Jane Clayton™, John Carter®, Dejah Thoris®, Carson Napier™, and David Innes™ being only the best known among them. In Burroughs' 80-plus novels, their epic adventures transported them to the strange and exotic worlds of Barsoom®, Amtor™, Pellucidar®, Caspak™, and Va-nah™, as well as the lost civilizations of Earth and even realms beyond the farthest star. Now the Edgar Rice Burroughs Universe expands in an all-new series of canonical novels written by today's talented authors!

JOIN THE ADVENTURE AT ERBUNIVERSE.COM

© Edgar Rice Burroughs, Inc. All rights reserved. All logos, characters, names, and the distinctive likenesses thereof are trademarks or registered trademarks of Edgar Rice Burroughs, Inc.

Edgar Rice Burroughs, Inc.

A whole universe of ERB collectibles, including books, T-shirts, DVDs, statues, puzzles, playing cards, dust jackets, art prints, and MORE!

Your one-stop destination for all things ERB!

VISIT US ONLINE AT ERBurroughs.com

© Edgar Rice Burroughs, Inc. All rights reserved. Trademarks Edgar Rice Burroughs®, Edgar Rice Burroughs Universe™, Tarzan®, Dejah Thoris®, John Carter®, and Warlord of Mars© owned by Edgar Rice Burroughs, Inc.

THE WILD ADVENTURES OF EDGAR RICE BURROUGHS™

In the Wild Adventures of Edgar Rice Burroughs series, today's authors innovate and expand upon Burroughs' classic tales of adventure in truly *wild* fashion in these brand-new novels, even moving his iconic characters and storylines outside the bounds of the classic canon to alternate universes!

AVAILABLE NOW AT ERBURROUGHS.COM

© Edgar Rice Burroughs, Inc. All rights reserved. Trademarks including Edgar Rice Burroughs®, Tarzan®, Pellucidar®, The Moon Men™, Beyond the Farthest Star™, and The Wild Adventures of Edgar Rice Burroughs™ owned by Edgar Rice Burroughs, Inc.

The Martian Legion: In Quest of Xonthron

- **An *Epic Adventure Novel in the Grandest ERB Tradition!***
- ***The Finest ERB Collectible Ever Produced!***

Written in spirit by Edgar Rice Burroughs with an assist from Jake Saunders.

- A quarter million words of high adventure! Like getting four ERB novels in one!
- Tarzan, John Carter, The Shadow, and Doc Savage battle the Holy Therns!
- First 100 copies signed by Saunders, Grindberg, Hoffman, Mullins, DeVito, Cabarga, and Cochran.
- Featuring 24 full color painting and illustrations, plus 106 spot illustrations by Tom Grindberg, Michael C. Hoffman, and Craig Mullins, including....
- Leather bound, full color, 11-1/4-in. x 12-1/4-in. x 1-1/2in., 423 pages.

The Martian Legion: In Quest of Xonthron, Copyright © 2014 Jake D. Saunders, all rights reserved.
Edgar Rice Burroughs TM is a trademark of Edgar Rice Burroughs, Inc. and is used by permission.
Published by The Russ Cochran Company, Ltd.

Now available at TheMartianLegion.com!

JOIN EDGAR RICE BURROUGHS® FANDOM!

The Burroughs Bibliophiles

The only fan organization to be personally approved by Edgar Rice Burroughs, The Burroughs Bibliophiles is the largest ERB fan club in the world, with members spanning the globe and maintaining local chapters across the United States and in England.

Also endorsed by Burroughs, *The Burroughs Bulletin*, the organization's official publication, features fascinating articles, essays, interviews, and more centered on the rich history and continuing legacy of the Master of Adventure. The Bibliophiles also annually sponsors the premier ERB fan convention.

Regular membership dues include:

- *Four issues of* The Burroughs Bulletin
- The Gridley Wave *newsletter in PDF*
- *The latest news in ERB fandom*
- *Information about the annual ERB fan convention*

For more information about the society and membership, visit **BurroughsBibliophiles.com** or The Burroughs Bibliophiles Facebook page, or email the Editor at BurroughsBibliophiles@gmail.com.

Call (573) 647-0225
or mail
318 Patriot Way,
Yorktown, Virginia
23693-4639, USA.

Trademarks Edgar Rice Burroughs® and Tarzan® owned by Edgar Rice Burroughs, Inc. and used by permission.

Printed in Great Britain
by Amazon